Jheraal had seen decomposed ~~~~ ~~~ concerned about the implications of the mold that fuzzed the dead man's bones, the sight itself didn't disturb her. Not compared to the others in that place.

Slumped behind a tattered curtain were three hellspawn, each with a fist-sized, cauterized wound burned into the center of his or her chest. Two, presumably the missing servants Chiella and Nodero, wore the colors of House Celverian. The third was a more obviously devil-descended woman dressed like a fishmonger from one of the poorer districts.

All three were missing their hearts—Jheraal had held a light to each of those gaping wounds and looked closely to be sure—and yet they lived. Their mutilated chests rose and fell in steady breaths. A ghostly pulse beat in their wrists. When the Hellknight brought her light to their eyes and held open their eyelids, their pupils contracted under its glare, and then dilated when she put the light away.

They seemed to be comatose. Jheraal pricked each hellspawn's fingertips with the tip of her dagger, prodding them hard enough to draw beads of blood from the pads of their thumbs, but none of them flinched. She clapped her hands sharply next to their heads and shouted into their ears, but none stirred. Their faces remained slack, their breathing slow.

"What do you want to do with them?" one of the rundottari asked. Two ruin wardens armed with swords and crossbows had accompanied her out of the Obrigan Gate to meet the one waiting to show them the bodies. As formidable as the Hellknight was, even she wasn't expected to venture into Rego Cader without protection.

"They need a healer's attention," Jheraal said. "These servants may be innocent victims."

The rundottari spat on the muddy floor, displeased by her answer. "Or they may not. No offense meant to you, but they're hellspawn. And whatever killed that moldy fellow might be contagious. This whole thing might be a trap."

The Pathfinder Tales Library

Called to Darkness by Richard Lee Byers
Winter Witch by Elaine Cunningham
The Wizard's Mask by Ed Greenwood
Prince of Wolves by Dave Gross
Master of Devils by Dave Gross
Queen of Thorns by Dave Gross
King of Chaos by Dave Gross
Lord of Runes by Dave Gross
Pirate's Honor by Chris A. Jackson
Pirate's Promise by Chris A. Jackson
Pirate's Prophecy by Chris A. Jackson
Beyond the Pool of Stars by Howard Andrew Jones
Plague of Shadows by Howard Andrew Jones
Stalking the Beast by Howard Andrew Jones
Firesoul by Gary Kloster
The Worldwound Gambit by Robin D. Laws
Blood of the City by Robin D. Laws
Song of the Serpent by Hugh Matthews
Hellknight by Liane Merciel
Nightglass by Liane Merciel
Nightblade by Liane Merciel
City of the Fallen Sky by Tim Pratt
Liar's Blade by Tim Pratt
Liar's Island by Tim Pratt
Reign of Stars by Tim Pratt
Bloodbound by F. Wesley Schneider
The Crusader Road by Michael A. Stackpole
Death's Heretic by James L. Sutter
The Redemption Engine by James L. Sutter
Forge of Ashes by Josh Vogt
Skinwalkers by Wendy N. Wagner
The Dagger of Trust by Chris Willrich

HELLKNIGHT

Liane Merciel

A TOM DOHERTY ASSOCIATES BOOK
New York

PATHFINDER TALES: HELLKNIGHT

Copyright © 2016 by Paizo Inc.

Maps by Crystal Frasier and Robert Lazzaretti

A Tor Book
Published by Tom Doherty Associates, LLC
175 Fifth Avenue
New York, NY 10010

www.tor-forge.com

Tor® is a registered trademark of Tom Doherty Associates, LLC.

The Library of Congress Cataloging-in-Publication Data is available upon request.

ISBN 978-0-7653-7548-3 (trade paperback)
ISBN 978-1-4668-4735-4 (e-book)

Our books may be purchased in bulk for promotional, educational, or business use. Please contact your local bookseller or the Macmillan Corporate and Premium Sales Department at 1-800-221-7945, extension 5442, or by e-mail at MacmillanSpecialMarkets@macmillan.com.

First Edition: April 2016

Printed in the United States of America

0 9 8 7 6 5 4 3 2 1

For Peter, with love.

Inner Sea Region

Westcrown

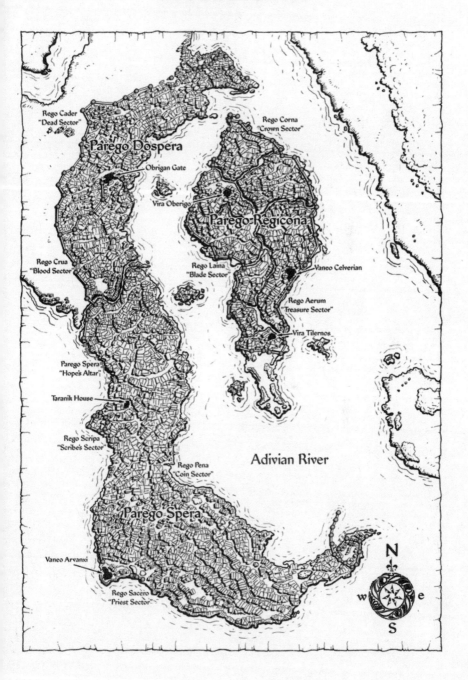

PROLOGUE

The devilheart chain was a cruel thing.

It lay across Sechel's palm and draped around her armored forearm like an iron viper, smooth and dark and deadly fanged. Each of its scale-shaped links was engraved with infernal runes and inlaid in gleaming red gold, evoking rivulets of magma running across the blackened landscapes of Hell.

One end of the chain terminated in a hollow golden cap designed to be locked into another segment. The other ended in a lupine devil's head, its gaping jaws stretched as wide as both of Sechel's hands spread together. Black diamond teeth fringed its maw, arrayed outward in a double row of curving hooks. A spiked iron band covered the wolflike devil's eyes, and another encircled its throat like a collar.

Even in their imaginings, they shackle and torment us.

The thought made her angry. Anger was not useful. She lifted her eyes and counted her heartbeats, willing them slower to match her breaths, until she was calm again.

Her contact, Hakur, watched her closely, his nervousness barely showing. No sweat beaded on his black-stubbled scalp. No lines of worry furrowed his sunburned brow. He might have gone apostate, but the man had been trained as a Hellknight, and the iron discipline of his order almost masked his concern.

Almost. He had taken a step back while she studied the chain, perhaps thinking she wouldn't notice. The corner of his left eye twitched, and the raw skin around his mouth—blistered by the scalding water and acids he'd drunk to purge his sins—was taut with unspoken worry.

"It's what you wanted," he said. The acid had roughened his voice to a gravelly baritone, but a quiver of trepidation ran through each word.

"It might be," Sechel allowed. She wrapped the chain tighter about her forearm, holding the blindfolded devil's head against her palm so that its black diamond fangs spread outward like extensions of her own fingers. The sensation pleased her. "It might."

With the chain coiled around her arm like a cherished pet, she crossed the derelict shack that she'd chosen for this meeting. The place was too small to have been divided into rooms, but a sackcloth curtain hanging from bent nails on the ceiling offered a semblance of privacy around what had been the sleeping area.

Three hellspawn huddled there, flinching as Sechel stepped past the curtain. Two women, one man, all tainted with the blood of devils. Rough brown rope circled their wrists and ankles, binding the three of them together like slaves being driven to market. Gags filled their mouths.

Two of them, the most human-looking of the trio, wore servants' garb in white and gold-slashed blue, the colors of House Celverian. Only subtle things—a faint odor of sulfur that trailed after the man like stale perfume; an opaque yellow tint to the woman's fingernails and a line of coarse boar's bristles down the center of her scalp, almost hidden by the rest of her hair—signaled the impurity in their blood. The third, whose snake-pupiled red eyes and sharp black fangs proclaimed her infernal ancestry, wore a scale-spattered fishwife's apron tied over her dress.

It was always easier for hellspawn to climb toward social respectability in Cheliax if they looked more human. Sechel had known that her entire life, and seeing these three confirmed it. The obviously devil-born woman would never have been permitted to darken the grounds of House Celverian, much less tend its lavish gardens or serve wine to its pious patriarchs. Never. She was fit to hawk day-old fish to Westcrown's poor, and that was all.

Almost all.

The three hellspawn watched her fearfully as she drew the ragged curtain. With the light of Hakur's lantern blocked off behind her, Sechel's eyes lit with their own infernal radiance. She felt the change, and she knew what the others would see. Blue sparks ignited and circled around her pale green irises like tiny fireflies, enabling her to see in the dark. It was a trait she went to considerable pains to conceal before most onlookers. But with these three, there was no need to hide.

Sechel saw the confusion on the hellspawn's faces, the befuddlement that wouldn't quite turn to hope. She was one of them. Her blood was tainted with Hell's legacy as surely as theirs. They saw it, they recognized it, and they knew it was the only commonality they shared.

But they didn't know why that had led to them being bound and gagged in this stinking hovel.

Sechel owed them no explanation, but it amused her to offer one—after a fashion.

With showy, theatrical gestures, she removed the second half of the devilheart chain from a pocket sewn into the inner lining of her cloak. One end matched the golden cap at the end of the segment Hakur had given her. Its opposite end was another fiend's head, but whereas the first chain ended in a fierce, snarling wolf's visage, this one was a horned and shackled skull that seemed to be dissipating into mist. Although it was wrought of solid iron, heavy in Sechel's hand, the fiend's face had been crafted with such exquisite skill that she could almost believe it was fading into fog before her eyes.

She snapped the chains' hollow ends together. They clicked into place with a loud snap; she heard Hakur jerk in surprise on the far side of the curtain. A hellish spark flared within the chain where the two parts joined, then thinned and stretched as the light was sucked to either end. The spark was gone in the space of a second, but Sechel could feel its echoes reverberating through the metal.

If it had been a viper before, it was a dragon now. Heat thrummed in the chain's core, pushing at the throats of the heads on either end. Hunger pulsed along with that infernal fire; Sechel felt it as clearly as if it were her own gut twisting in emptiness. The devilheart chain sensed blood nearby, and it wanted a taste.

"You'll get more than that," she whispered, caressing the wolf's head in its spiked iron blindfold.

Holding the chain as she had before, with the wolf's head poised in her palm, Sechel bent over the red-eyed hellspawn. She untied the woman's fish-speckled apron and pulled it off, crumpling the garment into the corner as she brought the devilheart chain toward her victim's chest. The fishmonger's jaws worked around the gag stuffed between her teeth, trying to form a word that Sechel couldn't hear but understood regardless.

Why.

Everyone she killed, if they had time to see death coming, asked the same question: *Why?* As if that *mattered.* As if the reasons for their deaths would somehow serve as a final soothing bedtime story, making it easier to go into that last long sleep.

It was absurd. But they all asked, every one, even as the knife was sliding in.

She never answered, unless whoever had paid for the blade had also paid for a message to be delivered with it. Even then, Sechel often slurred her words to keep them from being understood. The dead deserved no courtesy from her. If they wanted her answers so badly, they were welcome to walk out of their graves and ask again. Thus far, none had.

But this time—*this* time, out of all the souls she'd cut loose from their mortal moorings—she felt impelled to give an answer. Because this time was different.

"Your blood is a sin," Sechel said as she pressed the wolf's head into the cloth over the fishmonger's chest. "Your *existence* is a sin. You are a thing that should not be, you and all your line." Heat rose in the chain's belly. The infernal runes carved into its links shone brightly in the hovel's dimness as the magic flowed through the metal. The iron blindfold over the wolf's eyes began to smoke. The tips of its black diamond teeth burned pinpoint holes through the fishmonger's dress.

So are you, the fishmonger mouthed. Her jaw strained around the cloth gag. The tendons of her neck bulged. Tears of fear or frustration spilled from the corners of her crimson eyes. No sound escaped, but her meaning could not be mistaken. *So are you.*

"So am I," Sechel agreed. In her hand, the magic flared and reached its final form. The fiendish wolf's head opened its maw, black diamond teeth smoking, and bit into the fishmonger's chest.

In a blur of gold and glowing iron, the devilheart chain plunged into the woman's body like a tern diving into the sea. Its metallic scales clacked between Sechel's fingers as the chain skimmed across her palm, burying itself until its wolfish jaws closed around the hellspawn's heart.

There was no blood, no gore, nothing but a hiss of coppery-smelling pink steam. Flakes of burned cloth from her victim's dress drifted through the air like black snowflakes. The fishmonger's eyes went wide, and her nostrils dilated in shock, but Sechel read no pain on her face, only a jolt of sudden terror—and then, just as suddenly, nothing.

The light died in the woman's eyes, and the heat died in the chain's hellish core. From the hollow end of the devilheart chain, a glimmering oblong jewel emerged and dropped onto the hard-packed dirt floor. It rolled to rest against Sechel's boot, emanating a soft rosy radiance.

She picked it up. The pinkish stone was large enough to fill her hand, but it weighed next to nothing. It pulsed gently against her palm, echoing her heartbeat so closely that it took the hellspawn assassin several moments to realize that the translucent stone was not beating in time to *her* heart but to its own.

Shrunken and smoothed from raw red meat to a jewel that looked like rose quartz and felt like a glass bubble, it remained, all the same, a heart. A *living* heart, strange as that seemed. It was warm in Sechel's hand, it carried a beat, and it kept its owner alive.

For the fishmonger was still breathing, even after Sechel pulled the devilheart chain out of its smoking wound. A gaping hole yawned beside her sternum, as bloodless and smooth as if it had been burned by a cauterizing iron, but her breast rose and fell steadily under the black-fringed rags of her dress. The woman's heart was gone, transmuted into the gem that shone before her, yet she lived on without it.

After a fashion. She breathed, and the jeweled heart in Sechel's hand throbbed with a phantom beat, but there was a slackness in the fishmonger's body that suggested her mind, and perhaps her soul, had flown to judgment in the courts of the dead.

Did her consciousness linger in that maimed flesh? Was there anything left of the fishmonger that could feel, sense, *care* what happened to her shell of bone and skin?

Sechel didn't know, but she didn't need to answer that mystery to finish her job. She had been warned that killing the hellspawn might disrupt the chain's magic, so she left her victim bound and moved to the next stage of her task.

Unlatching the steel-ribbed, padded carrying case that she carried in a secret compartment of her pack, Sechel slid the ghostly jewel of the fishmonger's heart inside and tucked the top flap shut over it. Then she looped the devilheart chain around her forearm and strode to the other two other captives.

It went faster with practice. A little.

When Sechel emerged from the curtain, her hands were flecked with blood and soot. Three pale pink jewels nestled in her hidden case. Three not-quite-living hellspawn lay limp in her wake, their vacant faces tipped toward the ceiling and their wrists braceleted in coarse rope.

"Did it work?" Hakur asked. If the apostate Hellknight had been nervous before, he was frightened now. Under the coarse black stubble on his cheeks, the skin was gray as death.

Sechel took a pouch from her pocket and tossed it at him. Reflexively, Hakur put a hand up to catch it. Coins slapped against his palm, loud even through the leather.

His fingers closed around it, but there was too much money in the pouch for them to meet. "Is this all of it?"

Sechel shrugged, drawing her hood over her head and a scarf over her nose. "Count for yourself."

He hesitated only a second before unlacing the bag. A puff of gray dust came up from its open mouth, engulfing his face. Hakur staggered back, coughing, as the pouch tumbled from his fingers to spill gray-furred golden coins across the floor.

Quicker than understanding, Sechel was behind him, her knife in his neck. The former Hellknight's coughs turned to gasps, then to gurgles, then to silence.

She eased him to the floor. Already the fungus was spreading across his flesh, burying Hakur's lips and tongue under a thickening mask of gray. In an hour, the corpse would be unrecognizable. In a day, it would be reduced to teeth and bone.

Someone might find him before then, of course, and might even identify the dead man—but if they did, they'd likely assume that the killers had been working at the behest of Urgathoa, the Pallid Princess, whose domain encompassed death and disease.

Few outside her foul worship used such fungal spores. Sechel had collected that sample from the body of an Urgathoan cultist she'd killed. Following that clue would lead any pursuit down a perilous false trail.

Not as perilous as the true one, though.

Exhaling the breath she'd been holding since Hakur opened his poisoned pouch, Sechel pushed open the door and stepped back into the sunlight of Westcrown. She stripped off the scarf that had covered the lower half of her face and dropped it into a nearby canal. As it sank into the sluggish green water, trailing a fringe of bubbles, she turned north.

North, toward the Dospera, the shadowy, abandoned ruins of old Westcrown that were the stuff of local dread and legend, and that sometimes served as informal execution grounds for the condemned.

North, toward the gate that waited to carry the assassin back to her employer.

North, to Nidal.

1

THE SCHOLAR'S MURDER

JHERAAL

irds cared nothing for murder.

Sweetly they sang from the branches of the fig and lemon trees that wreathed the grounds of Vaneo Celverian, the city manor of proud, ancient House Celverian. Under the elegant tile roofs and gilded balustrades, all might be in panic, but nothing disturbed the birds among their sun-dappled leaves. They sang and sang, bright as joy, while down below, mortal men and women struggled to grasp the enormity of loss.

They'd suffered a staggering one, Jheraal knew. Master Othando Celverian, second and favored son of Lord Abello Celverian, heir to his house and hope of his family's future, had been murdered in the night. Others had been killed, too, but in Cheliax, only one of those deaths really mattered.

Out on the grand lawn, a semicircle of maids, grooms, cooks, and washerwomen in white and gold-slashed blue stood where they'd been turned out for her inspection. Every one of House Celverian's servants was a picture of shock and grief. The younger maids held handkerchiefs to their tear-puffed eyes, while the older servants muttered about what they'd do when they found their master's killer.

Both the sobbing and the plotting died abruptly when Jheraal rode into the servants' view. One did not cry before Hellknights, and one certainly did not conspire to commit crimes. A sullen hush fell over the Celverian household as Jheraal's chestnut destrier trotted across the graveled path, coming to a halt before the chief steward.

He was a tall man, spare and elegant and silver-haired, and although Jheraal was framed against the sun, he looked up into its full glare without blinking. "Sir?"

"I'm here to investigate the murders." Jheraal removed her fearsome, devil-visaged helm, allowing the servants to see her face.

It caused a stir, as she had known it would. House Celverian's people were well trained, and other than a gasp from one of the youngest grooms and a few tightened mouths and half-steps backward, none showed an overt reaction to her appearance. But Jheraal read their shock all the same.

The hellspawn taint ran strong in her. Jheraal's skin was white as snow and covered with fine, soft scales, each one edged with a faint shimmer of copper. A pair of four-inch horns, curved and sharp as a goat's, poked through her bronze-streaked black hair. They fitted into the hollows of the horns in her helm, and had indirectly served as inspiration for the same.

It was not unheard of for the devil-blooded to serve among the Hellknights, but neither was it common. In Cheliax, hellspawn were widely considered to be no part of proper society, and few of them received the training in arms or spellcraft needed to gain acceptance into the Hellknight orders' ranks. Yet here she was, armored in the scarred breastplate and horned helm that marked her as a full Hellknight sworn to the Order of the Scourge.

The chief steward, a consummate professional, tipped his head downward in an extremely correct nod, affording Jheraal precisely the degree of courtesy that her status warranted. "It is our honor. Should we be expecting any of your associates?"

As he spoke, his eyes flicked to the star of bleeding lashes painted on Jheraal's shield. That was the Scourge's sigil, and the steward's unspoken query was clear: *Will the Order of the Rack be coming?*

It was a delicate question. The Hellknight Order of the Rack, based in Citadel Rivad near Westcrown, was the primary order of Hellknights in the city. Jheraal's order, the Scourge, was less well known and much less strongly represented, which was both advantage and disadvantage: it gave her greater independence, but fewer resources to call upon.

Less currency with the common people, too. As Westcrown had long been troubled by rumblings of dissent, Her Imperial Majestrix, Queen Abrogail Thrune II, had granted the Order of the Rack wide-sweeping authority to detain, question, and even execute suspected rebels in the city.

And although the Order of the Rack held the preservation of peace to be its highest duty, the methods it chose to achieve that duty were not always peaceful. In much of Westcrown, the order had a fearsome reputation. Few Wiscrani were glad to see them coming.

House Celverian, Jheraal recalled, might have more reason than most to be wary where the Order of the Rack was concerned. There had been some trouble with the eldest son, who'd gotten caught up in the idealistic fervor of the young. He hadn't been accused of any serious wrongdoing, and his father's influence had hushed any whiff of scandal, but nevertheless the boy had been sent packing to a crusader's exile in Mendev.

That had been years ago. Well over a decade, in fact. But fear could take a long time dying, and Jheraal couldn't blame the servants of House Celverian for being cautious.

"The Order of the Rack has no part in this investigation," she said. Some of the servants relaxed visibly at her words. Out of long habit, Jheraal noted their faces, as well as those of the servants who didn't blink at all. "The dottari will assist in whatever capacity they can, but they will not send a separate investigator. In this matter, I serve both the throne and my order. All of us wish to see your master's killer brought to justice. You have my condolences for your loss."

"We are grateful for your kindness. I have the honor of being Belvadio, chief steward of this house. Lord Abello Celverian should be arriving late tonight or early tomorrow. In the meantime, the household staff is at your disposal." The chief steward clapped his hands, signaling the end of the assembly. In a flurry of curtseys and bows, the maids, cooks, and house servants dispersed. Jheraal dismounted, and one of the grooms led her horse away. Two servants, a pair of boys who looked no older than fourteen, remained behind at the steward's signal.

"Achio and Tirol were the first to discover the . . . the . . . what had been done," Belvadio said, clearing his throat. "They found Nappandi, one of our guards, lying in the hedges and came together to wake me a little after midnight. I hastened to wake the young master, and that is when we found him. Master Othando had been murdered in his study, where he was accustomed to read nearly until dawn. There are still two servants unaccounted for. We have not found their bodies, but I fear the worst." The chief steward took a breath, quavering only slightly. "Where would you like to begin?"

"Show it to me as you found it." Jheraal had no reason to doubt the steward's honesty, but if there *were* any gaps in his story, she expected that it would be easiest to find them by walking alongside Belvadio and seeing whether the evidence matched his words.

"Of course. Please, this way." With a courtly bow, Belvadio led his armored guest through the gardens' fragrant shade toward the honeysuckle-threaded hedges that encircled the vaneo. Overhead, the birds continued their merry, oblivious song.

Although House Celverian's main seat lay in the hinterlands, and its manor in Westcrown was not as grand or expansive as the sprawling estates called *vira*, it took several minutes for them to reach the bloodstained spot by the walls where Nappandi's body had been found.

There wasn't much blood. Only a few brownish drops, already mostly soaked into the earth, and a patch of crushed clover near the base of the hedges where the body had lain. In the darkness, screened by the dense thorned shrubs, it might have been a long time before anyone noticed a body at night.

Jheraal crouched and looked for tracks that might have been left by the killer, but found none. Either Nappandi's assailant had known how to hide them, or the servants had already trampled out those traces.

She straightened with a clanking of steel and leather. "Your guard kept a regular patrol?"

"Yes. Every hour on the hour. Nappandi was extremely diligent. He would never have missed a round, nor been a minute late on his circuit."

Predictable, then. Easily evaded. The lack of struggle suggested that the killer had never been seen. He could have slipped by if he'd wanted, but instead he'd chosen to kill the guard.

"Was anything taken from his body?" Jheraal asked.

"Yes. A ring of keys. Nappandi had keys to most of the vaneo, other than the master's private rooms and the wine cellar. That was the only thing I could see that was stolen. Do you wish to examine the body?"

"Later. Show me where you went and what you did after you found him."

Belvadio glanced at the two boys behind him. They hung back nervously while Jheraal examined the blood-speckled grass. "After Achio and Tirol told me what they'd found, and I had confirmed with my own eyes that this was no prank, we went together to inform the master. I also sent word to the captain of our household guard that there was a murderer at large in the vaneo."

"How many guards do you have?"

"Four." The steward grimaced, shaking his head. "Three, with Nappandi dead. But none of the others saw whoever did this."

Jheraal nodded. Three household guards were unlikely, in her estimation, to present much difficulty for someone who could kill one of their number so easily and silently. That they had seen nothing meant little. There was no need to insult their honor by saying so, however. "Show me to Master Celverian's study."

"At once." With another neat bow, Belvadio strode toward the manor, the two younger servants trailing him like puppies. A few steps from the servants' door, he hesitated. "Do you wish to follow precisely the same path we took? These halls are . . . not grand enough for guests, I fear. I would not wish to cause any insult."

He is worried about offending the Hellknights. Belvadio's concern about ushering her through the servants' door might have been reasonable if he'd been dealing with the touchiest of high Chelish lords, but she had no illusions that a steward who'd spent his entire life in service to a great house really believed that *her* rank was so exalted, or her skin so thin. This was caution and nothing but.

Jheraal snorted. "I'm not a duchess, Belvadio. I won't be insulted by walking through the service door. Just show me where you went."

"Forgive my presumption." Producing a ring of keys from some unseen pocket inside his blue coat, Belvadio unlocked the door and stepped aside to hold it open. "The young master's library will be up the stairs and to the right."

"Lead on."

He took her past the larder and buttery, through the kitchens, and up a flight of well-worn wooden stairs. No footprints stood out here, either.

At the top of the stairs, they reached the discreet little door that separated the servants' quarters from the nobles' halls. Quilted padding covered the servants' side of the door, insulating their superiors from any unwanted noise or smell that might drift up from the kitchens. The other side of the door, Jheraal noted, was painted white and adorned with gilded scrollwork. All the unsightliness—and all the function—was on the servants' side.

Although the servants' halls had been lit only by the daylight that streamed through their small, cloudy windows, enchanted lights shone serenely along the ceiling and upper walls of this corridor. Wide picture windows overlooked the manor's gardens, while carpets in faded blue and white sank under Jheraal's booted feet. The carpets were lush at the periphery but worn in the centers. That they hadn't been replaced suggested that House Celverian wasn't as rich as it had been in years past. No surprise. Failing fortunes were common among the old nobility that had declined to align strongly enough with House Thrune.

Nevertheless, it was lovely. The airy beauty of the upper hall was marred only by the faint whiff of blood that grew stronger as they approached an open door on the right.

"In there," Belvadio whispered. The color had drained from his face.

They hadn't moved the body. The mortal remains of Othando Celverian remained in the overstuffed armchair where he had presumably died. A linen sheet covered his slumped form imperfectly, trailing over part of the desk in front of him. A carafe and half-full wineglass rested on a silver tray near his elbow. Papers spilled across the floor by his side, along with a fallen candle stub trailing a comet's tail of wax spatters.

Jheraal stepped forward to examine him, taking care not to disturb the papers. "This is all as you found it?"

"Almost. There was . . . a cleric came before you. Udeno of Abadar. He looked over the master and said there was nothing he could do. Other than his examination, and the sheet I placed over the master, nothing has been touched."

The Hellknight nodded without looking up. With as much delicacy as she could muster, she lifted the sheet that covered Othando Celverian.

He had been a young man. Twenty-five, she guessed. Maybe a year or two to either side. Slim, handsome, with the soft hands and pale skin of a scholar who spent little time outdoors. Drying blood spilled from a single deep puncture wound on the side of his neck and darkened his sleeping robe in a crooked fan that widened as it stretched toward the floor. More blood painted the carpet behind him and to the side, and a single brownish-red fingerprint smudged his right arm near the elbow.

Othando's own hands were clean. That bloody fingerprint had come from someone else.

His face was buried in the pages of the book he'd been reading. When Jheraal lifted Othando's head, she saw that his eyes were wide and his lips slightly parted. The breeze from an open window fluttered dark blond hair across his brow. She couldn't tell if he had been talking, trying to cry out, or just gasping for breath in his last extremity, but it seemed that he'd been looking at someone when he died. The spill of blood from his wound suggested that he had turned toward, and then away from, something or someone at his back.

The killer? It was tempting to conclude that Othando must have seen his assassin. If he had, his shade might answer a cleric's prayer and identify his attacker.

Jheraal had been an investigator long enough to know that such hopes almost always proved futile. Something as simple as a mask or hood sufficed to prevent recognition, as every professional killer knew, and the dead were blessed with no more knowledge than they'd had in life. The Hellknight had worked on dozens of murders in the twelve years of her investigative career, all across Cheliax and its vassal states, and never once had she seen the spirit of an assassin's victim able to identify his killer. Amateurs might be named by the dead. Professionals never were.

That didn't mean she had no use for magic. Only that its use had to be less easily anticipated by her target.

She glanced at the open book. Drying blood gummed its pages and darkened the illustrations, but the lettering remained clear. It looked to be a collection of Taldan heroic stories—disgraced knights winning back the honor of tarnished houses, second sons and valiant daughters carving names for themselves in savage lands, heroes who vanquished monsters and won the love of their people. Tales to stir excitement into a quiet life.

The letters that had blown onto the floor appeared to be correspondence: invitations to various social events from other Wiscrani nobility, orders from his lord father at the family estate, and an unfinished letter from Othando himself to his exiled brother in Mendev.

Drawing the sheet back over the body, Jheraal stepped sideways to examine the desk. Two of the drawers were partly opened. One held signets in gold and bronze, sticks of sealing wax, unsharpened quills, a paring knife, and a wrinkled paper sachet of sugar-rolled mints. The other was empty save for a few faded stains at the bottom. The remaining drawers were locked.

She motioned to the desk. "Was anything taken from here? Or from Master Celverian himself?"

"I cannot be certain," Belvadio admitted. "The master's study was private. I did not notice anything stolen, but some small theft might have escaped my notice."

"How busy would the household have been at that hour?"

The steward took a moment to think it over. "We had no guests at the vaneo, and no entertaining planned for the next few days. Other than one or two of the under-cooks in the kitchen and the guards making their rounds, everyone should have been sleeping. Achio and Tirol were out only because they were making mischief."

"Was it Master Celverian's custom to leave that window open?" Jheraal gestured to the skylight, although she already knew the answer. That window was too high to be opened without the aid of a ladder, and she had seen none in the study.

Belvadio frowned, confirming her guess. "Pleasant as the weather is, no. The master was concerned that nothing should damage his books—not rain or sun or snow. The window was only to admit light to assist his reading. He never opened it."

"You said there were two other servants missing?"

"Chiella and Nodero." The steward fidgeted with a button, then caught himself and stopped, smoothing his coat. "Chiella was here when I sounded the alarm. I saw her with my own eyes. No one recalls seeing Nodero after he retired to his room last night. Both were gone by the time I found the master, or soon after."

"Do you believe they might have played some role in this?"

Belvadio shook his head vehemently. "Impossible. No one loved House Celverian more than Nodero and Chiella. Their loyalty is beyond question."

"You're sure of that? How?"

The silver-haired man exhaled. With a quick, uncomfortable glance at Jheraal, he said: "House Celverian has always been adamant that everyone in its service is to be dealt with fairly, as fits each person's talents and disposition, and that no one is to be slighted on account of their ancestry." Belvadio's eyes flickered to the carpet, avoiding her, on the word "ancestry."

The missing servants were hellspawn, then. No other reason for that discomfort. And not everyone on the staff was as accepting as their master had been, judging from the reception she'd gotten on the lawn.

"Those who offend this policy are dismissed without references, which is a death sentence for employment among the great houses. The young master, like his father, was an uncommonly enlightened man, and he was fiercely beloved by all who had the good fortune to serve him. It is inconceivable that either Chiella or Nodero would ever have done anything to hurt him, or to damage the honor of his house."

"As you say." It sounded like burnishing the virtues of the dead to her, but perhaps Othando Celverian really had been a saint among men. "I'll visit the church of Abadar to speak with the cleric who examined Master Celverian, and then return to the Order of the Rack's garrison. Please send word when his father, Lord Celverian, arrives in Westcrown."

"Of course." He followed her back out of the manor, keeping always two paces behind and a half-step to the side, like the most discreet of ghosts. As they reached the servants' door, however, the steward took a small step forward.

"Truly," he said, dropping his reserve for a moment and letting her see the real anguish beneath, "I don't believe Chiella or Nodero could have had any part in this horror, let alone both of them together. Never. In my bones, I know they are innocent. But I do believe someone might try to use them to discredit their kind. Not everyone approved of the master's views on hellspawn, and some of the servants I was forced to dismiss might seek revenge for their disgrace."

No servant could afford to hire an assassin with that much skill. They might have aided in the killer's plots, but they couldn't have been the driving force. "Did he have enemies among the nobility?"

"The young master? No. He was being courted by some of the lesser houses with marriageable daughters, but as yet he had chosen none, so no one had reason to be insulted by his refusal. He had no position at court and no place in political schemes, and his hobbies were harmless. Master Celverian was a dreamer and a scholar. He was no threat to anyone."

"What about the rest of his house?"

Belvadio opened the door. Outside, the sun was a glory and the birds were singing, and Westcrown's life went on. Even within the vaneo's walls, the rhythms of the day were returning. A washerwoman pinned damp sheets to her lines. Across the yard, a stocky, freckle-faced boy carted muck from the stables. Already, the night was beginning to recede in their memories.

"Their mistakes are in the past," the steward said, returning Jheraal to the city.

The cleric of Abadar had little to tell her. Yes, he had gone to the vaneo that morning. Yes, he had seen Master Celverian's corpse. No, he had no suspicions regarding how the murder might have been carried out, nor about who would have had a motive to strike at House Celverian's younger son.

"It's what they do, isn't it?" Udeno shrugged. "The courts are snake pits. No surprise when one gets bitten by a viper."

Jheraal hadn't argued, but as she walked down the temple's steps back into the canal-lined streets of Westcrown's Rego Sacero, she'd thought, *Not like this.*

It was true that the Chelish nobility spent an inordinate amount of time plotting against each other, and that espionage and assassination were well-used weapons in their arsenals. But it was also true that blatant, barefaced murder was considered extremely bad form.

Cheliax prided itself on being a nation governed by law. Its killers might disguise their doings as hunting accidents, food poisoning, or highway robberies gone wrong. The more cunning and ambitious might even go so far as to trump up criminal charges and let the royal executioners take their enemies' heads.

But they *did* disguise their murders, because otherwise they invited the full wrath that Cheliax visited upon all those who broke its laws.

The assassination of a well-born scholar in his study was precisely the sort of crime that offended Her Imperial Majestrix and insulted her rule. That it had happened in Westcrown, which chafed at its loss of prominence under House Thrune and needed little provocation to stoke its smoldering discontents into new flame, made the investigation more urgent. And that the victim had been an eligible young bachelor who was actively courted by several Wiscrani houses added an edge of intrigue. Jheraal guessed that there were several furious dowagers who were eager to learn which of their rivals might have destroyed their daughters' prospects.

For all these reasons, it was exceedingly important that she find the killer.

No one had said this, of course. Not explicitly. The mere fact of her assignment made it clear enough. Jheraal was of the Order of the Scourge, and she had been chosen to investigate a crime in a city where the Order of the Rack held sway. There were any number of messages bound up in that, but the key one was that Her Imperial Majestrix expected results. Failure was not to be countenanced. That was why Jheraal, of all the investigators available to the Hellknights, had been singled out and sent to serve. The Queen wanted answers, and Jheraal was meant to find them.

The obvious course was to question Lord Celverian. But the lord hadn't yet arrived in Westcrown, so Jheraal returned to Taranik House, the Order of the Rack's base of operations in the city, to see whether any messages had come.

There was one. The courier, a towheaded halfling boy, was standing in the foyer and filling his satchel with new missives when Jheraal arrived. He dropped the packet he was holding and waved excitedly when he saw her. "Jheraal! Hellknight Jheraal!"

Jheraal raised a hand to calm him. "What?"

"I have a message of utmost urgency. Utmost! From Durotas Tuornos. His rundottari found bodies in Rego Cader. Two from House Celverian. The durotas said you'd want to know immediately. Here—he wrote this for you, but it only says the same thing." The boy held out a folded slip. It had been hastily written. The ink soaked through the cheap paper.

"He was correct." The Hellknight took the letter, gave it a cursory look, and put her horned helm back on. Rego Cader, the long-abandoned Dead Sector of the city, was infamously perilous, full of thieves and murderers and worse. Even the dottari, Westcrown's city guard, didn't like to linger in those blighted ruins. Rego Cader was so dangerous that it had its own division of the guard—the rundottari, or "ruin wardens"—dedicated exclusively to holding back the threats that proliferated in that sector. "Bodies, you said. Where, exactly? Are they still there?"

"I don't know." The halfling said, fumbling to pick up the packet he'd dropped, "but Durotas Tuornos is on the Obrigan Gate. He hoped that you would hurry. He hoped, also, that you would send word to the capital. For a wizard."

"Why? Aren't there enough wizards in Westcrown?"

"I don't know." The boy shook his head in helpless confusion. He closed his overstuffed bag and went to the door. "The durotas didn't tell me, not really. All he said was that there was magic in this. Deviltry. And . . ." he swallowed, "and that the dead might not be dead."

2

THE CRUSADER'S FAREWELL

EDERRAS

The letter was brief. One paragraph in his father's bold forward-sweeping hand, surrounded by emptiness. *Your brother has been murdered. Come home.*

There were other words on the page, but they were meaningless. Ederras might have read them and might not. He remembered only those first two lines, black and lacerating and raw with grief. *Your brother has been murdered. Come home.*

He put the letter down on his desk and spread his hand over it, blocking the words from his sight. They didn't leave his mind as easily.

The last time Ederras had been in Westcrown, Othando had been an ebullient boy of eleven. Although conscious of his family duties, he'd been very much a child, daydreaming about himself as a wandering knight and champion of the downtrodden.

In the decade and a half since—and especially after Ederras's exile—those daydreams had given way to the reality of duty. The brothers had corresponded through letters over the years, and had met occasionally outside the city of their birth, but their paths had diverged that summer. Ederras had disgraced himself, and Othando had become the heir to House Celverian.

Ederras had always thought they'd have more opportunity to reconcile. He'd been close to his brother as a boy, but letters and visits were a poor approximation of knowing the man. And now even that was gone.

A gust of wind tore across his tent, dimpling the canvas walls and rattling the lamps so that their flames left black ribbons of soot along their glassy prisons. The wind smelled of brimstone and burning blood, as it too often did out here by the Worldwound.

When was the last time he had felt a clean breeze or breathed air that wasn't poisoned with madness and despair? When was the last time he'd walked through gardens given over to the luxury of flowers instead of crowded with the scraggly, stunted crops that sustained Mendev's defenders?

Ederras couldn't remember. The memories slipped through his grasp like smoke. He *had* seen and felt such things, he knew, and not that long ago. Queen Galfrey's advisors insisted that all the troops along the Worldwound be allowed periods of respite away from the front lines so that they might remember what it was they were fighting so fiercely to defend. But those days of rest might as well have been in another lifetime, and in someone else's life.

Westcrown, though . . . Westcrown was as vivid as if he'd left it yesterday.

"Will you be sending a message back, sir?" The adjutant was new to her post—new to the Worldwound altogether, in fact—and plainly nonplussed by Ederras's reaction to the letter.

"No. Thank you." He'd forgotten she was there. Lifting his hand, the paladin folded the letter neatly in two. The outlines of his father's script showed through the thin paper, but only barely. He could pretend they were but shadows in the dim light of his tent. "Please send Sorellon to my tent."

"Yes, Knight-Captain." The redheaded woman bowed and retreated, letting in another chilly gust of sulfurous wind.

Sorellon arrived a few minutes later. The old gnome had been drinking again. The smell of rotgut whiskey surrounded him like cheap perfume. He was upright, though, and his hands were mostly steady on his brass-capped walking stick, which meant he was about as sober as Ederras had ever seen him.

"Girl said you wanted to see me?"

Ederras gestured to a chair opposite his desk. "Have a seat."

"I'll stay standing, if it's all the same to you. Not sure how easily I'd get up again if I sat." The gnome leaned forward on his walking stick, swaying slightly. His eyes were yellow and cloudy, and his breath had a musty smell.

"You'll be dead in six months if you keep drinking like that." Ederras wasn't even sure where Sorellon got the rotgut. It was well known among the troops that their knight-captain had no tolerance for drinking anywhere near the Worldwound, where the slightest carelessness could doom an entire company. Wine was forbidden to Ederras's soldiers once they left town, yet somehow that had never stopped the wispy-haired old wizard.

The gnome snorted. "I'll be dead in six months with or without my bottle. Least this way I'll keep warm in the meantime. Now, what was so important you called me across camp for it?"

"I need you to send a dream message to Nerosyan. I don't care which of the commandants you contact, but do it tonight. Tell them I'm resigning my command as soon as we return to the city. They'll have to appoint someone else to lead the company. I give my recommendation to Kehora and Three-Tongue, but of course it's not for me to make the final decision. You'll have to help teach the ropes to whomever they choose, in any case."

"Three-Tongue?" Sorellon shuddered. "That bear-greased barbarian? He barely knows twenty words of any civilized tongue."

"They're twenty words worth hearing. Better than you can say for some officers."

"I suppose." The gnome squinted at Ederras from under his long, wispy eyebrows. "Better than most of your other alternatives, now that I think on it. Brave, got fair judgment, treats his soldiers well enough, in his way. Not sure how well them uppity Taldan knights are going to take to Three-Tongue handing them chunks of hacked-up silver bracelet as prizes for a good mission, but hopefully they'll see his heart's in the right place. That's more than most crusaders these days, and I count myself in that number."

"Indeed." The glory days of the Mendevian Crusades were long past. Once, the radiant army had been the flower of chivalry across the Inner Sea: paladins, clerics of every brave and goodly god, men and women whose virtue was equal to the strength of their sword arms.

Those days were gone. Today, a crusader was more likely to be a poacher fleeing the hangman, or a desperate bandit hoping for easy plunder, than anyone with a shred of either honor or skill. While a scattering of true souls remained, especially around Queen Galfrey and her stronghold in Nerosyan, the shining beacon of the Mendevian Crusade was neither as bright nor as clear as it once had been.

Ederras spent much of his time trying to coax the small sparks he found into light. Sorellon had spoken truly: Three-Tongue *was* a Kellid barbarian, given to eating the hearts of his foes and painting his face in their blood. He wore fetishes of hair and bone, prayed to a savage god in a strange tongue, and could scarcely write his own name.

Kehora, who had been born a poor farmer's daughter under the rule of a petty lord, was worse. At sixteen, Kehora had turned to banditry to survive when unjust fines claimed her parents' farm. She'd spent years as a robber queen, preying on that lordling's guards and tax collectors, until one of her own betrayed her and sold her to a company of low templars heading to Mendev. She might have escaped, but within weeks her traitorous underling had led her people into ruin, and nothing was left for Kehora at home but a choice between the hangman and the headsman. So instead the onetime bandit queen had come to Mendev, and eventually to Ederras's command.

Neither Kehora nor Three-Tongue had been paragons of knightly virtue when they'd come to the crusade. Both had initially thought their captain's codes and strictures foolish, and neither had been shy about saying so. But both the barbarian and the bandit had a core of the true steel at their hearts, and brought out the best qualities in those they led. Ederras had seen it, and had spent long months carefully strengthening and polishing it, while the hardships of the Worldwound burned away their old foibles until only that steel remained.

If he'd had years, he might have turned them into great generals. Instead, he'd had months, and could only pray that one or both of them had learned enough to keep their troops from disaster.

It would be no easy task. Whoever took his command would inherit a motley collection of the disgraced and desperate. Wet-eared novices, sellswords from broken companies, gutter rats who had knifed countless victims in the back but never faced a foe in open combat. Their company wizard was a drunk and their cleric was a disgrace.

Ederras hoped they would succeed, but in truth he didn't know. Able commanders were a rarity around the Worldwound, and his departure would be a blow.

Across the desk, Sorellon had reached the same conclusion. The gnome's expression had grown dark as the implications of Ederras's words sank in. "So you're leaving us, eh? Getting out while you've still got legs to walk away on? Can't say I blame you, but I never thought you'd be one to have that much sense."

"It's not that. There's been a death in the family. I have to go home." It stung to be accused of cowardice, however obliquely. Perhaps that hadn't been Sorellon's intent, but Ederras couldn't help but feel that the gnome was suggesting that he was abandoning his duty. His soldiers.

Or maybe that was just his own guilt speaking.

"Where *is* home for you, anyway?" Curiosity seemed to have cut through the air of inebriated indifference that Sorellon wrapped around himself. "Somewhere in Cheliax, isn't it? Egorian? I'd mark you for an Egorian man, myself. You have the air of a fellow who knows his way around the capital. I've been there myself, you know. Lots of good-looking girls around Egorian. Lots of devils too, of course. Must be hard for a fellow like you. Say, is that why you left? Why you came here? Because of the devils?"

Ederras sighed. "Send the message, Sorellon. Tonight. That will be all."

Too short a time later, they returned to Nerosyan, the Diamond of the North.

The sight of the city gladdened Ederras, despite his weariness. Nerosyan had been built for defense against fiends in all their forms, but the city was far more than a military bulwark. It was a place of beauty and harmony, where the crowning glories of all the civilized races were held aloft to serve as a spiritual rebuke to the demons' all-consuming destruction.

We will not go quietly. That was the proclamation in Nerosyan's white and gold towers. *We stand here, and we will stop you, and all the despair that you bring. We stand here, unbowed.*

Time and again, Ederras had ridden out from those shining walls to do his part in keeping that promise true. Often he hadn't expected to return. But always fortune had smiled upon him, and always he had felt his heart lift when the towers of Nerosyan came back into view. The defenders held. Their defiance burned. The Worldwound would not creep past their watch.

Today, however, his return to Nerosyan brought a pang of regret along with the joy.

With each step, Ederras came closer to abandoning the righteous cause that had restored his sense of purpose in the world and returned him to Iomedae's holy graces. With each step, he came closer to Cheliax, where it was almost impossible to live by the code that had strengthened and sustained him in the Worldwound.

It was in Westcrown that Ederras had failed and fallen. He had no wish to go back.

But his father had summoned him, his family needed him, and he had to obey.

At the gates, the white-cloaked guards waved his company in after a short exchange of passwords and a nod of approval from the cleric on duty, signifying that she had sensed no taint of supernatural evil and no masking magic among the returning troops.

"Commandant Monteyu is waiting to see you," the gate captain informed Ederras. "She's in the Cruciform Cathedral."

"Thank you." Ederras bowed his head in acknowledgement. He dismounted, handing his warhorse's reins to Kehora. The stallion was too well trained, and too valuable, for him to take from his command. He'd leave the horse behind to serve another master, and go on foot himself. Brushing the animal's flank in farewell, Ederras gave what he expected would be his last order in Mendev. "My troops: dismissed."

As they dispersed, Sorellon patted the paladin's leg. The old gnome looked completely sober. "You did well by us. Kept us alive, more often than not. I'm glad you're going, though. Glad you're getting out. You deserve better than this."

"This was the best part of my life," Ederras said.

The gnome pursed his lips in a soundless whistle. "Some life you've led."

"Indeed. Goodbye, Sorellon. Try to keep the new recruits out of trouble." Taking the reins of his pack mule, Ederras set off toward the Cruciform Cathedral.

It was, by design, a short walk. The Cruciform Cathedral stood at the heart of Nerosyan, its four great halls arranged so that its defenders could be deployed swiftly to any part of the city. The Cathedral served simultaneously as the center of faith, military leadership, and governance in Mendev, but like the city it ruled, it sought to lead as much by inspiration as by might. Its pennon-crowned towers and high walls were built in smooth, clean lines, as pleasing to the eye as they were effective in defense.

At the base of those walls, Ederras shrugged off his pack and handed the mule's reins to a dwarven stable hand. The dwarf must have been very young; although stout and burly, he had only scant blond fuzz around his chin.

"Do you want a stall?" the stable hand asked, hoisting the pack onto his own shoulders.

Ederras shook his head. "I won't be staying long. We'll be leaving within the hour."

"Very good, Knight-Captain. I will see that your animal is ready."

"Thank you." The paladin took off his helm and tucked it under an arm as he stepped into the shade of the Cruciform Cathedral.

Peace settled over him almost immediately. A whisper of sacred incense threaded through the cathedral's cool stone halls. Under one of the apses Ederras passed, a chorus was practicing sacred hymns, and their harmonious voices soared over the corridors. Marble reliefs wound around the support columns and covered the walls in broad bands, depicting the triumphs of the First Mendevian Crusade and narrating incidents from the holy scriptures of Sarenrae, Iomedae, and their allied gods.

More than Westcrown had ever been, this place was his home. *This* was where Iomedae had called him. This was where he was meant to do his life's work. He had never truly known peace except here.

Commandant Monteyu's guards stepped aside as Ederras came to her office, knocking to announce his presence before they opened the door. He nodded to each of them and stepped inside.

It was a clean, impersonal space, all in white and gold. Most of the north wall was dominated by an enchanted map of Mendev and the Worldwound. The wardstones glowed in tranquil shades of turquoise and sea green, a delicate strand of lights holding back the smoky pall that signified the Worldwound.

Some of the lights were weaker than others. A few flickered on the edge of extinction. *The war never ends.* And yet he was leaving.

The commandant rose to greet him as he entered. No one knew much of her history before she'd come to Mendev, but it was widely rumored that Commandant Monteyu had been a pirate of the Shackles before joining the crusade.

She certainly looked the part. Three heavy gold rings dangled from each of her earlobes, and her coarse black hair was twisted into dreadlocks that hung halfway down her back. Across her cheekbones, chest, and upper arms, whirling flames in vibrant gold, green, and scarlet had been tattooed upon her rich brown skin. When the commandant crossed the slash of sunlight that fell through the cathedral's windows, the ink of her tattoos sparkled like powdered diamonds.

Her accent, however, was pure Nerosyan. Not a hint of the Shackles colored her words. "Knight-Captain Ederras. I received your wizard's message. You're resigning your commission?"

"I am." It was no small sacrifice. Queen Galfrey herself had confirmed his commission—after he'd been knighted in the field, to be sure, but a considerable honor nonetheless—and Ederras held no illusions that he'd be restored to the same rank if he returned to the crusade. Not for a year or more, at least. "My family needs me in Westcrown. My brother was murdered, and his killer hasn't been found." *And I'm the last heir to my house.*

"I wish you swift justice. Will you return to us when the crime has been solved?"

"I hope to, if my obligations allow." He didn't think the chances of that were high, though. Without a son to carry on the line, his house would die with him—and Ederras's duty to his family outweighed his duty to the crusade. In Mendev, he was valuable, but not indispensable. To House Celverian, he was irreplaceable. This had the feeling of a final farewell.

"Your service to our cause has been exceptional. The queen can't offer you a wizard to take you directly to Westcrown, unfortunately. Not in Nerosyan. Their spells are needed for more urgent matters."

"I would never have expected—"

Commandant Monteyu cut him off with a quick shake of her head. The gold rings in her ears clattered against one another, swaying loosely in holes that had widened under their weight. "We can't spare a wizard here. But in Karcau, there are some who sell their spells for gold or favor, and who owe much to many in our crusade. You have passage on the *Raven's Daughter* down the Egelsee River to Karcau, if you wish to take it. There you should be able to find a wizard to hire at a fair price."

"Thank you. When does the ship leave?"

"This evening. If you need the time, however, the captain will wait a day or two."

"No. This evening will serve perfectly." Prolonging his departure would only make it more difficult. Best to make a clean break, and quickly.

The commandant nodded. "Good fortune to you, Knight-Captain."

Sunset found Ederras and his pack mule on the *Raven's Daughter*, watching Nerosyan recede along with the dying day. The Egelsee River, its waters luminous with dissolved silt, reflected a pointillist impression of the blue- and pink-streaked clouds overhead. The river's radiance grew as that of the heavens dimmed, until they floated through the starry night on a wide swath of liquid moonlight.

As the Egelsee carried them south and west toward Ustalav, the concentration of cloudy silt in its waters diminished, and so too did their glow. The change came quickly; by midnight, well before Ederras thought they had reached the border, the river had gone entirely dark. Only the churning bubbles in their wake shone white under the low full moon.

It felt like a mirror to his own journey. With each passing minute, the brightness of spirit that Ederras had felt in Mendev dwindled. Darkness lay ahead for him, and a duty far heavier than any he had carried by the borders of the Worldwound.

3

THE HEARTLESS

JHERAAL

In twelve years as an investigator, Jheraal had seen her share of horror.

The Hellknight had witnessed the worst that arsonists' flames and spurned lovers' knives could do to flesh and bone. She'd seen the ruin of children beaten beyond recognition by drunk fathers' fists. She had uncovered the remains of innocents subjected to the occult rites of Urgathoan cultists, and stood expressionless beside the gallows as the executioners of House Thrune tortured criminals to death in showy displays for the crowd's jeers.

She had thought there was nothing left that could frighten her. And then she had seen what the rundottari had found in that stinking, mud-floored hovel among the ruins of Rego Cader.

The dead man bothered her the least of the four bodies in that shack. The fast-spreading fungus that had consumed his flesh was troubling, but more for what it might signify than for its own sake. Jheraal had seen decomposed corpses before, and while she was concerned about the implications of the mold that fuzzed the dead man's bones, the sight itself didn't disturb her. Not compared to the others in that place.

Slumped behind a tattered curtain were three hellspawn, each with a fist-sized, cauterized wound burned into the center of his or her chest. Two, presumably the missing servants Chiella and Nodero, wore the colors of House Celverian. The third was a more obviously devil-descended woman dressed like a fishmonger from one of the poorer districts.

All three were missing their hearts—Jheraal had held a light to each of those gaping wounds and looked closely to be sure—and yet they lived. Their mutilated chests rose and fell in steady breaths. A ghostly pulse beat in their wrists. When the Hellknight brought her light to their eyes and held open their eyelids, their pupils contracted under its glare, and then dilated when she put the light away.

They seemed to be comatose. Jheraal pricked each hellspawn's fingertips with the tip of her dagger, prodding them hard enough to draw beads of blood from the pads of their thumbs, but none of them flinched. She clapped her hands sharply next to their heads and shouted into their ears, but none stirred. Their faces remained slack, their breathing slow.

"What do you want to do with them?" one of the rundottari asked. Two ruin wardens armed with swords and crossbows had accompanied her out of the Obrigan Gate to meet the one waiting to show them the bodies. As formidable as the Hellknight was, even she wasn't expected to venture into Rego Cader without protection.

"They need a healer's attention," Jheraal said. "These servants may be innocent victims."

The rundottari spat on the muddy floor, displeased by her answer. "Or they may not. No offense meant to you, but they're hellspawn. And whatever killed that moldy fellow might be contagious. This whole thing might be a trap."

Jheraal gave him a flat stare. She was taller than the rundottari, and she used that to her advantage, looming over him in the scarred steel of her Hellknight plate. "If Durotas Tuornos believed that, he wouldn't have sent for me. Those servants are wearing House Celverian's colors. You will, of course, have heard what happened at their vaneo last night. These two might have seen something, or might have other leads to offer. If we can't get them healed, we'll never know. And if I lose valuable information about the Celverian murders because you were afraid of a little mold, well, I can't imagine your durotas will be pleased. Nor will his superiors. What you should be wondering is not whether this is a trap, but where you might be able to keep these people."

Licking his lips, the rundottari looked away. "There are cells in Keep Dotar that might serve, and a few under the Obrigan Gate."

"I'll take the ones under the gate." Keep Dotar, where the rundottari were based, was located in the northeastern part of the Dead Sector, far from the rest of the city, and was too remote to be useful. Jheraal didn't want secrecy. She wanted a full investigation that would force the killer to light. But she also didn't want to keep them at Taranik House, where rivals in the Order of the Rack might try to interfere with or claim credit for her work. The Obrigan Gate was neutral, but accessible.

She unslung her pack and took out a large, flat box. It was much heavier than it looked. Although only plain wood showed on the outside, the interior was lined with a half-inch of lead and a thin coating of silver over the base metal.

Perhaps the precaution was unnecessary, but she didn't want to risk bringing some Urgathoan contagion into the city. Holding her breath and working quickly, Jheraal stacked the moldering bones into the lead-lined box. When the last of them had been tucked inside, leaving only a fuzzy shadow of white powder on the floor, she took out a long cylinder of soft white wax and held it over the rundottari's lantern.

It took only a few seconds for the cylinder's end to sag and start dripping. Quickly, while it was pliable, Jheraal scrubbed the wax against the box's seam. The molten wax flowed into the crevices and hardened in place.

After a few more rounds of softening and scrubbing, the seal was complete. Not a breath of air would get out of that box until she'd taken it safely back for inspection.

The Hellknight took a card out of her pocket and handed it to one of the rundottari. "Deliver this to Havarel Needlethumbs in Parego Spera. The card has the address. He's expecting the package."

The rundottari lifted the box, holding it as far away from himself as the length of his arms allowed. "I'll wait for you. Safer if we all go back together."

"Fine." It was cowardice, but she couldn't fault him. No one wanted to walk through Rego Cader alone. Jheraal hoisted the unconscious hellspawn man and slung him over her shoulder, motioning for the two remaining rundottari to grab the other hellspawn. It wasn't the gentlest way to carry them, but it was the fastest, and dusk was rapidly approaching. "Let's go."

They made their way back to the Obrigan Gate in silence but for occasional grunts and curses when one of the rundottari stumbled over a gap in the rutted streets while carrying the senseless devilspawn. Around them, the crumbling shells of Westcrown's former grandeur cast ever-longer shadows, while the red sun sank down between their broken towers.

For eight hundred years, the city of Westcrown had been the capital of Cheliax and one of the wonders of the world. Clad in shining white marble and gold, its beauty had been renowned from sea to sea. Beyond its architectural splendors, the city had been famed as a place of art, learning, and the high glories of religious faith.

Then Aroden, patron god of humanity and the nation of Cheliax, had died and cast his people into turmoil. Civil war tore the country apart, and when the fighting ended a generation later, the devil-binding House Thrune was ascendant. Queen Abrogail the First, new ruler of the empire, moved her capital north to Egorian, and Westcrown entered a long decline.

Its population shrunken, its splendors diminished, its streets and historic buildings scarred by years of civil war, Westcrown pulled back to its central districts and abandoned the poorer neighborhoods along the north shore to ruin.

Today, the sculpted fountains that had once flowed with fresh water for Westcrown's downtrodden were filled with weeds and cobwebs. Nothing remained of the sculpted angels that had once ringed the basins except empty plinths bearing mottled crowns of bird droppings. The angels themselves were gone, having been stolen and sold to art collectors who wanted the masterworks for themselves. It was, Jheraal supposed, a fitting symbol of the city's decline that the marvelous public works that had once served its most vulnerable had been scavenged and hoarded away by a wealthy few.

The other signs of Westcrown's deterioration were less poetic but more dangerous. The wooden bones of taverns, inns, and dilapidated stables lined the pocked streets around their little party. No law-abiding citizens lived among them, but some of those ruins were the lairs of squatters and bandits. Others were infested with all manner of bloodthirsty beasts. On their way out, Jheraal and the rundottari had seen nothing more dangerous than a pack of starved dogs, but not all visits to the Dead Sector were so peaceful.

The Obrigan Gate marked the point at which civilization began again in Westcrown. Until they passed through its portcullises and put Rego Cader safely on the far side of its wall, they remained vulnerable.

She hefted the senseless hellspawn on her shoulders and trudged along a little faster. The man's weight compressed her armor, and the edge of her chestplate was digging into her flesh, but Jheraal forced the pain out of her mind. She'd chosen to carry the male servant for a reason. As long as she carried a heavier weight than the rundottari, and did so without complaint, they wouldn't dare shirk their own burdens.

A Hellknight she might be, and devil-blooded to boot, but she was also a woman. None of the three men behind her would let themselves fall behind. It might be pure chauvinism that drove them, but if it drove them, Jheraal would use it. She hadn't survived fourteen years in Citadel Demain, and then in the wider world, by being blind to the levers that moved people's souls. And she wanted to get out of Rego Cader before dark.

Smoke drifted through the weeds that fringed the mouth of an alley to her left. Jheraal's skin prickled. There *were* relatively harmless transients living in the ruins, and the smoke might be from something as simple as a squatter's cookfire. But there were arsonists, too, and madmen, and creatures of shadow that crept out with the night.

And something that stole the hearts of its victims and consigned them to a living death.

She hurried her pace. The thirty-foot-high wall surrounding the Obrigan Gate was visible now, rising above the skeletal rafters and chimney stumps that made up the crumbling skyline of the Dead Sector. Torches and lanterns lined its parapets in golden ribbons of fire.

Jheraal led her companions into the swath of clear space that covered the last hundred feet around the wall. They were within crossbow range of the Obrigan Gate's defenders. Behind them, dusk blurred the ruins and filled every empty doorway with black menace, but it didn't matter anymore. They were safe.

One of the small portcullises in the gate's base opened. A rundottari waved them hastily through, peering into the twilight with his lantern raised high. As Jheraal ushered her escort into the Obrigan Gate, then followed them inside, worry slid off her shoulders like a blanket of lead. The thud of the portcullis closing behind them was the most welcome sound she'd heard in days.

"See anything dangerous out there?" the gate guard asked.

"Not as such." Jheraal lowered the comatose hellspawn to the ground. Her shoulders ached, but she refused to stretch them or adjust her chafing armor where the rundottari might see. Hellknights admitted no weakness. "Do you have a spare cell big enough to hold all three?"

The guard hesitated, but after a glance at the rundottari, he nodded. "This way. The cells under the Gate have held worse than hellspawn."

Another small insult. Accidental, probably. Ignoring the rudeness, Jheraal picked up her living burden once more and followed the guard down a set of winding stairs to a niter-streaked dungeon. Twice she bumped against the cramped walls, jolting her armor into bruised flesh, but she refused to wince. *You do not feel pain. There is no pain.* "Send a messenger to the Qatada Nessudidia." The Asmodean cathedral was the largest temple in Westcrown, and would have the most powerful clerics to be found in the city. "Durotas Tuornos was correct: there is some unholy magic in this. I require a wizard and a cleric, the best that they have, to examine these poor souls. Immediately."

"We shall send the request at once," the rundottari assured her, opening an iron-barred cell door. Damp and littered with moldy straw, it was far from welcoming, but Jheraal had stayed in worse. She didn't think her insensible charges were likely to complain.

She laid the hellspawn on the straw, cradling the man's head against her gauntleted forearm. Removing a roll of bandages from her pack, she spread the gauzy cotton over the wound that disfigured his chest. It would do nothing for his missing heart, but she felt the man deserved that much dignity. "Good. Send word to Taranik House when they arrive."

After ensuring that the heart-stripped hellspawn had been settled safely into their barred beds at the Obrigan Gate, Jheraal returned to Taranik House alone.

Night had drawn its cloak over the city, and in Westcrown that meant that the main streets were lined with pyrahjes, enormous torches as high as men, that filled the avenues with fiery heat. Smaller lanterns hung from the doors of respectable private homes, and lines of torches or enchanted spell-lights drew cordons of radiance around the viras and vaneos of the wealthy. Anything to keep the dark at bay.

Fire was a perpetual hazard in the city, and walking between the pyrahjes on a summer evening could be uncomfortably warm, but the Wiscrani had deemed these costs worth bearing in exchange for safety from Westcrown's nightly curse.

From dusk till dawn, throughout the city, shadows hunted the unwary. Those who broke the nocturnal curfew and ventured beyond the streets protected by torch and lantern took their lives into their hands.

The way to Taranik House was well lit, however, and Jheraal walked the streets without fear. She was deadlier than any hunter in shadow, and she knew it.

So did they. No challenges came from the night.

Back in the garrison, the Hellknight returned to her quarters, locked the door, and finally allowed herself a sigh of relief as she took off her heavy plate. The padding underneath was soaked with sweat, and the fine, soft white scales on her skin had been dented and deformed where the armor pressed into her. Some had chafed off entirely. They floated to the floor like snowflakes when she pulled the padded jerkin over her head, leaving angry pink lines behind.

Jheraal daubed a soothing ointment onto the raw spots along her shoulders and under her right arm, where the armor had bitten in, then tied a soft sleeping robe around herself. In the morning, when she had to put on her public face again, she would be as stoic as the honor of the Hellknights required. For now, she could allow herself a small measure of comfort without shame.

At her desk, she sprinkled a few drops of water on the block of compressed ink she carried with her. While waiting for the ink to soften, Jheraal sharpened a new quill and took out three sheets of good paper: one for the nightly report she sent back to her superiors in Citadel Demain, and two for a letter to her daughter.

The report took little time to write. In quick, broad strokes, Jheraal summarized her visit to Rego Cader and her interactions with Durotas Tuorno's rundottari. She detailed the condition of the heartless hellspawn as carefully as she could, keeping her opinions out of the factual descriptions.

As an afterthought, Jheraal included a request for a consultation with the most skilled wizard that the Order of the Scourge might be able to offer. Udeno of Abadar, the cleric who had examined the late Othando Celverian's body, hadn't impressed her, and she wasn't sure any Wiscrani wizard would be better. Durotas Tuornos had thought it best to request a wizard from the capital, and perhaps he'd been right. Even if she could find someone uninvolved in the local nobles' scheming, indifference and fatalism seemed to rule the day in Westcrown. Anyone with real ambition would have sought a post in Egorian, so her odds of finding a wizard capable of unraveling this mystery were likely better there.

She sealed the letter and set it aside. Then, more slowly, Jheraal dribbled another trickle of water across the eroded slope of her ink block and smoothed a new sheet between her white-scaled hands.

Dear Indrath, she began, *I hope this letter finds you well, and that the summer is not too hot in Egorian.*

Then she stopped, at a loss for what to add. The flame of her lantern crackled in the silence. A bead of ink grew bulbous on the tip of her quill. She caught it and moved it back to the block just before it would have spattered on the near-empty page.

What could she write to a daughter who didn't even know who she was?

The truth, a small, plaintive voice whispered, as it had since the day Jheraal had brought her infant daughter to Citadel Demain, claiming the girl was a foundling.

And just as she had then, and as she'd done every day for the fourteen years since, the Hellknight pushed that voice aside. The truth would do her daughter no good.

Indrath had been born with the blessing of a fully human appearance. No hint of her mother's infernal heritage showed in her face, her speech, or her soul. She was a strong, gifted, *good* child, a child who could live her life free of the prejudices that had hobbled Jheraal's own life—as long as the truth remained unknown.

Jheraal would have given anything for that blessing herself. She would not deny it to her daughter.

She scratched her quill against the block's softening ink. *I saw this book in a shop window,* she continued, agonizing over every word, *and thought you might be entertained to read it. A collection of tall tales and outright lies, I don't doubt, but perhaps someday you'll get to see for yourself, and tell me if there was any truth to such fancies.*

She stopped again, her mind as blank as the rest of the page. What could she write next? Was that enough? Jheraal had barely begun, yet she couldn't think of a single thing to add. Her current investigation was nothing that needed to trouble an innocent child's thoughts, and she'd done little else in Westcrown. She had no amusing anecdotes, no profound insights, nothing that she imagined other people wrote in their clever letters. The Hellknight felt like a hammer, all bluntness and force, when she wanted to be deft as a scalpel in dissecting the world into bites that could fit a child's mouth.

Even her gift suddenly felt too clumsy. It was a collection of the adventures of Durvin Gest, infamous Pathfinder, and his recovery of the legendary Scepter of Ages. Jheraal had seen many versions of Gest's adventures over the years, but this volume, unique among them, included numerous detailed descriptions of his travels into the ruins of lost Ninshabur. The accompanying illustrations were lavishly colored and easily tripled the cost of the book. She'd spent half a month's wages to buy it, and then she'd paid an extra silver for the shopkeeper to wrap the book in paper pressed with tiny, exotic dried flowers.

Since she could first read, Indrath had loved stories about Durvin Gest. She'd been particularly fascinated with the far-off continent of Casmaron, where the fallen empire of Ninshabur was said to be located. Once, she had delighted in telling Jheraal about how someday she was going to travel to Casmaron and chart its territories as an envoy for Imperial Cheliax. One of her most prized possessions was a small ivory elephant, supposedly carved by an artisan in those far-flung lands, which Jheraal had purchased for her in the markets of Kaer Maga.

But that had been three or four years ago, and Indrath was fourteen now. Almost fifteen. Maybe a storybook was too childish for her.

Jheraal didn't know. Her own daughter, and she didn't know. It had been months since she'd last seen Indrath.

I hope you'll like it, she finished, and signed: *Your friend, Jheraal.*

"Your friend." She stared at those words, so small and inadequate to carry the burden she wanted to put on them.

There was so much more she wanted to say, and nothing else she could.

Sighing, she sealed the letter with a daub of wax and tucked it under the string that the shopkeeper had tied around the paperwrapped book. She stacked the parcel next to the report she was sending back to her order. It, too, would go out in the morning.

Then Jheraal leaned back in her chair, folded her hands into her lap, and closed her eyes, trying to imagine who would tear the hearts out of hellspawn, and why, and what might be gained by leaving those maimed unfortunates alive.

4

REGRET AND REUNION

EDERRAS

It felt so strange to walk through Westcrown.

For years, the City of Twilight had been the center of Ederras's life. He had been born in Vaneo Celverian. His earliest memories were of sunlight streaming through the lace-curtained windows of his nursery and of birds singing in the lemon trees outside. As a boy, he'd stolen figs from the orchard and honeyed tarts from the kitchen, and had run out to the gardens to eat them in secret with his brother.

When he grew older, and more aware of life outside the privileged walls of his family's vaneo, Ederras had become better acquainted with Westcrown's beauty, and its sorrows. He'd spent countless mornings practicing swordplay along the canal bridges and upon the steep sides of the two-hundred-foot hill of Aroden's Rise; he'd spent innumerable evenings trying to fend off highborn debutantes at the Lord Mayor's balls. Faith had come to him late, but that too was indelibly associated with Westcrown, where he'd first heard the call to Iomedae's service.

And where he'd fallen from grace.

There was a memory he'd fought to keep from recalling, but as he walked steadily toward his family's ancestral estate, it loomed larger in his mind.

Other painful ghosts came close on its heels. His mother's wild grief at losing a daughter to stillbirth, and the listless shadow she'd become afterward. His father's cold rages. The fates that had befallen so many of his friends, and the mistakes Ederras himself had made that caused all those miseries.

That final disaster had happened during the last days of summer, just a little later in the season than it was now. The beach roses had been blooming along the shores of Parego Spera when the first rumors reached him. Their rebellion had been uncovered. There'd been a traitor in their midst.

He stopped, lost in regret and remembrance. The perfume of those pink and white blossoms mingled with the salt breezes of Gemcrown Bay and the cooler river winds, just as it had then. Ederras had breathed the same fragrance while waiting for his lover to die, and while waiting to find out if the imperial executioners would be coming for him.

She hadn't died. They hadn't come. But it hurt, fifteen years later, to breathe that salt-fringed scent of roses.

He shook the memories away and kept walking. Ahead, massive walls rose around Regicona, as Westcrown Island was known to its citizens. They shielded the opulent old palaces of the city's center from the common people who lived on the surrounding shores. Only the towers of the great estates and the domed roofs of the largest opera houses could be glimpsed above their reach.

Several skiffs-for-hire, each manned by a single rower, rested in the canals that separated Regicona from the shore districts. The ones that were meant for wealthy passengers were easily distinguished by their tassled canopies and padded seats; a few offered bottles of wine and other pleasantries for the ride. The smaller boats, available to servants and household guards, contained no such amenities.

At the wide stone steps leading down to the water, Ederras hesitated. In Mendev, he had worn his hair long and let his beard grow out, initially as a way of hiding from himself, and later because he'd found it more comfortable in that bitter northern climate. It was a far cry from his clean-shaven youth in Westcrown, and as yet, no one seemed to have recognized his return to the city. He hadn't dressed in his house's colors, and the armor he'd worn as a crusader was bundled up in his mule's packs. Nothing identified him as who he was.

It was tempting to cling to that secrecy a little longer. Just until he crossed the canals to Westcrown Island.

But he had come to resume the role that his family needed, and as soon as he recognized the temptation for what it was, Ederras knew that he had to forgo it. *The right choice is always the harder one.*

He waved down a canopied skiff, as befit a nobleman of his stature. No scion of House Celverian would return to his family home in a servant's boat.

The rower tilted his head as he pulled alongside the steps. He was a slender hellspawn man with a mustache that started red and faded to ash-gray past his mouth. The boat's ornate covering had been heavily scented with sandalwood and cinnamon, driving off the less pleasant smells of the canals. "My lord?"

Ederras pressed a gold coin into the rower's callused palm as he stepped under the boat's canopy. He was who he had to be. "Take me to Vaneo Celverian."

"Your lord father is waiting in the vaneo," Belvadio said. When Ederras had last seen the man, his temples were just beginning to gray. Now all his hair was silver. The precision of the cut, however, was exactly the same.

The steward clasped his shoulders in a stiff but heartfelt embrace, tears shining in his eyes. "It's good to see you again, Master Celverian. Welcome home."

"I'm glad to see you as well. How is my father?"

"Grieving, as are we all. It is a terrible loss."

"It is." Ederras stepped away, gazing up at the vaneo's stone facade. A blurry figure crossed the windows of the study where

Othando was said to have died. A moment later it crossed again, moving the other way. *My father.*

Something must have shown on his face, for Belvadio cleared his throat. "Whatever he says to you . . . it is not meant cruelly. You must know that. He has been devastated by sorrows."

Ederras didn't answer. As loyal as Belvadio was, and as much as Ederras loved the steward, there were some pains that needed no sharing. "Is my mother here?"

The steward shook his head. "Your lady mother remained in the countryside. She said she had no wish to set foot in Westcrown again."

Just the old bear, then. That would make things easier, and harder. Ederras sighed. "Thank you, Belvadio. I left a pack mule and some belongings at the Bent Blade. Would you have them brought to the house?"

"Of course." The steward's lips tightened around something he couldn't decide whether to say. "My lord, there is another . . ."

"Yes?"

"No, please excuse me. This is not the time. Forgive me for interfering with your grief, my lord. Other matters can wait." The steward bowed and was gone, vanishing with soft-footed grace.

With a final glance up at the study's windows, Ederras steeled himself and went in.

Time had hardened Lord Celverian and made him more brittle, like the stone trees in the petrified forests that Ederras had seen near the Crown of the World. Deep lines carved his brow, while a lifetime's unhappiness pinched the corners of his mouth. His features had grown thinner and sharper, and his once-gold hair had gone to gray. In his youth, Abello Celverian had been a lion. In his silver years, he had become a wolf.

Narrowing his rheumy blue eyes, the old lord lifted his head at his son's entrance. The scent of crushed wintergreen carried on his breath; it seemed Lord Celverian had kept his decades-long habit of chewing the medicinal berries. "Ah, you come at last. Too late to save your brother, of course."

"I've missed you too, Father."

Lord Celverian waved an age-spotted hand. "I have no time for your wounded sentimentality. If you gave a fig about your family, you would have left that crusade years ago. The Inheritor has servants aplenty. She hardly needs you, and you had duties here. Yet you remained. Othando died because you weren't here to prevent it, and you dawdled so long in coming that his funeral is past. As you could not be bothered to save your brother's life or attend his burial, at the very least, you will avenge it."

Ederras circled the desk, keeping it between his father and himself. He saw dark spots discoloring the worn blue carpet, and a few brownish spatters on the armchair's sides that the servants hadn't quite managed to get out. Othando's blood. "You're blaming his murder on *me?*"

"Othando was a scholar. A student of philosophy and the natural mysteries. A *gentleman.* He was no swordfighter. He saw what pursuing a life of violence did to you. Your brother was a peaceful soul, and he never stood a chance against his murderer."

Lord Celverian's hands were shaking with anger. He knotted them around the back of the bloodied chair to hide it, and his knuckles went white as his fingers dug into the padded leather. "If it had been *you* sitting in the vaneo as the rightful heir of House Celverian, your brother might not be dead today. But you were halfway across the world, serving a fool's exile. All your kind are the same. You, your uncle—off championing everyone but your own blood. And now? The best you *might* do is bring his killer to justice."

There was much Ederras wanted to say to that, and nothing that he could. He closed his eyes, wishing he were back among the demons of the Worldwound. "Have the authorities begun any investigation?"

"Of course." Even without looking, Ederras could see the contempt that curled his father's lip. "They've assigned a Hellknight to find your brother's killer. One Hellknight. I suppose I'm meant to take solace that she's not from the Order of the Rack. They've brought in an outsider. Perhaps she doesn't know about your old follies."

"Is she competent?" One good investigator was of infinitely more use than a squadron of brutes.

"I haven't met with her. I have no interest in speaking to some lackey of House Thrune."

Ederras bit back a retort that would have brought him nothing but grief. "Do you have her name? An address?"

"She'll be coming to the vaneo in three days' time. She wanted to come sooner, but I insisted that I required time to grieve." The frosty fragrance of wintergreen approached and receded as Lord Celverian strode past his son to the exit. "I intend to be gone by then. You may deal with her if you like. It would hardly be the first time you've consorted with Hell's disciples."

It took all he had to keep his voice calm. But calmness was the only victory he'd ever won against his father. "Yes, my lord."

The only answer was the thud of the door. With a mixture of relief and regret, Ederras opened his eyes.

He was alone. A thread of smoke rose from the single candle on the desk, which had gone out in the gust of the door's slamming. Around that gaunt black wisp, however, the study might have been preserved in glass, so perfect was its stillness.

The room had scarcely changed since his childhood. Some of the books on the shelves were new, and his brother had replaced their father's stern wooden chair with his own overstuffed armchair, but the light was the same. The musty smell of old maps, quietly yellowing books, and candlewax was the same. Their uncle Stelhan's tourney swords and lances still crossed on the walls. The aura of the study was just as it had been when he was a boy.

Even death, it seemed, couldn't change that. It was oddly comforting. The world went on, whether or not their individual lives did.

Holding on to that thought, Ederras made himself look, really *look*, at the chair where his brother had died. He didn't actually expect to find clues. It had been weeks since Othando's murder. His father had been through here, and the Hellknight investigator, and the servants with their brooms and brushes.

But faint brown stains remained in the carpet and where they'd soaked into the worn, cracked leather of the chair. The comfortable depression left in the chair's seat stayed behind, outlining the shape of his dead brother's body.

Who could have wanted to kill Othando? *Why?* It made no sense. House Celverian was of little importance in Westcrown. Their fortune had dwindled after years of civil war and disfavor by House Thrune. They held no political offices, owned no warships, fielded no significant military force. The better part of their lands had been taken in "settlement taxes" at the end of the Chelish civil war, and what remained was barely sufficient to keep them from penury.

As difficult as it was to imagine that anyone would have targeted their house, however, it was entirely impossible to think that Othando himself could have drawn an assassin's blade. The man who'd written those years of letters had been quiet, self-effacing, shy. Othando had written long, considered meditations on the writings of philosophers Ederras had never heard of. His brother was a man who compared rites of passage across varied religions and analyzed legends and folk stories for common archetypes. He was toothless as a turnip. He *couldn't* have had enemies.

Could he have stumbled on some dangerous bit of lore? It was possible, Ederras supposed, but unlikely. His brother's interests had been so benign. Even if he *had* accidentally blundered into some deadly secret, anyone who might have wanted it would have been able to coax Othando into sharing his discoveries simply by feigning a scholar's curiosity.

But what other reason could there be?

Ederras pulled open the drawers. Papers, pens, sealing wax. Nothing obvious was missing.

The letters on the desk offered no help either. Ederras flipped through the stack. Correspondence from his father, an invitation to a party thrown by some minor Jeggare, a letter to a fellow scholar concerning Desnan religious paraphernalia, and—

—an unfinished message that Othando had been writing to him.

The paper curled around his hand, but its first line remained visible. It was the only one his brother had finished. *Do they ever let you take any rest from demonslaying?*

There was no ending. There never would be.

His brother's last words were the only thing worth keeping. There weren't any clues waiting for him here. Ederras closed the drawers and smoothed the rumpled stack of letters, then reached up and rang the bell that would summon Belvadio.

Within moments, the steward appeared in the doorway. "My lord?"

"Has my father gone?"

"Yes. He took a carriage back to his inn just a few minutes ago."

"Good. Please send for a bath and a barber. It's time I started presenting myself as a proper scion of House Celverian again. Also, send a message to Taranik House. Let the Hellknights know that I'm ready to meet with their investigator."

The return message was as quick as it was unexpected: the Hellknight investigator was visiting a colleague in Parego Spera, and the Hellknights of the Rack did not know when she might return. They had the name and address of the colleague, however, and had provided it to Belvadio's messenger in case Ederras wanted to find her there.

"Havarel Needlethumbs?" he read aloud. "That sounds like a gnome."

"He is," Belvadio confirmed. "An alchemist of a sort. One hears unsavory stories about his work."

"Unsavory stories like how he cooperates with Hellknights?" Ederras strapped his sword on over his blue-and-gold tabard. It was a garment better suited for a knight than a Chelish noble, and it was for precisely that reason he had chosen it. He wanted to remind others—and himself—who he was, and why he was in Westcrown.

"Please be careful, my lord."

"Always."

In the waning light of late afternoon, the streets and canals of Westcrown glowed gold. Once again, Ederras was struck by the beauty of his city. The sunset ripples on the canal water, the painted silk canopies and carved poles of the wealthier skiffs and adels, the delicate soaring towers of Westcrown's bygone age of glory. It hurt his heart to look upon it, especially with the red and black roofs of the newer, diabolist-influenced buildings blending into the scarlet shadows of the dying day. He could ignore what House Thrune's rule had done to Westcrown and could pretend, for an evanescent moment, that the city still existed as it had before Aroden's Fall.

Once he had believed it was possible to restore Westcrown to that righteous path in reality, not just in these sunset daydreams. Once he'd known others who believed that, too.

Many of them were dead now. Others, like him, had fled into exile. But most still lived in Westcrown, keeping their heads down and their mouths shut, seeing every day that their hopes had died in ashes.

Could we ever have won? Would the city ever have changed? The question, unanswerable, followed him like a second shadow as he crossed into Parego Spera.

The address written on the card was located down a smoke-hazed street that rang with the cacophony of smiths' hammers. By the time Ederras reached its steel-barred door, he'd been deafened by the din.

He didn't expect that anyone would hear his knock over the smithies' clamor, but almost instantly the door's slotted window slid open, revealing a squat brass golem with a horned dog's head and clawed hands. Heat glowed between its curved teeth when the golem spoke, although its mouth never moved. Its voice was a slow, grinding rumble, like coals tumbled into a forge. "The master is busy."

"I'm not here to see him. I'm looking for the Hellknight Jheraal."

Firelight flared in the golem's eyes. "What is your name." Not a question. He didn't think the automaton had the capacity to ask questions.

"Ederras Celverian."

"I will tell him." The window slid shut, and the golem's thunderous footsteps receded. Ederras stood in the street for several minutes, trying to ignore the stares of passersby, until he heard the metal creature's heavy tread return.

A lock turned with a dull clunk, an unseen bar scraped across metal brackets, and the door opened. The golem stood just inside, occupying most of a low-ceilinged hallway lined on both sides with metal lockboxes recessed into the walls. Overhead, magical lights spun behind opaque golden domes like trapped dervishes.

"Follow." The golem lumbered down the hall. Its brass shoulders came within two inches of hitting the lockboxes on either side. There was no question of moving around or past the thing; it was as much barrier as guardian.

Four times the golem held up one or both of its clawed hands, raising its palms to the golden domes in the ceiling. Blue light flashed in its palms when it did. Once, as it lowered its arms, Ederras glimpsed an azure sigil shining like a jewel in the creature's hand. An instant later, the light was gone, and the runic marking was invisible.

"What was that?" he asked.

The golem offered no answer. It trudged on to the end of the hall, where two identical bronze doors faced each other across a brass-lined alcove. "That way," it said, pointing to the door on the left. The golem stepped into the alcove and rotated itself with short, shuffling steps until it had turned around to face Ederras. Then it went still. The glowing heat dimmed in its eyes and sank out of its throat, leaving the paladin with the unmistakable impression that the creature had gone to sleep.

Bemused by his host's peculiarities, Ederras pushed open the door.

A gnome with a bushy gray beard and rose-tinted spectacles stood next to a white-scaled woman wearing the Order of the Scourge's distinctive scarred armor. Sharp, curved horns jutted through her coppery-streaked raven hair. She had to be at least six feet tall, almost as tall as Ederras.

Offering a hand in greeting, Ederras strode forward. "Hellknight Jheraal? Am I interrupting you?"

The Hellknight glanced up from the glass-covered table she'd been studying alongside the gnome. A pendant lamp hung between them, presumably illuminating whatever it was they were looking at, but also making it difficult for Ederras to see anything beyond its glare off the glass. "Master Celverian. It's no interruption. I'm glad you could join us. I had hoped to speak to your father, but he seemed reluctant to make time for me."

Ederras tried not to wince. His father's intransigence had put him in a bad position already. Even the nobility of Cheliax didn't scorn the Hellknights lightly. In overlooking Lord Celverian's discourtesy, the investigator was being kinder than she had to, and that was never a good sign. "I apologize. He's asked me to represent our family in any further proceedings. If there's anything I can do to help—"

"There might be." Jheraal beckoned for him to approach the table. "See if this looks like anything you've seen before. Havarel, show him."

The gnome pressed a lever of fiery orange spessartite on the side of the table. Flames roared out under the glass top, consuming everything underneath in such an intense wash of heat that Ederras had to take a step back, eyes watering.

After a second, Havarel flicked the spessartite lever back up and pressed down one of nearly colorless aquamarine. The flames died, and a gust of wind sent the gritty ashes blowing away in a flurry that collected in a small curved tray attached to the table's side. After raising the aquamarine lever up again, the gnome emptied and replaced the tray, then lifted the glass tabletop on its hinges.

Using a pair of tongs, Havarel lifted a pair of dismembered fingers from a sack and placed them into the steel-walled compartment under the table's glass top. One of the fingers, rough and callused, had belonged to either a dwarf or a stout human who'd spent a lifetime at hard labor. The other was covered in leathery, brick red skin and had unquestionably come from a hellspawn.

"Where did you get those?" Ederras asked.

Havarel lifted a thick eyebrow as he set the fingers onto the table, placing them twelve inches apart. "Bought 'em off a grave robber, and I don't want to hear a word of lecturing about it."

"There won't be any trouble," Jheraal assured the gnome. "Just show it to him."

"I am, I am," Havarel grumbled, trudging over to a wooden box on the floor. He stooped to collect something from it, then eyed Ederras up and down. "You're not secretly dead, are you?"

"Not to my knowledge."

"Good." Returning to the table, Havarel dropped a sliver of mossy, discolored bone between the two fingers, then lowered the glass lid and set his tongs aside. "I'm allergic to mold, and this stuff's got a nasty appetite for corpses."

"I don't—" Ederras began, but then he saw what was happening under the glass.

The bone fragment that Havarel had placed between the dismembered fingers was coated in patches of fine-haired mold. Seconds after being set down, a cloud of spores puffed from the bone shard toward the two dead fingers. They clung to the human flesh and, with impossible speed, melted its skin and muscle under a cloak of fuzzy, grayish-white mold. The decomposition took hold so quickly that the mold rippled as the flesh under it dissolved. Almost before Ederras had registered what was happening, nothing was left but a second chunk of bone with a furry ruff of mold tufted around its joints.

But it never touched the hellspawn finger. A full minute passed, and not a speck of decay marred the burgundy skin.

"Fascinating, isn't it?" Havarel asked conversationally, flicking the spessartite lever to consume the moldy remains in a second incinerating flash of fire. Wind whisked it away a moment later, and he emptied out the tray containing the grainy remains. "Quite a feat of selective breeding. I'd guess it's Ristomaur Tiriac's work, or one of his disciples'. That speed and specificity bears all the hallmarks of the master's craft."

"Who?" Ederras regarded the gnome blankly. "What does this have to do with my brother's murder?"

Jheraal dusted specks of ash from her scarred plate mail. She'd been watching him closely throughout the gnome's demonstration, but he couldn't tell why. That inhuman face revealed nothing. "Someone in your house had formidable enemies. Your brother, your family, or maybe your servants."

"Our *servants?* How?"

The Hellknight gave him a tired smile. "Let's take a walk, and maybe you can tell me."

5

THE VALUE OF LAW

JHERAAL

Run through that again," Ederras said. He was taking the news far better than Jheraal had expected, but then he'd probably had plenty of practice absorbing strange and disturbing information while serving around the Worldwound.

She told him again what she'd found in Rego Cader—the skeleton covered in mold that Havarel had been analyzing, the hellspawn with their hearts stripped away—and finished: "They're still *alive*, somehow. The clerics say that they can't be healed, though. Unless we can restore their hearts, there's nothing to be done."

"Can I see them?" Ederras didn't break stride, but there was a slight hitch in his step, almost hidden by his turn around a fruit seller's stand. The fruit seller glanced at them, calculating the odds of a sale, and then continued packing up her wares. Nightfall was nearly upon them, and it wasn't worth the price of an apple to be caught on Westcrown's streets after dark.

Ederras *was* a paladin. Even when told there was no hope, he was determined to try. Inwardly Jheraal smiled, even as she kept her expression perfectly neutral.

She had decided that her best play was to treat him like an ally, at least until she had a better sense of who the elder Celverian son was. Given his Iomedaean faith and years of immersion in Mendev's military, she expected that he would cooperate easily with authority, or would at least pretend to. If he was what he seemed, that cooperation could be invaluable. If not, the pretense would give her time to make a more accurate assessment.

So far, Ederras Celverian appeared to be the genuine article. He carried himself like every other Iomedaean paladin Jheraal had ever met, simultaneously humble and arrogant. She guessed that he was about a decade older than Othando, putting his age around thirty-five. Tall, blond, uncommonly handsome, if a little weathered by his years in the crusade. Scrupulously clean-cut, to the point where she was almost tempted to flick a little mud onto that snowy shirt just to see if it stuck.

But it would have been a mistake to assume too much from that. That the older son of House Celverian was—or had been—a paladin didn't mean he'd had no involvement in his brother's death. Righteous believers weren't always peaceful ones, and the family was known to be on strained terms with one another. That Ederras had been at the Worldwound when Othando died might not mean much, either. Assassins could be hired anywhere.

She didn't think it was *likely* that Ederras had been involved, but it was a long leap from "unlikely" to "impossible."

"Of course," she said, turning north at the next cross street. "We can go right now, if you'd like. Along the way, perhaps you can tell me why you think your house might have been targeted. Whoever did this was a professional. Why would an assassin come after you?"

"I've wondered that myself. It doesn't make sense. Othando had no enemies, and neither did our house. A hundred years ago, even fifty years ago, we were a power in Westcrown, but no one would claim House Celverian holds much importance today."

Jheraal paused to let a company of dottari pass. All the guards carried torches in their hands and lanterns tied to their belts: the first to light the pyrahjes that illumined Westcrown's major avenues, the second in case their torches blew out. One of them hurried a pair of young, tipsy lovers along the cobbled streets, ushering them home, while her companions set their torches to a pyrahje's oil-soaked base.

The Hellknight waited until the dottari had moved to the next block before she went on. Ahead, the Bladewing Bridge stood limned in torchlight over the dark water of the frieze-lined Canaroden, Westcrown's oldest and most ornately decorated canal. Much of its beauty was hidden by the night, but the slashes of torchlight showcased small, firelit glimpses of Aroden's holy deeds and holy guises, which had been carved along the length of the ancient canal. "What if it was the vaneo that was the target, not the people in it?"

Ederras canted his head in confusion. "What do you mean?"

"None of the victims had serious enemies. Nappandi, your guardsman, was sleeping with a wine seller's wife, but the wine seller had—and still has—no idea his wife was unfaithful. Your hellspawn servants seem to have led irreproachable lives. The worst I could find about either of them was that the manservant occasionally annoyed his neighbors by feeding stray cats around their homes. And Othando, as we've discussed, gave no one any reason to want him dead.

"The innocuousness of the dead makes me wonder if we're not looking at this the wrong way. Perhaps we should consider another possibility: either that the murderer meant to strike against you or your father, as the two of you *did* have enemies, or that there wasn't any living target at all. Maybe everyone who died simply had the bad luck to be in the wrong place at the wrong time. Maybe the assassin wasn't acting as a hired killer, but as a saboteur or a thief."

"Of what?"

"That's the part I was hoping you'd be able to tell me." Jheraal altered her course to follow a better-lit avenue rather than venturing down a shadowed side street. While the Hellknight had little fear of the night in Westcrown proper, darkness tended to emphasize certain aspects of her infernal heritage, and she didn't think it would be helpful to overplay those traits to a paladin. Not yet, at least. "Was there anything in the vaneo that would have been worth killing to steal?"

Several minutes passed before the paladin answered. When he finally did, his reply was slow, as if dragged up from a deep well of memory. "I'm not sure. I can't think of anything, but it isn't impossible. Many generations of my family have lived there, and some of them were people of note. Wanderers, adventurers, champions of the faith. It's possible one of them might have left some legacy I was never told about. The history of my family has been troubled at times."

Jheraal had heard the same. Not about Othando, who truly seemed to have been a cloistered innocent, but about his father and brother. Both unhappy souls, according to local gossip. "Does that trouble extend to yourself or your father? Do you think there's any chance that the murders were meant to send a message to one of you?"

"No." Ederras's jaw set in a hard line. He stared into the fire-broken night, as if searching for enemies that weren't there, before shaking away the distraction and falling back into step alongside her. "I don't think so. My father is an unhappy man, but his misery is all turned inward. As for me . . ."

"You were involved with rebels as a youth." She'd dug up the old reports. They had been meticulously prepared; the Thrune agent who had infiltrated the rebellion had done a thorough job of it. The spy's work had resulted in sixteen convictions, with punishments ranging from fines to execution, and the complete destruction of that seditious group. "I found the records. You knew some of those who were convicted, even if there wasn't enough to make an arrest in your own case. Could that have been a motive for someone to strike at your family while you were out of reach yourself?"

Again, Ederras didn't answer for a long time. They crossed the Bladewing Bridge, passing between its grand carvings of sword-feathered pegasi in silence. Rows of torches burned on the bridge's low walls, their flames reflected on the dark water as liquid feathers of red. Under daylight, the bridge would have been crowded. After dark, it was empty except for the two of them and the canal-guarding condottari who stood watch at either end.

"No," Ederras said as they passed the last of the condottari. His voice was strained and distant, his face white under the moonlight. "No, that was dealt with before I left."

That was . . . fear? No, not quite. But something. The ghosts of the rebellion still haunted that one. Jheraal filed the observation away without reaction. "After leaving, you went to Mendev?"

"Eventually, yes. I didn't go there first. I tried to find other battles to fight, other wrongs that needed righting. I wasted a lot of time before I finally answered my purpose and went to the Worldwound." He shrugged uncomfortably. "That doesn't matter now, though. The crusade will go on without me. I'm here to find my brother's killer."

They passed another cluster of torch-carrying dottari and, a few minutes later, a woodcutter's cart that had broken its wheel and been abandoned by its owner. The cart's donkey had been removed from its traces, but the wagon bed remained piled high with a full load of seasoned firewood. If the woodcutter didn't return to the cart at dawn, it was likely that a week's work might be lost—but no one would brave the dark to steal that wood until then.

Would they?

A scab-knuckled hand lay between the spokes of the broken wheel. Had the driver fallen under his cargo? Or had someone tried to move the overburdened wagon and gotten injured? Puzzled, Jheraal took a step closer. "Hold a moment."

The hand twitched, reaching across the cobbles toward her. A powerful stench rolled out from under the wagon, reeking of corpses' curdled innards and the worm-infested mud of week-old battlefields. Yellow eyes, glowing like diseased moons, ignited in the shadows under the wagon.

Not just two eyes. Jheraal counted eight in the heartbeat it took her to slap her mace into her palm. The first of them was already crawling out, tasting the air with its gray, pebbled tongue. "Ghouls."

The emaciated creature turned toward them as if responding to its name. A hiss of raw hunger escaped between its yellowy-brown teeth. Beside it, a second ghoul dragged itself out from under the wagon. This one wore a thief's brand, withered and puckered black, across its sunken cheeks. Its belly, like the first one's, was covered with congealing mud. It must have been lying under the wagon for hours, waiting for darkness to fall and prey to happen by.

"In Rego Crua?" Ederras's sword had ignited with white fire, driving back the shadows and earning snarls from the emerging ghouls. The paladin moved to stand beside her, taking up an angled position to guard her back without needing a word. There was no fear in him. Only a restrained eagerness for the fight, like a hunting hawk waiting to be loosed on its prey. "What are they doing on this side of the wall?"

"At a guess? Trying to eat us." Despite the radiant sword blazing in their faces, the ghouls weren't retreating. Jheraal hadn't really expected that they would. Ghouls were notorious slaves to their appetites. Nothing but death deterred them from the chance of a feast. "Be careful. Their claws can paralyze."

He nodded absently, barely seeming to hear her.

The fourth and final ghoul emerged, dragging itself up from mud under the wagon's belly. As soon as the latecomer got to its feet, the first one attacked.

Jheraal met it with a swing of her mace. The ghoul's face crumpled under the spiked steel like an eggshell meeting a mallet. Its skull collapsed from nose to spine in a single continuous crunch, and the body dropped stinking at her feet. She kicked it away, both to get rid of the smell and so the carcass wouldn't trip her underfoot.

The thief-branded ghoul leaped at her side, trying to take advantage of the Hellknight's distraction. Jheraal met it with an armored elbow, smashing the spiked plate into its teeth. Squealing through bloody froth, the ghoul fell to its knees and scrabbled away.

The other two, wary now, circled around the Hellknight in opposite directions. Snarling and feinting, they stayed out of her mace's reach, trying to bypass the steel-clad hellspawn to reach the man beside her. Ederras wasn't wearing a penny's worth of armor. He probably looked like an easier target.

He wasn't. The paladin called upon Iomedae to aid him, and spectral golden fire blazed in a sudden ring around him. The wave of divine power rolled outward with Ederras at its core, and where it touched the ghouls, they *burned*.

Dead flesh went up in blinding, smokeless flame. Dead bones tumbled to the ground, bounced off the cobblestones, and were incinerated before they clattered down again. Even the stench of the dead was purified by the Inheritor's magic.

The two that had been circling toward him had just enough time to freeze, eyes wide, before the magic took them. The one that had been crawling away from Jheraal, clutching its ruined face, screamed as Iomedae's blessed fire seized its legs. Swiftly the golden flame leaped along the ghoul's body, consuming it from thigh to throat. Its gargled wail died as abruptly as it had begun, for in less than the space of an eyeblink, there was nothing left to scream.

Jheraal lowered her mace. Its spikes were spotless. The prayer had consumed even those small scraps of skin.

The Hellknight went to the wagon, peering under it for any sign of where the ghouls had come from or any victims they might have left behind. There was nothing, only rutted mud. Probably they'd come from Rego Cader and found a breach in the wall somewhere, then hidden here until the sun went down. She'd have the rundottari look for cracks or gaps in the morning.

Straightening, she raised a scaly eyebrow at Ederras, reassessing the man. "I'd heard stories that you fell from Iomedae's grace."

"I did." He didn't meet her gaze. The fire on his sword vanished as he sheathed the blade. "The Inheritor forgave me."

"So I see." An understatement. Jheraal was no expert on matters of religion, but she knew enough to recognize that a paladin capable of destroying three ghouls with a single prayer was not a novice in his faith.

If Iomedae showed Ederras such favor, then he probably wasn't her murderer. The goddess of honor and righteous valor wasn't likely to grant her blessings to a man who hired assassins to kill a harmless younger brother. Whatever else was troubling his conscience, it wasn't this.

Jheraal hooked her mace's haft back into its carrying loop. "Let's go."

As they resumed their march northward, the golden line of torchlight that fringed the wall around the Obrigan Gate began to wink into view occasionally, whenever a gap between the inward-leaning roofs of Rego Crua's poorer homes allowed. Higher yet, the moon shone silver and serene.

Their course was taking them past the Pleatra, Westcrown's massive slave market. At this hour, the auction blocks and blood-spattered testing grounds were empty, but the communal cells that ringed the market echoed with muffled moans and prayers. While valuable slaves were usually given better quarters, unskilled laborers and arena fodder were almost always consigned to the communal cells, frequently in conditions that made the city's prisons seem luxurious. Unsold slaves could spend days, weeks, even months in those cells, waiting for a buyer to take an interest and praying that their next home wouldn't be worse.

The wind turned, carrying the slaves' prayers. Jheraal saw the paladin's fists clench in response.

"Those aren't your worries," she said. "Those aren't your griefs. If you let yourself be distracted by the things you can't help, you'll lose sight of the ones you can."

Ederras shook her words away, but he relaxed his hands and kept walking. Together they circled around the spiked gates of the Pleatra's main entrance, their shadows crisscrossing and melting into one another as they passed the ever-burning lights of its watchtowers. "Is that what you tell yourself so you can stand to live in this empire of devils?"

"It's what I tell myself because it's true. The world is full of sorrows and injustices. Each of us is given the power to remedy some of them, but no one has the power to cure them all." She nodded to the arcaded walls of the Pleatra, receding in the shadows behind them. Each of the columns supporting its arches had been carved into the likeness of a slave. Men and women, humans and halflings. Porters, field laborers, dancers, scribes—all the slaves who supported Imperial Cheliax on their backs and brows. "Everyone has a place in the empire. Everyone has the protection of its laws. We are *civilized* here, Ederras Celverian, which is more than can be said for much of Avistan. Do you think those slaves would trade the Pleatra for the mad terrors of Galt? For the Worldwound?"

"Some would. Some did. I fought beside them."

Jheraal shook her head in disbelief. She had forgotten that Iomedaeans could be so foolish, sometimes, thinking it was worth bringing down the pillars of civilization if that meant everyone could stand equal amid the rubble.

It wasn't worth the argument. She wanted to win his trust, not a point of philosophy. He could think what he liked, as long as he cooperated.

The pungent smells of tanneries and slaughterhouses surrounded them as they continued north through Rego Crua. Here the streets were less well lit, and fewer of them had pyrahjes. Ordinary oil-burning lanterns, far dimmer, filled in the gaps, leaving large swaths of darkness between each uncertain oasis.

Past the Pleatra, they saw far fewer dottari on patrol. No one watched to ensure that the people of Rego Crua kept to curfew. Yet the streets remained empty because here—unlike in the wealthier central districts of Parego Spera—the peril was real and immediate. Here, people died to the dangers in the dark.

Jheraal hadn't realized how tense she was until they finally reached the Obrigan Gate. Ederras had, however, and he broke the silence as they crossed the archers' field leading up to the wall. "Are the shadows still so deadly here?"

"Thirty-four deaths since the beginning of the year," she said. "Documented ones, that is. The disappearances are harder to track, and no one counts the dead in Rego Cader."

"Is the Midnight Guard still supposed to be protecting them?"

"Yes."

The paladin's snort carried years of resigned contempt. "I'm glad to know they're as effective as ever."

Jheraal didn't answer, but privately she shared his disdain. The Midnight Guard, a loose cabal of Nidalese shadowcallers and Chelish wizards, was supposed to stand watch against the dangers in Westcrown's nights. Since its inception, however, disturbing rumors had swirled around the organization. Many believed that the Midnight Guard concealed its own murders behind trumped-up tales of monsters in the dark, and that any reduction in the number of deaths that Westcrown suffered was due to the curfew that kept its citizens inside, not the sinister wizards who claimed to be protecting them.

As little as she cared for the Midnight Guard, the Hellknight wasn't about to breathe a word of those seditious thoughts to a former rebel. Instead, she strode to the nearest of the Obrigan Gate's sally ports and rapped an armored hand against its steel-barred wood.

"Who comes?" a voice called out.

"Hellknight Jheraal of the Order of the Scourge, and Ederras of House Celverian."

The sally port opened. Inside, a stout dwarf with a coiled braid of raven hair piled atop her head raised her lantern to shine over their faces. It was a formality. Jheraal knew the dottari had recognized her immediately. With her white scales and sharp horns, she cut a distinctive figure. "Hellknight. What brings you to the Obrigan Gate?"

"I'd like to check on my guests." Jheraal squinted in the lantern's glare as they entered. "Has there been any change in their condition?"

"None," the dwarf replied. She locked the door behind Jheraal and Ederras, then opened the inner door that led into the fortified gatehouse. "But come, see for yourself."

The rundottari hadn't moved the three hellspawn from the cell Jheraal had chosen, although someone had brought in clean straw and wool blankets. All three lay limp on their makeshift beds, eyes vacant and breathing slow. Their clothes were no dirtier than they'd been on the first day. It seemed the hellspawn couldn't sweat or soil themselves. The pinpricks she'd made in their fingers had healed, though. Whatever magic gripped these unfortunates had transformed them into something like waxen dolls, perfect in their repose.

Making an inarticulate noise low in his throat, Ederras pushed between Jheraal and the rundottari. He knelt beside the insensible hellspawn, touching the hands of the Celverian house servants. The Hellknight wasn't surprised to see the light of a healing prayer surround the paladin, nor was she surprised when, a moment later, it died without effect.

"I told you the clerics couldn't heal them," she said. "Without their hearts, it's impossible."

Ederras shook his head helplessly, staring at the faces of the people he'd known. "I had to try." Straw pricked at his knees, and his fine white clothes were stained with dirt, but he didn't seem to notice. She could almost *see* the guilt wracking the man as he looked upon the eerie holes where the hellspawn's hearts had been.

That wasn't the look of a killer. His reaction confirmed Jheraal's growing opinion of his innocence. Either Ederras Celverian was an actor to put every member of Westcrown's theater companies to shame, or he hadn't had anything to do with this.

"We tried to feed them," the dwarf said, standing outside the iron-barred cell door, "but the gruel wouldn't go down their throats. Water, either. Durotas Tuornos was concerned that we'd choke or drown them, so he had us stop. They don't seem to need it, anyway."

"I won't hold you from your duties any longer," Jheraal said.

Acknowledging her dismissal with a nod, the rundottari stepped back into the hall. "You can lock it when you're done."

"You keep the key to their cell?" Ederras asked, straightening from his crouch after the dwarf had gone. "Don't you trust the rundottari?"

The Hellknight leaned against the niter-streaked stone wall, crossing her gauntleted arms. "I trust Durotas Tuornos more than I'd trust any other durotas in this city, but that doesn't extend to every rundottari in his command. Some of them might see an opportunity in these hellspawn. Some might see a threat. Both of those things can be dangerous. Better if no one besides the durotas and myself has a key to their cell. Keeps them safer."

"That's important to you?"

"It is." Jheraal pushed her hair back behind her horns, weighing the moment. She thought she had a good enough measure of Ederras to make her play. *Not an appeal to authority. Not Chelish authorities, not for this one. But an appeal to justice, and a little righteous anger . . .* "These people were law-abiding citizens of Westcrown. They paid their taxes, they didn't make trouble, they lived their lives as good people. They had family, friends. They didn't invite this upon themselves, and they didn't deserve it.

"Even if they had, it wouldn't matter. The rule of law is supposed to protect *everyone.* But maybe, I'm inclined to think, it should have protected them a little bit more." Stepping into the shadows, she fixed the paladin with an unearthly glare. From the slight golden tint to her vision, Jheraal knew that her infernal blood was showing. Her eyes glowed like the fires of hell when she called upon the legacy of her devilish ancestors—and right now, she wanted them to. "It offends me, personally, that the law failed some of its most vulnerable citizens. It offends me that people who lived ordinary lives were put through unimaginable horror. It is *wrong.* I brought you here so that you could see the profundity of that wrongness for yourself. Your brother wasn't the only victim. He might not even have been the most important one."

"Do you think the law in Westcrown is strong enough to see justice done?" Ederras tipped a hand toward the insensible hell-spawn. "There's magic at work here, and it's powerful. It isn't always easy to bring the powerful to justice in Cheliax, as you surely must know. What makes you think the throne will let you drag the culprits into the light? How do you know they won't just protect their own?"

"Because they gave the case to me," Jheraal said. And knew, from the grudging respect that crossed the paladin's face, that her answer had won her a measure of trust.

6

DEVILS

EDERRAS

"You can stay in the Obrigan Gate until dawn," Jheraal offered as they left the cell where the hellspawn lay. "There are spare beds in the barracks. Not as fancy as your vaneo, but they'll do."

"Thank you, but no." Ederras followed her up the spiraling stairs that led from the dungeons to the street. He felt sick leaving Nodero and Chiella behind in that state, but he saw nothing he could do to help them. For now, he had to trust that the Hellknight would keep them safe. She'd cared enough to tie bandages around their chests. It wouldn't help their wounds, of course, but it said something that she noticed and bothered to protect their dignity.

And she wasn't a Rack Hellknight. Ederras wasn't as familiar with the Order of the Scourge, but what little he knew gave him some hope that Jheraal might be an honest investigator. The Scourge's primary purpose was tracking down criminals and forcing them to answer for their deeds. The Hellknights of that order were reputed to be unyielding in their pursuit of justice, regardless of their quarry's title or station, and fiercely resistant to the throne's attempts to subvert their independence.

If those tales were true, he might be able to trust her.

He hoped they were. He didn't know where to begin hunting Othando's murderer on his own. Ederras was made to fight battles on the open field, not to chase hints and whispers across alleys and cloakrooms.

"Would you like me to escort you back to your vaneo?"

"No." What he wanted was space to think, and solitude in the clear cold air of Westcrown. As clear as it ever got with a thousand fires burning to ward off the curse of its nights, anyway.

After all else that had happened today, that loss felt abruptly like too much to bear. He'd lost his brother, his family's servants, his sense of place in the world. Why should he have to live with the stars taken from him too?

For as long as Ederras could remember, it had been impossible for the people of Westcrown to feel safe in their own beds. It had been impossible for them to stand in their streets and admire the stars. Moonlit walks, nighttime rides in the skiffs that plied the city's canals, the small mysteries and romantic intrigues afforded by anonymity in darkness—all of those things had been stolen from Westcrown for years.

If anything, it had gotten worse since he'd left. Thirty-four deaths in half a year, just among the ones that the dottari bothered to count. Ghouls inside the city walls. Intolerable.

"I'd like to go out to Rego Cader," he said.

Jheraal gave him a long look, flexing her white-scaled fingers as if she were weighing something invisible in her palm. Her eyes were no longer glowing gold, but the devil-blooded Hellknight in her scarred plate mail remained a profoundly inhuman presence: a walking reminder, whether she wanted it or not, of Cheliax's unholy alliance with the powers of Hell. "No."

"No?"

"I know that look. You're spoiling for a fight. With whom or what, I don't know, and I'd wager you don't, either. But I know the look of a brawler hunting for trouble. I can't stop you from finding it, if that's what you want. But I *can* stop you looking in Rego Cader." The Hellknight shook her head. "If you were one of my armigers, I'd have you confined to quarters. Maybe doused with a few buckets of cold water, ordered to run a few laps around the barracks while carrying a pack full of rocks. But you're not a cadet in training, and I can't do that, so I'll try appealing to your better nature. I need you alive. There's a crime to solve. Find your fight in Rego Crua, if you have to find one tonight."

"Fine," Ederras said. She was right, of course. He was ill prepared for the perils of Rego Cader. The paladin was dressed in silk and cotton, not the spell-forged steel he'd worn in Mendev. He didn't have a shield, and he wasn't carrying any of the trinkets or potions that he'd relied upon for years. All he had was his sword and his faith.

But this was Westcrown, not the Worldwound, and Rego Crua wasn't as lawless as the Dead Sector. Whatever lurked in its shadows, Ederras was confident he could face it.

"Open the gate," he said, turning back toward Rego Crua.

Jheraal signaled the rundottari with a raised fist. The portcullis groaned as the dottari cranked it up, letting Ederras back into the sally port. Behind him, the iron grate clanged back down. The second gate opened, and he walked out to the night-shrouded city.

Beyond the Obrigan Gate, the streets were dark and desolate. The torches and lanterns of Rego Crua, far smaller than the pyrahjes that lit Westcrown's wealthier districts, had mostly burned out in the hours since sundown. Moonlight painted the inward-leaning rooftops that crowded the district, but little of that light pierced the dense canopy of buildings to reach the ground.

A familiar, dangerous thrill coursed through his veins as he walked into the darkness. Under the stars and the cool, pale moon, Westcrown was a world in black and white, washed of all the complexities that complicated it by day.

The years fell away from him. Ederras felt impossibly light on his feet, preternaturally alert. In his youth, he had walked these same streets, hunting for the same faceless, shadow-born foes that he hoped to find tonight.

Back then, he'd believed he could defeat them. Now, he just wanted to vent his anger that they still held his city in fear.

Not even mice stirred in Rego Crua. There were no rats, no pigeons, no scrawny-ribbed cats hunting for squeaking morsels amid the refuse of the district's tanneries and slaughterhouses. Like the people who huddled in the shuttered homes around them, the street animals of Westcrown had learned to hide after dark.

Alone, Ederras walked through the deserted avenues of what had once been the most celebrated city in Cheliax. Only the wind's gentle whispers and the occasional sputtering pops of a dying lantern broke the night's silence. Only the flicker of moonshadows moved with him across the eerie, empty market squares.

He listened to the wind, and he watched those sighing moonshadows, and when he sensed a disturbance that was not of the natural night, he began his hunt.

He heard his quarry before he saw it. A reedy, high-pitched clicking echoed softly off the brick and stone walls of Westcrown's alleys, like an enormous ghostly cricket chirping in the dark. It wasn't a loud noise—Ederras would never have heard it during the day—but in the utter hush that was Rego Crua after midnight, even that small, spectral tremulation stood out.

That was the song of a shadowgarm.

Whether it really *was* a song, Ederras didn't know. He could think of no closer descriptor for that haunting noise, but who knew whether shadowgarms had any concept of melody, or any purpose to the noises they made? They were secretive and alien creatures, not native to this world. Although the Midnight Guard steadfastly disavowed any knowledge of how they'd come to infest the streets and sewers of Westcrown, the paladin had always believed that they were born of some wizard's summoning run amok. Nothing about their behavior or physiology was remotely natural.

As man-eating extraplanar menaces went, however, shadowgarms weren't especially deadly. Ederras had fought them since his first days in the rebellion, and he was vastly better with a blade now than he'd been then. Unless he stumbled into a rut-crazed throng of them, he didn't expect shadowgarms to give him much trouble.

Under a feeble street lantern, he saw the creature's prey: a young man, insensibly drunk, who had passed out in that fading pool of light. His clothes looked clean and well made, and his hair had been recently cut, but a pungent odor of alcohol and urine permeated his vicinity. Three empty wine bottles rolled on the cobblestones around him.

It was an unhappily familiar scene. Sitting out at night, alone, was one of the ways that a Wiscrani might court oblivion when outright suicide was too frightening, but life's burdens seemed too heavy to bear. It wasn't uncommon for people to drink themselves senseless under a streetlamp's steadily shrinking glow, half hoping and half dreading that the light would fail and a shadowgarm might swallow them before they woke.

Ederras had long since stopped trying to guess what drove people to do it. He'd asked, when he was younger. Sometimes they answered. One fierce old woman told him that she'd faced the night because she was dying of tumors and refused to let her children spend all their inheritance to buy a cleric's cure. A boy of seventeen had offered himself to the shadowgarms simply because, he said, he was too melancholy to go on.

Knowing those things did Ederras no good. He'd learned, eventually, to stop asking.

Whatever their reasons for doing it, however, one thing was always true: none of the people who sat alone in the dark really wanted to die. All of them were ambivalent enough that they'd chosen to gamble, and anyone who gambled on death secretly hoped for salvation.

So Ederras gave it to them.

He didn't have to wait long. The shadowgarm's song died as the creature crept closer to the unconscious drunk. As it edged toward the guttering lantern, Ederras caught his first glimpse of the beast: a mass of oily black tentacles that pulled a bulbous, spongy form across the cobblestones. Wisps of semi-solid shadow fluttered around its body like translucent scarves, further camouflaging the monster in the night.

Circling around the streetlamp's post, Ederras closed to within twenty feet of the shadowgarm before it noticed him. A knobby protuberance—perhaps a head, although it had no eyes or mouth—reared up from its fluid mass, turning in his direction.

Time froze between them for a split second. Then, soundlessly, the shadowgarm struck.

Three pincer-tipped black tentacles churned out of its body as it leaped, seeming to materialize out of the shadowgarm's body where no such appendages had been before. Ederras came forward to meet it, raising his sword. In the same instant, he prayed for Iomedae's favor, and holy white fire flashed across its steel.

It was over before it began. One blow, and the shadowgarm lay in oozing pieces on the cobblestones, its clawed coils twitching feebly as its body began melting into a puddle of murky fog.

Ederras hadn't even broken a sweat. Sheathing his sword, he knelt beside the shadowgarm's intended victim.

A quick check for wounds revealed none. Ensnared in his wine-soaked dreams, the youth moaned and cursed incoherently at whatever imaginary foes troubled his sleep. He hardly seemed happy, but he had sustained no harm.

Several hours remained before daybreak, however, and the streetlamp was down to a glowing wick in a shell of sooty glass. In the past, Ederras would have prayed for Iomedae's light to guard the sleeping drunk until dawn . . . but tonight he'd acted on the spur of the moment, and he hadn't thought to prepare those prayers.

Carrying the drunk back to an inn or guardhouse might be another option, but while shadowgarms weren't much threat to Ederras when he was ready for them, that calculation could change drastically if he were burdened with a helpless companion. The oily black slime that coated shadowgarms was a potent paralytic, and they could render him defenseless if they caught him unawares.

The best option was to wait until dawn was closer. Ederras could fend off whatever dangers might approach in the meantime, and then either escort the man to safety if he regained consciousness, or, if he didn't, leave him with enough light to shield him until morning.

Settling into the shadows, the paladin drew his sword, reached for Iomedae's blessing to help him sense encroaching threats, and opened his senses to the night. He relaxed into a familiar state, motionless yet alert, attuned to any disturbance that might herald danger.

The hours rolled by in long, slow stretches of quiet punctuated by brief bursts of violence. Two more shadowgarms emerged to feast upon the unconscious man, but Ederras dealt with them easily, reducing each to corpses that rapidly disintegrated into mist and darkness.

And then, in the last hour before he could safely leave, Ederras sensed a much greater evil moving through the dark. He saw nothing, yet, but he felt its aura pass across his prayer-enhanced senses like an eclipse across the sun.

That's no shadowgarm. The strength of the evil he sensed was far beyond those lowly scavengers. That was a true fiend, or more than one . . . and he was, at the moment, unprepared to confront a foe of such magnitude.

If it came to him, he would be bound to defend the helpless drunk to the best of his ability, but Ederras had no illusions about what that would mean. He had no armor, no shield, no chance. Clenching the hilt of his sword, he found himself hoping that the menace might just pass them by.

Luck didn't favor him. The odor of sulfurous smoke, hot iron, and burning fur wafted from an alley across the street. Two pairs of red eyes shone in the darkness, high and huge enough to belong to a team of draft horses. A moment later, they stepped forward in unison, revealing wolflike heads, ragged ebon ears, and soot-blackened iron barding.

No shadowgarm, indeed. No shadow creature at all. Those were the warhounds of Hell.

Ederras felt his knuckles go white on his sword hilt. If he'd been in his battle armor, with his goddess's divine power behind him and all the tools he'd had in Mendev at his fingertips, he wouldn't have hesitated to set himself against one of those infernal beasts. Two might have been chancy, however, even if he'd been fully prepared.

Making matters worse, the warhounds weren't alone. A third wolflike creature stepped out of the darkness between them. It wore no barding, and it was smaller than the warhounds. Its dark gray ears came up only to their elbows. Where the warhounds' eyes glowed like embers plucked from the bonfires of Hell, the third wolf's gaze seemed almost mundane at first glance: solid, unblinking brown-black, like the eyes of some ordinary dog.

But that was no dog, nor was it a wolf. Even if Ederras's spell hadn't told him the truth of the creature's diabolical nature, he would have known it by the ease with which it moved between the ironclad, fire-fanged warhounds, and the apparent deference with which the two hulking hounds stepped out of its way.

The paladin licked suddenly dry lips. He could fight them, but it would be a suicidal stand. If he died, the youth he'd been guarding all night was doomed as well, and his brother's murder might go forever unsolved and unavenged. The hellspawn who'd had their hearts ripped out might never be made whole.

It wasn't worth it. Not when he didn't even know what they wanted, or why they had come.

Ederras had heard that warhounds could understand spoken language, although he didn't know if they comprehended anything other than the tongue of devils. He had to try, though. "Who are you? What do you want from me?"

The warhounds didn't answer. Neither did the wolflike fiend between them. But they moved out of the alley, arraying themselves like sentinels at its mouth, and a fourth figure emerged from their midst. Slim, graceful. A woman.

Recognition shot through Ederras like a bolt of ice. He heard the *tink* of his sword's tip hitting the cobblestones, and wondered, distantly, how he had the strength to keep from dropping it altogether. The world seemed to have stopped where it stood.

Velenne was just as he remembered: petite, dark-haired, so slender that she looked like she could be broken by a stiff wind. Time hardly seemed to have touched her. Only her clothes were different. As she stepped into the open street, the moonlight gleamed on the polished leather of her dress: black with red piping. Diabolist's colors. The crimson shield-and-swords of House Thrune stood on her right breast. It suited her better than the greens and whites she'd worn when she'd pretended to be part of their rebellion, Ederras thought. More honest. Truer to what she really was.

Between the massive warhounds, she looked tiny as a child, but that fragility was as false as her smiles. The last time he'd seen her, she'd been lying in a sea of her own blood, gasping on the brink of death. If he closed his eyes, he could still see her red-streaked fingers trembling as she fought for breath. Fifteen years, and it was vivid as yesterday.

You should have finished it. You should have made sure.

But he hadn't, and here she stood. Unharmed, unchanged. Delicate and deadly.

"Are you here to kill me?" he asked.

She laughed. It was a warm, low sound, incongruous in the night. "Don't be absurd. I'm here to *help* you, Ederras."

"Is that why you came with an army of devils?"

"No." Velenne's amusement softened to a smile. "We parted on bad terms. I wasn't sure you'd hear me out if I came alone. I brought an escort to ensure that everything stayed civilized." She took a step forward, lifting her hands.

Immediately Ederras backed away, raising his sword as if to parry whatever spell she might be preparing. That made her laugh again, but he didn't lower his blade. "There's nothing I need to hear from you."

"Ah, so cruel." Her sigh was a sound of yearning. It made his hackles rise. "That's what drew me here, you know. I missed you. Everyone else is playacting their games of pain, but *you* . . . you really meant what you did. Nothing else compares, and oh, I've looked. For years. So. You've come back to Cheliax, and I've come back to you."

Slowly, Ederras let his sword down. He didn't trust a word she said, but he felt foolish holding a guard stance if she wasn't going to attack. "You sound like the Nidalese."

"I've spent some time with them."

"Maybe you should go back. Maybe Pangolais is where you belong. It isn't here. I don't need your help. I don't need *you*."

"That," Velenne murmured, "is entirely untrue. I know why you're in Westcrown. We received the Hellknights' message. We know you need a wizard to aid in the investigation of your brother's death. Naturally, I volunteered for the task. Regrettably, I will be the only one who does. In House Thrune's view, my offer of assistance is a considerable honor. You would insult us by refusing. Which, of course, may not be a concern for you, but would certainly be worrying to anyone else you might approach for aid. Prohibitively so, I should think."

"I see," Ederras said grimly.

"Do you? Good." She moved toward him again, and this time he didn't step back. Her perfume surrounded him. It was the same scent she'd worn during the summer they'd shared together, so long ago: rich red roses, verging on black, with a shimmer of pink pepper thrown over their crushed petals. Luxurious, sweetly bitter, intoxicating. "I've missed you. What we had. Don't you regret how we left things?"

He recoiled. The dream of her perfume snapped as he stumbled on a loose cobblestone. Reality surged back in his senses. "No."

"No? Not at all?"

He hadn't touched a woman since he'd left her. "No."

"You will." Velenne closed on the paladin, pushing his sword arm gently aside. He didn't resist. Couldn't, with her flock of devils watching him and his charge. She forced him back, step by step, until a rough masonry wall jolted his heels and put an abrupt end to his retreat. Then she paused, looking up at him with a strange, wistful expression. "When I heard you'd fled to Mendev, I thought I might never see you again."

"I wish that had been the case."

"Why? It would be entirely too stupid if we left matters as they were. I never bore you any malice for the manner of our parting."

"*You?*" He stared at her in astonishment. "Why would *you* be the one to harbor a grudge? You betrayed me. You betrayed my friends. Good people died because of you. Families were ruined. I should have killed you when I had the chance."

"It would have been worse if you had. Back then, I mean. Now . . . well." Mirth and moonlight glittered in her eyes. "What stops you now?"

Ederras snorted. He jerked his chin at the pair of hellish, armored warhounds and the smaller gray beast between them. All three of the fiends were staring at him without blinking, their hostility palpable from thirty feet away. One of the warhounds growled, leaning forward as if testing an invisible leash. "Them."

She laughed. And leaned up, and kissed him. Only once, lightly, but it burned. Her lips seared him like fire, or holy water on a demon's flesh. "Oh, my love. Don't be afraid of *them*. I've become a worse devil than any of those."

7

READING BONES

JHERAAL

I didn't ask for a diabolist," Jheraal muttered, annoyed. "This is a murder investigation. I wanted a wizard who could help me with that. Not a devil-binder."

Havarel shrugged philosophically. The gnome tended to view all wizards as much the same, Jheraal knew. To him, they were all foolish, meddling in powers they couldn't possibly understand or control when right in front of them the perfectly sensible paths of alchemy lay waiting to be explored. "At least she's a good one. Could be worse. Could be some stripling apprentice fumbling around with cantrips. And the Thrune name, that might open some doors for you. Anyway, no use worrying about it. You can't get rid of her. Might as well make the best use you can."

"Thank you, Havarel. You're a great help."

The gnome seemed oblivious to her sarcasm. He flashed an absent-minded smile, pushed his rose-tinted spectacles a little higher on his bulbous nose, and stooped to rummage through the drawers under one of his chemical cabinets. "Welcome, welcome. Always welcome. Now where was that thing I wanted to show— Ah! Here we are."

He straightened and smoothed the front of his stained leather apron with one hand, holding out a moldy chunk of bone in the other. "Take a look."

It looked like the bottom half of someone's jaw. A row of small, shrunken teeth poked loosely out of the grayish bone. Jheraal frowned, making no move to touch the thing. "What is it?"

"Jawbone from that skeleton you brought me. Human male. The one from Rego Cader, with the mold that only consumed human flesh? I was so impressed with the mold, I didn't bother looking at the bones that closely until now, but the other day I was going through my drawers and I examined them and—and—" Havarel was so excited that the bone bounced in his palm. He reached back into the drawer and pulled forth the rest of the skull. "Here's the top half. Look at the teeth!"

She did, taking the two pieces of the skull carefully from the gnome and carrying them back to his work table, where the light was better. The enamel of the front top teeth was chipped and almost lacy at the edges, having been worn through to translucence and then broken unevenly. The bottom teeth were flattened stubs, smoothed down to the gumline. Wide, uneven gaps separated all the teeth where their sides had been eroded inward.

There was one obvious conclusion to be drawn from that, and it wasn't one Jheraal wanted to make. "That isn't mold damage, is it." She couldn't make herself phrase it as a question.

Havarel shook his head, looking positively gleeful. "Acid."

"You could be a little less happy about it." The Hellknight sighed. "What are the chances it's coincidental?"

"Minute. Infinitesimal. Impossible!" The gnome plucked the skull's top section from her grasp and ran a stubby finger over its fringe of glassy-edged broken teeth. "Look how this has been worn down over time. You don't get this kind of damage from sudden trauma. If a black dragon spit in your face, you'd look entirely different."

"No doubt," Jheraal said dryly.

"Your *teeth* would, I mean. No, no. Either this fellow had the world's most delicate stomach and spent every morning regurgitating his breakfast into his chamber pot, or—"

"—or he was a Hellknight. Yes. *Thank* you, Havarel. You are, again, a great help."

The little alchemist beamed. He took his glasses off and buffed their pink lenses against a sleeve. "No question which is likelier in Westcrown."

"No, there isn't." Jheraal sighed a second time, placing the lower jawbone back on the table.

Acid-worn teeth meant that the skeleton had almost certainly belonged to a member of the Order of the Rack, and not a very good one. Each Hellknight order had its own reckoning, a ritual method of purging sins by which members could atone for acts of weakness or defiance. Jheraal's order imposed its reckoning by lash or scourge. Those who strayed from its strict code were subject to a half-hour of purification by whipping. The Order of the Rack had a different ritual: those who swallowed ideas not in accordance with the order's tenets were forced to drink solutions of acid or boiling water to scald the impurities away.

A man who had to endure that reckoning often enough to have damaged his teeth that badly must have been an uncommonly incompetent Hellknight—or one who was beset with a crushingly heavy burden of guilt. The latter, she guessed, was more likely. No one who suffered that many punishments for failure of duty would have been allowed to remain a Hellknight. His commanders would have drummed him out of the order long before his teeth reached that state.

But no one stopped Hellknights from flagellating themselves out of self-condemnation. Unless he crippled himself to the point where it interfered with his other duties—and that was difficult to achieve with the Rack's reckonings—no one would have said a word.

"So my mystery corpse is, or was, a Rack Hellknight with a troubled conscience," Jheraal said. "That's wonderful. The Order of the Rack is going to be *thrilled*." Rivalry between the orders was prickly at the best of times, and this was not looking like the best of times.

"Maybe they already know," Havarel suggested.

"Even worse. How *do* you manage to find ways to crush my spirits so consistently?"

"Must be a gift. I have quite a few." He coughed into a hand. "Speaking of gifts, I'm meeting with a new buyer tonight. Seems like a decent enough sort, but you never know with the new ones, and he's asking after some awfully expensive trinkets. So I thought, if you wouldn't mind standing on the docks and looking grim and scary for half an hour, that might go a fair way toward keeping everything peaceful."

"Fine." Even after years of trading favors with Havarel, Jheraal had to remind herself every time that she wasn't *really* acting as the man's enforcer. Deterring crime with her visible public presence was exactly what a Hellknight was *supposed* to do. If her presence happened to coincide with where Havarel wanted crime deterred, and if the specific crime he was worried about was being robbed by an unscrupulous buyer, that didn't actually change anything. She was still acting within the proper ambit of her duty.

But it always made her uncomfortable, even so. "When and where?"

Havarel replaced his spectacles and smiled broadly. "Sunset. Regicona. I'll write down the address."

"Half an hour. No more."

"I'm in your debt." Havarel scribbled an address on a scrap of paper, harrumphed happily to himself, and handed it to her. "So, what's next for you? Planning to go knock on the Rack's doors and ask which of their members might have been involved in murdering a bunch of hellspawn?"

"I'll save that for tomorrow. Today I have to meet with my diabolist. She's the only wizard I'm likely to get for this assignment, at least until she gets bored with it." Jheraal shook her head in deep resignation. "I hope she's worth the trouble."

Velenne of House Thrune was a slight, attractive woman in her mid-thirties with an elegant, self-possessed bearing. Dark hair, dark eyes, dark clothes. Her skin was lightly bronzed by the late summer sun, but fair enough to make it clear that she was no laborer who toiled in the heat. Everything about her radiated wealth and privilege, so deeply ingrained that she didn't bother to flaunt it. She looked like any other idle noblewoman, but Jheraal approached her with a measure of caution nevertheless.

She knew the diabolist by reputation, although she had never met the woman. Velenne had spent much of her career as a liaison to Nidal, and anyone who got along so smoothly with those pain-worshiping lunatics deserved a certain degree of wariness in Jheraal's mind. On top of that, she'd had some involvement with a paralictor in the Order of the Gate, whose career had advanced rapidly while the diabolist was in northern Cheliax and stalled as soon as she'd left. Several of her apprentices were rumored to have had similar trajectories. The prospect of having her professional fortunes tied to the whims of a politically connected devil-binder did not fill Jheraal's heart with joy.

But she couldn't refuse the assistance without insulting House Thrune or crippling her own investigation, and Havarel had been right about one thing: the Thrune name carried a great deal of weight in Cheliax.

Jheraal cleared her throat as she approached the table where Velenne sat alone, overlooking one of Westcrown's grand market squares. The diabolist had the balcony of a celebrated teahouse entirely to herself. While she hadn't formally requisitioned the place, the waitstaff had discreetly but firmly declined to allow

Jheraal onto the balcony until she explained that she was expected and her entire purpose was to meet with their guest.

It was an insult, but one that Jheraal refused to let prick her. She would not begin this meeting at a disadvantage.

"You must be Hellknight Jheraal." Velenne beckoned the Hellknight toward the empty chair on the other side of the wrought-iron table. Her smile was warm and apparently unfeigned. "Please, join me. There is tea, if you would like some. Green jasmine and honey. Cakes, too. This place has the most wonderful little cakes."

"Thank you." Jheraal sat and poured herself a cup of tea, taking a sip to be polite. It was much too sweet for her taste. She set the cup aside. "I understand you've come to assist our investigation."

"To the best of my ability, yes."

"May I ask why? This matter hardly seems to warrant the attention of House Thrune."

"Oh, I wouldn't be so sure. Your description of the hellspawn's condition was most intriguing. Living and breathing without hearts! How extraordinary." Velenne laughed softly. She broke apart a frosted lemon cake, neatly tearing out its center with her nails. "But, yes, I have some personal interest as well. Not my house. Only me."

"Ederras Celverian."

"An old flame." The diabolist's smile took on a self-deprecating twist, but her dark eyes gleamed with something far more predatory. "One I can't quite seem to let go."

"Will that interfere with my investigation?"

"Hopefully not very much. My spells are entirely at your disposal, I assure you, and I'll follow your lead in this investigation. Whatever you ask, I will do as best I can."

Jheraal nodded. That answer wasn't altogether what she had hoped for, but it was better than she'd expected. She felt a brief flicker of pity for Ederras, but a greater sense of satisfaction that she'd gotten the diabolist's cooperation so easily. "When would you like to begin?"

"Now, if that's convenient."

"It is."

"Marvelous." Velenne dropped a stack of silver and gold coins on the table, then finished her lemon cake and stood. Jheraal, taking the cue, rose as well and led the way down from the teashop's balcony to the streets of Parego Spera.

Two blocks from the teahouse, a large gray dog shouldered through the crowds to fall in beside the diabolist. At first glance, Jheraal took the creature for a wolf, but she soon realized that was wrong. Its body was too long, the head too heavy-boned, the eyes dark brown instead of lupine gold. A moment later, she realized that it wasn't a dog, either. The intelligence in its gaze was too keen, and the sense of controlled malice that emanated from it too strong.

"A pet?" the Hellknight hazarded.

"A friend," Velenne replied, resting a hand on the animal's shoulders. She buried her fingers affectionately in his coarse gray fur. "A loyal guardian given for good service. His name is Vhaeros."

"He's a devil?"

"We'll call him a dog. It simplifies matters."

The dog, who clearly was no more a dog than Jheraal herself was, swished his tail once and cast an openly amused glance at the Hellknight.

"Of course," Jheraal said. Masking any expression, she started toward the avenue that would bring them to Havarel's workshop. "Well, since I have you, I may as well show you what I learned today. The skeleton that was found in that shack in Rego Cader, along with the hellspawn, most likely belonged to a Hellknight from the Order of the Rack. Male human, but we don't have a name yet."

"Ah. That might answer one question I'd had."

"What was that?" Jheraal turned down a footbridge that spanned one of the smaller canals. Spiraling pillars supported a wooden lattice overhead. Flowering wisteria had been trained along those supports to cover the bridge with fragrant lavender blooms. In winter, the vines could look a bit barren, but in summer, the wisteria bridge was one of the thousand secret beauties of Westcrown. She hoped it would keep the lady in a good mood.

"How the killer got three captive hellspawn into Rego Cader without anyone sounding an alarm." The diabolist trailed her fingers along a low-hanging cluster of blossoms. She paused to indulge in their fragrance, then went on. "Teleportation seemed unlikely. If you had the capability to teleport your victims anywhere, why not take them out of Westcrown entirely? Then no one would recognize them, connect them to the murder at Vaneo Celverian, or care. But, instead, they remained within the city, which led me to believe that they traveled on foot. And then I wondered: how did they pass the Obrigan Gate without drawing attention? Surely the rundottari would have told you if they'd seen anything."

"Indeed."

"But they didn't. Therefore I concluded that either the rundottari didn't see anything, or they didn't recognize whatever they *did* see as relevant. The former is possible—the hellspawn might have been hidden under a spell of invisibility—but struck me as less likely than some form of disguise. Because that would explain why they were in Rego Cader."

"A Hellknight releasing convicts into the ruins." *Of course.* Jheraal felt stupid for not realizing it earlier. It was so common for Westcrown's dottari and Hellknights to effectively execute criminals by forcing them through the Obrigan Gate into Rego Cader that no one paid much attention to the daily exodus. Without the correct documents, even a Hellknight wouldn't have been able to force unauthorized prisoners through the gate itself, but smugglers and scavengers were always digging secret holes through the wall, and perhaps the hellspawn's captor had known where to find one. Once out in the ruins, the killer would have had all the time in the world to torture his or her victims without drawing the notice of authorities.

"Precisely. I'm only surprised to learn it was a real Hellknight who led them out." Velenne seemed sorry to leave the wisteria bridge, but she followed with one last glance at the flowers.

Past the bridge, they were soon engulfed by the city again. Yet although the streets bustled with scribes, barristers, and merchants, and every corner held a vendor hawking spit-roasted sausages, fresh apples, or fish pies to the prosperous denizens of Parego Spera, an empty space opened immediately around the Hellknight and the diabolist. It was as if an invisible bubble pushed the ordinary citizenry away.

Jheraal didn't mind. Intimidation had its advantages. For one, it allowed them to talk freely. "We're not sure it was a Hellknight," she cautioned. "He might have been a captive himself. Someone might have stolen his armor—we didn't find it with the skeleton. He could have been traveling incognito, or he could have been robbed. We don't know yet. But I think I've learned all I can from his bones, so maybe it's time to find out."

They had come to Havarel's workshop. Jheraal knocked at the door, waving to the golem when it slid open the slotted window. "You might want to leave your dog outside."

Velenne made a tiny gesture of one finger, not nearly enough to cue a dog, but sufficient to instruct an attentive servant to acquiesce to the suggestion. Vhaeros flattened his ears in vexation but took up a sentinel's position outside the door, watching the street with a mixture of boredom and resignation. Occasionally, if a child looked at him, the fiendish creature wagged his tail.

"He likes children?" Jheraal asked, mystified.

"He likes baiting them into trying to pet him. Vhaeros is not permitted to harm any citizen of Cheliax except at my instruction, or if one lays a hand on him first. It's an obvious loophole, I realize, but it does keep him entertained."

"Ah." It was a good thing there weren't many children on the smithies' street, and that they already knew to stay far from the alchemist's door. Otherwise, Jheraal would have had to invent some excuse to cancel the visit altogether, rather than leave that devil unattended. As it was, she made a note to keep it brief.

With a deep metallic rumble, Havarel's horned brass golem opened the door. It turned in place and trudged back toward the gnome's dual workshops. "The master awaits."

"That's an impressive piece of work," Velenne murmured, folding her arms as she followed Jheraal and the golem inside. She looked up at the whirling magical lights that lined Havarel's foyer, smiling faintly in recognition when the golem lifted its palm to negate the spell wards that the alchemist had set into the hallway. "And a paranoid set of mind."

"Everyone who's any good has enemies." Jheraal strode to the end of the hall and into the gnome's workroom, then stopped short as she ran into a blinding haze of smoke. The room was entirely choked in acrid gray. It smelled horribly of burning chemicals. "Havarel! I'm back. I brought a visitor."

"I see that. I'd come to say hello, but I'm a bit busy." The gnome, barely visible through the pall of smoke, was clad head to toe in a visored garment of oiled leather that distorted his voice into a nasal echo. It resembled a beekeeper's suit, although the resemblance stopped at the pincered metal claws that poked from either sleeve. Soot blackened the front of his garment and drew an ebon lace across the glass of his visor. "Might be some explosions here shortly. Or possibly now. Can you come back later?"

"We don't need to trouble you. I just want to take another look at the bones you showed me this morning."

"Other workshop. Lead-lined box in the quarantine cabinet. Take them if you want. Close the door on your way out, and make sure it's locked. It's important that it's locked."

"All right." Jheraal retreated back into the hallway. She pulled the door shut behind them, giving it a few extra tugs to ensure that it was completely sealed, and then coughed until her lungs were clear of the caustic smoke.

Velenne, who had stayed in the hall behind her, waved away a stray curl of smoke and wrinkled her nose delicately. "An odd friend."

Jheraal heaved open the opposite door while the fire-bellied brass golem looked on incuriously. "He's the best at what he does. I'll forgive a lot for that."

The workshop was dark when Jheraal opened the door, but magical lights glimmered into life on its ceiling when she stepped inside. The light glinted off a spotless glass cabinet, framed in mirror-bright silver, which stood against the far wall. More cabinets of wood and metal lined the other walls, but the shining glass drew the eye instantly.

Specimen boxes and enormous jars filled the glass cabinet's shelves. Among them was the lead-lined box that Jheraal had brought back from Rego Cader. Retreating from the room, she pointed it out to the golem. "Can you get that one for me?"

Crimson light flared in the golem's hollow eyes. It made a sound like the intake of a forge bellows as it inhaled. "Yes." Stepping past the two women, it entered the workshop alone.

The door closed behind the squat, dog-headed construct. A short while later, the golem exited, a sheen of moisture glistening on its brassy surfaces. The lead-lined box was lying on one of the tables, unopened. "It is done."

Jheraal went into the workshop, motioning for Velenne to follow. A medicinal odor of crushed marigold and spearmint lingered in the air. "The quarantine cabinet is best not opened by the living. Our box should be safe enough, probably, but I can't say the same for everything in there."

"Duly noted." The diabolist kept her arms crossed and stayed well away from the cabinets on the walls as she entered. "I'll let you arrange the skeleton. Is it mostly intact?"

"Mostly." Pulling on a pair of thin leather gloves, Jheraal raised the box's lid and began arranging the bones in a rough approximation of a skeleton. Most of the pieces were there: the skull with its eroded teeth, chunks of spine, a pelvis, the long bones of arm and leg. Some of the smaller bones from the fingers and feet were missing, either because she'd missed them on the scene in Rego Cader or because Havarel had used them in his mold-growing experiments. But the general shape of the skeleton soon built beneath her hands.

"Is that adequate?" the Hellknight asked, moving aside so Velenne could examine her work.

"Yes, thank you." The diabolist took a sleek black scroll case from a hidden pocket at her hip and twisted it open. From the papers furled tightly inside, she chose a rippled sheet covered in bronze script. She held it over the dead man's bones and read its incantation aloud, and as she recited each line on the page, its lettering flared up into sparks and smoke. A shower of copper and bronze motes fell around the bare bones, forming the spectral outlines of muscles, tendons, veins, and skin.

By the time she finished the scroll, the dead Hellknight had been restored. A greenish pallor lingered under his skin; a slight puffiness distended his abdomen. He looked, and smelled, like a corpse that had been three days dead.

Velenne lowered her hands and gazed down at the rebuilt corpse. "He should be intact enough for a cleric to commune with his spirit, if you wish." She glanced at Jheraal, raising an eyebrow at the Hellknight's expression. "Did you know him?"

"Yes," Jheraal said, staring at the dead knight's face. "Yes, I did."

8

KEEPING FAITH

EDERRAS

In the blue hour before dawn, Ederras returned to Westcrown Island.

He was utterly drained. After Velenne had left, he'd sat there for another hour, not really thinking about anything, just letting the night's solitude wash over him.

The drunk had twitched and cursed helplessly in his restless sleep, but that had only made Ederras feel more alone. Finally, when he judged that morning was near enough to make it safe, he'd summoned a wisp of divine light around one of the empty wine bottles and left that small blessing to see the young man through to daybreak.

And then he'd walked away, back into the silence of the city where the moon had set and the stars were falling, but no sun yet touched the sky.

Velenne's kiss still burned. He'd loved her, once. Or maybe he'd only loved a mirage of her, a version that shared his ideals and passions. A version that had never really existed.

The truth was red and black. House Thrune and devils. *That* was who she really was. Not the girl who had enchanted him with her smile and made him believe, for a short and glorious and terrible time, that together they could restore Westcrown to its long-lost splendor. All of that had been a lie, an illusion that she'd used to worm her way deeper into the rebels' secrets so that she could destroy them to a one.

And he, a fool, had let her.

The only question was why she'd come back. There was nothing Velenne could exploit him for now. Was she just that much a sadist?

He scrubbed the back of his hand against his mouth. The fire of her touch hadn't faded. It frightened him how easily she did that, and how readily he responded. Desire had been a stranger to him for so long that he'd forgotten how powerful its dictates could be.

It was a relief when the walls of the inner city rose before him. Ederras stepped off the skiff that had carried him across the dawn-silvered canals to Regicona, paid the rower extravagantly, and left the docks behind.

Around him, the first signs of life were beginning to stir. Maids from the smaller houses filled water jars at the communal fountains. Along the side streets, a handful of highborn stragglers, still dressed in last night's rumpled finery, returned discreetly from illicit assignations or secret duels. On the main boulevards, uniformed dottari took down the spent pyrahjes and set new ones for the evening to come.

No one paid Ederras much mind. He was just one more dissolute noble wandering home after a night of excessive revelry. A cluster of giggling young opera singers and courtesans, their hair tousled and lip rouge smeared, waved and called to him flirtatiously. Ederras ignored them, and after a few pouting protests, they moved on.

It's no sin to be happy, he reminded himself. They weren't harming anyone. The world would be a better place if pretty girls everywhere felt safe to express their vivacity freely and without fear. Wasn't that part of what he fought for? A world that was civilized enough to allow for such gaieties?

Yes. But he was glad for their joy without having any interest in it. What he wanted was in black and red. Iron and fire.

It always had been. Even when he'd tried so hard not to see that, some part of him had always known. That was the real reason he'd never been tempted in Mendev, or during any of his journeys before he'd joined the crusade. Not because he'd been concerned about the impropriety of engaging in liaisons with his commanding officers or taking unfair liberties with his subordinates. Because what he wanted, what he'd *always* wanted, was something much crueler.

He reached the gates of the vaneo. The household guards saluted and opened the spiraled iron gates, allowing him entry into his ancestral home.

One path stretched in front of the paladin. A line of pale crushed stone cut a swooping arc across the manicured trees and courtyards of Vaneo Celverian, leading to the manor's grand front doors. No branches, no forks. One clear line.

The orchard's fig and lemon trees draped long, crisscrossing shadows over the manicured grass. The ornamental vines and trellises that ringed the garden gazebo made their own tangled knot of blue shade. Around and through them looped the path, passing from sunlight to shadow and back to sunlight again.

It goes back to the light. He had to have faith in that.

Pushing through his weariness, Ederras started down the path.

He had scarcely gotten upstairs to his old bedroom when Belvadio knocked at the door. The steward looked more tired than Ederras had ever seen him. Both years and grief told on his face, but his coat was pressed and buttoned, and his grooming was impeccable despite the ungodly earliness of the hour. "Welcome home, Master Celverian. May I bring you anything? Tea? Or slippers?"

"Tea. Strong. Thank you." It would be an early morning, not a late night.

As the steward turned toward the door, Ederras raised a hand to stop him. "Belvadio, wait."

"Yes?"

"Yesterday, when I first arrived, there was something you wanted to say. What was it?"

"Ah." Again that minute tension flickered under the surface of Belvadio's outward composure, just as it had the first day. "It may well be nothing, but . . . when the Hellknight was here, she asked whether anything might have been stolen from the vaneo. I said that there had not, because it was not apparent to me at the time that anything was missing. Later, however, when we were preparing your brother for burial, I realized that one of his keys had vanished."

The hair prickled on the back of Ederras's neck. "Which one?"

"Not one of the house keys. None that was regularly used, which is how I missed it." Belvadio clasped his hands at his waist. A hint of a flush crept up along his neck. "It was a key to the Black Chest."

"My uncle Stelhan's chest?"

"The same."

"Was anything taken from it?"

Belvadio coughed. "I cannot say, master. Forgive me. The Black Chest remains in its accustomed place, and it does not appear to have been disturbed. The lid is shut, however, and lacking the key, I cannot open it. Moreover, I do not know what your uncle kept there. If anything were missing, I would not be able to tell." He waited a moment, then inclined his head to excuse himself when Ederras didn't respond. "I will see to your tea."

Ederras sat back on the side of his bed and raked a hand through his hair. The barber had cut it shorter than he'd expected, insisting that this was the current fashion in Egorian. It was startling to feel the difference, but that was the least of the things unsettling him.

Stelhan Celverian, his father's elder brother, had died when Ederras was just a boy. He remembered Stelhan vaguely as a towering presence with a booming voice and a great golden beard, but they'd never been close. Lord Abello Celverian had always harbored a certain tension toward his brother, and even on the rare occasions that Stelhan was in Westcrown, they had seldom visited.

What little Ederras knew about his uncle had come in bits and pieces of family gossip, mostly from his mother: that Stelhan had abdicated his inheritance as a youth, saying that there was no place for him in devil-ruled Cheliax; that Stelhan had spent the better part of two decades serving Iomedae as a roving paladin across the wastes and wilds of other lands; and, finally, that Stelhan had disappeared, presumed dead, somewhere in the River Kingdoms.

The Black Chest was all he'd left behind.

Built of black-stained wood and trimmed in tarnished silver, it had sat in a cobwebbed corner of the vaneo's cellars for as long as Ederras could remember. He and Othando had dubbed it the "Black Chest" as children, and the name had stuck. Supposedly it was enchanted, and held some of the keepsakes and trinkets that Stelhan had accumulated during his travels, but that was only family rumor. Ederras had never confirmed it for himself. He had never seen it opened. He hadn't even known that Othando owned a key.

Could the Black Chest have held something worth killing for?

He was still mulling over that question when Belvadio returned with the tea. A hot, lemon-scented facecloth and steamed hand towel in a silver dish accompanied the cup and teapot. Ederras took them gratefully, daubing some of the night's exhaustion away.

"What do we need to open the Black Chest?" he asked, returning the cloths to the tray. "A wizard? A locksmith? I'd like to know what was in there. Perhaps it bore some connection to the crime."

Belvadio shook his head before Ederras had finished speaking. He whisked the towel dish away deftly, carrying it toward the door. "Lord Stelhan was always most adamant that it could only be opened by the proper key. Any attempt to force it, whether by steel or spell, could be deadly."

"But if we don't have—"

"There is another. There was, at least. While your uncle left the original key to your brother, to be claimed upon his majority, he bequeathed a second key to Lord Kajen Tilernos for safekeeping."

"I see." Ederras poured himself a cup of tea, collecting his thoughts. Lord Tilernos was well known throughout Westcrown as an upstanding and pious man, one of the few to remain in power at the head of a great house after the Thrune Ascendancy. It wasn't entirely a surprise that his uncle would have been friends with the man. "Do you suppose Lord Tilernos might be willing to entertain a visit?"

"I'll send a messenger to ask. He is in residence at Vira Tilernos, so I imagine we will have his answer shortly."

Lord Tilernos's reply was brief and to the point: he had indeed been friends with Stelhan Celverian and had thought highly of the man, and he would be delighted to meet with Stelhan's nephew.

Later that afternoon, Ederras went to Vira Tilernos. He'd slept, washed, and changed into clean, simple clothes in white and gold-slashed blue. After a moment's indecision, he opted to wear his sword. He didn't think Kajen Tilernos would be offended by receiving an armed guest, and even Regicona was not without its hazards.

Vira Tilernos, unlike Vaneo Celverian, was a true estate, encompassing numerous buildings within its sweeping stone walls. The servants' quarters and stables were tucked discreetly to the sides. In the center, at the end of a driveway paved in swirling stone tile, the great house rose in gold-and-white terraces over an expansive formal garden.

Mulberry, orange, and bay trees framed a long rectangular pool that ran through the garden's heart. Lush-petaled flowers bloomed in carved marble vases, filling the garden with ethereal perfume. At each end of the reflecting pool, graceful sculptures depicting philosophers and muses stood as fountains.

It was a display of breathtaking wealth. Every statue and bench in the garden was a work of art, and every double-flowered lilac and silver immortelle in the vases was a botanical masterpiece. Ederras couldn't begin to fathom how much money House Tilernos must have poured into its vira over the years. It was a wonder they hadn't lost it all after House Thrune took power.

At the door, a halfling butler greeted him and escorted him to a cozy library off the main foyer. Two of the walls were lined with shelves of leather-bound books, their gilt-lettered spines gleaming in sedate dignity. Another held a glassed cabinet of brandy, rum, and other spirits in crystal-stoppered bottles. The last was adorned with ceremonial shields bearing heraldry from the great families of a century past, before the Chelish civil war had altered Westcrown so profoundly.

Lord Tilernos had curated his selection pointedly. His wall held only the families who had kept faith with the dead god Aroden, and then with the Inheritor, Iomedae. A third of the houses represented on those shields no longer existed. Some, like House Galonnica, had fled after the civil war, seeking refuge in Taldor or Andoran. Others, braver or less wise, had stayed and been destroyed. Most of the survivors, including House Celverian, had fallen from power, existing only as shrunken remnants of what they'd once been. None, save House Tilernos and its handful of allies and cadet lines, retained any real wealth or influence.

Ederras was studying those shields, hands clasped behind his back, when Lord Kajen Tilernos entered the library.

"Our city has changed a great deal since those days," the lord observed from the doorway behind him. "Not for the better, I'd say."

"Lord Tilernos. Thank you for making time to see me." Ederras crossed the room and offered a hand in greeting.

"Call me Kajen, please. Your uncle was never one for ceremony. Stelhan would have my head if he knew I let his nephew refer to me by title." Lord Tilernos clasped the younger paladin's hand in a strong grip and drew him in for a quick, one-armed embrace, then stepped back, smiling. "It seems a shame we never really met until now."

"It does," Ederras agreed. He had seen Lord Tilernos at formal removes a few times, of course: at the mayor's banquets, opera performances, and the glittering balls that opened and ended each social season. But Ederras had scarcely had time to become acquainted with Wiscrani noble life as an adult before he'd been forced to flee into exile, and he'd never had occasion to speak to Lord Tilernos privately.

He regretted that now, for having finally met Lord Kajen Tilernos, Ederras liked him immediately. Although the lord had to be well north of sixty, he remained vital and energetic. He was a compactly built man of middling height, with a wreath of close-cropped silver hair around a bald pate. Intelligence and good humor lit his rich brown eyes, and his mouth seemed perpetually quirked on the verge of laughter. Had Ederras not known of his reputation, he would have guessed that Lord Tilernos spent more time with books than blades. In fact, he was famous for his accomplishments with both.

"Sit," Lord Tilernos said. "May I offer you a drink? Brandy?"

"Thank you." Ederras accepted a glass from the lord, who poured another for himself and then settled into a red leather armchair opposite his guest. "You must be wondering why I came."

Lord Tilernos smiled over the rim of his brandy glass. "I have a few guesses. First, however, allow me to express my regrets for your loss. I knew Othando moderately well. I liked him. He was a good man."

Ederras bowed his head to acknowledge the kindness. "That's part of what brings me. Othando had a key to a chest that once belonged to my uncle. The key's gone missing. I don't know what was in the chest, but I wonder if it might have had something to do with the attack on our house. I was hoping you might be able to shed some light on that."

The lord didn't answer immediately. He swirled the brandy in his glass, taking a long and thoughtful sip. "I understand you spent some time in Mendev recently. Serving Queen Galfrey."

"That's true."

"What did you think of it? The crusade?"

Ederras frowned. It was his own turn to take a delaying drink of brandy as he pondered how to answer. Finally, as honestly as he could, he said: "It wasn't as simple as I had thought or hoped it would be. But it was important. I knew my purpose there. It rekindled my faith."

"Faith that you lost in Westcrown."

"Yes."

Lord Tilernos nodded, as if that answer was exactly what he had expected. "It's hard to hold faith here. The way of the righteous is not easy anywhere, but in Cheliax, we have particular difficulties. That's why Stelhan left. I imagine that's why you left, as well."

"How have you managed so long?" As far as Ederras knew, Kajen Tilernos had never faltered or fallen. For more than forty years, the patriarch of House Tilernos had been a paladin in Iomedae's shining grace—and yet, somehow, he'd also managed to navigate the treacheries of Chelish politics without losing his family, his fortune, or his head.

"By rarely leaving my vira," Lord Tilernos replied wryly. His smile faded after a moment, though, and he tapped his fingers reflectively on the brandy glass. "My apologies. You deserve a better answer than that. The truth is, I did it by caution and flexibility and luck. I've struck some bargains that I'm not sure really served the greater good, although I always tried to. I've doubted myself a thousand times over the years, and I've made some grievous mistakes. But the Inheritor recognizes and forgives our imperfections, and by her mercy I have never strayed too far from the light." His gaze returned to the wall of shields. "It's possible to do good in Cheliax. Even today. It's possible, and it's never been more important. There are so few of us left."

"I couldn't," Ederras said bitterly. "I failed almost before I began."

"You were alone. You need friends. No one is strong enough to stand in isolation, not against the world as it is today. That was the cause of my only real fight with Stelhan—that he abandoned you and your brother to be raised without proper guidance. But then, he always was more for playing the chivalrous mystery knight than for putting down roots. No matter how many times I tried to tell him that all our victories blow away in the wind if no one stands fast to secure them, he wouldn't listen."

"Is that why he gave you a copy of his key? To help secure whatever is in that chest?"

Lord Tilernos looked back at Ederras. A measuring glint came into his brown eyes. He leaned back in his armchair, raising the brandy glass. "After a fashion, perhaps. I think he did it so that whoever wanted to open the chest would have to either receive the key from him or come to me. So that one or the other of us would be able to judge their character."

"Why? What's in there?"

"An old, dangerous, broken thing." Lord Tilernos drained his glass and stood to refill it, his expression distant and enigmatic. "You've heard of Citadel Gheisteno?"

"I know the name." It was one seldom spoken in Cheliax, for it was linked to many old miseries. Once the headquarters of the Hellknight Order of the Crux, Citadel Gheisteno had been destroyed over half a century ago when its order was declared anathema by House Thrune and the other Hellknight orders.

Ederras didn't know what the Crux had done to earn the enmity of their former brethren, but it must have been a grievous sin, for the Hellknights had stamped those heretics out completely. Not one of them had survived the slaughter. Their fortress had been razed to the ground, their bones cast into unmarked graves, their sites of worship cursed by Asmodeus's clerics . . . and yet even that hadn't ended their miseries. Twenty-five years after Citadel Gheisteno's destruction, a ghostly replica of the citadel had materialized upon the fire-scarred mountain where the fortress had once stood. It was said to be a bleak and cursed place, its walls ringed by blackened skulls, its towers infested with wailing ghosts. Few mentioned that name now, and no one ever went there.

Lord Tilernos uncapped the crystal-stoppered carafe. "Your great-grandfather, Kelvax Celverian, was among those that brought down the Order of the Crux."

"I thought the Order of the Scourge led that crusade." Ederras hadn't had any idea that his great-grandfather had been involved in the attack on Citadel Gheisteno. One more piece of family history his father had never mentioned. He finished his brandy and offered his empty glass to Lord Tilernos.

"They did." The lord poured another splash of amber liquor for him and handed it back. "But they weren't alone. The Order of the Crux was a Hellknight order, after all. They made fierce adversaries, and the Scourge knights weren't about to turn allies away. Your great-grandfather was a formidable champion of Iomedae, and his name added considerably to the weight of law on their side. He was quite old by then, but nevertheless he volunteered to help them, because he believed they were fighting on the side of the righteous."

"Were they?"

"I think so. But I wasn't there. What I do know is that Kelvax found something in Citadel Gheisteno that he regarded with absolute horror. An indefensible sin, he called it. This was, mind you, in the judgment of a man who would work hand-in-hand with Hellknights if he thought he could serve the Inheritor by doing so.

Kelvax was not one who shied from hard measures. But whatever was in Citadel Gheisteno shocked him.

"It wasn't within his authority to pronounce judgment on the entire order, nor to decide what would be done with their possessions. Your great-grandfather, however, couldn't countenance the continuation of whatever it was he'd seen. In the chaos and confusion of the fighting, Kelvax seized a key part of its workings. He removed it undetected, and hid it away in secret. He meant to destroy it, I believe, but never found a way to do so before he died."

Ederras frowned. "That's what was in the Black Chest."

"Yes." Lord Tilernos settled back into his armchair with a comfortable creak. "Your great-grandfather never confided this secret to anyone other than Stelhan, and Stelhan never told anyone but me. Kelvax didn't want anyone to know unless he could trust them completely, and the only one he trusted was the grandson who followed him into Iomedae's faith. Even then, he never told Stelhan exactly what it *was*. Only that it was never to be revealed."

"And Stelhan just left it in the vaneo?" Ederras asked, baffled. "It's practically unguarded. It's just a dusty box in the cellar. Belvadio said it was warded, but I don't know whether that's true. I've never sensed any magic on the chest."

"There isn't any. Stelhan told his servants that to keep them from tinkering with it. But in reality there's no enchantment, and the key is just a key." Fishing around in his pocket, Lord Tilernos came up with a small steel key on a worn leather fob. He tossed it across the room to Ederras. "Both your uncle and I believed that there are two ways to keep a dangerous thing safe. You can lock it up in a ferociously guarded vault, ringed by traps and monsters. Or you can drop it quietly in an unmarked box, stow it in the least likely place, and hope the whole world forgets."

"That didn't happen, though," Ederras said. He weighed the key in his hand. It felt like almost nothing. Too small, by far, to be the reason for Othando's death. "Someone remembered, and they killed my brother for it."

9

DEAD SECTOR

JHERAAL

There were three messages waiting for Jheraal when she returned to Taranik House: one from her paralictor, acknowledging receipt of her reports and including a letter of credit to replenish her operating funds. One from Ederras Celverian, asking her to meet with him. And one from Indrath, her daughter, written in the girl's characteristically large, looping hand. A blob of beige candlewax, deeply pressed with a thumbprint, held it shut.

She wanted to break that seal as soon as she saw it. She didn't. Duty first. Indulgence later.

Jheraal pocketed the letter of credit and sent one of the armigers to Vaneo Celverian to inform Ederras that she would be available that evening. She sent another missive to the Asmodean church, requesting one of their clerics to commune with the corpse that Velenne had recently restored. Then she tucked Indrath's letter into her jerkin, close against her heart, as she carried it back to her quarters to read.

Alone, under lantern light, she broke the letter's seal and smoothed its creased pages.

> Dear Jheraal! Thank you for the book. Do you think the pictures are real? Not real-real, I mean, but drawn by someone who had really been to Ninshabur? Someday I'll find out. For now I'm still studying, though. Signifer Orielle says I have very good potential, which she hardly says to anybody. Today she let me try a spell . . .

Jheraal reread the letter twice, savoring each line, then folded it carefully again and put it into the box where she kept all her daughter's correspondence. Other than her arms and armor, it was the only possession that mattered to her.

Later she would write back. At night, when she could devote her full attention to finding the right words.

First, however, she had to trace that dead Hellknight.

She'd recognized his face, but she didn't have a name to put to that face, and she had no idea what he might have been doing in Westcrown. When Jheraal had encountered the man, he'd been serving in Citadel Rivad, the Order of the Rack's stronghold in the Turanian Hills northwest of the city. He'd just been another rank-and-file Hellknight, no one who'd stood out for doing his job particularly well or poorly. If she hadn't been blessed with a gift for recalling faces, she likely wouldn't have remembered him at all.

Ordinarily, identifying a man with that much information would have been trivial. She knew his face, she knew his affiliations, and she knew where he'd been based. Tracing his identity should have been as easy as finding an artist to sketch his likeness, then showing his picture to his former comrades. Once that was done, solving the mystery of why he'd died in Rego Cader might not be much harder. It should have been simplicity itself.

But it wouldn't be, because those comrades were Hellknights. Not only that, but Hellknights of another order. And whatever the dead man had been doing in Westcrown, Jheraal doubted it was anything that his commanding officers in the Order of the Rack would want known.

Above all else, and no matter their order, Hellknights prized three things: discipline, duty, and honor. Those were the basis of the Measure and the Chain, the belief system that guided all Hellknights. The Measure codified their ideals into absolute laws, and the Chain bound them to follow with total obedience, yielding to neither mercy nor fear.

And just as there was no greater sin for a Hellknight than dereliction of duty, so too was there no greater insult than to suggest that one had failed to uphold his order's honor.

The problem was that the dead Hellknight *had* unquestionably failed, one way or another. If he'd been threatened into cooperating with the plot to kill Othando Celverian and tear the hearts from those hellspawn, then he was guilty of cowardice. A true Hellknight would have chosen death before dishonor. If he'd been magically coerced, then his weak will was a mark of shame.

And if he had *voluntarily* cooperated, and had chosen to abscond from his post in Citadel Rivad in order to take part in such crimes, then the disgrace that would fall upon him and his entire order would be unfathomable. A failure of that magnitude reflected not only on the one who committed it, but on all who had a duty to prevent it and had allowed it to happen.

Jheraal didn't believe that the Order of the Rack would deliberately impede her investigation. She was in the right, according to law and tradition, and no true Hellknight would defy that. Not to protect someone who had potentially brought dishonor upon their order.

But she didn't think they'd be eager to help her, either. Not until she had amassed too much proof for them to deny.

That meant she might have to begin her investigation outside the walls of Citadel Rivad. Hardly impossible, but more difficult. Potentially *much* more difficult, depending on how secretive the man and his associates had been.

What are the levers to break the bonds of loyalty? Jheraal's first teacher had asked that, as almost her very first lesson.

She'd recited the answer immediately and with confidence, having learned the litany well: *Anger. Greed. Fear. Guilt. Resentment. Love.*

Fourteen years later, Jheraal had seen all the foul fruit that could spring from those seeds, and she still believed her teacher had given her the correct answer that day.

There weren't seven deadly sins. The traditional litany missed the mark entirely.

Pride, without resentment, never led anyone to murder. Gluttony and lust could be sated without crime. Sloth tended to *prevent* violence, if anything. But fear, guilt, and corrosive jealousy, the sins seldom cited by the priests—those could drive an honest citizen to kill.

As could love, which few people considered a sin at all. But it was deadlier than any of the others, because love could carve a space for treachery where nothing else would. Love of country, of political ideals, of imagined virtue—those could erode loyalties and divide otherwise impregnable hearts.

Which of those might lead a Hellknight astray?

Any of them could. She'd seen them all over the years. But some were more common than others.

Anger she discarded immediately. Anger led to tavern knifings and bloody rages between lovers. It had spurred some of the ugliest crimes she'd seen in her career, but it burned too hot to have produced something like this. What she'd seen in Rego Cader were the leavings of a crime planned and executed in cold blood.

Fear and greed were possible, but unlikely. It was a Hellknight's honor to embrace death in the service of duty, and to accept hardship and privation as tests of strength. Some always failed in those ideals, but not many.

Love seemed improbable as well. The life of iron discipline imposed by the Hellknight orders left scant opportunity for that delicate flower to flourish.

That left guilt and resentment. And those two could be fertile ground indeed.

Some Hellknights were killers without conscience. But many weren't, and not all of them could put their personal guilt aside when carrying out orders that seemed too harsh for reason. That shame could simmer for years, boiling just beneath the surface, only to erupt at some tiny provocation. Jheraal had seen it many times, and she wondered if perhaps the reason the dead man's teeth had been eaten away by so many reckonings was because he'd punished himself over and over in futile attempts to expiate guilt over some long-ago wrongdoing.

Or it might have been resentment. Hellknights' honor could be prickly. Many were acutely sensitive to any insult that cast doubt upon their discipline or dedication, and slow to forget such slights. Although their doctrine emphasized subservience to one's order and the negation of individual vanity, the Hellknights were a warrior elite. From their first days as armigers—cadets who hadn't yet been recognized as full Hellknights—they were drilled in stoic dignity and the proud refusal to show fear, weakness, or pain. It was impossible for them to avoid arrogance entirely.

And where there was pride, there was the potential for that pride to be wounded.

Could that have been what drove the dead man out to Rego Cader? The need to retaliate for some festering grievance?

Against whom? Not the hellspawn, at least not personally. Jheraal had found nothing in the histories of those poor souls that suggested any reason a Hellknight would bear a grudge against any one of them, much less all three.

But against hellspawn as a race . . . maybe.

She was turning that thought over in her head, trying to find an angle that might allow her to approach the Order of the Rack without betraying her intentions, when a knock sounded at her door.

"Come."

It was one of the armigers, a boy of sixteen or seventeen years, with brown hair and thick, expressive eyebrows. "A message, Hellknight Jheraal."

"What is it?"

"Velenne Thrune wishes you to know that she has found something in the ruins of Rego Cader. She requests your presence at once."

The message wasn't entirely unexpected. After they'd left Havarel's workshop, the diabolist had asked Jheraal to show her where the Hellknight's bones and the heart-thieved hellspawn had been found. Although weeks had passed since that initial discovery, Velenne had wanted to stay behind to continue searching for clues in Rego Cader, and Jheraal had neither the authority nor the inclination to stop her.

She hadn't expected the diabolist to find anything, but she wasn't surprised to be wrong. "Did she want me to come alone?"

"She didn't say. There is a . . . dog, however. To lead you there."

"Show me."

Vhaeros was waiting on the street outside Taranik House. He sat in the shade to the building's side, watching the flow of passersby on the street with a silent intensity that was eerie to behold. The Hellknights posted at the door watched him carefully, well aware that the gray beast before them was no dog.

"You're here to show me something?" Jheraal asked the wolf-like fiend.

Standing, Vhaeros gave his tail a lazy wave that was, she felt, less a wag than an indifferent acknowledgement of her presence. The gray dog sauntered into the crowds, ambling with an exaggerated lope that was surely meant to convey his boredom with her slow two-legged walk.

"Do you talk?" she asked the dog when she thought no one was in earshot. The street traffic was thinning steadily as they passed northward through Rego Crua, and the noises of livestock being penned and put through the slaughterhouses would easily cover conversation.

The dog flicked a pointed ear in her direction. A low huff escaped him, almost a laugh, but he didn't look back.

"Fine," Jheraal muttered. "I can see you don't. Not if you went to that much trouble working out other ways to communicate your contempt."

Vhaeros swished his tail again and continued northward. He wasn't heading toward the Obrigan Gate, she realized, but to another point, five blocks away, in the high wall that separated Rego Crua from the rest of the city.

"Where are we going?" the Hellknight asked.

The gray dog gave her an amused look over his shoulder. His jaws parted in a canine grin as he trotted toward a pile of discarded planks heaped at the end of an alley that backed onto the wall.

As Jheraal followed him into the alley's shadows, the gifts of her infernal blood caused a golden glow to appear in her vision, clearing the darkness from her sight. With its aid, she could clearly see the crevice in the wall, just large enough for a crouched person to slip through, that the boards and planks masked from casual view. It would be tight, but she thought she could get through without removing her armor.

Vhaeros didn't wait. With one last wave of his tail, the gray dog bounded through the crack, leaving the Hellknight to curse and clamber through after him.

On the other side, the ruins of the Dead Sector rose like crumbling tombstones over the city's fallen greatness.

It was only early afternoon, but Jheraal felt a chill of apprehension as she brushed dirt off her palms and stood. There was little risk that shadowbeasts would menace them. Not with the diabolist and her pet devil present. But there were other threats in Rego Cader, and some of them—especially the strongest and fiercest of Westcrown's condemned criminals, who'd survived the Dead

Sector and each other long enough to gather in savage bands—held a burning hatred for any symbol of Thrune authority.

Jheraal didn't fear any of them in a straight fight. But she also didn't expect that they'd be foolish enough to try that. Ambush was a real danger.

Scanning her surroundings continually, she followed Vhaeros down the pocked, weed-choked roads into Rego Cader.

They passed through desolate squares where trees grew through gaps in the flagstones and birds nested in the shelter of abandoned market arcades. Occasionally Jheraal glimpsed some fragment of Westcrown's lost finery, startling as a tatter of gilt lace in a robin's nest: a religious mosaic veiled by climbing ivy, shards of jade-green celadon scattered amid the leaf litter, a single stained-glass window shining beneath a fringe of stone at the top of a shattered tower.

But nothing living, and nothing threatening, until at last they came upon Velenne.

The diabolist sat on a tilted slab of stone outside the beige marble pillars and vine-clad arches of a ruined bathhouse. She stood and closed the book she'd been reading as Vhaeros and the Hellknight approached. "I'm pleased you could join me."

"What have you found?"

"Another group of victims." She pointed to the bathhouse entrance with her book. "All hellspawn. No fungal skeleton this time. Go, look for yourself."

Jheraal didn't move. "How did you find them?"

"I didn't. Scavengers did. They're always crawling through these ruins looking for scraps to eat or barter. I had Vhaeros find a few of them, and then I asked them whether they had found anything of interest these past several weeks. Much more efficient."

"I'm sure they were delighted to cooperate." Jheraal had some guesses as to how Velenne might have persuaded those scavengers to be forthcoming.

"Eventually." The dark-haired woman smiled pleasantly. "Anyway, one of them spotted a group of prisoners being led into this area by a Hellknight. She supposed that they'd been condemned, so she and her comrades lurked in wait, intending to strip the corpses—or, if necessary, finish them off—after some other menace brought them down. What the scavengers found when they went back, however, frightened them so badly that they didn't even rob the dead."

"And that's what's in the bathhouse?" Jheraal glanced at the entrance again. It was a gap of blackness framed between green-garlanded marble, entirely unrevealing.

"Yes. According to the scavengers, these hellspawn were brought into Rego Cader eight days ago. Therefore the Hellknight they saw cannot be the one whose bones you found. Either our killer had another contact among those Hellknights, he is one himself, or he stole the armor that belonged to the skeleton you found. In any case, I haven't disturbed what's left of the victims. I thought you'd want to see them in their original state."

"I do," Jheraal said. Lowering her head, she stepped into the darkness. The golden haze of her infernal vision took hold once more, comforting in its familiarity.

The abandoned baths smelled of moss and mud and mineral salts. The archway opened to a split foyer that branched right and left. Marble friezes, chiseled away in places by vandals and thieves, showed men in various states of undress on the right, women on the left.

Jheraal went left. After descending a short flight of scalloped stairs, she came to a series of cavernous, empty basins that had once allowed the poorest Wiscrani to enjoy the luxury of warm and cold baths, and which were now home to rats and scuttling vermin. Enormous cobwebs, ghostly in her magical sight, billowed over the doorways and cloaked the vaulted ceilings.

She found nothing else. Turning back, she returned to the entry foyer and chose the branch on the right.

This time, her search ended almost immediately.

The hellspawn were piled into one of the old baths on the men's side. Their limbs were tangled over one another like trees in a deadfall, spilling over the basin's marble lip. Their upturned faces stared sightlessly at the mossy ceiling, empty-eyed as dolls. A spider had woven a tented web between two of them. The dry husk of a moth lay trapped in the strands that crossed the hollow of one man's open mouth. Jheraal brushed it away carefully, more disturbed than she wanted to admit by the warmth of his breath puffing over her hand. Then she pulled them out, one by one, and examined what their killer had left in the bath.

There were five victims: three men, one woman, and a girl of six or seven with mottled, toadlike yellow skin and, under her curly brown hair, the large orange ovals of tympanums on either side of her head.

All of the victims were maimed like the ones she'd found earlier. Gaping holes plunged into their chests, showing where the hearts had been carved out of their living bodies. Their clothing had been crisped to flaky black lace around the entry wounds, but there was no soot on their skin and flesh. Only the smooth, clean ripples of cautery.

And around those fatal, impossible holes, every one of them still breathed. Insensible, trapped in a nightmare without waking, they lived.

All five victims were hellspawn who showed their tainted blood openly, but that was the only thing Jheraal could see that they had in common. Two of the men wore the coarse, sweat-stained clothes of common laborers, but the third was dressed in the velvets and stiff brocades of an affluent merchant. A blocky gold ring weighed down the smallest finger of his left hand. Their killer hadn't even bothered to rob him.

The woman wore a plain silk dressing robe and no jewelry, but her hair had been curled into a polished, ornate coiffure, and her hands were soft as baby's skin. Whoever she'd been, she hadn't been poor.

The child was the hardest for Jheraal to examine. *That could have been Indrath.*

She made herself do it, though. Duty demanded that she look.

The girl's attire held few clues. A cotton smock, simple but well made, with smudges of dirt that might have been picked up in Rego Cader and might have predated it. No shoes, but no calluses on her feet, either. There was webbing between her toes, and they were long and thin like a frog's. Her only jewelry was a little band of yellow stones around one finger. Glass and tin, maybe, or golden sapphires in platinum—Jheraal wasn't familiar enough with jewelry to tell.

But someone had loved that little girl enough to give her a ring to make her feel beautiful, and she had loved them enough to believe them and wear it.

The Hellknight blinked back tears as she walked out of the bathhouse. For a moment she paused in the darkness, struggling to pull her mantle of stoicism back on, before she let herself emerge into the light.

"It appears to me that someone's hunting hellspawn," Velenne said. "That whatever happened in the first group of victims, it might not have been sufficient. That our killer—if we wish to use that word—is continuing to seek new victims. Would you agree?"

Jheraal nodded. Once. Curtly. She didn't trust herself to speak.

"Then we're not trying only to solve murders that have already happened. We're trying to stop a predator on the hunt."

"*How?*" The word burst out more vehemently than Jheraal had intended. She struggled to regain control as the diabolist raised an eyebrow at her. "We don't have enough information. We don't know who's doing this, or why, or *how.*"

"We know that the killer returns to Rego Cader to dispose of his victims. That's something, if not much. And we may have a chance to catch another lead, with luck."

"How?"

"Vhaeros is a very good tracker. Eight days is too long even for his nose to follow, unfortunately, so this trail is too cold. However, if this Hellknight comes back again, and if the scavengers' information comes to us more quickly, then we'll be able to track where he goes afterward—and where he went before."

"But then we have to wait for him to find more victims. Probably kill them, too. I doubt your scavengers will be able to get a message to us quickly enough to stop that, even if they're willing to cooperate."

"They will cooperate," Velenne assured her with perfect serenity. "Oh, yes. They'll help. You are correct, however, that we'll have to wait for the killer to return before we can act."

"How many will die when that happens?" Jheraal's fists tightened in helpless frustration. She didn't look at the bathhouse entrance. Couldn't. "Three the first time. Five this time. What's next? Seven? Ten? Twenty? You just want to wait and find out?"

"Do you have a better alternative?" the diabolist asked.

"No," the Hellknight said. "Not yet." *But I will.*

10

THE BLACK CHEST

EDERRAS

With shaking hands, Ederras set his lantern down on the cellar floor and approached the Black Chest.

It was smaller than he remembered. In his childhood memories, the Black Chest had loomed enormous: an ominous presence in ebony and silver. It had been easy to imagine that it held all the wonders and terrors of his uncle Stelhan's adventures across the world hidden in its belly.

But when Ederras looked upon it with adult eyes, the Black Chest was just a plain box of dark wood, its bindings simple, its lock ordinary. It was the sort of chest that one might inherit from a seafaring relative and then use to store mismatched silverware and moth-eaten furs. Amid the cobwebbed wine racks in the cellar, it looked quite convincingly forgotten.

It hadn't been, of course. Whatever his great-grandfather had hoped to hide was likely gone, but he still had to look. To see whatever there was to be seen. A clue, maybe. An explanation. Something to tell him *why*.

Willing his hands steady, Ederras fitted Lord Tilernos's key to the lock.

It opened on the first twist. He lifted the lid, holding his breath.

Inside was a jumble of oddments: a case of dead butterflies impaled on silver pins. Kellid hair fetishes. Animal figurines and religious icons fashioned from Qadiran brass or chiseled out of mammoth tusks from the snowbound Crown of the World. The painted likeness of a beautiful, white-haired woman with an icy severity to her face.

Old maps. Older books. A perfume vial of iridescent purple glass. A silver and copper bracelet, its metal tarnished into a hoop of black braided around spotted green, that depicted a serpent and a dragon strangling one another as they fought.

All exotic, all of little value. All, he guessed, intended to disguise the presence of something less innocuous in the collection.

What?

Nothing stood out as visually different, and he couldn't tell if anything was missing. Ederras drew upon Iomedae's power, fashioning a simple prayer that would reveal any magical resonances in the chest or its contents.

That, too, proved fruitless. There wasn't anything enchanted in the Black Chest.

Does that mean it was stolen or that it isn't magical?

Lord Tilernos had said that Kelvax Celverian had hidden a *piece* of some terrible relic in his home, but a mere fragment of a powerful artifact might not possess any magic on its own. Further, Ederras didn't know for certain that whatever his great-grandfather had taken had been magical at all. Maybe its power existed in a more abstract form: a chronicle of damning secrets, or a repository of forbidden knowledge. Not everything that drove people to murder was enchanted.

What had his great-grandfather seized from Citadel Gheisteno?

A smudge of dimness along the inner rim of the upper lip caught his eye. Invisible from the angle at which he'd been previously viewing the chest, it was just the faintest suggestion of a blur from here. Bringing his lantern closer, Ederras craned his neck for a better look.

It was a fingerprint.

Two, actually, pressed close together as someone had gripped the lid to lift the chest open. The lantern's yellow glow transformed their color to an ill-distinguished brown, but Ederras felt certain that under daylight, that murky smudge would show itself as rust. Or blood. Dry now, fresh then.

Lord Tilernos had been right. The killer *had* stolen something from the Black Chest.

Ederras let the lid down gently, staring at its blankly curved expanse with unseeing eyes. He had expected, somehow, to feel a glimmer of satisfaction upon confirming his guess. Urgency, maybe. *Something.*

Instead he only felt hollow. His brother's assassin had come here, pried open the lid with hands soaked in Othando's blood, and stolen . . . what?

There weren't likely to be any hints elsewhere in the vaneo. Kelvax Celverian had never recorded any of his exploits.

As a child, Ederras had always believed that his great-grandfather was too humble to be caught bragging, and that his father had been close-lipped about the prowess of the family's paladins because he, who had never been praised for valor, envied their heroism. But it seemed, instead, that Kelvax had been trying to bury his secrets. And while Ederras still believed that jealousy and discontent had twisted his father's heart, he was beginning to understand some of the other reasons for Lord Abello's silence.

The cost of heroism was seldom borne only by the hero himself. Othando had been murdered and their servants were suffering grievously because, before any of them were born, one of the paladins of House Celverian had joined the crusade against the heretical Order of the Crux. Unquestionably, Kelvax had fought on the side of good, but sixty years later, innocents were dying for what he'd done.

What would be the consequences of Ederras's own choices? Today, tomorrow, in a hundred years? Who would pay the final butcher's bill when Ederras was long in his grave?

He couldn't possibly guess. The question would paralyze him, if he let it.

What he needed to know, here and now, was what Kelvax Celverian had taken from Citadel Gheisteno—and who would have wanted it. That meant he needed to talk to Jheraal, because he wasn't going to find the Order of the Crux's secrets in Vaneo Celverian.

He wasn't even going to find his own family's secrets here.

After sending a message to the Hellknight investigator at Taranik House, Ederras sought out an Iomedaean chapel for prayer. He needed to unburden his conscience.

There was a small chapel near Taranik House, unpretentious in its service. Once the building had belonged to another faith— the dead god Aroden's, maybe, or that of some other congregation forced out of the city by punitive taxes and restrictive policies meant to favor Asmodeus's worship and cripple all others in Cheliax. While the official policies of House Thrune permitted other religions to exist under their rule, they weren't subtle about manipulating the laws to gut them.

The Inheritor's faith often reclaimed those abandoned chapels before they could be turned to less worthy purposes. House Thrune might starve its temples and slight its priests, but Iomedae's worship was rooted too deeply in Westcrown to die so easily. Cheliax had been theirs before House Thrune rose to power, and someday it would be theirs again. As long as they kept hope alive, the powers of Hell would not defeat them.

Ederras held that thought. It warmed him as he stepped onto the cobblestoned path leading into the chapel. A tidy garden hemmed in the humble shrine, drawing a flurry of white and yellow butterflies. He recognized the plants as healers' herbs: comfrey and feverwort, elderberry and blessed thistle, all of them suitable to serve the Inheritor's faithful.

In that garden, a young man knelt, snipping prickly seed heads from a furry-leafed shrub and collecting them in a basket. His black hair was tied back in a neat, short ponytail, emphasizing the sharpness of his features.

As Ederras entered the garden, the man stood, brushing cut leaves from his clothing. "May I be of service?" There was a fractional pause, scarcely noticeable, as the gardener registered the finer details of Ederras's clothing and added: "My lord?"

"Is there a cleric in the shrine?"

"Of course. Mistress Develya is with a petitioner at the moment, however. Would you care to wait in the garden?"

"Certainly." There was a bench of carved gray stone in the shade of a linden tree nearby. Idly, Ederras turned his attention to the gardener. "May I ask your name?"

"Aedan. I have the honor of serving this chapel as an acolyte."

"You're a cleric of the Inheritor?" It was strange to see one of Iomedae's faithful tending to garden herbs. The crusader goddess's servants trained for righteous combat; weeding and watering were chores more often left to lay worshipers.

"Not yet. I hope to prove myself worthy soon." Aedan brushed dirt from his pale cheek. He had the classic Chelish coloring—fair skin, dark eyes, and silk-smooth black hair with a faint sheen of blue—and an aristocratic crispness to his words. "But first, they say, I need to learn humility. The thorns and bugs are meant to teach me patience in the face of provocation. Digging in the dirt is a meditation on the true price of grave-bought glory. Only when I've grasped these lessons will I be permitted to turn a blade on anything other than dead flowers." He flashed a quick, wry smile. "Forgive my impudence. You see why I'm doing penance in the garden."

"I do." Ederras had to laugh. "You sound like me, twenty years ago."

"Then I shall continue to cherish the hope that in twenty years' time they'll let me hold a sword." The young man dropped a last pod into the basket and stood, placing his clippers on top of the seed heads he'd collected. "I'll see if Mistress Develya is free."

Several minutes passed before Aedan returned. "I'm sorry," he said, "but the petitioner she's tending is in greater need than I'd realized. It may be best if you return another day."

"Is there anything I can do to help?" Ederras asked. "I have some skill in the healing arts."

"You're very kind to offer. The matter seems to be well in hand, though. It's just that it will likely take Mistress Develya the rest of the day to finish her spells, and she'll be exhausted afterward. She isn't a young woman anymore. I'm sorry. I hope your need wasn't too urgent."

"No, not really." Ederras rose to go, then hesitated.

Ordinarily, he would never consider making confession to an acolyte. The hierarchy of the faith was clear, and for him to set his sins before a novice was nearly as absurd as a duke offering penance to a stable hand.

On the other hand, the acolyte didn't seem to know who he was, whereas any senior cleric in Westcrown certainly would. He might get a purer sort of truth from Aedan, in that case, while also maintaining his privacy. "Maybe you can counsel me. If you feel comfortable advising those in need—"

"I would be honored," Aedan said, eyebrows shooting upward in surprise. He ushered Ederras to a small room just inside the shrine. It smelled of fresh lavender, sun-warmed resin, and the lemon oil used to polish the wooden floors. A round table sat in its center. The table held a devotional book and a soapstone tray, upon which a ceramic pitcher and three cups sat. Three mismatched chairs surrounded the table, none new, but all painstakingly repaired. Everything was simple and of humble make, but immaculately clean.

The acolyte closed the door. "What troubles you?"

Where to begin? With his guilt over Othando's death? His worry about the heart-stripped hellspawn? His sorrow at seeing Westcrown still bowed under House Thrune's yoke fifteen years after his own failed rebellion? Should he ask this young apprentice how to navigate the mysteries of long-dead Citadel Gheisteno and his great-grandfather's secret treachery against the Hellknights, or how to capture an assassin who took his victims' hearts but not their lives?

What could he ask a budding priest who hadn't even been initiated into Iomedae's full mysteries yet? Already Ederras regretted his suggestion. Most of his secrets were too deadly to share. What burden could he possibly set on Aedan?

"I need counsel about an old lover," he decided.

Aedan nodded solemnly, his dark eyes lighting with eagerness as he steepled his fingers and leaned forward. This, it seemed, was a subject he felt comfortable addressing. "How so?"

"Fifteen years ago, I was involved with a young lady in Westcrown. I was—I was infatuated, to put it bluntly." *We were in love.* "It didn't go well. She had . . . other commitments, other allegiances, which she kept hidden during our relationship. I would never have allowed myself to become involved with her if I'd known, but of course that's why she hid them from me. Eventually, a friend forced me to confront the truths I didn't want to see, and the lady . . . betrayed me. Badly. There was . . . I did ugly things. Afterward, I left the city for many years, as did she."

"But you've returned. Obviously."

"Yes. So has she. And she wants to rekindle some part of what we had."

Aedan sat back in his chair, quietly surprised. "After she betrayed you?"

"*Because* she betrayed me, I think." *Because I almost killed her, and that one has a shard of Zon-Kuthon embedded in her soul.* It hadn't surprised him to learn that Velenne had become an emissary to the shadow-sworn nation of Nidal after she'd left him. That entire country worshiped Zon-Kuthon, the mutilated Prince of Pain, and it seemed a natural haven for her. "But perhaps for other reasons as well. I don't know what those might be, exactly, but she doesn't seem to do anything unless it profits her somehow."

"Ah." The acolyte frowned intently, working it through in his mind. "Do those differing allegiances remain a conflict between you?"

"Yes."

"Can you reconcile them?"

"I don't think so." Ederras poured a cup of water with a shaking hand, holding it carefully until it stilled. When the last ripple had smoothed, he lifted it to his lips and let the water's coolness wash away his agitation. "I wouldn't know where to begin, and I doubt it would be wise to try. But she has me trapped. I need her help. I can't afford to offend her station. And yet I can't be near her without going mad."

"Do you think she intends to exploit you? Your title? Your faith, perhaps?" The delicacy of Aedan's tone suggested that he was trying to tread carefully around the issue, but his pointed glance at Ederras's sword said he knew full well that his visitor was a paladin, whether or not Ederras wanted to announce it openly.

"She has no need of my title. As for my faith . . . no. She was always careful to protect me in that way." It was peculiar to remember that, but he was certain that it was true. When they were lovers, Velenne's counsel had always guided him toward the righteous path. Up until the very end, Ederras had never suspected that she'd had blood on her own hands.

Not back then, anyway. Afterward that had changed. For both of them.

"But your beliefs are not compatible."

"She is . . . very loyal to the crown."

"Ah. Still, if she has such influence over you, then you must have some over her."

"Doubtful."

"You must," the acolyte insisted. "She came back, you said. *She* was the one who sought *you* out."

"What if she did? Why's that important?"

"Because it means you have an opportunity. You might, anyway." Aedan sat straighter, holding Ederras's gaze earnestly. He sounded cautious but excited, like a scout who thought he'd glimpsed a way out of an ambush. Only a possibility, but hope. "What if you could convert her?"

"What?"

"Change whatever allegiances conflict between you," Aedan said patiently. "The harms of the past cannot be undone, so one must look to what good can be worked in the future. The Lady of Valor teaches us that love breaks the chains of the soul. Is that a possibility? Even distantly?"

"I have no idea." He'd never considered it. If the acolyte had any inkling who they were discussing, Ederras thought, he'd never have suggested it either. The idea of wresting Velenne away from her loyalties was more than a little absurd. She was a woman of formidable will and fierce intelligence, and if she was sworn to Asmodeus, then he hardly expected to coax her from that infernal lord. Better—and safer—to assume that her oaths were sealed in iron. Better to treat her like a devil herself.

"Is it not worth trying? If you truly cannot avoid her, then why not glean some good from what can't be changed? Should you fail, nothing is lost. Perhaps she might even soften in small ways, if not absolutely. But should you succeed, think of what might be gained! Why close off the possibility before you try?"

"It's impossible." But even as he said it, Ederras found himself drawn to the idea. What if he *could* win her over? What if, knowing what she was, he could change her?

Be careful you aren't making excuses for temptation.

But he didn't think he was. Not yet.

"Consider it," Aedan urged. "I can't tell you what to do, of course. But you asked for counsel, and that is mine. Consider it."

"I will," Ederras said, standing. "Thank you. That might be the answer I needed."

An hour before nightfall, Ederras went to a trattoria near Taranik House, where Jheraal had indicated she would take her evening meal after she'd finished her other work for the day.

The Hellknight was sitting alone at a bare wood table in the back of the crowded common room, halfway through a meal of coarse bread and stewed fish in white sauce. A flask of water sat before her. There was no wine.

She nodded in greeting as Ederras joined her. A white-aproned halfling waiter, almost invisible amid the press, materialized beside their table. "Your order, my lord?"

Ederras glanced at the slate board hung high on one wall, between narrow shelves of wine bottles and ornamental plates. "The lamb, please."

"Of course. Wine?"

"Yes." He didn't bother specifying what he wanted. The trattoria offered only a nameless red and a nameless white, and with lamb roast the servant would certainly bring red. Those who were more particular about their pairings would bring their own bottles.

The halfling bowed and vanished again. Jheraal chuckled. "This place not quite up to your standards?"

"There were times by the Worldwound when I'd march two miles through the snow to get a hot meal," Ederras said. "I'm not about to complain if the wine selection here wouldn't make a Jeggare swoon."

"But you notice. You can't help but notice. Birthright matters." The Hellknight hid a smile behind a lifted soupspoon.

Ederras was spared having to make any reply by their waiter's return with a platter of roast lamb and potatoes. A second halfling carried a tray with a decanter of deep red wine, almost purple, and two silver-rimmed glasses. The glasses were considerably finer than the wooden cup sitting next to Jheraal's elbow. As soon as the food was laid out, and the paladin indicated with a nod that nothing more was required, both halflings retreated noiselessly.

"They could teach my scouts a thing or two about stealth," Ederras observed, cutting into the roast. It was dry, and the potatoes over-salted, but he'd told the Hellknight the truth: after his time in Mendev, a middling meal in Cheliax was an unimaginable luxury. He tilted an empty glass toward her, offering a pour. "Maybe I should suggest a training camp in Westcrown."

"Mayor Arvanxi would be delighted." Jheraal waved away his offer with a white-scaled hand and finished her fish stew. She pushed the empty bowl aside, and the halfling servants made it vanish in a twinkling. "Your message said you had something to talk about?"

"Is this place safe?" The trattoria had become even more crowded since Ederras had entered. Patrons were packed elbow-to-elbow, and the constant din of conversation made it hard to hear Jheraal across the table. Adding to the chaos, a quartet of minstrels had begun singing on a raised dais near the largest of the commons' three fireplaces.

"Anyone who cares enough to eavesdrop through this noise would have to be using magic. Anyone who cares enough to use magic would find a way to spy on us wherever we went. Is it that sensitive?"

"It might be." He relayed what Lord Tilernos had told him and what he had seen when he unlocked the Black Chest, although he was careful to skirt around using any names or identifiable details. By the time he'd finished telling the tale, Jheraal's scowl was deep enough to show the tips of her pointed canines.

"You think your great-grandfather had something belonging to those heretics?"

"I do. I hoped you could help me find out what."

"Maybe." The Hellknight raked her hair back behind her goatlike horns. "I think I'll have a glass of that wine after all." She quaffed it in a single motion, thumping the empty glass down like someone who'd spent a lifetime drinking among soldiers. Probably she had. "I can look into it. Won't be easy. People get more close-mouthed about the secrets of the dead than their own. But—yes, I'll try. It'll give me something to do while I wait for our killer to strike again."

"What?"

"Another crop of hellspawn turned up in Rego Cader. Same as the last. Hearts gone, bodies breathing. I'm planning to follow up with background investigations tomorrow, but I don't expect to find much. I think they were just targeted because of their ancestry, not because they knew anyone or did anything. But it's possible that their friends or family might have glimpsed the assassin, so that was going to be my next line of inquiry." She stared at the empty glass, looking tired.

"That's not what I meant. You're waiting for the killer to attack more victims?"

Jheraal breathed a soft, whistling sigh through her fangs. "I don't like it, but I haven't thought of a better plan. Velenne says her dog can track our killer, but only if the trail is fresher. I'm hoping to find a quicker way, but I don't have one yet."

"I see." Ederras finished his own wine. He lifted the decanter, offering what remained to Jheraal, but the Hellknight shook her head, so he poured the last of the dark red for himself. Dregs swirled and settled at the bottom of the glass. "Is there anything I can do to help?"

"There might be. Your great-grandfather didn't go out there alone. I wonder if it might be useful for you to pretend you're looking to research his past deeds. Writing a biography for the glory of your house and faith, that sort of thing. Might open a few doors that'd stay closed to me."

"It's worth trying," Ederras agreed. "I might be able to get a few names from L— from the friend I saw today."

Jheraal's amber eyes crinkled in mirth at his near slip. The trattoria had grown dark as night fell around its windows, and the Hellknight's eyes had begun to glow with their own inner fire. "Should I ask Velenne to go with you? She might be able to persuade the ones who don't find your credentials as impressive."

No, Ederras almost said, before he thought back to Aedan's suggestion.

Did he really want to try redeeming a diabolist?

That diabolist?

"Yes," he decided.

11

THE CITADEL
OF THE RACK

JHERAAL

The high walls of Citadel Rivad cut a forbidding silhouette. The granite fortress loomed sternly above the ragged rise of the Turanian Hills, standing atop a foundation that had been built untold centuries before, when all this land had belonged to the empire of Taldor. Over the years, the world had shifted around it. One empire had faded and another had risen. Armies had flowed through those gates in rivers of iron and blood. Innumerable storms had battered the walls and flung spiked javelins of lightning against the citadel's towers.

But the stone had endured. The fortress had endured. And although Jheraal came to Citadel Rivad as an ally, not an enemy, she couldn't help feeling a pang of apprehension as she rode into the view of its defensive towers.

The first line of sentinels stopped her at an outpost fifty yards from the outer walls. Her credentials were checked politely but thoroughly, her passes examined with a critical eye. They knew who she was, of course, but Hellknights made no exceptions in their security.

Three more times she was stopped at checkpoints before the Rack Hellknights allowed her entry into Citadel Rivad. Never a smile, never an idle word. Always the same correct, efficient courtesy, just this side of chilliness, as they saluted and waved her onward through gate after gate.

She wasn't the only visitor to the citadel. At the last gatehouse, she passed a Hellknight of the Scar riding out in mithral plate, shield slung over his back and rapier clattering alongside an armored leg. Four vicious gouges cut across the cuirass, continuing up to the gorget, where they vanished abruptly. The original gorget had been ruined past repair and replaced, but by the cuirass's furrows she recognized the wearer as Ursion Nymmis.

Based in the Taldan city of Cassomir, the Scar was one of the smallest Hellknight orders. It counted fewer than forty members under its banner, and Jheraal doubted there was another knight with such distinctively damaged armor among them. Given how rarely its members worked outside the nations of Taldor and Qadira, there probably wasn't even another Scar Hellknight in Cheliax.

The pins in the cloak accompanying the knight's dress uniform—one of several subtle ways Hellknights denoted rank—suggested he'd moved up in the world, which didn't surprise her. Three years ago, Jheraal had helped him solve a trail of mysterious assassinations that stretched all the way from Cassomir to Egorian, eventually tracking down the wizard responsible. She'd fought at the Scar knight's side against the necromancer's beasts of bone and shadow—one of the most desperate melees of her career—but as they rode past one another in Citadel Rivad's gatehouse, neither offered more than a curt, wordless nod. No Hellknights, in any order, would pause in their assignments for mere socializing. Not even for a comrade who had saved one's life.

At the gates of Citadel Rivad, Jheraal dismounted and handed her passes to the Rack Hellknights standing guard beside the massive iron doors. The Ennead Star, a nine-pronged black-and-crimson starburst that represented the core tenets of the Hellknight orders, stood proudly on each of the citadel's great doors. The starburst's center showed the Rack's spiked wheel, and another breaker's wheel encircled the entire design. Above each symbol, smaller wheels crowned the flagpoles flying the Rack's grim banner.

It made for an intimidating entrance, as it was meant to. After a long moment, during which Jheraal had ample opportunity to contemplate the forked black banners flapping over the citadel's granite walls, the Rack knights returned her passes and waved her onward. Jheraal took up her horse's reins and continued afoot.

In the large courtyard beyond the gates, squires and armigers piled books up into towering stacks over hollow cores of kindling. Most of those were old editions of disapproved histories, or texts from prohibited religions. They'd be burned once the sun went down, so the light of the fires carried further. The Hellknights of the Rack were famed for those bonfires, which they called "clarity pyres." *The venoms of the mind poison the body,* they said, and fire was its cure. Sometimes they burned the books' owners along with their texts.

On the other side of the courtyard, a Hellknight of the Chain, clad in manacle-like gauntlets and plate armor worked to resemble coiled chains bound in place with heavy locks, stood watch over a group of shackled prisoners. Jheraal didn't recognize the Hellknight, but the scenario was clear enough. The Chain knights wore helms faced with iron prisoners' masks and made it their mission to track escaped prisoners, retrieve runaway slaves, and ensure that none of the criminals consigned to their prisons ever had a prayer of escape. Some of the most dangerous prisoners in the world were kept at Citadel Gheradesca, and none, to Jheraal's knowledge, had ever gotten free.

From the layers of old whip scars on their backs and the welts of lost collars around their throats, Jheraal guessed that the captives in the courtyard were slaves who'd tried to run and had been recaptured, and who were now bound back to their former masters. Most likely those masters were in Westcrown, and the Chain Hellknight was overseeing the return of the slaves to their rightful places.

Jheraal took no joy in the slaves' suffering, but their fate was none of her concern. As she passed the stables, Jheraal handed her horse's reins to an unsmiling armiger. The steely song of combat echoed from a smaller yard to the right, loud enough to make her battle-tested destrier flatten its ears in protest, and she turned to watch.

Under the hard eyes of Kassir Voidai, Citadel Rivad's Master of Blades, a would-be Hellknight was testing himself against a devil. He was black-haired and golden-skinned, suggesting ties to the Dragon Empires of the far east, and he was being sorely tried.

To be an armiger was no easy task—even that level of acceptance within a Hellknight order required a candidate to embrace the Measure and the Chain, and to endure years of rigorous study and self-mastery. Yet to win the armor and title of a true Hellknight, a candidate had to slay a devil in single combat—and had to earn that victory under the eyes of a sworn Hellknight.

A single witness sufficed in times of necessity, but when an armiger took the test in one of the citadels, the formal rituals of ascension called for more. The courtyard for this test was lined with Hellknights of the Rack. Men and women in heavy black armor, its design made to resemble flensed musculature, watched without expression as their young trainee fought for his life against a crimson-skinned, heavily muscled fiend.

Jheraal paused in the archway, remembering her own test. The fiend she'd faced had been similar to the one that the Rack armiger was squared off against: a squat, glaive-wielding devil with a scraggle of blood-soaked beard that left dark streaks glistening across his bare scarlet chest.

Her long-ago opponent had blistered her ears with infernal curses and threats, trying to rattle her nerves. This one, however, fought in silence. So did the armiger, tight-lipped and determined despite several minor wounds that dotted his leathers with blood. There were no battle cries, no shouts of pain or pleas for mercy that would never come. Only stoicism, fierce determination, and skill.

This one will succeed. Jheraal only needed to watch a few minutes to see that. There was skill behind his sword and steel in his spine, and the young man didn't flinch when the devil leered close enough for the blood-crusted tendrils of his beard to caress his cheeks obscenely. The youth answered with a thrust of his longsword, drawing the devil's blood.

She left the armiger to his battle, removing her helm as she continued through the interlocking yards of Citadel Rivad. It wasn't until she'd passed through another shaded stone arch and back into the sunlight that she finally found the Hellknight she'd come to see. Or, rather, he found her.

"Well, if it isn't my favorite scourgey hellspawn. Hunting criminals in Citadel Rivad, are you? Close your eyes and throw a rock, you'll hit a dozen."

Jheraal turned toward the familiar voice. Only one Hellknight in the entire Order of the Rack talked like that. "Merdos Rasdovain. They haven't drummed you out of the order yet?"

"Ha! Far from it. I've been promoted. It's *Paralictor* Rasdovain now." Merdos came down one of the enormous staircases that swept up from the citadel's formal entrance hall. He hadn't changed much since the last time Jheraal had seen him, other than a few more strands of gray in his red-blond hair and the new pins of steel and gold on the shoulders of his flayed leather cloak to go along with his increase in rank.

Although he was over thirty, her old friend still seemed almost too boyish to be a proper Hellknight. There was a spring to his step that no weight of formal armor could diminish. His blue eyes glinted with mischief, and his open, broad-nosed face always seemed on the verge of cracking into a smile. It was a jarring contrast to the harsh, fanatic asceticism that surrounded him.

Part of that was calculated, Jheraal knew. Merdos's good humor was invaluable in convincing the common people of Westcrown to trust him. He could find witnesses, win their confidence, and persuade them to testify openly before magistrates when no other Rack Hellknight could coax a word out of entire neighborhoods.

But it was genuine, too. He truly did care for his people, both the Hellknights and armigers under his command and the Wiscrani they were charged with safekeeping. He could be as merciless as any Hellknight when necessary, but he didn't let that hardness define him. It was why Jheraal had always liked him, and why she had hoped to find him here. Merdos was the only Hellknight in the Order of the Rack that she could trust with her current task.

"Did they give you an office with that promotion?" she asked.

Merdos raised an eyebrow, taking her meaning immediately. "They did. I'll show it to you, if you don't believe me."

"Seeing *is* believing."

The paralictor swept a hand up the staircase, mimicking a courtier's grand gesture. "Then come, and I'll make a convert out of you."

His office was small, spare, impersonal. The only natural light came from two east-facing windows that were crisscrossed with iron bars despite their height and the narrowness of their apertures. Panels of dark wood covered the walls. They depicted the Order of the Rack's spiked-wheel insignia, alternated with carvings of criminals being brought to justice and seditious writings piled into pyres.

"It's a bit gloomy," Jheraal observed, clicking her clawed fingertips on a corner of his desk.

"Never said it wasn't. I promised an office, but I never said it was a *nice* one." Merdos closed the door. His voice dropped and lost its levity once they were alone. "What brings you to Citadel Rivad? You surely didn't ride all the way out here to congratulate me on a promotion I won three months ago."

"A promotion I didn't even know about?" Jheraal snorted. "No. Congratulations on that, but no. I came because I need access to certain records. *Accurate* records."

The emphasis did not go unnoticed. The Order of the Rack was entrusted with keeping—and, when necessary, concealing—true accounts of all that transpired under their watch. Common sentiment held that the Order of the Rack destroyed all disfavored ideas that came into its grasp, regardless of their merits, and that only fawning, Thrune-approved propaganda survived its pyres.

While popular among the order's enemies, these beliefs were far from accurate. The Order of the Rack indeed bottled up truths that were too dangerous for the populace to hear. But it seldom destroyed them.

The truth was too valuable a weapon to lose. A fact that might be inconvenient in one age could easily become indispensable in another, as anyone who held power long enough eventually learned. Nothing shattered lies and heresies more conclusively than the truth; nothing dispersed rabble-rousers' exaggerations more quickly. Accurate information was the first, best, and sometimes only antidote to the myriad poisons of the mind.

The Order of the Rack understood that better than anyone. Its Hellknights, accordingly, were tasked with maintaining the discipline of information—which meant, in part, that they hoarded secrets the rest of the world had long forgotten.

They weren't quick to share those secrets, though. Merdos was her one chance to break through the Rack's wall of silence, and Jheraal wasn't sure their friendship would go that far. Not if whatever she was trying to find was as lethal as she'd begun to suspect it might be.

Merdos's brow creased. "Records about what?"

"The Order of the Crux."

"That seems a bit historical for your interests, doesn't it? It's been more than fifty years since those pretenders were crushed. I'd think they were out of your jurisdiction."

Jheraal sighed. "It's not them I'm trying to track down. I just need to know what happened around the time of Citadel Gheisteno's fall. I wouldn't ask if it weren't important, Merdos. I have reason to believe those records could be relevant to my current investigation."

"The killings at Vaneo Celverian?" He laughed at the startlement that crossed her face. "Don't look so surprised. Knowing other people's business is my job. So you believe there's some connection between Citadel Gheisteno and that unpleasantness?"

"I'm not sure. I *do* think there's a connection between the Rack Hellknights here in Citadel Rivad and the murders in Westcrown, though."

Merdos's smile vanished. "You can't be serious."

"I am. Unfortunately." She described the Hellknight whose body they'd found in Rego Cader, watching Merdos closely as she detailed the dead man's build and features. When a wince of recognition passed across the paralictor's face, so fleeting that Jheraal would have missed it if she hadn't been watching for a reaction, she knew her guess had been on the mark. He'd known the man.

"His name was Hakur," Merdos said. "We'd thought he deserted. His last assignment was serving as a guard in the library collections. He'd served honorably for years, but recently he'd been . . . troubled. That happens, from time to time. His superiors thought that perhaps a few weeks of quiet in the archives would help. Evidently not." He shook his head, grim-faced. "Does anyone else know?"

"Not yet."

"I would be grateful if you could keep it that way. At least a little while longer." The paralictor paced across his office. There wasn't much room for it. Three short strides, and he had to turn around, adding to his barely contained agitation.

Jheraal leaned against a wall, giving him as much space as possible without being obvious about it. The wall carvings jabbed her back, but she refused to shift her weight away. Doing so would have been an admission of discomfort, and beneath her dignity. "Do you know if he had any friends outside the citadel? Any family? Lovers?"

"A sister in Westcrown. I can give you her address." Merdos stopped pacing. "What was he *doing* in Rego Cader? Was he captured? Did he actually desert the order?"

"I don't know. That's part of the reason I'd like to see the archives. Knowing what Hakur was doing during his last days here might help me piece together what happened to him, and why."

The paralictor nodded, unhappy but satisfied. "I'll show you where he was assigned."

The secret libraries of Citadel Rivad were dark, dusty, and densely packed. Although the rooms were enormous, their vaulted ceilings lost in shadow, only a cramped warren of tunnels was accessible from the ground. Overloaded shelves and unmarked boxes crowded in on every side, leaving gaps so narrow that Jheraal had to walk sideways to fit through. Enchanted lamps cast a steady, bluish illumination at the end of each row, but the clutter was so thick that the light invariably failed before reaching the centers. Sometimes it lasted only a few feet.

Still, there was more than enough to show Jheraal that while this part of Citadel Rivad might be formally designated "libraries," the spaces more closely resembled evidence rooms. Mostly the shelves held stranger things than books or scrolls: bones, religious icons from outlawed cults, bottles with poisonously colorful, unlabeled contents. She saw a wand with a baby's skull impaled upon its handle, and another made of clear, hollow glass beside it. The glass wand was filled with what looked like fresh-spilled blood, and within it swam a dozen tiny leeches, none longer than the smallest of Jheraal's fingernails. Each of the leeches had a shriveled, eyeless human face.

And all these things, hideous and horrible and unexplained, hemmed her in so closely that she had to pull her elbows close to her body to keep from knocking them onto the floor. Even when she made herself as small as she could, her shoulders brushed against them constantly.

The Hellknight didn't consider herself claustrophobic, but the secret libraries were threatening to change her mind. "*This* is what Hakur was supposed to guard?"

"Hakur and eleven other Hellknights. Yes."

"Why does this place need a dozen guards? How would anyone even know where to find anything in order to steal it?" Jheraal plucked at the cloth covering a nearby box. Under it was a stack of flat brown leaves covered in curling script that seemed too miniscule to have been penned by any human hand. An ugly, squat stone figurine sat atop the leaves. It looked like a toothy, cross-legged frog, or perhaps a demon of some kind. Blood, apparently wet and fresh, stained its broad-toed feet. She pulled the cloth back over it, wondering what the Order of the Rack had seen in those leaves and that statuette that warranted locking them away.

"There's an order to the collection. The Rack would leave nothing so disorganized." Merdos's smile, likely meant to be wry, was cold in the blue-tinted light. "But it's deliberately obscured." He pointed to a shelf three rows down. "Anything we have pertaining to Citadel Gheisteno will be there. Or in that general area. It might be moved around a bit."

Jheraal nodded. "How long do I have?"

"This is dated for a week." He handed her a small scroll: a pass authorizing access to the secret archives, signed with his name and affixed with the seal of his rank. "I can't imagine you'll need longer."

"A week." She tucked the scroll into a belt pouch, hoping it would be enough.

Merdos started back toward the stairs. Paper rustled as he moved. The library's books and papers were piled so high around him that even the small motion of turning around threatened to knock mountains loose. "You owe me a favor for this one, Jheraal. A big favor."

"And here I thought I was doing you one."

"Time will tell," he said, leaving her to the gloom.

When his footsteps had receded up the staircase, Jheraal ventured down the row he'd indicated. Its shelves bowed under the weight of dust-cloaked crates. They'd been hastily built, the nails angled in carelessly and hammered with enough force to splinter the cheap wood. Old stains, greened and faded by time until she couldn't tell blood from mud, smeared across their sides and bottoms.

If there really was any secret order to the jumble, as Merdos had claimed, Jheraal couldn't see it. The boxes' markings were indecipherable, and she couldn't find a catalog or list of their contents anywhere on the shelves. Sighing, she resigned herself to going through each of the crates by hand.

The first few boxes held nothing of obvious interest. Blades, saws, scalpels, retracting hooks. Braziers for cautery tools and stained glass jars for holding blood. Torture implements, she assumed, kept to prove that the Order of the Crux was as red-handed in that respect as any other Hellknight order. Some were curiously made, with blades shorter and stouter than most of the similar implements she'd seen, but none of them stood out otherwise.

There wasn't anything revelatory about proof that the Order of the Crux had used torture. Nearly every major power in Cheliax did that. It was widely known that House Thrune even sent some of its royal executioners to Nidal so that they could study the most sophisticated techniques devised by the church of the pain god. Far from hiding the fact, they extolled it across the continent, so that all would know what it meant to break the laws of Cheliax.

Nothing in there could explain what had happened at Vaneo Celverian. Nor could it explain the five hellspawn who'd turned up, weeks later, in the ruined bathhouse of Rego Cader.

Jheraal moved on, extricating another crate from a high, overcrowded shelf. She pried off its splintered lid, lifted up the sackcloth under that, and then stopped dead, the breath caught in her throat.

It held bones. Ten sectioned sternums and frontal ribcages, sawn out like bony breastplates and stacked one atop another, neat as saucers in a cupboard. The next crate held more, and the next beyond that. Jheraal pulled them down one after the other. When she finally ran out of boxes of bones, she was surrounded by more than a dozen of them, holding the remains of nearly a hundred people.

Most of them looked human, although a few had the stouter proportions of dwarves or the slight, small bones of halflings. One partial skeleton was the milky green of jade. Another was striated with scarlet ripples like tongues of living flame.

Whether or not they showed their infernal heritage that plainly, however, the Hellknight knew that not one of the ribcages in those boxes had come from an ordinary person. Their condition made that clear. All of them, every last one, had a smooth-bored gap in the bones, cauterized neatly at its edges, where something had burrowed into that person's chest and ripped out his or her living heart.

What did this? Why?

The bones offered no answer. Jheraal traced the polished rim of one ruined ribcage, marveling at the molten smoothness of the bone, even as she shivered inwardly at the clinical horror of it. Then, numbly, she began stacking the boxes back up on their shelves, because the rows were too cramped for her to move otherwise.

When the last of them had been replaced, Jheraal rested her forehead against a bare spot on the shelf, hoping that the cool wood might leach away some of the heat that pounded behind her temples. The hellspawn she'd found weren't the first victims. The bones proved it. Someone had done the same thing at Citadel Gheisteno, decades earlier.

Was that the Order of the Crux's heresy? Was that why they were stamped out of existence?

The bones didn't answer that question, either.

With luck, however, someone else would. The fall of Citadel Gheisteno remained within living memory. Some of those who had marched against the fortress could still speak of what they'd seen.

It was Ederras's task to find them, though, as it was hers to investigate the archives of Citadel Rivad. Returning her attention to her duty, Jheraal stooped to the next pile of unmarked boxes.

There were only three left in this section. Two were large, one small. Jheraal pulled out one of the larger boxes and lifted its lid, then pulled aside the layers of sackcloth and brittle straw that cushioned its contents.

Jewels gleamed amid the straw. Dozens of them, each the size of a large apple. Some were dull and gray. Others were pink and pale as dewy roses. Cautiously, with quick, light touches, Jheraal brushed their shining surfaces clear.

A ghostly throbbing reached her ears. The Hellknight bent closer to the straw-cradled jewels, unsure what she was hearing. Then she pulled back abruptly, eyes wide in the blue-tinted gloom.

The stones were beating like hearts. Not all of them. Only the pink ones, never the gray. It was only a faint echo of the true sound, as muted and distant as the roar of waves trapped in a seashell—but it was there. She was certain of it. Those jewels held heartbeats. How and why, she couldn't begin to guess, but there was no doubt in her mind as to what they were.

Jheraal's hands shook as she replaced the lid and returned the box to its rightful place. Tense in anticipation, she pulled out the second large crate, and took only a moment to confirm that it, too, was filled with row after row of cabochons, rose pink or lifeless gray, nested in decades-old straw. Again, the rosy ones thrummed with spectral heartbeats, while the dull ones made no sound. The box's jewels drummed in an unearthly chorus from the moment she revealed them until she replaced the lid on their crate and pushed it back onto its shelf.

The last box sat between them. It weighed almost nothing in her hands as she pulled it out. The smudged tracks of fingerprints showed as clear streaks in the dust on its pinewood lid.

Filled with foreboding, Jheraal fitted her fingers to the tracks of whoever had gone before, and lifted up the dust-cloaked lid.

The last box was empty.

12

THE WINTER OF WHITE ROSES

EDERRAS

W e need to set the terms of our agreement," Ederras said stiffly, looking anywhere but at Velenne. It felt surreal to be so close to her, in the pleasantly civilized setting of a Wiscrani restaurant, with the windows thrown wide to a balmy late summer morning and pots of geraniums, white and red and brilliant pink, hanging between the filmy curtains. It was easy to imagine, or pretend, that none of the ugliness of their past parting lay between them.

A lie. But a tempting one.

"Our agreement?" Velenne toyed with the handle of her porcelain teacup. Today she wore a dress of frothed silk in green and gold, betraying not the smallest suggestion of her infernal vocation. Her smile made his chest clench. "About what?"

"If you insist on being part of this investigation, then I must have certain assurances. I won't have the citizens of Westcrown suffering because of you."

"Ah. You want me to avoid offending your code?" She lifted the teacup to her mouth, her dark eyes dancing above its rim. "Fine. Consider it agreed. At least for the duration of our work in Westcrown."

Ederras scowled. "This isn't a joke."

"Did I give you the impression I thought otherwise? I apologize if so." Setting the teacup aside, Velenne reached languidly for his hand. The diamond on her white gold ring flashed in the sun, ostentatious in its size and brilliance.

He recognized it with a pang. That ring was an heirloom of his house. Ederras had given it to her after the first time they'd lain together, when he was smitten and foolish and had actually believed that one day they might marry.

He jerked his hand away before she could touch him. "I don't need your apologies. All I want is your word that you'll not indulge in your usual perfidies for as long as we're forced to work together."

"You have it. As I said. For as long as we share this endeavor, and remain in Westcrown, I'll maintain your code impeccably. Whatever restrictions you care to impose, I will obey. I'll be very nearly a paladin myself, if that's what you want."

"Why only while we're in Westcrown?"

"Because it's *easy* here. I have all the weight of the law on my side, the arms of the dottari to call upon, the resources of House Thrune awaiting my whim." Laughter warmed Velenne's voice and crinkled the corners of her eyes. "I'd have to be a complete idiot if I couldn't accomplish everything I needed to do in this city with one hand tied behind my back. Which is good, because that's essentially what you're asking. But when we leave Westcrown, I'll give up all those advantages, and then I may want my hands untied."

"When? Not if?" Ederras found himself both irritated and grudgingly amused by the diabolist's nonchalance. She'd been like that every time they'd worked together in the past: acceding easily to much of what he wanted, while telling him exactly why it didn't matter. It should have been infuriating, and sometimes was, but it also had a way of melting his annoyance. How could he stay angry when she conceded so readily, and when the concessions seemed so trivial?

Her shrug was an iridescent shimmer of green-gold silk. "It may be that our assassin has remained in the city and will be caught here. But I suspect we're dealing with a professional, and in that case it would be foolish to assume that his or her behavior will be quite so predictable. Moreover, our road seems to be pointing toward Citadel Rivad, or even to Citadel Gheisteno—to answer some of our questions, if not to capture our culprit."

"Jheraal's already gone to Citadel Rivad. She'll find whatever there is to find in that place. There's no reason for us to go as well."

"Marvelous. I love nothing more than reclining in idleness while others do my work." Velenne studied the silver plate of pastries between them, eventually selecting a flattened, flaky dome crowned with small sour cherries and a lace of white icing. "In any case, are you satisfied with those terms?"

"For now." If they left Westcrown, he'd have to renegotiate, but he'd deal with that eventuality when they came to it. Perhaps by then he wouldn't need her anymore.

"I'm delighted to hear it. Now, did you have a plan for where to take our investigation? Vhaeros remains in Rego Cader, waiting to see whether our assassin drags more hellspawn into the ruins. I had planned to assist him, but my pet is more than capable on his own. If you have another task for me, I am entirely at your disposal."

"I do, actually." Ederras paused. He still wasn't sure he wanted to let Velenne involve herself. *This is probably a mistake.*

And yet . . .

"I'd like you to come to a party with me," he said.

Lord Mayor Aberian Arvanxi was famous for three things: the incompetence of his political scheming, the spite he showed to defeated enemies, and his love for the pomp and grandeur of Chelish opera. Since becoming the titular ruler of Westcrown, he'd expended enormous sums from the public coffers to expand and gild the city's opera houses, hire the most acclaimed performers from across the continent, and host notoriously hedonistic open-ing-night galas.

It was widely rumored that the Lord Mayor was more interested in the starlets than their singing. Even in the short time since his return to Westcrown, Ederras had heard no shortage of scandalous tales. Aberian Arvanxi was a man of sizable appetites, and he indulged them extravagantly.

That extravagance bought the tolerance, if not the affection, of the ever-mercenary Wiscrani nobility. The Lord Mayor's parties were infamous as orgies of sybaritic excess, and invitations were coveted among Westcrown's wealthy. The first gala of the season was virtually mandatory for all the great houses, and for all who aspired to join them.

Even so, Ederras would have preferred to minimize his appearance—or, like Lord Kajen Tilernos, to avoid it altogether and send a frivolity-loving relative in his stead—if not for the fact that the guest list included several people who might have information about the fall of Citadel Gheisteno. The Lord Mayor's gala represented a rare opportunity to introduce himself to them.

It also represented a rare occasion when he might actually *want* Velenne on his arm. Ederras was in no mood to spend the evening dodging debutantes' snares and dowagers' schemes, and he knew that the new heir to House Celverian was likely to prove an irresistible target. The only way he expected to get any peace was by pretending to already be claimed—and by a scion of House Thrune, no less.

If that is a pretense. He didn't know how much longer that would be true. Every time he saw her, his desire burned hotter. A small devil voice had begun to whisper: Why not give in? Plainly Velenne wanted him. She had come back to Westcrown for him, had forced her way into this investigation for him. Why not use that, as Aedan had suggested?

The world was full of stories where brave souls were seduced to evil. Why couldn't it work the other way?

His carriage slowed to a rattling stop, interrupting that line of thought. Loud laughter and genteel conversation drifted through the carriage windows. Straightening the stiff blue brocade of his surcoat and the gold-and-sapphire belt that cinched it tight about his waist, Ederras pulled aside the curtain to see what he was about to step into.

It was a crowd, and a very large one. All of Regicona seemed to have turned out for the premiere of *The Winter of White Roses*, the opera that would open Westcrown's social season.

Twenty years ago, it had been the norm for the season to begin in mid-autumn, when the heat had dissipated enough for the aristocratic families to return from their summer homes and for the crowded theater houses to become bearable. The Lord Mayor's extraordinary devotion to the opera, however, and his willingness to spend public funds on such niceties as enchanted breezes and misting fountains, had expanded the season considerably. Now the opening performance came in the waning days of summer, and the social importance of the opera had climbed to loftier heights than ever before.

Resplendent in their finest jewels and fabrics, Westcrown's citizens thronged the street around the Regiconan Opera House. The oldest and stateliest of the city's theaters, it was widely accounted to have the best acoustics to be found anywhere outside of Oppara or Egorian. Up to fifteen hundred people could crowd into its audience.

It would be crammed to capacity tonight. Ederras recognized a handful of Hellknights, stiff and uncomfortable in civilian dress, sprinkled among the scholars, tradespeople, and lawyers who waited to gain entry through the public doors. Whether they were genuine lovers of the opera or merely hoped to push their stars higher in Westcrown's social firmament, no one with the money and connections to procure a ticket to the opening night's performance had stayed home. The carriage driver had to use all his skill to navigate the milling crowd and reach the canopied entrance reserved for high nobility, on the opera house's west side.

Once he did, however, the carriage stopped. A footman opened the door, and Ederras disembarked into a world of plush and polished luxury.

Boiseries of mahogany and cherrywood, touched with gilt and lightened with mirrors in baroque gold frames, covered the walls of the western wing. Fanciful chandeliers hung from the ceiling, each one a controlled burst of firelight caught in crystal. The carpets were crimson and lush, shot through with glittering threads of silver and gold. Portraits of Thrune royalty and the opera stars of bygone decades looked down over the night's illustrious guests, while servants wove through the mingling crowd with silver trays of sparkling wines in pink and diamond yellow.

Velenne was standing before a portrait of the first Queen Abrogail, a flute of pale rose wine fizzing in her hand. She was dressed in black and burgundy, her dark hair pinned up in a twist and adorned with a brilliant diamond-and-platinum clasp that was, in its spikes and swirls, almost certainly Nidalese work.

Her perfume, however, was pure Cheliax: a rich, opulent amber, inflected with the incense and smoke of Asmodean ritual. It was far headier than the scent she'd worn as a girl, at once more overtly sensual and more formal. As much closer to the truth of her as the red and black of her diabolist's dress. *The perfume of a wanton empress.*

He came up behind her and touched her waist lightly, as if pulling her into a dance. *Let everyone think we're closer than we are.* "Have you been waiting long?"

Velenne turned smoothly, the silk of her dress warm under his palm. Kohl and silver dust accented her eyes, shimmering when she smiled. "Fifteen years, more or less."

Ederras couldn't think of anything to say to that. He was spared from having to make a reply by the appearance of a crimson-liveried usher, who bowed and addressed the glittering gathering as one.

"The Regiconan Opera House welcomes the distinguished lords and ladies of Westcrown to the inaugural performance of *The Winter of White Roses.* If you would be so kind as to proceed to your boxes, the curtain will rise in five minutes."

"Lord Tilernos has offered to share his box," Ederras said as the crowd began to filter out of the gathering hall.

The diabolist shook her head, slightly but decisively. The diamonds flashed in her hair. "He isn't here. He's sent his sister Sascar to represent House Tilernos in his stead, and I can't abide that cackling drunk. She always chatters through the entire performance. Besides, you don't need to court favor from Lord Tilernos. You already have it. Better to focus our efforts elsewhere."

"Where?"

Her eyes flickered past him. Disengaging his hand from her waist, she approached a balding man who appeared to be in his late middle years. Black peacock feathers accented his silken robe, echoing the iridescent black pearls that adorned his belt and marched down the front of his surcoat in regimented bands. "Lord Oberigo! What a delight to see you here."

"Lady Velenne." Lord Eirtein Oberigo's face creased in an easy smile. His voice was warm and mellifluous, so beautifully modulated that it had been rumored for decades that the patriarch of House Oberigo had secretly trained as a bard. "A rare honor to have you with us in Westcrown."

"Your city has some compelling attractions." Velenne glanced through her lashes at Ederras, who took the cue and stepped forward. "Lord Oberigo, please allow me to introduce Ederras Celverian."

"A pleasure," Ederras said stiffly, offering his hand. He knew Lord Oberigo by reputation, and had no liking for the man. Eirtein Oberigo cut a sinister figure in Westcrown's higher circles. He'd been linked to innumerable scandals and blackmail schemes that had ruined more upstanding citizens. While no one had ever accused him directly, the rumors and innuendoes were too widespread, and too enduring, to ignore.

"Likewise." Lord Oberigo took his hand briefly and released it. His touch was dry as snakeskin. "My condolences on your loss."

"Thank you." Ederras wondered what Lord Oberigo knew about his brother's death. It was said that he heard every whispered secret in Westcrown.

"Will the Lady Auvadia be joining you this evening?" Velenne inquired. Auvadia Oberigo, Lord Eirtein's elderly aunt, was one of the nobles Ederras had listed as likely holders of information about the fall of Citadel Gheisteno. Her late husband had been a Hellknight in the Order of the Scourge, and had participated in the march that brought down the citadel.

"Ah, no. Aunt Auvadia doesn't care for the opera. Too wearying, she calls it." Most of the guests had gone to their boxes, and Lord Oberigo glanced at the emptying hall. The ushers would never be so impolite as to interrupt the nobles' conversation, but it was clear that the performance was about to begin. "Does House Thrune maintain a box here?"

"We do not. The Lord Mayor has been gracious enough to invite us to share his, but . . ." Velenne left the sentence hanging. A tiny shrug of her slim shoulders underscored the point. Aberian Arvanxi's buffoonery scarcely needed elaboration.

Lord Oberigo understood her perfectly. "If it would not be too presumptuous, might I extend an invitation of my own? The Lord Mayor's box has, of course, the best view of the stage, but House Oberigo's is not far behind. It would be a privilege to share your company."

He wasn't lying about that, Ederras knew. Poaching Velenne from the Lord Mayor's box would be a social coup: a very public affirmation of House Oberigo's status and favor with House

Thrune, an insult to a rival whom no one much liked anyway, and a chance to angle for news and gossip from Egorian, where all real power lay.

"We would be delighted to accept." Velenne laced her hand through Ederras's arm and followed the black-feathered Lord Oberigo up the carpeted steps to his opera box. Lady Oberigo and two of their daughters were already in the velvet-cushioned seats, a bevy of silent servants standing at attention behind them.

As Lady Oberigo murmured greetings and introductions on behalf of her clan, their patriarch leaned in toward Velenne. "Why did you ask about Aunt Auvadia?"

"Oh," the diabolist replied artlessly, draining her wine flute and exchanging the empty glass for a servant's full one, "I had hoped to ask her counsel on a minor scandal concerning one of the Henderthane boys. His betrothal is quite irreparably ruined. There's talk of sending him out of the capital. Perhaps to Westcrown."

"Is that so?" Lord Oberigo's face remained unrevealing, but Ederras noticed his wife's gaze flick to the two girls seated with them. Granddaughters, or maybe nieces, he thought, correcting his earlier guess. Not daughters. And unmarried, or they would have been with their husbands. No doubt they were here to meet eligible young bachelors—and, certainly, news that one had become available from House Henderthane would pique their family's interest. If the youth was too stained to be marriageable, then the scandal itself might be worthwhile.

No obvious gesture passed between Lord and Lady Oberigo and their servants, but one of the maids slipped discreetly away through the back of their opera box.

"Perhaps we're in luck," Lord Oberigo said, his eyes on the curtain. The first chords rose from the orchestra pit. "It's true that Aunt Auvadia doesn't much care for the opera, but she loves a good party. I expect she'll be at the Lord Mayor's gala tonight."

"Wonderful," Velenne said, settling back to watch the singers come onstage.

From the shocked whispers that swept the audience when the lead female singer appeared, and Lord Oberigo's hastily murmured explanation, Ederras gathered that the star they'd all anticipated had been replaced by an unknown ingénue; from the rapturous sighs and applause that greeted the end of the new singer's first solo, he assumed that the unknown had just become a star in her own right.

Beyond that, however, he understood little and appreciated less. The music struck him as artificial, the performances as overwrought, the plot as absurd. When the curtains finally came down at the end, Ederras breathed a silent sigh of relief.

Velenne's carriage came to bear them away from the opera house. It was a sleek ebony affair drawn by a pair of matched black horses, each one crowned by a pouf of blood-red feathers and harnessed in crimson traces. The driver was a handsome hellspawn woman, horned and tailed, but dressed like a man in trousers and a split frock coat. She asked for no instructions, and her mistress gave none. As soon as the two of them were inside, they were off to the Lord Mayor's vaneo. Cobbles rattled under the wheels, and then the smooth creaking stillness of the barge across the channel.

Alone in the carriage, Velenne pressed into him, silk rasping against brocade. Her perfume filled the close space between them, drowning him in opulence. "You like this one, don't you?" she murmured, running a jeweled hand along his thigh. "It excites you."

He looked away, lifting a corner of the carriage's black curtains so he could catch a glimpse of the streets. "It reeks of Asmodean temples."

"Ah. Then it's the reminder of diabolism that you find so enticing? Is it the scent of sin that enthralls you?"

"I hardly need a reminder of what you are."

Velenne laughed, but she withdrew her hand and leaned away, looking to the opposite window. Ederras was as much disappointed as he was relieved. "What I *am* is the reason you'll have the opportunity to talk to Auvadia Oberigo tonight. Some thanks might be in order."

"They might," Ederras agreed. "Depending on what she says."

"We'll soon find out," Velenne said serenely. She gazed out the window until they reached Vaneo Arvanxi. The strains of a string quartet filtered through the cool night air, while colored lanterns cast a multihued glow across the vaneo's lawns and shimmering magical lights darted through the trees like fireflies.

The house beyond those gracious trappings, however, was anything but elegant. Aberian Arvanxi had put his own stamp on the traditional dwelling of Westcrown's mayors, and it wasn't a particularly tasteful one. He'd clad the manor's exterior in ochre and black stone and crowned its gables with squat, dancing gargoyles in clumsy imitation of the fashion in Egorian. The old, graceful lines of the roofs were now marred with spiky protrusions in rusting iron.

None of the guests seemed to mind, though. Their carriages rolled up to the gardens. Footmen helped them disembark, and then they drifted through the gardens and between the floating lanterns and vanished into Vaneo Arvanxi.

"Shall we go?" Velenne asked, taking his arm.

They joined the rest of the Lord Mayor's guests in the grand entryway, then followed the mingling crowd to the banquet hall. That, too, had been altered to reflect current fashions. The walls were painted with unsettling scenes that showed Westcrown under the rule of devils. The support pillars had been carved into immense tangles of fanged black serpents.

It hardly seemed to make for a festive mood, yet once again Ederras had to wonder whether he was the only one who noticed. The other guests seemed entirely untroubled. Gaily they gossiped and chattered and feasted on the extravagant courses that arrived in an endless procession of domed silver plates. Velenne moved among them with a grace Ederras neither possessed nor particularly envied, often abandoning him when his presence might hinder her work, yet always returning.

Crimson-pickled hydra eggs, rabbits in ivory sauce, rare fruits cut and interleaved into sugar-trimmed fans: all came and went and were replaced by other, ever-stranger concoctions. Some of the spices seemed to be as much drug as seasoning. There was a rack of lamb crusted in peppery red seeds that burned the tongue and hazed the wits, and tiny roast quail stuffed with bitter, prickly leaves that left the guests flushed and giddy.

Wine and stronger spirits flowed in profusion, and although Ederras tried to keep his intake modest, he was more than slightly dizzied by the time the Lord Mayor stood and clapped his hands to signal that dinner was at an end. There was a short speech, none of which the paladin caught, and then the stars of the evening's opera stood in a line and bowed to the assembled guests, to thunderous applause.

But the party wasn't over. The minute that Lord Mayor Arvanxi finished his speech, servants came forward to escort his guests to the hedonists' paradise that served as Vaneo Arvanxi's inner gardens.

There, under an illusory, perfect sky, wildflowers bloomed around a crystalline stream and a rustic wooden bridge. In another part of the gardens, hedges of scarlet roses encircled a pool of golden honey. A third garden held a babbling fountain ringed by enchanted trees that produced half a hundred exotic fruits. Mangos and papayas nestled on the same branches, even the same twigs, as caimito and brilliant, green-tongued pink dragonfruit. Above them all, a sandalwood-screened balcony invited voyeurs to stop, linger, and watch the nobility of Cheliax at play.

Already there was much to watch. Inflamed by drink and drug-laced food, many of the guests had cast their dignity aside along with their clothes. Ederras turned away, acutely discomfited by the other nobles' excesses, and accidentally locked eyes with a tiny, shrewd-looking dowager in a towering white wig.

"Lady Auvadia," Ederras said, striding toward the old woman. He had glimpsed her at the feast tables earlier, but there'd been no opportunity to speak to her then.

The elder Lady Oberigo tipped her chin up in greeting as he neared. White powder blanketed her face and dusted the elaborate curls of her formal wig. She was seated in a horsehair-padded armchair at the gardens' edge, her green and black skirts arrayed around her with military precision. Fragile as a bird and less than five feet tall, the old lady wouldn't have reached Ederras's shoulder if she had been standing, but an undeniable aura of power radiated from her. "Master Celverian. I understand you wished to speak with me."

"Did Velenne tell you that?"

"She did." The old lady snapped out a painted silk fan with a flick of her wrist and fanned herself vigorously. Not a hair in her wig stirred. "A fearsome lady, that one. She'll make your house great. If you let her."

Ederras laughed. The drink had gone to his head completely, loosening his tongue past the point of foolishness. "She is. Terrifying. Did she tell you what I wanted to discuss?"

"The Order of the Crux. She also said that my answering your questions was the price for her answering mine. A fair exchange, I suppose. If anyone's being cheated there, it's you. Old secrets are seldom of equal weight to new ones." Lady Oberigo shrugged. "Still, a bargain is a bargain, and my Ferdieu is long in the grave. It'll cause him no trouble to have those tales retold. This doesn't strike me as the place to discuss such things, however, and you're in no condition to hear them. Tomorrow, perhaps. Or the next day, if you exert yourself too much to recover on one day's rest. Come to the vira. We'll talk then."

He wasn't drunk enough to need a second dismissal. "My lady." Sketching an unsteady bow, Ederras left the elder Lady Oberigo and made his way back into the gardens proper.

The debauchery was in full swing there. One of the Dioso ladies was painting a footman's bare chest with honey, while on the other side of the shallow pool, a distinguished-looking gentleman licked more honey from her giggling sister's toes. Others were wading—or writhing—in the pool, heedless of their ruined finery.

Ederras watched longer than he meant to, embarrassed for them but finding it strangely difficult to pull away. The feast had cast a peculiar haze over his senses. Everything was blurred and yet achingly acute.

Vividly—too vividly—he remembered how soft Velenne's hands had been the first time she'd drawn him down like that. How warm her breath had been in his ear. How suddenly she'd buried her nails in his back, clawing at him in a hot red flash of pain that had ignited him beyond reason and set the course for everything that came after.

Shuddering, he turned away.

He didn't know where Velenne had gone. The diabolist had vanished around the time the servants were bringing out the last course of cheeses and pastries enveloped in clouds of sweetly narcotic cream, and he hadn't seen her since. She wasn't in the honey pool, which was at once deflating and a relief. Nor was she under the branches of the enchanted fruit trees, although quite a few others were entangled in knots around the laughing fountain.

He found her on the banks of the silvery stream, reclining on the flower-strewn grass. She was alone. The Nidalese pin gleamed in her hair, reflecting the artificial stars in the garden's false sky.

Velenne lifted a slender hand in greeting, or summons, as Ederras crossed into her sight. Her eyes were dark and dilated, her smile full of mystery. "Where have you been?"

"Talking to Lady Auvadia." He knelt in the grass beside her. Standing suddenly felt too difficult. His knees had gone to water.

"Good." Velenne reached up, twining her fingers around the brocade on his sleeve. He could feel the warmth of her hand like a shadow passing over his wrist. "So you have what you wanted."

Ederras nodded. Forcing words past the knot in his throat was nearly impossible, but he managed: "I do."

Her fingers slid from the cloth to his skin. The edge of a nail touched him, just barely. "Then it's time I got what *I* wanted. Don't you agree?"

Ederras closed his eyes. It was too much. The wine, the drugs, the licentiousness all around them. Her scent, her smile, the familiar curve of her neck. For fifteen years he'd wanted her and hated her in equal measure. Since his return to Westcrown, she'd troubled his waking moments and stolen his sleep. He felt his restraint snap, almost audible in his mind.

"Yes," he said. "I do."

13

THE CITADEL'S MIRROR

SECHEL

The smell of death surrounded Citadel Gheisteno.

Not the foulness of carrion or the cold, musty breath of a subterranean ossuary, although those were the odors that most people took to be the smell of death. It was the actual scent of *dying*—of the last, surrendering sigh to escape from a mortally struck body—that enveloped the castle's barren stones and whistled through its lifeless courtyards.

Every time she walked into the citadel's dismal aura, Sechel wondered how many of its other visitors recognized that unsettling exhalation for what it was. How many, even among the handful who came to this desolate place, had killed often enough to know that scent? How many had stood close enough to their victims to breathe it in?

Perhaps she was the only one.

There were another dozen deaths in her carrier right now. Sechel shifted the pack on her shoulders. Twelve jewel-like hellspawn hearts, torn out and transmuted by the devilheart chain, beat softly within the case's padded walls. She could hear their muted murmurings whenever the wind died enough to let that haunting drumbeat through.

Once again, she wondered why her employer wanted them. It wasn't uncommon for Sechel to be asked to take something from those she killed, but usually it was meant to prove that the target had been slain. An ear, a head, maybe a patch of tattooed skin.

This was something different. Her employer hadn't given her a single name. None of her targets had been assigned; all had been taken simply because they happened to be available. And because they carried the taint of Hell in their lineage.

Twelve anonymous hearts from twelve nameless hellspawn. That was all the graveknight had wanted, so that was what Sechel had brought. For what he'd offered in return, she would have killed ten times as many.

Citadel Gheisteno feared no invaders. The castle's gates were wide open, its great portcullis lifted, as they had been on every one of Sechel's previous visits. She'd been coming to the fortress for over a year, and never once had she seen those massive bars dropped.

Under its immense iron teeth, a single figure waited. He listed steeply to the right, bent as a half-melted candle carved by the wind, yet he stood nearly seven feet tall despite the stoop of his spine. A shapeless, dirt-stained linen wrap flapped loosely about his gaunt form.

Sechel tensed when she saw him. Her fingers tightened on the straps of her pack, although she didn't slow her step. "I'm here to see the lictor, not you, Ochtel."

"He is . . . busy," the man replied in a breathy, slurred voice. Most of his teeth were missing, and his lips were seamed with layers of scars from having been repeatedly sewn shut and torn free. It left Ochtel's speech as disfigured as the rest of him. "I will . . . I am assigned to greet you."

"I don't want a greeting. I want to be paid." Sechel crossed the last few feet of the bridge with a long, swift stride. Impenetrable mist roiled across the chasm. She had no idea whether there was any water under the bridge. That cold, foul-smelling fog had never cleared enough for her to see.

The charred skulls on the Bridge of Memories stayed inert as Sechel passed over them. It wasn't always so, she knew. The skulls' fire awakened for those who passed in either direction. It was they who held Lictor Shokneir and his graveknights captive in their castle, for none of the three could stand to face the condemnation of the dead, nor their own memories of failure. For them, the bridge was an impassable barrier.

The Crux-marked amulet that the lictor had given her hung heavy around Sechel's neck. It was enchanted to protect her, she knew. From the skulls embedded in the cursed bridge, the lesser undead that infested the citadel—even from the lictor's own aura of life-sapping sacrilege.

Maybe it did, maybe it didn't. She wore it, because she was no fool, but if Citadel Gheisteno was this bleak even when she wore the lictor's amulet of soot and steel, she couldn't imagine what its aura of misery must be without.

Ochtel watched her mournfully, never moving. His greasy black hair seemed even longer and more unkempt than it had on her previous visits. It tumbled over the gaping pit where the man's right eye should have been, not quite hiding the hole. It didn't hide the slashed scar where his nose was missing, either, or quiet the painful whistling that accompanied every breath he took. "You . . . will be. But not . . . tonight."

Sechel's eyes narrowed. She took off the pack and whirled it across the floor at the maimed man's feet. "Why not tonight? I got what he wanted. Twelve hearts. In there. Count them yourself."

"I . . . believe you." Slowly, painfully, Ochtel stooped and hooked the strap of her pack on an impossibly long and bony finger. Ridges of stitching showed around the swollen knuckles of that digit, marking where pieces of Ochtel's other fingers had been severed and added in. He only had three left on that hand, two on the other, all of them extended to twice their natural length. "But it doesn't . . . matter. He wants . . . more. The work is . . . difficult . . . he says."

"Mine isn't?" Sechel inhaled deliberately, struggling to master her temper. It was useless to shout at Ochtel. He had no power or influence in this place.

Once the man had been a great druid, but since falling under Lictor Shokneir's control, he had been reduced to a wretched slave, mutilated in body and mind. His presence in Citadel Gheisteno was meant as a warning to all other mortals who dealt with the graveknight: *overstep your bounds, and this is what will become of you.*

She was almost too angry to care, though. Twelve deaths—twelve *hearts*—had been their bargain.

Twelve hearts, and the chain, for her freedom.

The maimed druid offered her a shaky, lopsided shrug. Bloody bubbles of saliva popped at the corner of his mouth. His voice cracked with the strain of speaking for so long. "Nothing . . . attaches to your refusal. There will be no . . . penalty . . . if you go. Only . . . that what was promised . . . will not be given." With the same agonized slowness of motion, Ochtel turned back toward the Citadel's looming doors. "The lictor . . . left one other thing. A vision . . . for you."

"What do you mean, a 'vision'?" Sechel stole a glance upward. Forty feet over her head, a single window in the blackened fortress glowed with crimson firelight. That was no torch's glow, she knew, nor that of lamp or lantern. It roared and died in wracking waves, fluctuating from bonfire to eclipse and back.

That was Lictor Shokneir's presence, and the agony of his curse. It was a vision, and a terror, that she had no wish to see.

"Come." Mercifully, Ochtel didn't try to explain further. Instead, he receded into the shadows, beckoning with his three-fingered hand for Sechel to follow.

She did so reluctantly, eyeing the portcullis as she passed beneath its heavy spikes. Behind her, the moat and drawbridge melted into indistinct blurs, veiled by the fog and shadow that blanketed Nidal.

Ominous as that landscape was, it didn't compare to Citadel Gheisteno's interior. In the emptiness of its unlit halls, Sechel's footsteps sounded tiny and forlorn. The weight of its stone walls pressed down on her so tangibly that she wondered whether that was the reason Ochtel had been crushed into a permanent, sideways stoop.

No tapestries softened the citadel's grimness. There were no paintings, no mirrors, no silk-upholstered furniture against its walls or soaring frescoes on its ceilings. Only drafty black stone, coated in a constant layer of soot, stretching its march onward in every direction without the slightest hint of relief.

They saw no one else in those corridors. The stale chill in the air, long undisturbed by living lungs, told Sechel that no one was there to be seen.

It didn't surprise her. More than half a century ago, after the other Hellknight orders marched upon and slaughtered the Order of the Crux, Citadel Gheisteno had been torn down over the bones of its defenders. The fortress she walked through had risen mysteriously from the ashes and crumbling stones of the original citadel, supposedly overnight, and Sechel had never entirely believed that it was real.

Deadly, yes. But not *real*.

Ochtel stopped before a bare wooden door that embodied all Sechel's doubts about the nature of Citadel Gheisteno. It was a door out of nightmares: plain wood, a tiny barred window, a hefty ring of hammer-dented iron. That ring was worn smooth on the bottom curve where it had been grasped by thousands of hands over the years, even though it was impossible that so many should have used it during the citadel's short existence.

But there it was, perfect as the iconic image in a sleeping mind.

"Your . . . vision. In there. Of what . . . could be." The mutilated druid lifted a broken hand to the door. His face was empty of emotion under the shaggy fall of his black hair.

Sechel scowled and yanked the door open, covering her fear under a show of impatience.

A single mirror stood in the windowless room inside. Black cloth draped its glass, but the round silhouette was as distinctive and recognizable as the dungeon door that led to it. It, too, seemed to be a thing that had been imagined into existence rather than having been made by mortal hands.

Wishing that she could shake off the persistent sense that she was walking through someone else's dream, Sechel strode to the mirror and snatched the black drape from its face.

In its glass she saw herself . . . but not as she'd ever really been.

The reflected eyes that stared back at Sechel were blue, only blue. They didn't show the whirling motes of viridian light that spun through her living irises. Sandy hair fell to her shoulders in relaxed waves, not the bone-hard spikes that she shaved back weekly. Her fingers didn't end in soft, scarred nubs where she'd pulled out her Hell-given claws. They had nails, *human* nails, weak and white and ordinary.

Everything about her was ordinary, even the tears that welled hot in her eyes at the sight. In the mirror's glass, she was human. Only human.

Shaken, Sechel put the cloth back over the mirror and retreated from the room. It wasn't real. It was only a vision, as Ochtel had said. Her eyes were flecked with the legacy of devils. Her fingers were stubbed and scarred. *And stained with so much blood.*

Gently, even reverently, Ochtel drew the door shut as the hellspawn dashed her tears away. The druid stood there, passive as a tree, until she turned on him. "Lictor Shokneir can make that happen? Not just a vision. He can make it real?"

Ochtel's head moved in a tortured nod. "That is . . . his promise. If you meet . . . his price."

Sechel's lip turned up in a half-conscious snarl. Deep in her bones, she didn't know if she believed that Lictor Shokneir truly had the power to purify the taint of Hell from her flesh. It was too convenient a promise, too mesmerizing a lure. The world wasn't that generous with her kind.

But what if she was wrong? What if he *could* do it? Was it worth the risk of throwing away her heart's desire because she doubted?

"What does he want?" Sechel asked.

"More . . . hearts. And. There are . . . hunters on your trail. Three . . . in particular. A Hellknight, a paladin, a binder of . . . devils."

"He wants them shaken off the track? Killed?"

Ochtel shook his head. Gingerly, as if he was afraid of it falling off if he moved too vigorously. Maybe he was. "He wants . . . you . . . to bring them here."

14

CONQUERORS OF THE CRUX

EDERRAS

The warm touch of sunlight roused Ederras from slumber.
For a long, disorienting moment, he didn't remember where he was. The angle of the light was wrong. The color of the sheets was wrong. His head throbbed from too much wine, and unfamiliar aches plagued his muscles.

Then he sat up and saw Velenne sleeping beside him, her dark hair spilled over the slim bare curve of her shoulders, and the memories came flooding back.

The riverbank. The carriage. Again and again in her bed. She'd been shameless, utterly insatiable, and he had—

Wincing, Ederras pulled back the burgundy sheets, trying not to disturb her. Livid red bruises marred Velenne's smooth, sun-gilded skin in a dozen places. She sighed in drowsy contentment, nestling closer to him as he drew the sheets back up again to cover what he'd done.

There is a shard of Zon-Kuthon in that one's soul, he thought again, stricken. And maybe not just hers. He had done what she'd wanted, *everything* she'd wanted, because the night had left him powerless to resist. He'd hurt her, badly, in half a hundred different ways.

I have to atone.

He extricated himself from the bed. The amber of her perfume lingered on his skin, heavy and sweet.

His clothes lay in a heap on the floor. The front of his shirt had been torn open, and there were grass stains on his trousers. *Belvadio will weep to see what I've done to them.*

As Ederras was pulling on his boots, he heard the diabolist rouse behind him. Her voice was low, sleepy, luxuriously sated. It sent a chill down his spine. "You aren't staying?"

"Of course I'm not staying." He laced his boots and stood. Only when he was out of arm's reach did he turn to look at her. "This can't happen again."

She stretched languidly across the bed and laughed, although he thought there was a flicker of hurt in her eyes. "Ah, my love. It's your cruelty that makes me adore you."

"Don't call me that. Or say such things. We aren't—"

"Lovers?" Velenne finished for him, sweetly. She reclined onto an elbow, watching him with an open appreciation that made Ederras deeply uncomfortable, even though he was the one who was dressed.

That half-lidded smile was too easy, too intimate. Too *much*. It was a smile that said no one had ever pleased her so well, and he didn't believe it for a second.

Ederras was clumsy with her, and knew it. How could he not be? He hadn't touched anyone else, not in all the time they'd been apart, but he had no illusions that she'd done the same. And she, a daughter of Egorian's courts, had been frighteningly experienced their first time.

His first time. Not hers.

In fifteen years, how many others had seen that smile? He surely wasn't the only one. Her ease amid the debauchery at the mayor's gala, and the familiarity with which some of the other male guests had addressed her, told him that much. Nothing there had made her blush. Why would it? What scandalized him was nothing to her.

He hated that it made him jealous, but it did. He hated that it excited him, but it did that, too. Everything about her put him off balance, and he hated that most of all. "Yes. That."

"We were and we are, and you seemed to enjoy yourself well enough. Why deny it?" Rolling over on the sheets, Velenne reached for a water glass on the table near her bed. As much as Ederras wanted to, he couldn't keep from looking at her. Sigils from the Asmodean Disciplines had been inked into her flesh, stark black against her skin. She hadn't had those marks when he'd known her before. The sight of those infernal symbols should have made him recoil, yet somehow they didn't. Impossibly, outrageously, they only fanned his desire anew.

She wore those inked sigils like jewels, like fragrance. Ornament and artifice, but also a natural part of her being, one he couldn't imagine her without. Velenne inhabited the decadence of Chelish courts as easily as a fish moved through water, and its trappings shone on her as inseparably as scales. He'd thought to convert her, to open her eyes to his faith, but now that he stood before her, it seemed as impossible as asking a stone to swim.

Worse, he wasn't sure he wanted to.

Ederras had spent his life fighting against everything she represented. He'd abdicated his inheritance, joined a rebellion, fled his homeland. And yet he wanted it. Wanted *her*.

Who was not only a daughter of Cheliax's ruling house, but one of its enforcers. A torturer, an assassin, a summoner of fiends.

"Because it's impossible. You are what you are—"

"Yes."

"—and I am what I am—"

"Yes?"

"—and *this can't be*," Ederras said in frustration.

"I fail to follow your reasoning." Velenne rested her cheek calmly against a forearm. "I've never asked you to change. I would never *want* you to change. That would spoil everything. You must be what you are. It delights me immeasurably, and I'd be heartbroken to lose it."

"Why? Because then you wouldn't be able to keep torturing me?"

"Or you me. Yes." The diabolist's smile was radiant. "That's the point precisely. And you crave it as much as I do."

To that, Ederras said nothing. He folded his surcoat over an arm and walked out of her bedroom, down the stairs of her borrowed townhouse, and into the sober light of day.

He didn't return to his own home immediately. First he sought out a temple, wanting to unburden his soul.

The cathedrals of Regicona were places of grandeur, but Ederras walked past all of them. He went to the little chapel near Taranik House, seeking out the acolyte he'd talked to before.

Aedan was standing outside the church's nave, washing its stained-glass windows. His sleeves were rolled up over his elbows, and a bucket of sudsy water sloshed between his feet. When he noticed Ederras, he dropped the rag in surprise, splashing himself with soapy water. "Master Celverian. Did you wish to see Mistress Develya?"

So the apprentice priest had learned his name. Ederras supposed he should have expected as much. "No. I came to see you."

"Why?"

"For counsel and confession."

"I—of course, my lord." Aedan fished out the rag, wrung it out, and draped it over the bucket's handle. He left the bucket just inside the door, no doubt so he could resume his chores as soon as their meeting was over. "The chapel's empty this early. We won't be disturbing anyone."

Inside, the sacred sweetness of frankincense drifted among the church's empty pews, along with the warmer undercurrents of wood resin and lemon oil. Morning sun streamed through the rose windows, and although they were made only of the murky glass that a poor congregation could afford, they seemed to shine as gloriously as the jewel-toned windows of Regicona's cathedrals.

Perhaps that was a trick of the light, or perhaps Iomedae's favor gave them beauty beyond their means.

Aedan continued through the pews into a small, private apse. Folding screens of pierced wood, oiled and subtly scented, provided some privacy from the rest of the church, but did not fully obscure either Ederras or his confessor.

The acolyte sat on a bench, motioning for the paladin to kneel on the prayer rug before him. Outside, Aedan had been deferential, but in here, Ederras sat as his supplicant, and the novice took on a priest's authority, clearly enjoying the novelty. "Do you require magical intercession or only confession?"

"I don't know," Ederras admitted. "I don't know how grave my sins are, or will be, in the Lady's sight. I only know they *are* sins, and that I must atone."

"What have you done?"

There was only kindness in the young priest's voice, not a trace of condemnation, yet Ederras had to force himself to speak. "I have . . . I've lain with a servant of Asmodeus. The lady I spoke to you about before. I considered your advice, and I had hoped to follow it, but that wasn't why I did it. I acted out of desire. I . . . I hurt her, too. She likes that; she wanted me to do it. I should have refused, though, and I didn't."

A long and thoughtful silence stretched between them. Then Aedan touched his shoulder, lightly and with great empathy. "Did you dishonor her? Lie to her, make false promises?"

Ederras coughed out a mirthless laugh, unable to help himself. "No. Nothing of the sort."

"Did you exceed what she asked you to do?"

"No." He wasn't sure if that was even possible. Certainly nothing he'd done last night began to approach Velenne's limits.

"Do you care for this woman?"

"Maybe." Ederras's mouth twisted as he said the word. "I don't know."

"How do you mean?"

"I *want* her, but that isn't the same thing. I want her to want me back. Truly, without guile. I want her to honor my faith. I want her to care for me, and for it to be something more than passing desire. Something more than—whatever she's had with others. Is that an answer?"

"It is," Aedan assured him. "And there's no dishonor in it. In any of that."

"It feels like there should be."

"Why?" The acolyte's brown eyes were wide with honest curiosity. The bench of the confessional creaked as he leaned forward. "Have you been derelict in your duties or neglectful of your faith as a result of this? Have you contributed to, or turned a blind eye toward, any act of evil?"

"No. Other than what I've told you. She has agreed not to offend my code, at least temporarily. As far as I know, she's kept that agreement."

"Then where is your sin?" The young priest's gaze was steady and compassionate, but matter-of-fact. "Why do you believe you've done wrong?"

"Because of what she is." What Velenne had become was the full flowering of her potential, as far beyond what she'd been in her youth as the black roses of Egorian were from green buds. There was power in her, and cruelty, under that glittering veneer. He felt it every time he touched her.

And he wanted it. *That* was the sin: that he knew exactly what she was, and that it hadn't stopped him. That he had forsaken his duty for desire.

His jaws locked around the words. Some thoughts he couldn't confess, even in a chapel. Even to a priest.

It didn't matter. Aedan seemed to hear everything he hadn't said. Maybe his silence was the only answer the acolyte had needed.

"She's a woman," the priest said. "She's not an angel, or a monster, or the entire empire of Cheliax made flesh. She is a *person*, Master Celverian. Which is both simpler and much more complicated than whatever you seem to imagine."

Ederras looked away. He had to, against the earnestness of that argument. Taking refuge in an arrangement of white roses in an alcove, he asked the flowers: "What does she want with me?"

"Apart from the obvious?"

"It can't just be that."

"You can't be so modest as to ignore the possibility."

"No, I mean for me. It can't just be . . . that. If that was all I wanted, none of this would matter. It wouldn't have to be her, and if it *was* her, I wouldn't have to confess it. I could just shrug at the memory, and go on with my life. Isn't that what people do?" He took a breath. "But instead I'm here. Looking for an answer."

"The answer will come clear in time. There's no need to rush to judgment. Not in this, not in anything. A wise man once said: When the world gives you time to make sure, take it. Always take it."

Those were his words. Years back, he'd given that advice to a green recruit at the Worldwound, and he'd repeated it several times since. Ederras raised his eyebrows at the priest. "Just how much digging into my past have you been doing?"

"A little," Aedan replied. "Enough to think that you'd do well to heed the same wisdom you gave to others. There's no fault in being conflicted, nor in finding your pleasure as you both will. And there's no fault in being unsure of what you want, provided you never misrepresent that. What matters—what *really* matters—is honesty. With yourself, with her, and with the Inheritor. Honor those three things, and you have done no wrong."

Ederras mulled over the acolyte's words all the way back to Vaneo Celverian.

When he returned, just as he'd feared, Belvadio went into throes of despair at his ruined clothes. The steward never *said* anything, of course, but his pronounced exhalations as he examined the grass stains were suspiciously close to sighs. The deeply resigned bend of his finger when he lifted the torn shirt, handing it off to another servant for mending, made his point more eloquently than words.

Ederras tried not to smile. Watching Belvadio's reaction, one would think that his house was too poor to afford shirts. Or thread to mend them. "I'll need the carriage this afternoon. I'm calling on Lady Auvadia Oberigo."

Belvadio's mouth snapped shut with an almost audible click. For a rare instant, he was visibly flustered. "You're going to Vira Oberigo?"

"Is that a problem?"

"No. No, of course not, my lord." Belvadio had miraculous powers of recovery. Already he appeared the very image of unruffled calm. "I had not expected you to take an interest in Wiscrani politics, that's all." He hesitated, visibly trying to find a way to phrase his next question.

"What?"

The steward cleared his throat, smoothing the front of his shirt. "When you didn't return with the carriage last night . . . I had heard . . ."

There was no point denying it. If the servants didn't already know, they would soon enough. The servants of Westcrown knew everything about the liaisons of the upper classes. "I spent the night with Velenne."

"Ah."

"You needn't look so concerned. As you can see, my arms and legs are all still attached, and I even appear to have my head."

"Of course, my lord." Belvadio didn't seem entirely convinced, but he refrained from voicing any further concerns. He stepped aside from the door as the other manservant returned, having exchanged the torn shirt for a light cotton robe. "Your bath has been drawn. We'll see that you're ready."

The bath's hot water restored Ederras immensely. After he'd washed, the steward trimmed his hair and shaved away the night's stubble, then helped him dress in fresh clothes.

Belvadio had chosen a sky-blue doublet, white shirt, and white trousers, adorned only with a sparing touch of braid about the doublet's hem and shoulders, but well-tailored and cut from the finest fabrics. The material conveyed wealth without boasting it, and the cut emphasized his broad shoulders and narrow waist without being overtly military in its design.

"I should let *you* talk to Lady Auvadia," Ederras observed as he held out his arms for the steward to pull on his shirt. "You seem to be a master of coded messages."

"One does not rise to become head of staff in a great house without some skill," Belvadio replied. He straightened the doublet and stepped away, examining his work with a critical eye.

"Will I do?"

"I'll summon the carriage."

The ride to Vira Oberigo was excruciatingly slow through the city's traffic. It would have been faster to take a skiff across the canals rather than deal with the delays on the bridges, but the etiquette of a formal visit wouldn't allow it. An afternoon call on Lady Auvadia meant arriving by carriage, which in turn meant spending an hour watching the streets and towers of Westcrown Island roll by at a snail's pace.

His city had changed so much, and yet it was all the same as he remembered. Graceful ladies in lustrous silks swept past hard-faced Hellknights and pompous scribes on the avenues of Regicona. Small children played in the water of a marble fountain, its carvings of nymphs and unicorns timeworn but beautiful, while their halfling caretaker looked on indulgently. Clusters of black-clad barristers argued or laughed on the steps of the district's courthouse, feigning both anger and smiles.

Everyone was polite, everyone was prosperous. From the windows of his carriage, there were no signs of hardship to be seen.

If one looked only at Regicona, Ederras thought, it would be easy to conclude that Westcrown had not suffered in the slightest under Thrune rule. Those who lived among the privileged might even consider their fortunes to have improved. It was the weak and poor who endured the worst. Not the wealthy of Regicona, who trod on their slaves' whipped backs with silk slippers and chattered about how lovely it was that their feet never touched mud.

Velenne would crush a hundred souls into the mud before she dirtied a toe. He had no doubt of that.

Did he have any obligation to change it?

Could he?

"Vira Oberigo," the driver announced. The horses took a turn to the left, and the carriage's wheels smoothed as they rolled from the bumpy city cobblestones to the flat paving stones of the vira's private driveway.

Ederras didn't open the curtains or look out as the carriage slowed to a stop. Doing so would have marked him as a provincial, easily overawed by the splendor of his hosts' home. Instead, he stayed inside, rehearsing what he intended to say to Lady Auvadia, until a servant in green-and-black livery opened the door and set a footstool out for his descent.

Yet another servant, impeccable in green and black, escorted him to the elegantly appointed sitting room off the main foyer. There Lady Auvadia waited on a silk-upholstered settee, the satin skirts of her day dress fanned out around her to show off the subtle, iridescent pattern of roses woven into the rich fabric. A triple strand of black peacock pearls draped over her lace collar, emphasizing its snowy whiteness.

"Ederras Celverian," the servant said formally, looking at neither of them.

"I can see that," Lady Auvadia replied. Her face was once again powdered nearly as white as her collar. "Fetch us some tea." She turned to Ederras. "You'll have tea, won't you?"

"Certainly." He sat on an armchair to her side. Its cushions were covered in the same patterned silk as the settee, beautiful but so slippery that he had to catch himself to keep from sliding off. *A trap.* He wondered how many of House Oberigo's guests had been so heavy, drunk, or ill-prepared that they'd been unable to keep from tumbling to the floor, doubtlessly to considerable humiliation.

Lady Auvadia's expression gave him no hint. The old lady's eyes were sharp and bright in her powdery mask. She wore a too-sweet perfume of violets and pink roses. Like the spots of rouge on her wrinkled cheeks and the dead, stuffed bluebird pinned into her white wig, it might have come off as sad or absurd on a lesser lady. On Lady Auvadia Oberigo, however, it perfected the picture of a dowager who had been a tigress in her youth and hadn't changed a stripe since, despite her muzzle having gone to snow.

"Good," she said. "We needn't wait for the tea to begin, however. So. My dear, late Ferdieu served as a Hellknight with the Order of the Scourge in his youth, as I presume you already know. Back then he wasn't an officer, though, just an ordinary Hellknight.

"In . . . oh, was it 4662? It's been so long, and I never was good with dates. It was the year I took sick and had to be confined to bed nearly the entire winter, I remember that. We spent a small fortune on clerics, but I never got better for long. Later I found out someone had bribed one of our cooks to poison me, the ungrateful little slip. It came to an end when we caught her, of course, but I suffered for months before that. That was a bad year."

"For Ferdieu as well?" Ederras prompted.

Lady Auvadia lifted her chin icily. "Yes. It was the same year. 4662. The Order of the Scourge received word that Lictor Shokneir, and the Order of the Crux under his command, had done something monstrous—a crime so huge and wrong that the entire order was implicated as lawbreakers of the most egregious stripe. Throughout that winter, I remember, Ferdieu's mood grew darker as their investigators accumulated more and more proof. Finally it was too conclusive to be ignored, and Lictor Shokneir refused their demands to cease, so it came to open warfare between the orders."

"Do you know what that crime *was?*"

Lady Auvadia shook her head. "Not exactly," she began, then stopped as two liveried servants came in with the tea service. With quick, neat motions, they unfolded a parquetry table, then set out a silver tray with a teapot and two saucered cups of eggshell porcelain. Next to that, they placed a tray of tiny scones, each one painted more delicately than the next with swirls of colored icing. They followed it with a second tray of boiled, slivered eggs; soft white bread; and cured meats rolled into flutes and fans like so many salt-glossed flowers.

The entire operation concluded in less than a minute, after which the servants bowed and left without a sound. The old lady had never even glanced at them.

"It was a kind of murder, I think," she said, gesturing for him to pour the tea. "But it wasn't exactly that, at least not the way Ferdieu described it. Early that spring, before the frosts ended, he was ordered to join the march on Citadel Gheisteno. He was gone for a month. When he came back, he was different.

"You must understand, my Ferdieu was never a voluble man. He was stoic. He kept his troubles silent. He'd been like that from childhood, but becoming a Hellknight made it a thousand times worse. A pillar of stone would have been a more revealing conversationalist." Lady Auvadia accepted the teacup Ederras offered her, blowing on it to cool the steaming liquid. "But after he came back from Citadel Gheisteno, he would twist and kick in his sleep, fighting enemies who weren't there. Sometimes he screamed. Twice I caught him crying. When he was awake, he admitted to nothing, but when he slept, he was consumed."

Ederras poured a cup of tea for himself. It was pale pink and smelled of currants and cinnamon. "What did you do?"

"What could I do? I asked him to unburden himself. For years he refused, and for years he shouted and wept at his dreams. Finally he could endure it no longer, and told me what he'd seen in Citadel Gheisteno. Some of it. Not all. Just enough to let himself sleep."

"And?"

Lady Auvadia smiled crookedly over her teacup. She took a scone covered in crystallized violets and dipped its corner into the tea. "If what he told me was a tenth part of what the Order of the Crux was doing, I can see why he couldn't rest.

"Ferdieu told me of fighting their way past heretics who wore the skulls of the condemned on their helms. Not one surrendered. All chose to die, and all fought with a ferocity that he might have respected if it had been in the service of a better cause. But they came, and they died, and finally Ferdieu's Hellknights crossed into Citadel Gheisteno over a flowing carpet of its defenders' blood.

"They went into the citadel as conquerors, and they left it broken. In the dungeons of that place, they found cells crammed with people. Well, I say 'people,' but really they were hellspawn. Dozens of them, piled on top of each other like plague victims in the grave. Their hearts had been torn out of their chests, but they weren't dead. They still had heartbeats, even without their hearts, and they could breathe and bleed. If Ferdieu poured water down their throats, he told me, they'd swallow. If he dropped sand in their eyes, they would weep. But they couldn't talk or hear or even respond to pain, and they certainly couldn't be healed."

Ederras's spine prickled. "They couldn't be healed? Not by any means?"

"That's what he told me." Lady Auvadia shrugged, nibbling at her tea-soggy scone. "I never saw them for myself. But that's why I say it was a kind of murder. They weren't dead, but from what he described, they might as well have been."

"Do you know why they were there?"

"Not precisely. Ferdieu did say that the Order of the Crux had declared all those hellspawn to be criminals. 'Crimes against nature,' he told me, and 'delusions about the proper order of the world.' Lictor Shokneir had declared them anathema. Said their very existence was a violation of natural law—proof of the perfidy of House Thrune. You can imagine how that went over in Egorian. Anyway, I suppose they were there as criminals, and whatever was done to them was meant to be their sentence."

"What became of the hellspawn if they couldn't be healed?"

"If Ferdieu knew, he never told me. But he said that in another part of the dungeon, they found chests full of beating hearts. Boxes upon boxes of them stacked in the dark, many more than the bodies that they found. The hearts were clear as crystal, he said, and hollow as blown eggshells. But they beat with phantom life.

"Even that wasn't the worst of it. The heretics did more to some of those hellspawn. Something that forced them back into what their lictor thought was the correct order. It was *that,* more than finding all those sightless and senseless people piled into cells, or their hearts gathered into boxes, that really troubled Ferdieu. But he never spoke of that to me, not in any detail. Only the part I've told you."

"Might he have kept a journal? Any written record of his thoughts?" Ederras tried to hide his desperation. What she'd told him so far only confirmed that they were on the right trail—that what they'd found in Rego Cader did, indeed, go back to Citadel Gheisteno. But he still didn't know why it had happened, or how, or what he could do to stop it.

Lady Oberigo reared back, nostrils dilated in distaste. "Certainly not! Ferdieu would never have put any of that nastiness to paper. Although it might have helped him if he had. Until the day he died, he was angry that they'd marched on Citadel Gheisteno without completely ending its crimes."

"Because the citadel rose again as a ghost?"

The old lady shook her head. She set her teacup down, the half-eaten scone balanced precariously on the side of its saucer. "Not that. He died before that happened. No, what angered Ferdieu was that they spent so many lives to stamp out the Order of the Crux, took all those heretics' heads, tore down their fortress, and yet failed to destroy the awful device that enabled the Crux's sins. They could have. But they didn't, because their orders were to capture it instead. Intact. It was too powerful to forsake, they were told. Too valuable. Regardless of the cruelty and horror it caused."

"Who gave those orders?" Ederras asked, although he felt with sinking certainty that he already knew.

"Who else?" Lady Auvadia picked a soggy violet off her scone with a hooked fingernail. She flicked it onto the saucer, where it crumpled into a damp, discolored heap. "House Thrune."

15

AN INHERITANCE OF SIN

JHERAAL

It took Jheraal another full day to finish exploring the Order of the Rack's stockpile of evidence from Citadel Gheisteno.

She had to make her own catalog of what she found, recording her discoveries as they came. The shelves held more dusty crates of instruments that she now guessed were surgical tools used to extract the hellspawn's hearts, not torture implements as she'd first thought. Later those tools had been replaced, Jheraal knew. But in the beginning, when the Hellknights of the Crux were refining their designs, the tools had apparently seen frequent and grisly use. Next to them were boxes of personal belongings: clothing, boots, wedding rings and mourning lockets, dolls and toy animals stitched out of worn fabric.

Initially Jheraal assumed that those were the private possessions of the Crux Hellknights, although she was puzzled by the children's toys. When she found the yellowed ledger that explained them, however, her heart sank.

The boxes didn't hold belongings taken from dead Hellknights after Citadel Gheisteno's fall. They held the things that Lictor Shokneir and his underlings had taken from the prisoners they'd killed.

Year after year, the ledger's entries tracked across the brittle pages, listing forfeitures as substantial as courtesans' jewelry collections and titles to ships or buildings, and as small as a farmer's worn pair of boots. According to the Order of the Crux's records, all those items had been seized from the condemned.

That was a violation of every Hellknight order's code, and further evidence that damned the Crux as heretics. Of course prisoners could be executed, and often were. Of course their possessions were forfeit when that happened. But those possessions were supposed to be assigned according to the law. In cases of theft, the stolen goods had to be returned to the victim. In cases of injury, the wrongdoer's valuables were to be sold and the coin used for clerical spells that might heal the victim's wounds. If the victim was dead, then the killer's possessions would be sold to pay for a funeral.

Only in the rarest instances were a criminal's belongings forfeited directly to the Hellknights. Any other rule created too much temptation to arrest and convict people in service to greed, not the law. Yet the Order of the Crux, if their own records were to be believed, had practically been looting its victims' pockets before they stopped swinging on the gallows.

It made Jheraal's skin crawl to read through those pages. She had dedicated her life to the Hellknights because she believed that their strict adherence to the rule of law was the best and fairest way to balance the competing interests in society. She hadn't always been perfect in upholding those ideals, but she'd tried. She had always tried.

The Crux hadn't.

What Jheraal found in those ledgers was not merely evidence of theft from the dead, but an attack on the very essence of what it meant to be a Hellknight. They suborned the law to their own desires. All their other crimes were almost secondary to that.

Almost.

On another unlit shelf she found a heavy book, bound in drab brown, with no name on its cover and no title on its spine. In its pages, set forth in a clear strong hand and signed by Lictor Shokneir himself, she read words that took the breath out of her lungs.

The creatures known as 'hellspawn' represent a profound perversion of natural law. Their infernal heritage poisons their souls. Evil is bred into them, blood and bone, innate to their beings as it is to devils.

Yet that very same taint may prove their salvation. For evil is not the only flower to blossom from the seed of devils. There is obedience to the law as well.

Jheraal closed the book. Her hands were shaking on its cover. She watched them as though from a great distance away, observing the fine white scales across the backs of her fingers, the larger pebbled scales on her knuckles and wrists, the sharp claws that dug into the book's dull brown leather.

There was nothing human about those hands. Nothing, and everything. Five fingers, a palm, a thumb. The power to wield a sword or wrap a bandage.

But not, according to Lictor Shokneir, the power to choose.

His words broke open an old, unhealed pain. All her life, Jheraal had struggled to know how much of a shadow her heritage cast over her soul. The blood that ran through her veins, the heart that thumped in her chest—they weren't like those of ordinary mortals. Hell was her inheritance, and Jheraal had spent three decades trying to understand exactly what that meant.

How much was she her own person? Was her will as free as those of elves and humans and halflings? Or was it a wagon with a crooked wheel, always veering to the side unless she constantly forced it straight?

Was she destined to darkness?

Had she doomed her daughter to the same?

Ever since she'd been old enough to understand that she was different from the other children, Jheraal had circled around that mystery, never knowing its truth. She had become a Hellknight in part because she believed the discipline of her order would strengthen her resolve against whatever taints and temptations were embedded in her ancestry. And while Jheraal didn't believe that her destiny had been written before her birth, or that Indrath was cursed with an inborn taint of evil, she was also painfully aware that she could never be sure. Not completely.

Even if she was, the rest of the world wouldn't be. It *hurt* to be reminded of that. Yes, the Order of the Crux had been heretics. They'd been criminals, outcast, their false beliefs crushed and cast out on the refuse heap of history.

But before that they'd been Hellknights, and they had believed her kind was cursed.

The ghostly thumping of the boxed hearts reverberated in her ears. She knew why some of them were gray, and wished she didn't. She knew why some of them were pink, and that was worse. Almost as soon as she'd found them, Jheraal had returned the jewel-like hearts to their crates, and the crates to their shadowed shelves, but their spectral pulses had surrounded her the entire time she'd been working in the evidence archives of Citadel Rivad.

Why had the Order of the Crux singled out and slaughtered all those hellspawn?

Steadying her inhuman hands, Jheraal opened the lictor's book again.

She had to know.

"It was called the devilheart chain," Jheraal told Ederras as they walked together along the sculpture-hemmed canals of Westcrown. It was very early, and the Hellknight had just come off the long ride back from Citadel Rivad. Her eyes were gritty with sand, her mind was bleary, and the familiar weight of her armor felt clumsy and ill balanced. She turned her face into the wind, letting its coolness cut through her stupor.

"That's what they used to tear out the hearts?" the paladin asked. He seemed preoccupied and oddly tense. His eyes stayed on the canal water, glass-smooth at this hour and largely undisturbed except for the birds that splashed in the shallow puddles on the stairs at the water's edge.

"Yes. It was meant to purify them, in a way. To separate the devil part of them from the rest, and to bind all that infernal taint into their living hearts."

"Why? I have difficulty imagining that Lictor Shokneir cared about doing that for the hellspawn's benefit. What did he get out of it?"

"Slaves." Jheraal's mouth twisted distastefully at the word. "He had them declared criminals and their lives forfeit. Then he chained their spirits as slaves. Their mortal natures made that possible, and their infernal tendency toward order made them easier to bind."

Ederras raised a golden eyebrow and looked up from the water, curious despite whatever distraction had him so moody. "That offends you? You were quick enough to tell me to ignore the prayers of slaves at the Pleatra."

"That was different."

"Why?"

Jheraal ran a clawed hand through her hair, trying to find the words. She shifted her helm under an armored elbow, seeking steadiness in the grim steel. After a moment, she shook her head. "Because they were stealing."

"I don't follow."

"In Citadel Rivad, there were ledgers where the Order of the Crux recorded all the things they stole from criminals they condemned. They didn't pay restitution to victims. They didn't offer compensation for thefts or provide funerals for the families of the murdered. They kept what they confiscated for themselves. They stole. It was *wrong*—a violation of the law that they were sworn to uphold. What they did with the hellspawn was worse. They weren't just stealing coins. They were stealing souls.

"Most of those people were ordinary citizens. The scrolls of condemnation listed what they were accused of, but most of the crimes were either petty or highly unlikely. Some of the accused were just children." Jheraal's lip curled in disgust. "Even if they were truly criminals, that wasn't the penalty for their offenses. If they were supposed to have been fined, they should have been fined. If they were supposed to have been branded, they should have been branded. If they were supposed to have been hanged, they should have been sent to the gallows."

Pages upon pages of names. Jheraal scowled, remembering. "*None* of them faced a sentence that began to compare to what they suffered. Having one's heart torn out and one's soul bound past death is not a permissible punishment for any crime, however heinous. Therefore sending them to that fate was illegal. What the Crux did wasn't in service of the law. It was just another theft."

Ederras let out a disbelieving little laugh. He stooped and skipped a small rock across the canal, watching its ripples until the last of them died. "*That's* what bothers you? Not that they tore the hearts out of innocent people and enslaved their spirits, but that they did it without . . . what? A proper hearing? Notice?"

"Without the authority of law," Jheraal said firmly. "It makes all the difference in the world. The law, and *only* the law, distinguishes the executioner from the murderer. The Order of the Crux chose to ignore that."

"I suppose we agree on the important part, at least," the paladin said. Straightening, he continued down the stone-paved walkway. The high towers of Westcrown Island receded behind them as the path curved away from the canal, turning toward the busier, more vibrant commerce of Parego Spera.

Here, the streets were alive despite the early hour. Shopkeepers were setting the day's fruits and vegetables onto dew-damp wooden stands. Baker's apprentices dodged through the streets, cradling covered baskets of warm bread, to make their delivery rounds. As the night receded into misty morning, the people of Westcrown took down the burned-out remnants of the pyrahjes that had warded off the terrors in the dark. Freed by the safety of sunlight, they resumed the normal rhythms of a city.

"So we know the Order of the Crux made this devilheart chain," Ederras said, "and we have some idea why. But we don't know what it's doing in Westcrown, or who's using it. As far as I'm aware, Lictor Shokneir remains shackled to his citadel, and no one's reported an undead knight in a shroud of poisonous mist to the local dottari. I think we can reasonably conclude that someone else is using the chain."

Jheraal nodded in assent. She moved her horned helm to her other arm, wiping away the dew that had collected on its steely brow. The mist that rose from the canals was so dense that mornings in Westcrown could be like walking through clouds. "I believe it's the same one, though. The chain was stolen from Citadel Rivad, and the dead Hellknight we found in Rego Cader had been assigned to guard the archives where it was kept. Presumably he stole it, handed it to an accomplice, and was then murdered, most probably by the same accomplice."

"Do you have any leads on that accomplice?"

"Maybe. The Hellknight had a sister in Westcrown. She might know something about his associates, or might even have been involved herself. I plan to visit her tomorrow. And you?"

Ederras didn't answer immediately. He glanced back, she noted, to the white spires of the Iomedaean cathedral behind them on Regicona. "I spoke to the widow of a Hellknight who'd been part of the march on Citadel Gheisteno. She told me that the Order of the Scourge captured the devilheart chain—although she didn't know that name for it—and wanted to destroy it. But they didn't, because House Thrune ordered that it be preserved. Awful as it was, they wouldn't give up its power."

"Didn't you tell me that your great-grandfather stole it?"

"Not exactly. He stole *part* of it. Maybe it was a small part. Enough to keep the device from working, but not enough that anyone would miss it. Anyway, that's not the point. House Thrune wanted it before. Presumably they're still interested now. So what happens if we find it?"

"You're worried that Velenne joined our investigation because she wants to seize the chain? That her goal is to reclaim it for House Thrune?"

The paladin nodded slightly. His jaw worked through a knot of tension. "It makes sense, doesn't it? Why else would she be here?"

Jheraal shrugged. The sun was rising high enough to slant its light through the surrounding buildings. She put her helm on and lowered its visor to shade her eyes. "Maybe she was telling the truth. Maybe she came to see you. Don't you have spells to reveal lies?"

"I do. And they're easily countered by other spells, which it's safe to say Velenne knows." He skipped a second stone into the canals. This time his frustration made him throw it too hard, and the rock vanished with a glurping splash. "I couldn't catch her in a lie last time, and it cost my friends their lives. What will it cost if I let her deceive me again?"

"How should I know? That's up to you, isn't it?"

Ederras tipped his chin, flushing slightly as he acknowledged his fault. "I'm sorry. I'm dwelling on my own small concerns. This must be much harder for you. Learning that the Order of the Crux preyed on your kind can't have been easy."

"It isn't."

"Is there any way I can help?"

"We can stop whoever's stolen the chain. That would be the obvious answer."

The paladin ran a hand across a low stone balustrade over-looking the water. The pillars were of an older style, predating the Thrune Ascendancy. They were worked into simple, graceful vaselike forms, without the ostentatious ornamentation that later designers favored. "Of course. But I meant to ask whether there was anything I could do to help *you*."

"You're not doing enough already?"

Ederras paused, studying one of the carvings with closer attention than it warranted. She'd stung him, she could see, although he tried to brush it off. "Maybe. Maybe not."

Jheraal sighed. She leaned against the whitewashed wall of a nearby house. A window opened on the second floor above her, and a head poked out. Probably the owner or a house servant, ready to tell these loiterers to leave.

Whoever it was, he or she withdrew immediately upon glimpsing the Hellknight's armor. Jheraal didn't even have time to register a face. "I apologize. I'm tired, and I'm being unfair. But my personal feelings have nothing to do with our investigation."

"What does that mean? That you're not allowed to *have* personal feelings? Does your order expect you all to be automatons inside your armor?"

"More or less." Jheraal let a wry smile surface briefly through her weariness.

"Well, I don't. I'd like to think that we're friends—or headed that direction—and that you'd tell me if something were troubling you, whether or not it has anything to do with our investigation." Ederras glanced up from his study of the balustrade, his blue eyes guileless. "You don't have to bear your burdens alone."

"You really believe that, don't you?" Jheraal marveled. "You really do." She looked away, watching a brown-speckled bird splash in a puddle. The bird ruffled its neck feathers and threw glittering droplets up on its wings, then made a little hop and flew away. When it was gone, she exhaled a soft breath, staring at the empty step where it had been. "There was a time—a long time ago, long before I became a Hellknight—when I would have given a great deal to find that kind of friendship."

A silence fell between them, not quite uncomfortable but not far from it. A small, flat-bottomed boat floated by on the canal. It sat low in the water, heaped high with crates of fruit, jars of wine and oil, and other sundries destined for some wealthy household on Regicona. Opposite the rower sat a second man, hard-eyed and unsmiling. His knuckles were permanently swollen, and his ears were lumpy as unfinished pastry, signifying a lifetime of rough-and-tumble brawls.

He was security, obviously. Protection against the risk that someone might try to steal his employer's apples and oil jars. Not a grave risk, in the richer parts of Westcrown, but one substantial enough to be worth paying a guard to avoid.

The man with the battered ears looked around, incurious but professional, as his rower pulled him past. Jheraal watched him in turn, thinking about all the different meanings that 'security' took in the world, and all the different ways people tried to obtain it.

When both the skiff and its attendants had turned around a bend in the canal and vanished behind a greening garden wall, Ederras cleared his throat. "You have it now. Friendship. If you want it."

"That easy?"

"It doesn't have to be that hard."

"Maybe not for you. It's never been easy for me. Even before I became a Hellknight, I spent most of my time . . . lonely." That was understating it, but Jheraal didn't feel like trying to explain the full depth of her isolation. Not to a man who had been highborn, handsome, and virtuous all his life. She didn't hold those things against the paladin—he had no more chosen his blessings than she had chosen to be born without them—but she knew he could never understand.

Another boat floated by, this one not a skiff but an adel: a barge covered by a silk canopy painted with cavorting fiends. Its rowers were a pair of strapping young men who had, like carriage horses, been chosen for their matched builds. One wore the laughing mask of comedy. The other wore the plaster grimace of tragedy. Both of their masks featured devils' horns and pointed goatees. A plump woman in a yellow silk dress lay prostrated on a heap of satiny pillows behind them, a young girl fanning her and holding a wilted sachet to her nose. The angle of the boat concealed the woman's face, but her tower of elaborate curls was crumpled on one side, and there were wine stains about the bottom of her dress.

An opera diva returning from an assignation. A noblewoman would have been more discreet. Her adel would have lowered its canopy to conceal her identity altogether, and would never have been that garishly decorated. But a singer or an actress, particularly one whose star was beginning to sink, might want to fan the flames of gossip. One way to do that was to keep a boat so distinctively designed that it was easily recognized across Westcrown's canals.

Ederras had seen the adel as well. A curious play of emotions crossed the paladin's face as he watched it float past. He was staring at the canopy paintings and the devil-masked rowers, not the insensible diva on her silken throne.

When it was gone, and its ripples had smoothed away on the canal, he turned back to the Hellknight. "Do you want to change that? Do you *want* a friend?"

"I . . . I don't know." It was surprising to realize that, but once she'd said the words aloud, Jheraal knew they were true. "I don't know that I've ever really had one. Even with my old comrades during my mercenary days . . . there were always some walls between us. Small things, easy to overlook when we were fighting, impossible to bridge when we weren't." She thought of Merdos, and how even their association came with a certain amount of professional caution.

Ederras regarded her with open surprise. "You've never had anyone that you trusted completely?"

"Not in the way you mean. The Measure doesn't encourage such sentiments, and even before I became a Hellknight, it would have been . . . complicated. The closest I ever came was just a different kind of lie."

"How so?"

"Back when I was a mercenary, I found something that had belonged to a dead bandit. A hat." When she closed her eyes, she could remember it exactly. It had appeared as a green hood embroidered with grapevines in glittering gold thread. The wool had been soft and scratchy against her skin, the golden grapevines smooth as satin. "It had the power to change who you were. It wasn't just a disguise or some spell-woven mask. The hat changed *everything*. Your voice, your scent, the way your skin felt when touched. As soon as I realized what it was—what I had—I ran away from the company. I couldn't risk them taking what I'd found, and I wanted the chance to start over. As someone else."

"You stole from your employers?" Scandalized amusement creased the corners of the paladin's eyes. Jheraal could read his thoughts as plainly as if he'd spoken them aloud: it was inconceivable to him that *she,* a duty-bound Hellknight, had once been selfish enough to snatch a treasure and run.

"I was a different person then," she said. "And I wanted to see what life was like without the curse of my blood."

"How was it?"

Jheraal rolled her shoulders wearily against the wall. The early morning left this side of the building in shade, and the whitewashed stone retained the night's chill. It crept through her armor, stiffening her bones, but she was far too tired to move. "You don't realize what a burden you've been living under, as someone *different,* until it's gone. It's like . . . a shell of stone that grows over you, bit by bit, each increment so tiny that you don't notice it.

Maybe it's meant to protect you from the world, and maybe it even does, but the weight of carrying that shell around for years will crush you into the dirt, no matter how strong you are.

"When I put on the hat, all of that weight just vanished from me. I didn't have to carry around that shell anymore. I didn't *need* it. I wasn't different. No one stared at me. No one whispered. Shopkeepers didn't tense when I came through their doors. Guards didn't glower when I walked past. And I felt so unbelievably free, so light, as if every step I took might launch me into the sky. The air was sweeter, the water cleaner, the whole world a sunnier place."

"Why did you give it up?"

The Hellknight breathed a sigh through her small, curved fangs. They'd gotten to the point of her story—the reason she'd begun telling it in the first place—and she found herself hesitating before plunging off that precipice. She'd never whispered a word from this part of her story to anyone. It had been a secret for so long, and the weight of that secret had grown immeasurably over the years.

She was tired. It was time to let go.

"Because I found someone that I could trust. Someone I could open myself to without fear of judgment or rejection. I fell in love, which was something I hadn't ever really thought possible. You might be shocked to hear this, but there aren't that many men interested in courting six-foot-tall scaly hellspawn. Most of the ones who do, they don't really want *you*. They want a fetish. An object. Not a person. I'm not interested in that. So I thought it would never happen for me. And it didn't, until I found that hat.

"Even more impossibly, he loved me back. But, as I said, it was all founded on a lie. Our entire courtship took place behind that mask. I didn't dare remove it, not for an instant. He never knew who—*what*—I really was. But in other ways I was truer and more open with him than I'd ever been with anyone in my life. That was

HELLKNIGHT 207

the closest I've ever come to having a friend, I think. And then it all just . . . went away."

Ederras frowned. Not at her. It was inwardly directed, that frown. About something else entirely. But he shook it off, whatever it was. "What happened?"

"Fear. Just . . . fear." She trailed off, mystified by her own confession. Jheraal knew the measure of her own bravery. There was no battle she'd run from, no peril she couldn't face. Except that one. Half a lifetime, and that hadn't changed. "I didn't know how he would respond to the truth. I didn't dare find out. The way he looked at me, the way he spoke to me . . . it was too precious. I couldn't risk losing it. Maybe he would have accepted me as I really am, and maybe he wouldn't, but I couldn't face the chance that it would ruin what we had. So I ran. I never told him anything. I just disappeared. Because I was that afraid. That ashamed."

Jheraal exhaled, closing her eyes in an attempt to escape the intensity of that old emotion. It didn't work. It never worked. Even now, so much later, thinking about that time set her temples to pounding in shame and confusion. "After I left him, I threw away that enchanted hood. I joined the Hellknights, so I'd never have to be that vulnerable again. Embracing the Order of the Scourge gave me a different kind of armor. A different shell. One that I could bear honorably, and that left me enough room to breathe."

The paladin's frown deepened. This time it *was* at her. She saw him sort through his questions, put some aside, settle on one. "Do you regret it?"

"Sometimes. I don't think there's any way not to regret that decision, whichever way you choose. But if you're asking whether I would decide differently, if I had it to do again, the answer is no. I'm as much a coward today as I was then. Maybe more so."

Ederras studied her armor in silence, following the web of deep, ridged scars that the armorer had cut into the steel. Most of the marks evoked the scars of lash and scourge, as befit the

Hellknight's order, but there were claw gouges and the puckered stars of tooth punctures as well, and the rippled, shiny sheets that followed burns. A thousand imagined wounds, more than any living bearer could have survived, marched across those blackened plates.

"I don't believe," he said at last, lifting his gaze from the armor back to Jheraal, "that you are, or have ever been, a coward."

You have no idea. She bit down on the protest. It had been an unthinking reflex, and it wasn't fair.

Would it hurt so much to have a confidant? A friend? Remembering Indrath's father had brought back a pang of nostalgia. Jheraal *had* been happy, then, and had been glad to have someone she could trust, even if only partway. Did it make her weak that she wanted to have a friend again?

Or was the greater cowardice in keeping her secrets, and refusing to confront uncomfortable truths?

She decided to test it. "I have a daughter."

Ederras's eyes widened. "You do?"

"I do. Fathered by the boy who only knew me with the hood. I never told him about that, either. Her name is Indrath. She's fourteen now. Bright, vivacious, full of adventure and love of life. She lives at Citadel Demain, and thinks I found her as a baby in a basket somewhere. She knows none of this. No one does, officially, though I suspect a few of my superiors have figured it out."

"She doesn't know? Your daughter?"

Jheraal shook her head. She lifted a hand, flexing her clawed and scaled fingers as she brought them out of the wall's shadow into sunlight. It was an inhuman hand. A monster's. She waited until she was sure Ederras had seen it, and then she let it fall back into the shade. "The curse doesn't show in her. She can *pass*. I won't take that from her."

"Do you think that's what she really wants?"

She heard the care in his voice. The caution. The unspoken questions that hovered beneath the surface of the one he'd voiced.

"I don't know," Jheraal admitted, "but I do know that I'm not willing to shatter the simplicity of Indrath's childhood to find out. Maybe that's cowardice, too. Or maybe it's understanding of how profound a gift it is to live with uncomplicated allegiances. Indrath's life will have challenges and hardships. I can't protect her completely. But I can protect her from that one, at least. I can give her a life free from the curse of my blighted blood."

Whatever the paladin thought, he didn't say anything. After another moment, the Hellknight pushed herself away from the wall. The morning was wearing on, and there was still much work to be done.

Ederras fell in beside her. They walked together in silence for a while. Then, as they turned a corner, he ventured a quiet question: "Is it worth giving up a mother?"

"Yes," Jheraal answered without a trace of hesitation. "Yes, if the mother is the cause of your curse. Then it's no sacrifice at all. Only a blessing. That's what it means to be a hellspawn in this world, with or without this devilheart chain."

16

DISSOLUTION

EDERRAS

They walked the rest of the way to Taranik House in silence. Around them, the morning warmed toward day, and the life of the city rose into full, buzzing bustle. The drivers of donkey carts cursed one another vigorously when they crossed paths at intersections, each refusing to give way to the other. Flower-sellers, pie vendors, and peddlers hawking luck charms and love potions crowded the approaches to the major bridges, chanting their wares to a steady stream of passers-by. Alchemists sold luminetti—small glass pendants that could be opened and shaken together to create an hour's worth of light—along with more exotic concoctions.

As the squat bulk of Taranik House came into view before them, Ederras paused. "When we first met, you mentioned that you'd looked up the old records from—from my indiscreet youth."

"I did. I thought it was important to know who you were."

"Can I see them?"

The Hellknight chuckled. "You don't already know what you did?"

"I know what I did. That doesn't tell me anything about what the reports say, though. If it wouldn't be too much of a favor—"

"It's fine. It's an old investigation. The convictions are well past appeal, the sentences long carried out. The records have been public for years. I'll have one of the armigers deliver my copies of the reports to your vaneo. Keep them if you want. I don't need them anymore."

"You're not going to ask why I want them?"

"Because everybody likes to see their name in print?" She laughed at his expression. "No. I try not to ask questions about favors. Not unless I have to. Havarel's taught me that excessive curiosity is rewarded only with headaches."

Two stone-faced Hellknights saluted and stood aside at the doors as Jheraal approached. Before either she or Ederras could announce their arrival, a female signifer in a ridged steel mask and flayed leather cloak stepped out to intercept them.

As a spellcaster in the Order of the Rack, the signifer didn't wear the heavy plate that the other Hellknights did. Although her armor was as ornately spiked and precisely fitted as theirs, it was far lighter, more ornamental than functional. Instead of the Rack's standard sleek helm, she wore a black steel mask that concealed the upper half of her face, hiding everything above the tip of her nose. "Hellknight Jheraal. You're needed immediately at the Obrigan Gate. Something's happened to your prisoners."

Jheraal's mood changed instantly. The tips of her teeth showed in her frown, and she didn't correct the signifer's mischaracterization of the hellspawn she was protecting as 'prisoners.' "What's happened to them?"

"Lady Thrune didn't say. Only that you must come at once. She left a scroll to hasten your arrival."

Jheraal raised an eyebrow and held out a clawed hand for the scroll. Even for House Thrune, a scroll of that power was no trivial expense. "It's that urgent?"

The signifer nodded. "So she said."

After giving the scroll a brief inspection, Jheraal curled it in her palm and looked at Ederras. "Teleportation. Can you use this?"

"No." Wizardly magic had always been beyond him.

The signifer stepped forward. "I can. Sir."

Jheraal looked the woman over, lingering on the dark leather of her cloak's shoulders. The signifer only had one pin on her left shoulder, and that one was a plain length of brass. Ederras wasn't versed in the nuances of the Hellknights' ranks, but he guessed that meant Jheraal ranked higher than this masked spellcaster—an impression soon confirmed by Jheraal's peremptory tone. "What's your name?"

"Baliah," the signifer replied. She sounded young, maybe not much over twenty. Ederras wondered about that—teleportation spells were no easy matter, even with a scroll to guide the caster—yet the woman must be skilled to have survived the Hellknights' tests and earned induction into their ranks.

Evidently Jheraal agreed, because she tossed Baliah the scroll. "Take us there."

The signifer smoothed the page and began reciting its incantation. As she spoke each syllable aloud, the inked letters on the fine white paper ignited into golden flame and burned away, washing Baliah's steel mask with spectral firelight.

Near the end of the spell, Baliah reached out to touch Jheraal's right shoulder. The Hellknight, in turn, clasped Ederras's arm with her gauntleted left hand. At once the paladin felt the magic envelop him, gathering power and intensity. He closed his eyes, offering a heartfelt prayer to Iomedae that the Rack signifer would be able to keep control of the spell.

Around him, the world dropped away. Ederras felt a disorienting lurch in the core of his being, as if he had plunged without warning from a great height and just as suddenly been jolted back up again. Bile burned at the back of his throat.

Swallowing its bitterness, he opened his eyes.

Baliah had calculated their arrival perfectly. They stood on the cobbled street fifteen feet outside the Obrigan Gate, facing two dottari and a slack-jawed ox-cart drover. The dottari, although initially astonished, seemed to have been forewarned of the possibility that Jheraal and her companions might arrive so abruptly.

Recovering from their surprise, they gave her a pair of crisp salutes. "Hellknight."

Jheraal nodded perfunctorily in return. "I'm told something has happened to my guests?"

The dottari exchanged a glance. There was more than apprehension in those looks, Ederras thought. Neither of the dottari was a wet-eared new recruit. They looked to be closer to forty than twenty, their faces seamed with the lines of sun and wind. Veterans, both of them.

And visibly afraid, both of them.

"Yes, ah, mistress," the nearer of the dottari said, fumbling for a title. "It began early this morning."

"*What* began?"

The guardsman took an unconscious half-step away, shifting his weight toward a defensive, placating crouch. "Best you see for yourself, mistress. Lady Thrune is with them. In the cells. They haven't—I mean, *we* haven't moved them."

"Show me," Jheraal said. Her face had become a mask, her voice steady but toneless. Ederras could feel the anger coiled inside her, pulled back on a tight rein.

The dottari could sense it too. Without another word, they led the Hellknight and her companions into the cells she'd commandeered under the Obrigan Gate, where the maimed hellspawn had been put for safekeeping.

Two dottari stood watch at either end of the torch-lit corridor. Between them, Velenne paced before the cells in the black-and-red attire of her office. Yet despite their guards and the formidable fortification of the Obrigan Gate itself, Ederras's apprehension increased with every step he took toward the hellspawn's iron-barred cells. There was too much tension in the air, too much brittle silence.

"What's happening here?" he whispered roughly to Velenne.

The diabolist gestured to the iron-barred window in the door nearest him. Ederras peered in, pulled back in surprise, and looked again.

It was empty.

No, he realized an instant later, not empty. The coarse straw pallets remained on the floor, each one covered by a tousled knot of blanket. There were clothes tangled up in that blanket, too: the fishmonger's dress, speckled with the iridescent white wrinkles of dried-up scales, and the livery that Nodero and Chiella had been wearing on the night of Othando's death. The clothes were slightly rumpled and deflated, as if they'd been draped over ice sculptures that had melted away.

"Where—?" he began, but before he could finish the question, Velenne seized his wrist and pulled him over to the next cell.

"*Now*," she hissed. "This is why I called you. This is what happened to the others. Watch."

Shuffling a half-step to the left so that Jheraal could stand alongside him, Ederras bent his head to the window and watched.

The five hellspawn from the bathhouse in Rego Cader had been separated into two groups, since the cells under the Obrigan Gate had been designed to house single inmates and didn't have enough space to hold all five together. The three men had been put on pallets in one, and the woman and child had been laid side-by-side in another.

He was looking into the cell that the woman and child had shared. The woman lay unmoving on her pallet, but the little girl, like the hellspawn in the previous cell, was gone. Her simple cotton dress, shapeless and empty, peeped out from her rumpled blankets. The ring she'd been wearing had tumbled into the straw. Its tiny yellow gems twinkled in the magical light that Velenne had conjured to illumine their view.

Next to him, Jheraal exhaled. It was quiet, probably quiet enough that the others missed it. But Ederras heard and understood: whatever was happening to these people, whatever horror they were about to see, he too was glad that they didn't have to watch it happen to that child.

It wasn't much easier watching it happen to the woman, though.

A second after Velenne pulled him to the cell, Ederras saw the hellspawn woman's mouth twitch. Her brow wrinkled, and she shook her head, slowly at first but with increasing fervor, as if she were arguing with someone in a dream. Her stiff, glossy curls, which had remained undisturbed since her arrival, flattened and tangled in the straw as her agitation grew. A breath puffed out her lips: a long, miserable moan, clearly shaped but drained of sound.

"What is this?" Ederras asked, turning to Velenne. Nothing they'd done to the hellspawn had been able to rouse any reaction from their insensible bodies, and now the woman seemed to be in great distress without any visible cause.

The diabolist lifted her right shoulder minutely. "I can't be certain. This is no magic that I know. I would *guess*, however, that something is being done to their missing hearts. Something that frightens and hurts them. Badly."

Jheraal glanced away from the window. The enchanted light cast her scaled face into sharp relief, emphasizing the curves and shadows of her horns. "Can you stop it?"

Velenne shook her head. "I couldn't do anything for any of the ones who went before."

The noise of the woman's body thrashing across her bed of straw drew Ederras's attention back to her struggles. She was flailing, her back arched high and wild into the air like a fish fighting an angler's hook. Every muscle in her neck and shoulders was clenched hard. Her legs kicked desperately as she strove to get away from something none of them could see.

Most devastatingly, her eyes were open. She didn't look at any of them—her wide, panicked gaze was fixed on some empty spot past the ceiling of her cell—but for the first time since she'd come to the Obrigan Gate, the hellspawn woman's eyes were open and focused.

And the terror in them was unbearable.

"Unlock this door," Ederras demanded, turning to the nearest dottari. "I have to help her. Give me the key!"

The guardswoman shrank away from him, looking at Velenne to forestall his fury.

"You can't," Velenne said. There might have been a note of compassion in her voice, or perhaps he only wished there was. "Healing doesn't work. Dispelling doesn't work. I've tried everything that you could do, and more. The magic that's affecting them cannot be countered here."

"No." Gripping the window's iron bars, Ederras stared into the cell in frustration, then flung himself away. The hellspawn's misery was impossible to watch. He couldn't conceive of how Velenne had been able to stand by and watch four other people go through this pain. Four innocents. One of them a child. "You're wrong. There has to be *something!*"

"There is." Jheraal crossed the distance to the dottari in two long strides. "The key. Now."

Hands shaking, the woman gave it to her and backed away.

Immediately the Hellknight turned on a booted heel and unlocked the door. "The rest of you may wish to turn your eyes away."

"You need to see it," Velenne protested, her eyes widening in alarm as she realized what Jheraal intended. "You can't—"

"I can and will. I don't need to see what happens next. You can tell us whatever we need to know." Drawing the long, flame-marked knife from her belt, Jheraal stooped beside the thrashing hellspawn woman. The Hellknight grabbed one of her flailing arms to hold her steady as she knelt in the straw. "There's no need for this poor soul, or any of the others, to suffer."

Despite Jheraal's invitation, Ederras did not look away as the Hellknight slashed deep across the agonized woman's throat. It was important to bear witness, to engrave this on his soul so that he would remember, always, what was at stake. *This is the cost of failure. When this is the greatest mercy we can give, we've lost.*

It was worse than he'd imagined. Cutting the hellspawn woman's throat didn't end her struggles. Blood gushed across her throat and chest in a crimson apron, but it made no more difference to her than if the Hellknight had wiped a damp cloth over her brow. The hellspawn kept thrashing and gasping through her voiceless screams, spraying scarlet mist over Jheraal's face and the scarred plates of her armor.

Grimly, her face frozen in an alabaster mask, the Hellknight kept cutting.

Both of the dottari fled, first one and then the other, neither able to bear the sight. Baliah made no sound, but angled her blank mask away. Ederras himself had to grip the window bars to stay standing. Without them, his knees might have buckled at the grisliness of Jheraal's work.

Only Velenne, who courted Kuthites in the smoky-crystalled palaces of Nidal, watched without flinching.

Finally, after a grueling eternity, it was over. The hellspawn woman's suffering had ended.

But not before Jheraal had taken off her head. Without the space to properly swing a blade, it had been slow, brutal going. Nothing else had worked, though. The woman had flailed and writhed and fought her invisible tormentors until the last wet shred of sinew snapped loose.

Breathing heavily, Jheraal left the cell. She wiped the blood from her face and the knife's blade. Sweat cut wavery, pink-streaked lines through the crimson spatters on her neck.

She didn't look at anyone, and she didn't say anything. Ederras tried to meet her eyes, willing the Hellknight to let him offer strength, empathy—*something*. But she never glanced his way.

Instead she held a clawed hand out at Baliah, who went to fetch a cup of water. Jheraal took it from the signifer and drank slowly, in small sips. Ederras couldn't tell whether she was rinsing the taste of ugliness from her mouth or simply too exhausted to drink quickly.

Velenne broke the silence. "Why did you do that?"

"What?" Jheraal finished her water and stared blankly into the empty cup.

"Take off her head. When slitting her throat didn't work. Why did you keep cutting?"

The Hellknight turned the cup around in her hands. Her fingers left sticky red prints on its wood, layering over and over each other. She didn't seem to see the blood, keeping her gaze focused on the darkness of the cup's interior instead. "I knew that killing her would stop the magic. Not exactly *how*, but that it would. There were accounts in Citadel Rivad that spoke of it, and hearts to corroborate it. The ones whose bodies were destroyed before the magic finalized its hold turned gray. The others didn't."

"What will become of the others?" Ederras asked. He didn't have the stomach to sit through that again, and the three hell-spawn men who'd been brought back from the bathhouse were still in their cell. Still waiting to suffer.

Velenne stirred. She pushed herself off the wall she'd been leaning against and went into the cell to examine the decapitated body more closely. "If they follow the same pattern as the others, then in about an hour, one of them will begin to moan and twist, as this woman did. Their struggles will accelerate over the course of perhaps twenty minutes. Then they will dissolve."

"Dissolve?" Ederras echoed.

The diabolist nodded, glancing back over her shoulder at him before bending to the bloodied corpse. "They . . . melted. Like snow on a warm day, or paper eaten by fire. Their flesh seemed almost to turn to fog. With each of them, the dissolution began at the edges of the wounds in their chests, then spread outward. It moved at a variable rate, slowing in some places and accelerating in others, so that there was always an equal amount of flesh left in all directions. I don't believe any of them stopped fighting until the end, but given how little was left, I can't be certain."

"That's what you wanted us to watch," Jheraal said dully, addressing the blood-smeared cup. "That's what you wanted us to come here to see. That suffering."

"Would you have believed me if you hadn't seen any of it yourself?"

The Hellknight didn't answer. She held the empty cup out, and Baliah dutifully retrieved it.

"More water?" the signifer inquired.

Jheraal shook her head. Baliah nodded, retreating gracefully to return the cup to wherever she'd gotten it from. The signifer's step was smooth but swift, suggesting that she was glad to leave the dungeon's tension behind. She hid it well, and none could have accused her of showing fear, but even for a Hellknight, it seemed, what they had just witnessed was unnerving.

"What will we do with the others?" Ederras asked.

"We'll take them out of here," Jheraal answered. She finally raised her head. Her eyes were haunted, unearthly. Ederras felt that he was looking into something dangerously close to madness. Hysteria burned at the edges of her gold-rimmed irises, not quite overtaking the hellspawn but close. Very close. "We'll take them outside and end them humanely. It's the only mercy we can give. But it will be a mercy."

"I'll do it." It was the least he could do to take some of the burden Jheraal was carrying. He knew that what he was offering wasn't the same as what she'd done, not remotely. The other hellspawn were insensible, and likely wouldn't feel his blade any more than they'd felt the little pinpricks that the healers had tested on their fingers. Their ends would be swift, merciful, nothing like that hard-fought bloody horror.

But it was still going to hurt him to do it, and he knew it would hurt Jheraal worse. *These are her people.*

"Thank you," the Hellknight said. That eerie emptiness hadn't left her eyes. She rubbed her hands blindly over her thighs, over and over, trying to scrub away the blood that stained them well past the wrists.

"What next?" Ederras asked quietly. "After that's done."

"We find the killer," Jheraal answered. "Without allowing him to strike again. I'm not waiting for him to gather another pile of victims so we can track him out of Rego Cader. I will not allow anyone else to suffer as these people have. I *can't*. I have to find a way to stop it."

17

FISHBONE ALLEY

JHERAAL

It took hours for Jheraal to scrub the blood off herself.

Her scales were the problem. Blood caught under their edges and wouldn't come out. She either had to soak herself in a hot bath or scour herself raw to get clean. Quite often, the Hellknight didn't bother. She simply waited for those last stubborn traces of blood to dry and flake away.

That wasn't an option today. The sight of the hellspawn woman's blood, even reduced to a ghostly, near-invisible pink tinge limning each scale, filled Jheraal with shuddering revulsion.

There were no bath facilities in the Obrigan Gate, only the buckets and rags and cheap, slimy brown soap used to wash the inmates in its cells. Jheraal soaked the rags and squeezed them over her skin to flush as much of the blood out as she could. Then she took a block of pumice stone and scraped it across the residual stains, over and over, until her scales were frayed and flaking, and the rosy taint underneath was not her victim's blood but her own.

Tears ran down her cheeks as she scrubbed. Jheraal didn't notice them at first; she had no idea when they had begun. Once she realized she was crying, however, she couldn't seem to stop it. The tears fell faster and hotter, raining into the bucket of pinkish wash water until it blurred too much for her to see.

She sank to the floor and sat numbly on the cold, water-slicked stone, crying into her bent knees for the cruelty of the world. For eight hellspawn citizens, innocent of any crime, who had tried to make lives for themselves in a city that hated them, and who had suffered and died for other people's sins. For the little girl with the froglike face who could have been her daughter, had fate taken the smallest of twists.

And for herself, too. For what she'd done, and what she had yet to do. For her shameful weakness in crying, and her inability to stop.

Since becoming a Hellknight, she had never wept. Not once. Hunger, cold, heat, privation—these were the privileges of a Hellknight, a chance to measure themselves against hardship and overcome it by discipline and force of will.

Jheraal could endure pain. She had. She would do so again. It held no fear for her. Pain was nothing but a challenge to be overcome, and she knew her own measure there.

But what she'd done in that cell was different. Nothing in her training had prepared her for that. Nothing *could*. And it was the unfamiliarity of her own emotions that terrified her, as much as the awfulness of what she had done.

Finally the storm passed, leaving Jheraal feeling scoured as raw inside as she was on the outside. Her tears dried. Her breathing steadied. She put the pumice stone back on its shelf, dumped the dirty water down the drain in the floor's center, and wrung out the washrags before hanging them on hooks to dry.

The towels were as poor as the rest of the washroom's furnishings: stiff, dirty rags trailing knots of frayed thread at each corner. They served better than nothing, but not by much. In winter, washing in the Obrigan Gate's guardhouse would have been a true hardship. In late summer, it was merely unpleasant.

No matter. She'd lived through worse. Jheraal picked out the cleanest of the dingy towels and dried herself, then strapped her underclothes, padding, and armor back on. Blood had soaked through some of the chinks in her armor and spattered the padding, but none of it had reached the light tunic and trousers she wore underneath. None of it would touch her skin.

She'd replace the quilted jerkin and burn her old one when she got to Taranik House. For now, it would have to be endured.

Shouldering her mace and scarred shield, the Hellknight left the washroom. The air outside was a welcome breath of freedom. The sunlight lifted her spirits. Clad in the familiar comfort of her armor and her discipline, she felt restored to her place in the world. She felt like *herself.*

Ready to find and face a killer.

Ederras and Velenne were waiting for her outside the Obrigan Gate. They'd found an abandoned courtyard, strewn with weeds and cloudy, glittering tiles of glass and ceramic that had rained from the ruined walls of the shrine that had once overlooked the yard. Nothing was left of that shrine but those scattered tiles and a ring of fallen foundation stones, wreathed by dandelions and low, creeping brambles.

The paladin and the diabolist sat on the foundation stones, not together, not apart. There was a subdued air to them, a shared exhaustion that Jheraal knew meant that they'd emptied the cells under the Obrigan Gate.

There was no blood on their hands, though. It washed more easily off human skin.

Both of them turned toward the Hellknight as she approached. The afternoon sunlight caught the golden embroidery of Ederras's blue surcoat, bringing out a rich sheen from the intricate designs. Near him, Velenne sat in the lacy, dappled shadow of a cherry tree that had grown tall in the rubble of the shrine.

This isn't their fight, Jheraal thought, and then stopped, wondering where that idea had come from. It wasn't like her.

It was true, though. Despite the weariness that etched lines in the paladin's brow and left shadows under Velenne's eyes, both of them were clearly born to wealth and power. It was in their white teeth and glossy hair, the confidence of their stride and the easy, unquestioned assurance in their voices. Even if they'd been dressed in sackcloth and rat skins rather than silk and gold, no one could have mistaken Ederras Celverian or Velenne Thrune for anything other than the Chelish nobles they were.

The ugliness of the hellspawn's deaths could never touch them as profoundly as it had her. They stood too far apart. They couldn't see what she saw, feel what she felt. Jheraal had no doubt that Ederras *wanted* to empathize. Equally, she was sure that Velenne didn't care. But whether the paladin and the diabolist strove to understand her or not, Jheraal was certain that neither of them ever would. Not really. Not in this.

It didn't matter. They didn't have to stand in her shoes. They just had to walk beside her.

Ederras stood respectfully as she joined them. Velenne cast the paladin an amused glance, but didn't stir from her perch on the moss-greened stone.

"It's done," the diabolist said. "The bodies will be burned and the ashes sent to their kin. One of the families wanted to have their father's body intact for burial. I told them I'd defer to your decision."

"Can you cover what was done to him?" Jheraal didn't want to subject anyone's family to that sight. She also didn't want rumors to spread about the fell magic that the hellspawn had suffered. Panic was poison to a careful investigation.

"Cosmetically? Yes. It would be trivial. Unless they went digging with knives to find the truth, no one would know."

"Is that useful in your line of work?" Ederras asked acidly.

"Very." Velenne gave him her most charming smile, which deepened as the paladin looked away from her. She glanced back to Jheraal. "I'll make the arrangements tonight. Is there anything else you need from me?"

"Not if your dog is still in Rego Cader." She hadn't wanted to wait for the killer to take his next group of victims, but there wasn't any point calling the fiendish beast away from his post yet.

"Vhaeros's watch continues." The diabolist stood, brushing specks of moss from her divided black skirts. "I will leave you two to make your plans, then. Good evening, Hellknight. I will call on you later, Ederras."

After she had gone, Jheraal gave the paladin a dry look. "Something to look forward to?"

"I'll look forward to capturing our killer," he replied stiffly. "Do you have any thoughts on where to go next? Earlier you'd mentioned that the renegade Hellknight had a sister in Westcrown."

"Yes. I'd like to pay her a visit. Would you care to accompany me?"

He stood. "I would be honored."

"It isn't an honor. It's a job."

The address that Merdos had given her was on a cramped, foul-smelling street in the bowels of Rego Crua. Filthy water, cloudy with blood and manure, ran downhill from a slaughterhouse perched higher on the street. It puddled in shallow holes around the alley's mouth, drawing swarms of fat black flies that stirred up angrily as Jheraal and Ederras strode through them.

Covering his nose and mouth with a sleeve, the paladin squinted dubiously down the crooked street. The largest building seemed to be a ramshackle tenement. Laundry lines, lumpy with the knots of a thousand repairs, crisscrossed between its windows. Dingy sheets and heavily patched undergarments flapped like huge gray bats in the gloom. "Are you certain this is the correct address? I can't imagine a Hellknight would have left his own sister to live in such squalor. Surely he'd have found her better lodgings."

"He might not have had a choice." Jheraal made no attempt to hide her own doubt. "Maybe she was too proud to accept his help. Maybe she's a drunkard who feeds all her money into bottles. Or maybe she doesn't live here at all, and lied to her own brother about her whereabouts. I don't know anything about the woman. This is the place, though."

"Then I suppose we'd better find our answers directly." Batting the flies aside, Ederras went to the door and knocked loudly.

A pinch-faced woman with a mop of greasy brown hair pinned into a loose topknot answered. The accent of Rego Crua's poorest neighborhoods was heavy on her tongue. "What?" Her eyes flickered to the Hellknight, and her expression darkened considerably. "Who're you 'ere to arrest now?"

"No one. We're just looking for next of kin."

"Oh, somebody's dead, is that all?" The clouds cleared from the woman's face. "Well, who's to be told? One of my lodgers? What's the name?"

"A woman named Katia. It's her brother who's passed. We're told she lives at this address."

"I don't know a Katia," the woman said, shaking her head. She tried to close the door, only to be stopped by Ederras's boot lodged firmly in its path. "Never had one. You got the wrong place."

"I don't believe we do." Jheraal stepped forward, drawing herself up to use the full six feet of her height. The fearsomely scarred armor of her order added even more bulk to her presence. Standing shoulder-to-shoulder with Ederras, she blotted out all the sunlight from the doorway. The hellspawn's eyes lighted in the darkness, burning with golden flame. She let an edge of iron menace creep into her voice, making sure that the tips of her teeth showed when she spoke. "This is the place. The woman's name is Katia. We wish to speak to her. Now."

The pinch-faced woman shrank back. A lanky strand of brown hair fell across her brow, shaking as she trembled away from the Hellknight. "There's none here by that name. I weren't lying. I wouldn't lie!" Her eyes darted to Ederras. "You tell her."

"Perhaps you might recognize her brother," the paladin suggested, gentling his manner to provide a more inviting counterpoint to Jheraal's intimidation. "His name was Hakur.

He was a strong, well-built man, but with very bad teeth. Glassy and eaten away."

"Him I know." The woman's head bobbed eagerly. She was almost pathetic in her sudden, fawning helpfulness. "He's got no sister here, though. He had a room in his own right. Different name, but the same man. Haven't seen him in weeks. Always knew he'd come to a bad end. You said you was here to find next of kin? Suppose he's dead, then. Don't surprise me none."

"What happened to his room?" Jheraal asked.

"I let it out again." The woman cringed at the admission, hurrying to explain herself. "The time he paid for ran out, and I had customers waiting. He had a few things. I sold most of 'em. Not everything. You're welcome to poke through what's left. Take it. Keep it. It's yours. I don't want none of it."

"Did he have any friends? Any kin?"

"Not hardly. He was a lonesome type. Unfriendly. Kept to himself, mostly just drank. He saw a girl sometimes. The paid sort, you understand? One of Colphina's lot, from down Fishbone Alley. Loose wenches." The woman sniffed, brushing her bundled skirts.

"The same girl or different ones?" Some men developed real affections for their favorite companions, and sometimes those affections were reciprocated. A lonely Hellknight, starved for warmth and isolated within his order, might well have come to view that as the most important relationship in his life. He might even have said something useful to the girl.

"The same one."

Jheraal kept her face impassive, but inwardly she was exulting. *That* was why Hakur had lied about having a sister: to explain his visits to this place, and the woman he might have been spotted with if anyone had bothered to follow him. There was a very good chance that he'd confided in the girl if he'd been here regularly enough to bother inventing a cover story. "What's her name?"

"Olivine. Like some kind of gemstone, she claims, although I never heard of any jewel called that." The woman spat across the doorway into a puddle, then blanched and retreated another fidgety step as she realized how close she'd come to spattering Jheraal's boot. She glanced into the dirty corridor behind herself, clearly longing to retreat from her unwanted guests.

The Hellknight decided to give her the mercy of drawing their interview to a close. "Down Fishbone Alley, you said?"

"I did. Will you be wanting what's left of his belongings?"

"Yes."

"Was it really necessary to frighten that poor woman so badly?" Ederras hefted the sack the landlord had given them. All it held was some spare socks, a battered old hat, and a handbill for an opera performance that had ended its run two months ago. Nothing useful. The cloud of flies parted a second time, buzzing in renewed displeasure, as they walked out of the alley.

Jheraal didn't answer until they'd left the noisome insects behind. Then she shrugged, unconcerned by his reservations. "It was faster. Probably cheaper and more trustworthy, too. There's a good chance she would have asked for a bribe if we'd tried to play nice, and then she might have lied to us anyway. With that one, I'd trust her honesty more if it were spurred by fear rather than greed." She paused, tilting her head to the side as she saw that he was trying to suppress a smile. "Is that funny?"

"No. It's just that Velenne would have given me exactly the same explanation if it had been her terrorizing that tenement keeper instead of you."

"You'd have handled it differently?"

"I'd have tried. Most people aren't bad folk, not really. They don't take pleasure in evil. They want to be virtuous, or at least to think of themselves that way. If you have enough empathy, enough understanding of who they are and what they value, you can help them become better versions of themselves. It doesn't always work, of course, but nothing *always* works. I'd rather try to inspire than rely on threats."

"That's—" Jheraal bit her tongue. *Ridiculous,* she'd been about to say. But as she glanced at the paladin, his golden hair alight in the sunshine and his blue eyes filled with earnest certainty, she thought: *oh,* that's *how he does it.* By showing people a reflection of themselves that was so bright and perfect, so flattering and yet so honest, that no one could possibly resist trying to become whatever it was Ederras saw in them. Who *wouldn't* want to earn his admiration? He was a paragon of divine grace—just one more blessing he had that others didn't.

He lifted an eyebrow. "That's what?"

"Not something I can do," Jheraal answered, more curtly than she'd meant to. She paused, grateful for the interruption, as they came to the midden heap that had given Fishbone Alley its name.

Since Westcrown's founding, the discarded mollusk shells and fish skeletons produced by the daily catch had needed a place to go. In the modern age, many of those shells were crushed and sold as paving material for the nobility's viras and vaneos. Others were pulverized more finely and sold to farmers in the hinterlands as fertilizers and chicken feed.

But in earlier years, and still occasionally during times of trouble when the value of those discards collapsed, the accumulated shells went to the midden heaps of Rego Crua.

The largest and oldest of these was the one that had bestowed its name on a neighborhood midway between the Obrigan Gate and the slave markets of the Pleatra. It stood nearly ten feet high and more than thirty feet across. There must have been hundreds of thousands, possibly millions, of clam and oyster and mussel shells heaped into that mound. Occasionally an optimistic gull hopped across the clattering pile, poking at the shells in hopes of finding a tender scrap, but mostly the animals left it alone. The remnants in that pile were old, and held nothing of interest to them.

The heap was interesting enough to many of Westcrown's citizens and visitors, though. Jheraal had heard a dozen different stories about how Fishbone Alley had begun. Some said the ladies-for-hire had picked through the midden heap for scallop shells to wear as jewelry. Others claimed that the ladies liked to work the streets around the midden heap because the dottari made so much noise marching across all those shells that it gave them ample warning to hide.

However it had started, Fishbone Alley today was known across Westcrown as a place to find gambling havens, fighting pits featuring everything from imps to cave scorpions, and brothels where patrons could reasonably expect to wake with their heads and purses intact. Crude entertainments and bawdiness ruled Fishbone Alley, but by and large, the neighborhood lacked the nastier edge that characterized the slave pits of the Pleatra or the dealings in the Dusk Market. These dens of vice paid their taxes and maintained their licenses, more or less. They were as safe as such things could be.

"Are you familiar with Colphina's girls?" Jheraal asked as they walked around the periphery of the midden heap, dry shells crunching underfoot.

"Of course not." Ederras sounded surprised by the question, maybe even offended.

He was really too easy to bait. "Well, then. You might be in for an education."

"I don't think we have time for that."

"They can be quite persuasive, I'm told. Colphina began as a courtesan in Regicona. Silk gowns, feathered masks, diamonds and the finest Opparan perfumes—all that nonsense. All the training, too. When she got older, she invested her savings in a house she called the Jewel Box. That's where we're headed."

"She didn't choose to stay in Regicona?" Ederras shooed a seagull away from pecking at the shining embroidery on his collar.

"She saw an opportunity to fill a niche in the market. No one had girls with those skills working outside Westcrown Island. No one had a house that tried to maintain the same atmosphere, either. Safe, clean, luxurious . . . but in a way that a commoner might be able to afford. It isn't quite diamonds and Opparan perfumes, but Colphina makes her magic work with paste and rosewater. And it is *exactly* where a lonely Hellknight might go to enclose himself in a warm illusion of love."

Jheraal stopped before a pair of large, plain doors. They were unmarked except for a single raised diamond on the paneling of each one. The brass knockers were worked with diamonds too. She raised one and slammed it down on its plate. "This is it."

The door opened, letting the scent of sweet roses waft from the crimson-carpeted foyer beyond. The walls were upholstered in pale pink paper and accented with brass-framed mirrors and candelabra that stopped just a hair shy of gaudiness.

In the center of that foyer, framed by its soft pink hues and made radiant by a strategically placed lamp behind her, stood a petite, pretty woman with a waterfall of red curls falling over the shoulders of her gauzy white dress. She smiled and held her hands out warmly as she saw the two of them. "Welcome to the Jewel Box. How may we serve you tonight?"

Jheraal heard Ederras stir behind her in quiet surprise. She understood his reaction. Most brothels in this part of town posted a large, imposing man as the doorkeeper. It was a simple and effective measure to keep away most of the kinds of trouble that a madam might expect. No one saw any of the ladies until they'd been cleared by the doorman.

The Jewel Box was different. That had surprised her, too, the first time she'd visited. But Colphina put great stock on creating a genteel atmosphere from the moment her clients first laid eyes on her house. Everything in the place had been carefully chosen to say: *Aren't we all civilized here? Far too civilized for any of that nastiness outside?*

And if that didn't work, the redhead was wearing a pair of enchanted rings that held enough fire and lightning between them to drop a company of orcs in its tracks. Colphina might wrap her guests in a mantle of velvet luxury as soon as they stepped through her door, but she was no fool. There was plenty of steel hidden behind that soft touch.

"We'd like to speak to Olivine," Jheraal told the redhead. "Privately. We'll pay for her time."

"I'll see if she's available," the woman replied. "May I offer you anything while you wait?"

"Tea, please," Jheraal said, understanding immediately. While there was nothing overtly illegal about Colphina's business, the sight of a Hellknight standing in the foyer was likely to make other guests uncomfortable. Best for everyone if they stayed out of view.

Gracefully their hostess led them away to a small private parlor off the side from the main lounge, where a pair of half-elves, one fair and one dark, danced sinuously to the notes of a single reed flute. A curtain of shells and cloudy glass beads strung on green and gold threads separated the parlor from the rest of the house. Despite its inexpensive materials, it was attractively designed, and conveyed an impression of far more wealth than it held.

"The tea will be here shortly," the redhead said, letting the strands of the curtain tinkle musically against one another as she released them from her fingers. "Please make yourselves at home."

"Interesting design," Ederras said, looking around the parlor when they were alone. "Having a curtain instead of a door, I mean. Blocks sight but not sound. Trivial for anyone outside to eavesdrop on private conversations or hear any hint of trouble. It's secluded enough to set one's mind at ease, but impossible to barricade. No rowdy customer would be able to pin one of her girls alone in here. Very practical."

"Colphina is."

"I'd like to meet her someday. She sounds like a fascinating woman."

"Maybe when all of this is over." Jheraal felt a brief, odd pang of melancholy, saying that. It hardly seemed possible that this investigation would ever be over, or that anyone would be brought to justice for what had been done.

A silly thought. She shook it away as the curtain's shells and beads chimed apart, letting in a young woman with a tea tray.

Strands of tumbled, olive-green peridot chips wrapped around the girl's swanlike neck, bringing out subtle highlights in her soft brown hair and accentuating her hazel-flecked irises. A light, pleasant perfume surrounded her. Jheraal couldn't identify the fragrance, but it put her in mind of a field of wildflowers on a brisk, sunny autumn day.

"Olivine?" The Hellknight motioned to an empty chair that faced them across the low table. "We're here about Hakur."

The girl poured two cups of tea, setting one before Jheraal and the other before Ederras, then settled on the chair that Jheraal had indicated. She moved with a reasonable facsimile of a Regiconan courtesan's grace—less precise, perhaps, and not quite as effortless, but more than sufficient to awe her patrons here in Rego Crua. "Is he dead?"

"I'm afraid so."

The girl nodded, seeming sad but not surprised. "He thought that might happen. He told me never to expect him again."

Jheraal leaned forward, clasping her hands. "You had a relationship?"

Olivine shrugged, looking away in wordless demurral. The peridot chips of her coiled necklace clicked softly. "He was lonely. A wounded soul, I always thought. He'd served his order for years, and had served it well, but the weight of the things he'd done and the horrors he'd seen . . . after all those years, it was too much." She glanced at Jheraal through her long lashes and quickly away again. "Hakur was the one who arrested Master Peregoma."

"Ah." That had been an unfortunate incident. Master Peregoma, given the derisive sobriquet "the Butterfly" after his death, was an elderly and eccentric scribe who had been accused of secretly copying and distributing prohibited religious texts throughout Westcrown. When the Hellknights came to his door to verify their informants' allegations, Master Peregoma had angrily refused to allow them into his home. He had, in fact, raised a weapon to them. Jheraal wasn't sure what the weapon had been, exactly—some said it was a letter opener, while others claimed it was a bookend—but it hardly mattered. One did not defy the Hellknights and live.

For that act of disobedience, Master Peregoma had been executed in the public square. His arms and backs had been flayed, the skin spread apart and pinned into bloody butterfly wings. Then he'd been burned atop a pyre of books, including the texts he'd been so desperate to protect.

The part that mystified Westcrown was that, after Master Peregoma's death, it was discovered that he hadn't even been guilty of the original transgression. He had *owned* a few banned books, but there was no evidence that he'd been copying or disseminating them, nor was there anything to suggest that he'd belonged to any forbidden religion. Had he allowed the Hellknights into his home, Master Peregoma would easily have been exonerated. He'd have been fined, and his handful of minor books would have been confiscated, but the matter would have ended there. Instead the old man had died a martyr's death for no reason beyond stubbornness.

Stupid. The whole affair had been stupid. But Jheraal was surprised to learn that Hakur had been so badly affected by it. The fault was the scribe's, not his.

Perhaps it's different if you have to watch him burn. Or be the one pinning his skin into wings as mockery of a faith he hadn't had. Even that, in truth, was something a Hellknight should have been able to withstand without flinching . . . but yes, it was possible that such a case could be the first of many cracks in one's soul.

Olivine nodded at her recognition. "By the time I knew him, Hakur was like a ceramic cup that had shattered and been glued back together. He looked strong and whole, but he wasn't. He tried to hide it, and maybe he fooled some of his comrades, but deep inside, he hated knowing that he wasn't what he had been. I believe that shame destroyed him as much as the weight of his memories did. Perfection is too much to ask of any mortal soul, but the Hellknights' demands are merciless. Hakur broke trying to bear a burden that no one could carry, and that he was too proud to set down. That's what I think, at least. He never said any of this.

"Anyway. He needed a friend, so I tried to be that for him. I don't think he had any real illusions about what we were, or weren't, but . . . he deserved kindness."

"You said he expected he'd die?"

"Yes. I . . ." The girl fiddled with the peridot chips of her necklace, rolling them between her fingers like prayer beads. "He gave me instructions, you know. In case his worries came true." She motioned to Ederras's cup of tea, which he had not touched. There was no third cup. She hadn't brought one for herself. "May I?"

"Please," the paladin said, pushing the ceramic cup toward her.

"Thank you." Olivine took the cup and sipped it. She'd practiced that movement, too. It seemed to be a kind of ritual, settling her nerves. "Over the last few weeks I saw him, Hakur was angry and afraid. He was being threatened by a woman. A strange one, he said. She had no hair, no fingernails. She wasn't human, but she didn't know *what* she was, beyond dangerous.

"She pressed him to steal things from the secret archives of Citadel Rivad. She promised him money and freedom at the end of their dealings, enough that he could live somewhere else as a new man, but he never really believed it. He always said she'd kill him when she had what she wanted.

"Hakur was . . . shamed, deeply shamed, that he didn't report the woman's offer to his commanding officers the moment that she approached him. He was ashamed that he was tempted by the prospect of leaving, even if he didn't really believe it could happen. When we last spoke, he told me that his superiors were getting suspicious, and that he feared discovery, but he couldn't bring himself to admit his weakness to his commanders. He hadn't actually *done* anything, yet, but merely holding silence was a sin. So he said nothing, except to me. He told me to store away a few words, and give them to whoever came looking after he died."

"What were those words?" Jheraal asked.

Olivine pressed the cup to her lips and closed her eyes. Tears glittered along her lashes. "The thing she made him steal—it was called a devilheart chain. He didn't tell me what that was. He said anyone who came asking would know." She dashed the tears away with a practiced flick of one finger, pushing upward along the lash-line to avoid ruining her paint. "Is that so?"

"It is," the Hellknight assured her.

The girl nodded. She returned the teacup to its saucer. It trembled and clinked in her hand. The cruder accents of Rego Crua began to break into her speech as her anxiety eroded the artifice of her Regiconan manners. "Then the next thing I'm to tell you is that she took it to Nidal. He caught that in her thoughts, the only time he dared use a spell on her. He was trying to find out what she wanted, and why. What he saw was a vision of gray mountains, all in shadow, and a castle with blackened skulls in its walls. A creature of walking darkness with eyes of fire. It wore Hellknight armor—the Order of the Crux, he said.

"She was afraid of the creature in that armor, Hakur told me. More afraid than he was of her. More fear than he'd ever felt in his life. He was glad he'd be dead before those burning eyes ever found him. Whatever terror there might be in dying, he said, meeting that one would be worse."

"Did Hakur learn why the woman wanted that chain?" Jheraal asked.

Olivine shook her head. "She never did. It wasn't her that ordered the theft from Citadel Rivad. It was the master behind her. The walking shadow in Hellknight armor. That's who wanted it, all along. That's what Hakur wanted you to know."

18

LETTERS FROM
AN OLD FRIEND

JHERAAL

The reports from his old rebellion were waiting when Ederras returned to Vaneo Celverian.

He carried them to the library's desk and broke the string with a flick of Othando's letter opener. His brother had kept a Taldan dagger for the purpose. With its filigree crossguard, solid gold hilt, and green tourmalines embedded in a line along the center of the fanciful blade, it certainly looked impressive. But its balance was abysmal, its poor steel couldn't keep an edge, and that golden grip would slide out of its wielder's hand as soon as it got slippery with the first splash of blood.

It was, all in all, a fine example of the state of Taldan weaponry. Ederras supposed it was a measure of Othando's gentle life that his brother had never noticed.

Setting it aside, he fanned out the pages that Jheraal had sent him. In keeping with government convention, the infiltrator's name didn't appear anywhere on the reports. Their anonymity was meant to instill a sense that anyone could be watching, anywhere in the world, and so spies and informants used coded numbers as identifiers instead.

He didn't need a name to identify her work. Velenne's handwriting—small, neat, and emphatic—hadn't changed a bit. He'd know it anywhere.

Ederras took a breath, steeling himself. He'd never wanted to look at any of these old things again. These pages held the stupid, blind, foolish infatuations of youth, and the disaster of his first attempt at leadership, dutifully recorded in ink and paper and set forth for the entertainment of the empire. All of his worst failures had been immortalized in the court chronicles of Imperial Cheliax.

The humiliation was crushing. But he had to know. How badly had she used him?

Abadius, 4700.

That was two full months before he'd met her. She'd been patient in setting her snares, but not overly so. Velenne never was.

The hours slipped by, unnoticed, as he read. By the time Ederras reached the last page and looked up, the library's skylight was purpling with sunset, and the vaneo's enchanted lights were beginning to awaken.

He shuffled the pages into an untidy stack and set them squarely in the center of the desk. Then he leaned back in the chair and stared at them without seeing a word.

Velenne had lied for him. More than that: she'd lied to protect his friends. The reports held less than half the information he knew she'd possessed, and fewer than a third of the names. The most damaging accusations were aimed at those already dead or discredited, with little or nothing said about people he *knew* had plotted violent treason against House Thrune. She'd managed to make his own role sound like a series of unfortunate coincidences and ill-considered friendships that led to a mistaken impression of involvement, when in fact he had been one of the rebellion's ringleaders.

None of that was obvious from the reports. To an outside reader, Velenne's work must have seemed exhaustive in its detailed observations. She'd amassed mountains of evidence to crush the conspirators she'd named.

But she hadn't named many of them, and those mountains of evidence were a thimbleful of sand next to what she could have produced.

Why?

Why would she have risked herself to protect him? Back then, Velenne had been barely more than a girl, without any real power or influence to exert. House Thrune had dozens of unknown, untested scions, and none of them were worth anything to their family until they'd proved themselves. She would have been gambling any hope of a career, and very possibly her life, by lying to hide his transgressions.

She'd done it all the same. And he had never known. The reports had been public for years, but Ederras had been too caught up in his own shame to look.

A knock sounded at the door. "Come."

It was Belvadio. "Lord Tilernos would be glad to accept your invitation to visit. A late morning call?"

"That would be ideal."

"I shall send your reply at once. Additionally, ah, you have an unannounced visitor, my lord." There was a hint of extra formality in the steward's bearing, and a reserved note in his voice, that warned Ederras of exactly who that visitor had to be.

He wasn't ready to deal with Velenne yet. But, as usual, she hadn't left him a choice. "Where is she?"

"In the lower study, my lord. She has been here for some hours, but I did not wish to disturb your reading."

You wanted to keep her waiting, you mean. Under other circumstances, that insult to a guest of Velenne's stature would have cost Belvadio his position—at the least—but, of course, the circumstances were exactly why he'd done it. "Thank you. Have dinner set for two."

Belvadio inclined his head in a stiff, correct nod that made no secret of his displeasure. "Shall I have a guest room prepared as well?"

"It couldn't hurt." He had a suspicion that if she stayed the night, however, she was not likely to do so in a guest room. Ignoring the steward's audible—and entirely calculated—sniff of disapproval behind him, Ederras went to the library to find Velenne.

She was curled up in an armchair by the fire, a fur-trimmed blanket over her lap and a book laid across her knees. Her dark hair hung loosely about her shoulders, filtering the firelight into a ruddy halo. It was such an absurdly domestic vision that Ederras paused for a moment in the doorway, trying to wrap his mind around what he was seeing.

Velenne raised her head, greeting him with a smile. "I was wondering whether you ever planned to come down from your tower."

"What if I hadn't?"

"I would have waited. At least until morning." She closed the book. "I probably wouldn't have waited quite that long for dinner, though. Your servants have been tormenting me with the smell of that chicken for over an hour."

"It'll be ready momentarily." Ederras paused, trying and failing to find a way of making the subject sound less fraught. He went for directness instead: "I've been reading your reports. From the rebellion. Before my exile."

Her smile flickered, froze, and then smoothed into her usual self-possession. "Those old things? Why? It's all long past changing."

"I'd never read them before. Why didn't you *tell* me?"

"If I spent all my time trying to correct your ignorance, I'd never get anything else done. Besides, it was more fun the other way. You hit harder when you're angry." She lifted a hand in a wave of perfect, airy indifference. Her ring flashed in the firelight. Diamond and white gold, the one he'd given her. Had she ever taken it off? "Anyway, you weren't missing much. My early literary endeavors were not, alas, very good."

"I missed everything. You lied to cover for me. To protect my friends."

"Out of sheerest pity for your incompetence. It's unsporting to send halfwits to the hangman, my love."

"I begin to suspect you're more sentimental than you let on."

"You're the only halfwit I take pity on. Still, you might be right."

"Then pity me enough to tell the truth. Why did you do it?"

Velenne sighed. "Because I'm fond of you. Don't ask me why. Obviously some things defy all rationality and common sense. But I am. Can I be allowed that?"

"I suppose so." Ederras extended an arm with mock-grave courtesy. Mirroring his exaggerated formality, Velenne dropped a small curtsy and twined her hand across his forearm.

It felt *right*, having her there. Comfortable. Which was its own seduction, Ederras knew, in some ways more insidious than the more overtly sensual ploys she'd used on him before.

Was it possible that they hadn't been ploys? It seemed unlikely, but doubt was beginning to crack his confidence.

What *did* she want? Him? The chain? Both?

With the diabolist on his arm and turmoil in his mind, Ederras led the way to dinner.

It had been ages since Vaneo Celverian's formal dining room had seen use. Othando had been in the habit of taking his meals alone and irregularly, often while immersed in his studies. Ederras had followed his late brother's custom, when he'd eaten at the vaneo at all. It seemed a waste to set the table or use the good silver when there were no guests to honor.

Despite the lack of recent opportunities to practice, however, Belvadio's skills remained sharp. The steward had set the table with the gimlet eye of a master tactician.

Two brass candelabra burned on the table, each holding three beeswax tapers: too bright for romance, but stopping well short of grandeur. Ederras was quite sure they were the cheapest candlesticks his family owned. Between them, a single vase served as centerpiece. It was glass, not crystal, and it held nothing but a handful of chamomile flowers, probably cut from the kitchen garden—an arrangement so sparse and ordinary that it paused only briefly on the precipice of insult before leaping right in.

"Your steward really doesn't want me here, does he?" Velenne sounded tremendously entertained. "He tried to throw me out before you came down, you know. Several times. With the utmost politeness, of course. But no subtlety at all."

"He thinks you're a bad influence." Ederras escorted her to a chair and pulled it out, pushing it back in after she'd sat. Her perfume touched him as he bent over her. Amber and rich incense and smoke, the same scent she'd worn at the mayor's party.

"He's right. So, were you planning to spend the entire evening discussing these dull and dusty old reports, or might you prefer to talk about something more current? The immediate investigation, perhaps?"

Ederras took a seat at the table's adjacent corner. "We could do that. What do you know about Lictor Shokneir?"

Velenne laughed, but it didn't touch her silver-dusted eyes. "Lictor Shokneir. A graveknight in a cursed castle? Do you suspect *him* in these murders?"

He couldn't tell if her disbelief was genuine. "Indirectly, perhaps. Our investigation suggests he has some involvement in these crimes. Can you think of any reason why he might want hell-spawn hearts?"

"No. I know very little about him, really. I can surmise that the late lictor must have been a thoroughly unpleasant fellow for the gods to curse him with undeath. I also know he had a particular hatred for my house. Of course, lots of people did back then, so that doesn't mean much. Devils! Damnation! Fie upon the Thrice-Damned House of Thrune! Sore losers, the lot of them. But the Order of the Crux was particularly determined about their spittle-flinging. Tiresomely so."

"Is that why the Crux is gone? Because they offended House Thrune?" *Or was it because you wanted what they had?*

She sat back in her chair, smoothing the linen napkin over her lap. "Yes, darling. Isn't that why you're so astonished about those old reports? As a rule, we're not so forgiving to those who plot against us. You're lucky that you chanced across the softest-hearted—or maybe softest-headed—member of my house."

"Was that the only reason?"

Velenne shook her head, parting her lips to say something, but then the first course came in, carried by a liveried manservant who maintained a resolutely formal air. He set silver bowls before each of them and poured an opaque, spicy-smelling broth over the fresh herbs, crumbled white cheese, and toasted croutons that had been laid in artful designs at the bottoms of the bowls. After each bowl was full, he inclined his head correctly and departed, having never said a word or glanced at his master's guest.

"Such gracious service," Velenne murmured, tasting the soup. "The steward's campaign against me continues. I'd complain that he refused to send out any wine, but I've never cared for wine anyway."

"No. I remember. You only ever liked sweet ciders and punches. Much too sweet for me, however much I tried to acquire the taste." Ederras stirred a spoon into his own bowl, momentarily wistful for the easy comfort of those days.

He cleared his throat. "Anyway, you were saying? About the Order of the Crux?"

"I was saying that they were bloody-handed heretics, and that's why they're gone. *Not*, in fact, merely because they offended my house. Although they did." Velenne's gaze was cool and inscrutable through the prickly steam that rose from her soup.

"Do you know what that heresy was?"

"I know what's in the records. I know what the historians of House Thrune claim. But as you appear to have finally discovered for the first time today, my cherished halfwit, what's written is not always what's true."

That night she stayed. Not in the guest room.

Having her there, in his own bed, was a strange thing for Ederras. She'd never visited his family home when they'd known each other before. Back then, he would never have dared to bring Velenne under his parents' roof. Given his position, an unaccompanied female visitor of her age would have caused a minor scandal. In good society, one's paramours were always kept at a respectable remove from one's family name.

That was part of the reason he'd never invited her to the vaneo. The other—and greater—reason for his secrecy, even then, was the nature of those dalliances. Paladins of Iomedae were *not* supposed to hit their lovers.

But Velenne demanded that. She always had. Fighting excited her, and pain inflamed her, and although Ederras didn't pretend to understand what it was in her soul that drove her to such extremes, it had been there for as long as he'd known her. She liked to hurt and be hurt, and her desire was so intense that it ignited his, too.

That night in his vaneo, however, marked something different: the first time Ederras understood both what she was and what she wasn't, and the first time he let that guide what happened between them.

He *wanted* to hurt her. He hated her allegiance to House Thrune, her diabolism, and her penchant for sadism, which was hardly restricted to the bedroom. If they'd met anywhere else, in any other way, Ederras might have tried to kill her—as in fact he had, all those years ago. And she would very probably have tried to kill him, too.

Instead they'd come together as lovers, and the tension between them found flame in other ways. It was tempered, for him, by the discovery of what she'd written after he'd caught her original deception. Velenne had risked herself to show him mercy, however much she tried to shrug off what she'd done. Beneath her cold and bladed edges ran a thread of kindness. He knew that now.

But that didn't entirely extinguish his desire to punish her sins, nor did it remove his unspoken conviction that he deserved the same for accepting her. It made for a strange kind of intimacy, feverish as battle, laced with a tenderness that lacerated.

There *was* tenderness in it, though. Ederras no longer doubted that. Velenne's gentler touches were layered and leaved with cruelty, but he felt them keenly—perhaps more so for the contrast. It wasn't purely violence between them, not anymore.

Afterward, Velenne lay curled beside him, nestled against the side of his chest. She traced idle patterns across his skin, following the lines of the scratches and welts she'd left on him. Appreciating her handiwork, he thought.

Ederras lifted his head, watching her. "Why me?"

"Why what?"

"Why are you here? Why did you come back? Is it really just about tormenting me?"

She clicked her tongue in chastisement, raising herself onto her elbows to regard him more evenly. Her hair tumbled over her shoulders, black in the moonshadows. "Do you always have so many questions of your bedmates?"

"There is no 'always.' There never has been. There's only you."

"Really?" Velenne's eyes widened in surprise. She laughed in delight and disbelief, running a hand along his side. "You *do* flatter me."

"I'm glad you're pleased." Rolling away from her touch, Ederras filled a glass of water at the bedside table. She'd bloodied his lip earlier. The water stung the cut.

"Oh, don't sound so wounded. I meant it. I'm flattered."

"Don't be. It wasn't out of devotion. Quite the opposite. After you betrayed me—"

"But I never did." Velenne reached past the water glass, pressing a finger to his lips. She touched him directly on the cut, splitting it open again with a sharp sting of pain. The note of impish mockery had faded from her tone. Something else shone in her dark eyes, bright as the moonlight that fell through his windows. "You know that now, so remember it. I never did. Even after you stuck a knife in me and left me for dead."

"It was a sword."

"Why yes, so it was. *Much* better than a knife. Do you still have the same one?"

"No. Leave off the absurdity for a moment. I need to know this. Why are you with me?"

"I've answered that question a thousand times," Velenne said, sighing, "and you never seem to hear me. Which makes me wonder why you keep asking."

"Because you never really answer. You dodge and deflect. Why can't you just say it?"

Velenne didn't answer for some time. She plucked the water glass from his hand, drained it, and silently offered it back. When he took it, closing his fingers over hers, the diabolist finally met his eyes again. The armor of cynicism that she showed the world—and that she wore even here, alone with him—slipped away, and for a moment Ederras glimpsed what was underneath.

"Some things are tremendously unwise to say, my love," she murmured. "My loyalties are what they are. What they've always been. I have my house. You have yours. I have my god. You have yours. I admire your passion, your faith, your dedication to your causes . . . but you must surely see that those very same things mean we'll be on opposite sides of the blade eventually. As we were before. What's the point, then, of putting voice to something we can't have?"

He'd never seen Velenne so vulnerable, or so openly longing. This was more than transient desire, more than a game she was playing to entertain herself. The fragility of the moment, and the sense that something great hung in the balance, arrested him.

If he could make her say the words, Ederras thought, it would be real. Words had that power sometimes. If she said it, he could bind her. "So we'll know it was there."

"We already know. Well. *I* already know. You, we have established, are considerably slower." She smiled, a little sadly, and trailed her fingertips along his wrist. Down and up and down again, following the path of his veins. "Of course I care for you, Ederras. I *love* you. I always have. You're the only one I've ever been able to trust entirely, the only one who didn't want something else from me—money, power, prestige. Safety, sometimes. They all fear me, and they all want things, and they're all waiting for the first sign of weakness. Except you.

"You have no idea how rare that is for me. How much of a comfort it is to have one person, just *one,* who would never put a knife in my back to climb a step higher at court. No one like you exists in my world.

"So yes, I came back for you. Of course I came back. I adore you, you great confounding idiot, and you have no prayer of keeping yourself safe in Cheliax. I will protect you as best I'm able, and I will stay with you as long as my position allows. But eventually it will take me from you, or yours will take you from me. We both serve greater masters than ourselves. This is all the happiness we're allowed."

"Lord Kajen Tilernos," Belvadio announced. Pride shone from the steward's voice and puffed his chest a little, despite his best efforts to hide it. A visit from a preeminent lord was a rare occasion at the vaneo, and a considerable honor.

Ederras couldn't remember the last time Vaneo Celverian had been graced by a guest of such importance. His mother had hosted occasionally, but by the time he was old enough to remember anything about those events, she'd lost her stillborn daughter and fallen into her long grief.

After that, the parties stopped. Abello Celverian had seldom hosted anyone other than his dwindling handful of friends for card games and drinking sessions, and since liquor sharpened the old lord's tongue past its normal lacerating edge, he usually ended each of those nights with one fewer friend than he'd had at the beginning. Ederras didn't know as much about Othando's habits, but it hardly seemed likely that his brother, modest to a fault, had been a favorite of the social set.

Lord Tilernos's visit didn't mark a turning point in that pattern, precisely. But some of the servants seemed inclined to interpret it as a promising harbinger.

They might be right. Ederras had been thinking hard about his house's fortunes over the past few days, and more after the past few nights. If he was going to fulfill his obligations as heir, he had to do better.

"When you first asked me to go through the church's archives, I must confess, I didn't expect to find much," Lord Tilernos said. He'd worn a plain riding outfit of cambric and leather, unadorned except for a light cloak in his house colors of purple and silver and a clasp worked with the Tilernos shield-and-blades crest. The relaxed nature of his dress signified a friendly visit, not a formal one, and added to the honor being done them. "Not that I minded, of course. It was a welcome chance to relive some of the intrigues of my youth. The spice of mystery, all that. But I wasn't especially convinced that anything would come of it."

"I wasn't, either. My great-grandfather was a secretive man. So was Ferdieu Oberigo, apparently. They didn't tell anyone much of anything, and they wrote down even less. It seems the march on Citadel Gheisteno attracted a stoic sort." Ederras led the lord into the lower study.

Gone were the too-warm blankets and insipid books with which Belvadio had tried to bore Velenne out earlier. The steward had replaced them with more appropriate furnishings. He'd unlocked the liquor cabinet, too.

"It did. But your intuition was correct: a crusade of that size, involving that many disparate forces, doesn't get organized without *some* recordkeeping. And those records were in the Dorjanala's archives." Lord Tilernos settled into an armchair. He took a paper-wrapped bundle out from under his cloak and set it on a nearby table. "As was a recitation of the crimes for which Lictor Shokneir was condemned."

"Excellent." That was one of the things he had most hoped Lord Tilernos would find. "What did it say?"

"Not very much, actually. Rote recitations of 'heresy' and 'offenses against the crown.' They were accused and convicted of violating the Measure and the Chain, and of subverting the Hellknight code of 'order, discipline, and mercilessness' to suit their own needs rather than the strict letter of the law. Understandable enough, if abstract. But there's no detail as to what the Crux actually *did*. Odd, given the recordkeepers' enthusiasm for recording all their murders." Lord Tilernos tapped the paper-wrapped packet. "I brought you a copy. Most of that is the list of their victims' names. Hundreds of them. The ones I could identify were mostly hellspawn. But beyond that, it's silent. There are no details beyond the names of the crimes. No mention of any devilheart chain, or cells full of bodies without hearts, or any of the other things you mentioned."

"Peculiar." The Dorjanala, Iomedae's largest temple in Westcrown, was one of the few repositories of information in the city where Ederras had thought they'd have a fair chance of finding unedited records. While the Rack Hellknights and the official historians of House Thrune were prone to constantly revising their accounts to reflect the political winds of the day, the Iomedaeans still believed in making—and maintaining—as complete and impartial a record as they could.

Given that Lictor Shokneir had been an outspoken and vicious enemy, it should have been in House Thrune's interest for the Iomedaeans to keep a detailed litany of his offenses. No one could doubt that the Lady of Valor's servants would be truthful in their telling, and the horrors of what the Crux had done could only make House Thrune look better for standing against them. There was no reason for Cheliax's ruling powers to force Iomedae's faithful into silence. Not about that.

So why wasn't that information in the Dorjanala?

"There were a number of such oddities," Lord Tilernos agreed. "Another is that what few records I found of the Crux's membership didn't list any positions along with the names. No distinctions drawn between even armigers and Hellknights, let alone between officers and the rank and file. The only ones who had their positions listed were the Master of Blades, the paravicar, and, of course, Lictor Shokneir himself."

"Any useful information in that?"

"Not especially. It's what you would expect. Most of their members were either foundlings raised by the Hellknights or scions of the noble houses. The Master of Blades was Behrion Khollarix, and the paravicar was Corellia Leroung. Neither of them was noted for anything else in their careers, as far as I could tell from the records in the Dorjanala. Only this."

Ederras nodded. Khollarix and Leroung were among the old noble lineages, and both had been much more successful in navigating the turbulence of Chelish politics than his own family had. House Khollarix remained prominent in Westcrown and maintained holdings across Cheliax. House Leroung had soared even higher: it was among the leading families of Egorian and had placed influential members in high places across the continent.

Most noble families, if they could, sent members into the various Hellknight orders. It gave them a certain amount of insight and influence in the orders' doings—which was virtually impossible to obtain otherwise where Hellknights were concerned—and the orders were glad to receive recruits who'd already been trained by the best possible tutors in spell- and swordplay. There was nothing unusual about the fact that members of Houses Khollarix and Leroung had stood high in the Order of the Crux. The only real surprise was that Lictor Shokneir hadn't been of noble birth himself.

Lord Tilernos paused, watching Ederras for a moment. "Speaking of names, your great-grandfather's came up. In an entirely different context, of course."

"Oh?"

"The Dorjanala keeps a list of all the knights who serve Iomedae in Westcrown. The records include each knight's prominent deeds. Their squires, too, at least if they're nobly born or otherwise noteworthy." The older lord hesitated again, uncharacteristically cautious. "Kelvax's name was in the record. So were his squires.'"

"Is one of those squires in the city?" If so, and the squire was still alive, that might provide another useful avenue to investigate.

"No. One of them was Corellia Leroung."

"I see." So his great-grandfather had marched on his former squire. Not, perhaps, as grievous as going to battle against one's own child, but close. A knight wasn't merely responsible for teaching a squire to handle arms and armor. He was supposed to instill the values and virtues of chivalry, shaping the youth into a champion of the faith.

In Corellia Leroung, it seemed, his great-grandfather had failed. Profoundly. As paravicar of the Crux, she would have commanded all arcane and divine spellcasters in her order. Any magical contributions to their crimes would have been hers, or undertaken at her direction. Given what he knew of the Crux's deeds, Ederras guessed that those would have been no small atrocities. "Do you suppose that's why he went? To absolve himself of that dishonor?"

"I would have," Lord Tilernos said. "Wouldn't you?"

"Yes. I suppose I'd have to." If one of his junior officers at the Worldwound, someone he had personally trained and promoted, had betrayed his comrades and gone over to the demons' side . . . then yes, Ederras would have felt responsible for correcting that wrong. Even across the distance of decades, he felt a ripple of Kelvax's shame. "No wonder he never spoke of it."

"It wouldn't really have been his fault, but no one could be proud of that. Still, Kelvax did what he had to do. He joined the march. You shouldn't feel that this brings any dishonor to your name."

"I don't. I'm just sad for him. It couldn't have been easy." Ederras paused reflectively, then remembered himself and turned a hand to the silver bell that would call Belvadio. "Forgive my poor manners. Might I offer you anything?"

Lord Tilernos shook his head slightly at the bell, smiling. "Too early for brandy, and I've had all the tea I need for the morning. But if you're inclined to humor an old man's presumption, I'd welcome a receptive ear."

"You could never be guilty of presumption."

"I'm afraid you're mistaken about that." Lord Tilernos tipped his chin at the doorway, casting a meaningful glance at the stairs that led up to the vaneo's second floor. "Word has it that you've been entertaining a guest recently."

Ederras inclined his head, trying to ignore the heat that crept up his collar. He was glad Velenne had already left for the day, conducting her own researches on graveknights and tactics that might serve against them. "Lady Velenne. Yes."

"She is worthy of her family name." Which was, Ederras knew, as explicit a warning as even Lord Tilernos could make in open company without risking accusations of treason.

"Maybe not as much as I'd thought before."

Lord Tilernos fixed him with a penetrating stare. "Yes, I suppose she might have convinced you of that. And I suppose you're still young enough to want to believe it. But innocents don't have devils walking at their heels, and the creature that follows her is no mere imp."

"I know."

"Then, if you'll pardon my bluntness, what are you *doing*?"

Ederras ran a hand through his hair. There was no hope of concealing his flush any longer. He got up, took a step toward the liquor cabinet, and then thought better of it and sat back down. "Neither my father nor my uncle was a good steward of this house. My lord father is a small and bitter man, and uncle Stelhan just . . . left. Othando might have been able to revive our ailing fortunes, but he never had the chance. Our line is nearly at an end. I want to do better. I *have* to do better. I have an obligation to the family, to our servants. To Westcrown."

"You're not going to serve any of them by handing them over to House Thrune." Compassion tempered the lord's tone, but his conviction was unwavering.

"I don't intend to. But neither do I have the skills to keep them safe myself. The courts, the opera, these games the lords and ladies play with poisoned words and daggered smiles—those aren't battles I know how to fight. Velenne does. It's *easy* for her. It's natural. That's what she was born to do. One of the things I learned at the Worldwound was that a wise commander knows when to assign tasks to operatives who can do what he can't. Another was that a good commander can win loyalty from the unlikeliest recruits. Not always. Not from everyone. I'm not naive enough to think that. But sometimes. It can be done."

"So you're going to try to . . . to what? To treat Velenne Thrune like some cattle thief shipped out to Mendev?" Lord Tilernos shook his head in mystification. "I don't know whether to applaud your audacity or cringe at your misplaced trust, my friend."

"I don't think it *is* misplaced," Ederras said. *Not if what she said was true.* He held up a hand to forestall the lord's protest. "In any case, I need her. I agree with you: she's no innocent. But no innocent would be able to lead a great house in Cheliax. And a woman with a devil at her heels might."

19

THE COST OF HUMANITY

SECHEL

Y ou disobey."

Every syllable of that sepulchral voice sent a drumbeat of fear along Sechel's bones. The words didn't come from the shrouded figure in the blackened armor standing on the balcony before her. They emanated up from the stones of Citadel Gheisteno, rumbling beneath her feet like the low growls of an approaching earthquake. *Anger me and be crushed.*

She was glad for the hood that concealed her disquiet, and gladder yet for the years of training that had taught her to keep her voice cold and her hands steady even while terror was yammering in her brain. "I'm not one of your underlings. I don't *have* to obey. If you want my continued cooperation, I need to know more. I don't work blind."

Another rumble sounded from the castle's depths. That one might have been laughter, inexorable as an avalanche. "You killed blind."

"Killing's different." Dealing out death was easy. Even this kind, with the devil-fanged chain and the jeweled hearts and the peculiar focus on hellspawn, was the same game. The bodies just looked a little different when she was done.

Sechel didn't ask questions about killings because she didn't care. What was someone else's life to her? But her own . . . "If you want me to play the broken-winged bird, then I want to know why.

What's so important about these three that you want me to lure them up to the castle? Why not just kill them?"

"Could you do that so easily?"

"Yes." *Maybe.* Sechel had studied her targets carefully, as she always did. The paladin would be easy. He was living in the vaneo where she'd killed his brother, and he'd done nothing to improve its security. That one would be as simple as a knife while he slept.

The other two might be harder. The Hellknight was staying in Taranik House, which offered no easy paths to her target. The building was secure, and the Hellknights who guarded it couldn't be intimidated or bribed. Sechel would have to hit her on the street, and she'd never seen the hellspawn without her armor outside.

A knife might not get through all that steel. An explosion, maybe. Or poison. It would be difficult, but not impossible.

The Thrune woman might be a problem. Sechel disliked taking assignments on wizards. Protective enchantments made her job harder. Wealthy wizards could purchase all manner of unpleasant surprises, and no one was wealthier than House Thrune.

Worse was that dog. As soon as she'd realized the dog belonged to the Thrune woman, Sechel had examined him through the lens that she used to break illusions and study her target's enchantments. What she'd seen had made her revise her estimation of the target substantially.

Not just difficult. That *was* impossible. Even for her.

But the Thrune woman had been sending the dog out to Rego Cader and spending her nights with the paladin in the vaneo, which made her potentially easy again. If Sechel could catch her target alone, without the dog, she had a better-than-fair chance of success.

Given enough time, Sechel was confident she could kill all three. People made mistakes. They always made mistakes. All she had to do was wait until one came.

Baiting them, however, was a very different game. One she hadn't played as often, and didn't know as well. One where the risks were substantially greater.

Capture, torture, death. Maybe not in that order. Maybe not the last one at all. She knew the stories about the Thrune woman's tastes.

"Why do you want them?" she asked again, resisting the urge to shiver. The wind was chill on the balcony. Summertime in the mountains wasn't supposed to be this cold, but summer never touched Citadel Gheisteno.

Lictor Shokneir turned away from his view of the night-shrouded mountains. His burning eyes scoured her soul. Venomous shadows veiled him like mist, clinging to his tattered cloak and swirling about his ironclad heels, but it never obscured the graveknight's fiery, fanatic gaze.

Sechel wanted to quail before that crushing stare, as she always did. Instead, she willed her spine upright and her muscles slack, counting her breaths to force them slow. Her posture was all deception—inside, terror tightened her vision to pinpoint acuity and set her heart racing three times faster than her breaths would show—but she made herself do it. Every time. *I'm not your underling.*

She could never tell if it worked. Nothing showed of the graveknight's face beneath his skull-crowned helm. Sometimes, through the slits of his visor, she glimpsed taut, dead white flesh around his burning eyes. Sometimes she saw charred black skin, cracking over bloody muscle. Mostly it was just shadow, empty and amorphous, and those fiery eyes blazing through the steel-barred darkness like an inferno in the night.

"The hellspawn," he said, making the word sound like a curse, "wears the armor of the Scourge."

Sechel waited for further explanation. When none was forthcoming, she made herself shrug. "And?"

Lictor Shokneir's eyes flared in fury. "The Scourge claims to be the true keeper of the Measure and the Chain. The Scourge presumes to declare us anathema. Yet who are they? Weaklings. Fools who refuse to correct violations in the natural order. Whimpering lapdogs of thrice-damned House Thrune. That one of their own is a hellspawn, and is serving a devil-binder in Westcrown, proves it. Through them, I will show the world that the Scourge was blind to the treachery of the tainted in its midst and powerless to defend against it. That *we* were correct in shouting the truths the Scourge was too soft to let Cheliax hear."

Sechel absorbed the lictor's anger without answer. Deciphering the graveknight's outbursts was like trying to read the allegory in a church window after vandals had smashed it to bits. Once that might have been brilliance, but all that was left now were splinters of sharp-edged madness.

She knew that the Order of the Scourge had been the leading force in crushing the Hellknights of the Crux, and that their dispute had arisen from some disagreement about the Thrune Ascendancy, which seemed to lie at the heart of every quarrel in Cheliax. She knew, too, that the lictor's hatred for hellspawn burned nearly as brightly as his enmity toward House Thrune. None of the rest of it, however, made much sense.

Thrune, hellspawn, Order of the Scourge . . . the answer was in there somewhere. She could puzzle it out later, once she got away from that disconcerting stare. "What about the paladin?"

"His ancestors thought they walked on the side of the righteous. As does he. They were wrong, and they wronged me. I wish for him to know the failure of his line. Before I take my vengeance through his corpse."

"Sounds pleasant."

The lictor's gauntlets creaked, shedding flakes of char, as his hands tightened into fists. "You will bring them here."

"What are you going to do with them? And why does it have to be here?"

"I will take the hellspawn pretender's heart. I will kill the other two. Their deaths will serve to remedy the damage their ancestors caused. I want them to see it, and hear it, and *know,* from my own words, why they must die."

And you can't leave the citadel. Sechel nodded. So it was revenge, then. She understood that. This was a game she knew how to play after all.

Silently, she calculated the risks. Capture, torture, death. Maybe not in that order. Maybe not the last one at all.

Then she weighed the price Lictor Shokneir was willing to pay. *Humanity.*

"I'll do it," she said.

20

MARCH INTO MEMORY

JHERAAL

We're being baited." Jheraal stared down at the sleek, steel-ribbed helm of a Rack Hellknight. It lay atop a folded cloak and a pair of crossed gauntlets, arranged like a battlefield memorial on a cairn of stones in Rego Cader.

After nearly two weeks of silence, during which none of them had found any leads fresher than what lay in the yellowing pages of the Dorjanala's archive books, Vhaeros had finally alerted them to a discovery in the Dead Sector. Velenne had summoned the other two, and her dog had led them to a cairn outside the ruined bathhouse where they'd found the second group of heart-stripped hellspawn.

The armor on that cairn, Jheraal felt certain, had belonged to Hakur.

She had no real reason to think that. Within the same order, one Hellknight's armor looked like another's, barring distinctive adaptations like the hollow slots in her helm that cradled her horns. Nothing about the cloak, helm, or gauntlets distinguished them from pieces that might have belonged to any other Hellknight of the Rack.

But she was sure of it all the same. Those were Hakur's. His killer had stolen them, used them to lead her captives into Rego Cader, and then left them here.

A handful of loose pages fluttered under the crossed gauntlets. They hadn't been out there for long. It had rained yesterday, but the papers were dry. Vhaeros had probably found them within hours of their placement.

They'd been that close to the killer, and they'd missed their chance.

"Bait," Jheraal said again.

"Yes, I believe that's obvious." Velenne swept a jeweled hand toward the papers trapped under the gauntlets. "Do you wish to read the message we've been left?"

With a grunt of wordless assent, Jheraal lifted the helm, pushed the gauntlets aside, and picked up the sheets.

There were three pages. She read each of them aloud. The first said: "I won't be needing these anymore. You can take them, with my thanks, back to Citadel Rivad. There's an empty box in the library that they should fit nicely."

Jheraal's grip tightened. Inhaling, she smoothed the crumpled paper and shuffled that message to the back.

The second one, written in the same scratchy hand, said: "I bought a few new toys recently, but they're already boring me. I'll keep them just a little while longer, and then I suppose I'll say farewell. Come to Citadel Gheisteno if you care. Don't dawdle, or they'll look just like your servants."

The third page was written in a different hand. Its crisp clarity marked it as a professional scribe's work. It was a bill of sale, duly recording that Sechel of Citadel Gheisteno had purchased seven slaves from Calphex Redhammer for use without restriction, had paid all taxes and tariffs on the sale, and was now legal owner of the seven specified persons.

Jheraal read the names aloud. She listed them with gravity, as she would have recited the names of the honored dead after battle, but no one recognized any of them until she came to the names of the buyer and seller.

Then Velenne stirred. "Calphex Redhammer?"

"You know him?"

"Of him. He's a slave dealer in Nidal. Hellspawn. Most of his trade is also in hellspawn."

"I could have guessed that last part." Jheraal reshuffled the pages into their original order and put them back on the cairn, using Hakur's helm to weight them down again. She didn't want to hold them any longer than she had to.

"Mostly they're children." Velenne's lips pursed. "He recruits runaways from the slums of Cheliax. The hungry, the desperate, the hopeful. He gains their trust, lures them across the border, and then puts them into chains. There's little demand for such slaves in Cheliax, and one cannot simply kidnap children off the streets and sell them at whim. But in Nidal, the children aren't citizens and have no rights, and any living thing that can suffer has value. So that's where he sells them."

Seven hellspawn children. Seven helpless *children.* They were being used to taunt her, and the assassin had left her with no legal recourse. *Bait.*

Jheraal snarled. The display of open anger was untoward. It was a failure in her self-control, and she knew it. She snarled anyway. "We have to go to Citadel Gheisteno."

"Which is, of course, precisely what our assassin wants. Sechel, I presume."

"It doesn't matter. We have to go."

"I agree," Ederras said. He looked to Velenne. He didn't move, but she canted her head toward him, softening minutely, as if he'd touched her. Something had changed between those two in the past few weeks. There was a warmth in them that hadn't existed earlier. But a tension, too. "Can you take us there?"

The diabolist snorted, crossing her arms. "I *can,* yes. That in no way implies that I think I *should.* It would be purely idiotic to go there under ordinary circumstances. To go when you know there's a trap waiting—that is stupid beyond all words. Even for you."

"We can't just leave them."

Velenne stared at the paladin. "Yes, we can. I'm very good at that. I am an *expert* at abandoning the helpless. Please believe me when I tell you that it's the easiest thing in the world. Hardly any work at all. If you didn't know better, you might think you weren't even doing anything."

"Very droll. We still have to go. You told me once that you admired my passion. My faith. This is what those oaths *mean*. We can't abandon those children in the citadel. If you meant what you said, then help me."

"Had I known you were prone to throwing my compliments back like weapons, I would never have given you any. A lesson for another time." Velenne sighed, immensely resigned, and flicked a hand in a wave of surrender. "Fine. If you're so determined to kill yourself, I suppose I might as well go along to watch the screams."

They didn't leave immediately. Ederras wanted to get his armor back from the smith who had been repairing the dents and tears he'd accrued in Mendev. Velenne needed to prepare her spells, and mentioned something vague about collecting on a few debts that she and Vhaeros were owed around the city. She hadn't explained how her dog owned debts, and no one had asked, because neither of the others really wanted to know.

Jheraal went back to Taranik House.

She didn't need the time to prepare herself. Not as the others had. Hellknights were expected to be ready for everything from escaped fiends to city riots at a moment's notice, and Jheraal was no exception. She could have marched on Citadel Gheisteno the minute they'd found those messages.

But she was glad she didn't have to.

Alone in her spare little room, Jheraal unlocked the box where she kept Indrath's letters. There hadn't been any new ones in the past two weeks, and only one since Indrath received the book. Probably that meant her daughter was busy with her studies, nothing more—the teachers at Citadel Demain were nearly as hard on their foundlings as they were on the armigers—but she wondered. She couldn't help but wonder.

Are you well? Healthy? Happy? Safe?

There was no way to know. Days of hard riding separated Jheraal from Citadel Demain. If it had been a part of her official duties, she could have sent a message by magic, or perhaps even requisitioned a wizard's services to teleport, but there was no reason for a Hellknight to take an unexcused leave from an investigation to visit a foundling girl.

Not even if that girl was her daughter. Not even if she might never see her again.

At least, Jheraal supposed, there was some cold comfort in the knowledge that this would be true even if she'd acknowledged Indrath as her own. The Hellknight code was hard on anyone's family. She wasn't special there.

And maybe it was better this way. If Jheraal failed and fell in Citadel Gheisteno, Indrath wouldn't lose a mother, just a friend. Not so devastating a loss, really. Nothing that would break her.

Jheraal could consider that another protection. Maybe.

She breathed a sigh through her teeth. It had been a long time since she'd doubted whether she would come through a mission alive. She trained as hard as any Hellknight—harder than most, really, to make up for being hellspawn—but in practice she was an investigator, not a warrior. Mostly she tracked down murderers and malcontents, and mostly the fight went out of them as soon as she kicked down their doors.

This was different. This wasn't going to be a hard knock and an easy arrest. This was going to be a fight every step of the way.

But there was a crime at the core of it, and Jheraal had her duty.

She lifted the lid of the box, breathing in the familiar scent of sandalwood, aging paper, and old wax. The letters were well worn from reading and rereading, their paper soft as baby's blankets in her hands. The little buttons of candle wax that Indrath loved to use for seals were brittle and dry, crumbling away in hard chunks no matter how carefully Jheraal tried to preserve them.

Tomorrow, she would put aside all sentiment, wrap herself in steel, and march against an evil greater than anything she'd ever faced.

Tonight, for a little while, she could read.

A week later, they gathered on the grounds of Vaneo Celverian. Ederras was resplendent in the silvered plate of a crusader, Jheraal grim in her Hellknight armor. Velenne wore a dress of black leather paneled with dark chain, accompanied with enough jewelry to suit a royal wedding. Dark pearls in silver filigree swung from her ears, rings glimmered on both her hands, and an ornate choker with an enormous black sapphire wrapped around her throat. Only the suite of wands banded in crimson leather on her hip indicated that her attire wasn't purely ornamental.

"Have the two of you done any research on graveknights?" the diabolist asked, one eyebrow lifted as she looked from Ederras to Jheraal. "In particular, Lictor Shokneir and his servants? They'll be formidable foes. According to the accounts of those few who've entered the citadel and escaped—or more likely been released— they're impervious to several different types of elemental energy, and all but impossible to harm without powerful spells and enchantments. And even if we defeat them, we have no prayer of truly killing them. All graveknights are arguably deathless, as their spirits are bound to their armor . . . but the Hellknights of the Crux are cursed beyond that. They cannot be destroyed by any mortal hand. Slain, they will rise again within days. And, of course, they have an army of undead at their command."

"I'm aware," Jheraal said. She dug the bottom of her heavy shield into the grass and rested a gauntleted hand atop it. "Are you trying to talk us out of going? It's a little late for that."

"No. No, I'm resigned to letting our charming champion of Iomedae march bravely into doom. I understand he's made a career of it. What I'm wondering is why, if you had any idea of what we'll be facing, the two of you arrived alone. Do we have no Hellknights marching with us? No crusaders clad in faith and glory? This is terribly disappointing. Also stupid. It took the entire Order of the Scourge to bring down Citadel Gheisteno last time, I'll remind you, and *they* had allies. We, by contrast, are three people and a dog."

Jheraal lifted her visor, meeting Velenne's mockery with a flat stare. She *had* asked for aid, from both the Rack and the Scourge, and had received nothing from either. "The Hellknight orders feel that this would be a poor use of their forces. Lictor Shokneir remains imprisoned in his citadel, which is isolated in desolation and poses no threat to any civilized realm. Sending Hellknights against him for the sake of seven hellspawn children who may or may not actually be there would be foolish. They'd lose far more lives than they saved, even assuming the whole thing isn't simply a false trail concocted by our murderer. Therefore they will send no one."

"How unexpectedly sensible. I'm delighted the Hellknight orders are led by such rational souls." Velenne turned her acid little smile onto Ederras. "And you, dearest? Your people tend to be much worse at math. Throwing away dozens to save seven is exactly the kind of idiocy they love, especially if the dozens are well trained and the seven are worthless—I'm sorry, 'innocents.' So why aren't they here?"

"I didn't ask." Ederras pushed his own visor up. He seemed untroubled by her nettling. "Many Iomedaeans in Westcrown would have come, if I'd asked. But it would have been folly. Not one of them would stand a chance against Lictor Shokneir or his lieutenants, and I won't lead soldiers to suicide just because they're brave enough to go."

"But you'll lead us? I'm touched you value me so highly."

"It's not suicide for us. We're not just three people and a dog, Velenne. You know that as well as I do. Each of us has fought foes most of Westcrown can't even imagine. We're blessed—if you can call it that—with that skill and experience. We can do this."

"I do love watching you believe that." The diabolist shook her head in resignation, pearl earrings gleaming through her hair. "Please pause and reflect that I brought *my* army. In our hour of need, the only allies that marched with us were the devils of Hell. I would like both of you to remember that, should we survive this. We didn't get the Hellknights and we didn't get the virtuous crusaders. But the devils?" She tapped the scroll case buckled next to the wands on her hip. "They obey."

"I'm profoundly reassured," Jheraal said. "Let's go."

"Attend." Velenne raised her hands, beginning her invocation. At its conclusion, a pane of darkness opened in the air before her, wavering in the air like a curtain of deep gray silk. "The shadowlands can be dangerous. Stay close."

Jheraal nodded, lowering the visor of her helm. Clasping hands with the others, she walked through the wizard's gate into the dark.

They passed through the shadowlands swiftly, crossing a starless nightscape that reflected the real world in darkened, distorted form. Mountains rolled across the distance, their peaks tapering indistinctly into sky. Rivers swam between the hills like shining ebon snakes, sleek and predatory and strangely alive within their gray-grassed banks.

And then, too soon, the cindery bulk of the citadel rose before them, solid and immovable in a land of mist and shadow.

"I cannot bring us into Citadel Gheisteno," Velenne said. "There is a magic around it that blocks my spell. This is as far as the shadows will take us. Are you ready?"

Ederras slid his shield onto his arm. The golden wings painted on its face, bereft of sunlight to reflect, were dulled to bronze in the shadowlands. "Yes."

Jheraal remained silent. A hand of iron had closed about her core, allowing nothing more to pass. She knew this feeling well: the touch of dryness at the back of her throat, the unnatural acuteness of her sight. Time seemed to slow around her, allowing her to see and feel everything with an intensity that thrilled across her marrow.

"Walk with me into light." Velenne took their hands again, and the shadows fell into brightness as she carried them back to the world.

One moment, they were standing amid a vale of sourceless shadows that rose into half-real shapes. The next, they were in the Menador Mountains, a crisp breeze blowing from the far-off snow-caps and a mantle of dark green pines, almost black, stretching across the slopes below. There was a hint of blue to the overcast sky, and the shrubs that grew between the mossy rocks around them showed spidery red veins in the center of each green leaf. The presence of brighter colors in the world told Jheraal that they were near or in Molthune. In the heartlands of Nidal, under the oppressive influence of the Midnight Lord, colors often seemed to drain to gray.

Citadel Gheisteno stood to the northeast. A natural chasm, spanned by a slender thread of stone, separated the fortress from the surrounding mountains on three sides. The fourth backed against a forbiddingly steep peak that loomed above the citadel and cast it into deep, unchanging shadow. Both the fortress and its surroundings were blackened and charred as if they had survived an incalculable fire.

The Order of the Crux's stronghold had no visible weaknesses. Its towers looked out upon all sides, allowing its archers to strike down anyone who had the temerity to approach. The curtain walls were high, thick, and impregnable; there were no usable positions where siege engines could be mounted effectively around them. Short of an assault by a full company of battle wizards, or the devastating aerial fury of a flight of dragons, Jheraal couldn't imagine how anyone had taken Citadel Gheisteno by force.

Not when there had been archers in those towers and standing along those parapets, at least. Not when there had been armed and armored Hellknights on the walls and behind the gates, ready to lay down their lives to fight back invaders.

As she looked up at the fire-scarred fortress, however, Jheraal saw no defenders anywhere. The gatehouses were desolate, the battlements empty. No lights burned in the windows. Five flagpoles rose from the citadel's towers, but none of them flew a banner. Three stood barren. The other two held burned black rags, so weighted with soot that they hung lifeless in the mountain wind.

"They're waiting," Ederras said, starting toward the bridge. Vhaeros loped alongside him, sure-footed on the mountain rocks. Velenne followed more cautiously, using her hands to steady herself along the path.

No guard towers watched over the near end of the bridge. Huge, ragged scars in the mountainside showed where they had been torn out to the foundations, but whatever magic had brought back Citadel Gheisteno didn't seem to reach this far. The chasm beneath the bridge was full of roiling dark mist. Not white, as natural fog should be, but an opaque black that seemed to carry the viewer out of the reality of the waking world into a land of nightmare.

Near their end of the span, the bridge was an unremarkable gray, the same color as the mountainside itself. As the bridge neared the fortress, the scattered specks of black dotting its stone thickened into a pointillist storm of darkness. From the halfway point until it reached the citadel's foot, the bridge was entirely black.

A flare of magic beside her told Jheraal that Velenne had summoned some protective enchantment to ward herself. The aura expanded to include Vhaeros, settling into his coarse gray fur with a shimmer. Without breaking pace, the diabolist and her dog went on.

They reached the bridge. The wind blew hard across the unprotected stone, stinging Jheraal's eyes through the gaps of her visor. Vhaeros's nails scratched behind her as the dog lowered himself against its push.

She came to the first wavering line of black specks. They were skulls, human skulls, coated in soot and embedded in the bridge like ornamental stones. All seemed to have been blasted by flame. The holes of their nostrils were charred, their craniums were cracked, and many were missing teeth that had exploded from the force of the heat they'd suffered.

As Jheraal stepped over the nearest skull, its eyes ignited. Spectral green fire, virulent as burning venom, lit in its hollow sockets.

I see you.

Jheraal froze. She took a breath. Walked past.

I see your sins.

Another voice that time. A second skull, ten feet away, had lit as she passed it. This voice sounded female, somehow, whereas the other struck her as male, even though neither of them made any actual sound. Their words reverberated in her mind, booming within her skull. Closing her ears would have made no matter. The dead didn't really speak.

She ignored the second voice as she had ignored the first. But she could not ignore the third, for it drove an icy shard of remembered vision into her mind along with its words.

I see your weakness.

And Jheraal saw herself, as through outside eyes, wearing the enchanted hood that had let her pretend to be human for a time. She saw herself laughing in the sunlight, rolling in the sweet grass with the boy who'd become Indrath's father. Who had never seen her real face, never known her real name.

I see your thefts.

Another voice. Another fragment of memory. This time Jheraal saw herself, pregnant at seventeen, stealing toward a farmhouse in the dead of night. The farmer's daughter had left her wash drying on the lines after dark, and Jheraal wanted one of her blankets. She had nothing so fine of her own, and no money to buy a blanket that might be warm and soft enough for her child. So she had stolen what she needed, and then the winds of chance had blown her away, and she had never repaid that debt.

I see your lies.

Jheraal at eighteen, barefoot and desperate outside the gates of Citadel Demain, holding a tiny girl baby swaddled in that stolen blanket. It was filthy and threadbare by then, but still the warmest thing she owned. She had given Indrath that blanket, her name, and a hope of a better future . . . and nothing else. No truths, because truths would destroy that hope. She had given her daughter a shield of lies instead.

The Hellknight came to a stop on the bridge, brought to bay by the fiery skulls and the memories they wrenched from her past. Tears ran freely down her cheeks under her horned helm. Pride kept her from retreating, but she couldn't go on. *I'm a disgrace to the Scourge. I've never been strong enough. I've never been worthy.*

A hand closed on her wrist. She didn't feel it at first, but eventually the tugging became too strong to ignore, and Jheraal looked to see what it was. If it had been Lictor Shokneir himself, in that moment, she would have surrendered without a fight. She wasn't worthy to fight.

It wasn't. It was Velenne, her temples damp with sweat, her voice frayed to the edge of breaking. Green flames, stretched into starved crescents, reflected from her choker's black sapphire. "Go on. You must go on. Follow Vhaeros. Ignore everything else. He can guide us across. None of this affects him."

"How—"

"Vhaeros is a devil. It's not in his nature to go against law. Ever. Not because he's stronger or better or truer. Because he has no free will, and thus he has no capacity to sin." Velenne's smile was small, tight, and bitter. "That's what this is, you realize. A showing that none of us can live up to the Crux's measure. That we're all failures against their ideal of perfection—because you and I *do* have free will. Because we're not devils or angels, but people. And people do not exist in absolutes. *That's* the flaw they find so abhorrent. Choice, and the capacity to err. Freedom, and the chance of failure."

Cracks in the stone where flowers might bloom. Jheraal had read that somewhere. She couldn't remember where. It didn't matter.

The Crux's skulls had tried to make those cracks her greatest sin, and indeed many of her life's regrets were linked to those early years . . . but she would never have traded any of them. Not for anything. Not if it would have cost her daughter.

Jheraal looked across the bridge. The dog was there, his gray fur backlit with green fire. Inhuman. Infernal. But untouched.

She fixed her eyes on the devil, and she went on.

21

THE DEAD GATES

EDERRAS

The dead were waiting for them on the other side of the bridge. They didn't cross the line drawn by the skulls' fire. Citadel Gheisteno's defenders stayed in a mass outside the flames, which gave Ederras time to both recover from the gauntlet of bruising memories he'd walked through and to study the foes awaiting them.

Skeletons clad in rusting armor stood in the shadow of the citadel's gates. They weren't drawn up into ranks, just clumped together in a mob. Many were missing ribs, jaws, or entire limbs. Dented helmets, loose without skin or hair to pad them, hung lopsided on a few of their heads. Other skeletons showed the bare dirty bone of their skulls, sometimes intact, sometimes cracked open by a killing blow. A few, rising like islands from the sea of dead, sat astride lifeless horses.

Most of them were human, or close to it, and most were dressed in scraps of leather and rust-gnawed steel, all at least sixty years out of date. They wore leather, chainmail, or tattered, quilted padding with blind white worms peeping from the filth-filled pockets.

Not one of the skeletons wore Hellknight plate. *These are the invaders, not the defenders.*

But behind them, two hulking forms did.

They came out from the portcullis side by side, silent and enormous in black-enameled plate and charred, crumbling cloaks.

One carried an immense greatsword, the other a wickedly spiked flail. Their skull-crowned helms towered over the skeletons around them, and the mass of walking bones parted where they passed.

Ederras drew his sword. White fire engulfed the blade as Iomedae's blessing awoke in the steel. Beside him, Jheraal swung her shield in a slow arc to loosen her muscles. Velenne whispered her invocations behind him, brushing her fingers across the back of his cuirass. A moment after her nails clicked against the silvered steel, Ederras felt new power surge through his body. With her magic behind him, he was faster, stronger, deadlier.

He strode out to meet the dead.

They surged toward him, enveloping him in waves of mindless hunger. Finger bones scratched at Ederras's breastplate and tugged at his elbows. The shards of broken swords stabbed at him, but their blows were so clumsy that the skeletons slapped him with the flats as often as they scraped the edges over his mail. Fleshless faces surrounded him, their dead jaws slack and clattering. In the chaos, he could barely keep track of Jheraal, although she loomed like an iron mountain at his side. He couldn't see Vhaeros or Velenne at all.

Ederras didn't even try to fight with finesse. The arts of feint and parry had no purpose in this horde. Instead he swept his sword through wide horizontal arcs, like a peasant cutting wheat, and bones tumbled around him in a grisly harvest.

Even so, there were too many. The skeletons grabbed at his shield, hurled themselves into his body, clawed at his armor with unthinking hands. The sheer weight of them forced him back, preventing him from carving his way into the center of the horde.

Jheraal was better able to withstand them. The Hellknight was stronger than he was, and more accustomed to using the bulk of her armor as its own weapon in battle. They weren't pushing her back. She was pushing them.

"Cut a path for me!" Ederras called. "To the center! I need to get to the center!"

The Hellknight's horned helm dipped in a nod. She bulled through the press of bones, slamming skeletons aside bodily with her shield and crushing any stragglers under her mace. A path opened, fleetingly, in her wake.

Ederras took it. He angled his stance to protect Jheraal from retaliatory attacks while the Hellknight continued her dogged march into the heart of the skeletons' ranks. Beyond his sword's reach, the horde closed in again, cutting off any chance of retreat to the bridge.

It didn't matter. He had no intention of retreating.

A few steps more and they were in the swarm's center, battered and assailed on all sides. The hulking Crux Hellknights waded through the press to reach them, smashing any of the lesser undead that got in the way.

Ederras waited until the enemy Hellknights were almost within reach, and then raised his sword to the heavens in prayer.

Iomedae's glory filled him in a rush that ignited his soul. Golden light erupted around him, tearing through the massed skeletons in a coruscating nova. Bones exploded into dust as the divine fire seized them. Rotted leather and rusting mail, unable to protect their wearers from the Inheritor's wrath, burst apart into flying scraps. The force of his prayer leveled the horde, devastating all but a few wobbling stragglers at its fringes.

In the suddenly empty space, the two Crux Hellknights stood alone. Dark smoke seeped from the joins in their plate. The stench of burning carrion filled the air.

A searing ribbon of fire struck the Hellknight on the left. Ederras raised his shield to block the wash of its heat from his face. At the same time he charged, rushing the temporarily stunned knight and calling upon Iomedae's grace as he ran. The blessed fire wreathing his sword intensified until it was bright as the heart of the sun.

He plunged it into the weak point under the graveknight's arm. Cold blood, wriggling with tiny pale vermin, spilled from the rent plate in black clots. The wound stank as if it had festered for weeks.

Gagging, Ederras drew back and slashed at the Crux knight again, this time aiming for the gap at the bottom of his gorget. His blessed blade overmatched the graveknight's steel and sheared into his foe's flesh with enough force to kill any living man.

And, it seemed, a dead one. The graveknight sank to his knees with tarry, verminous blood spreading sticky fingers across the side of his breastplate.

Ederras stepped away, turning to see how Jheraal fared. The hellspawn was hammering the other graveknight brutally. She'd caught his flail on her shield and driven it up, opening a space for her to slam her mace into the Crux knight's side again and again. Her opponent, moving his shield as slowly as if it were made of lead, was far too ponderous to stop her. Jheraal smashed her weapon into the crushed plate one last time, and the second graveknight fell.

None of them had been scratched. Velenne and Vhaeros had barely stepped off the bridge. Ederras lowered his sword, letting the congealed black blood run off its blade. "I hadn't expected that to be so easy."

"It wasn't." Jheraal straightened from where she'd bent over the Hellknight she'd felled. She moved aside, letting the others see what she'd discovered when she'd lifted the downed knight's visor. "They just wanted to fool you into wasting your spells."

It wasn't a graveknight. What had been inside that armor was a stinking, verminous corpse. Its face was a pulped mass of meat, so distended with crawling worms that Ederras could barely make out the contours of a skull. It didn't look human, whatever it was. Maybe an unusually large orc, or some stripe of ogrekin.

Velenne's face darkened when she saw the ruse. "Well. That was clever. Perhaps I'll take more pleasure than I'd anticipated in destroying them."

"Let's go." Jheraal stepped over the reeking body. "If we're quick, we might be able to find those children and deal with the lictor before these enchantments expire. One of the two, at least."

"The children first," Ederras said.

Velenne nodded and waved two fingers at her dog. Vhaeros stretched, yawned pointedly at Ederras, and trotted past him to the castle's open gates. Fearlessly the fiend loped under the portcullis's iron teeth, vanishing into the shadows of the citadel.

Keeping his sword loose in his hand, Ederras followed.

Past the portcullis and its flanking gatehouses stood a barren inner courtyard. Once, the Crux's horses might have been stabled there, and armigers and Hellknights might have tested their skills and discipline against summoned fiends. Nothing remained of the horses save a handful of pale equine skulls on the hard-beaten earth and a few flecks of colorless straw tumbling in the wind, and nothing remained of the armigers or their trainers at all.

Vhaeros put his nose to the earth, and then to the air. Hackles bristling, the gray dog made a low, huffing snarl and went to Velenne, his tail switching stiffly in agitation.

"What is it?" Ederras asked.

"The smells are wrong." Velenne frowned, stroking her dog's ears and looking around the courtyard as if she could see whatever he'd scented. "He's found the children's trail, but the shape of it . . . To Vhaeros's nose, you must understand, scent is not a straight line. It pools. It shifts in the air. It moves along walls and ceilings. But here, even with the breezes in the courtyard, it *is* a straight line. It's as if someone who had no idea how he perceives a scent trail had decided to invent one, and they'd drawn a single clear line hanging static in the air."

"Could it be an illusion? Some kind of trick?" He didn't want to think that the children had been sacrificed to the devilheart chain before they'd arrived, but they had no proof that the assassin had brought them to the fortress safely. She'd never bothered to bring any of the others back alive.

"No illusion. False scents obey the same patterns as real ones. Otherwise they wouldn't be remotely convincing. It does, of course, suggest some other trick. Probably the obvious one: we're being baited." Velenne nodded to the dog, acknowledging unspoken words. Vhaeros trotted off, heading straight across the courtyard toward the inner keep. "He's certain that the children are alive. Seven hellspawn, both boys and girls. Not poisoned, not sick. Very frightened. Some are injured. There's a scent of fresh blood mixed in with them. But it's not much. I assume you still want to follow them?"

"Yes." Jheraal's helm distorted her voice with the visor down, but it couldn't conceal the Hellknight's agitated intensity. "We have to find them."

"Then Vhaeros will lead you."

The wolflike dog paused at the entrance to the inner keep. The doors stood ajar, revealing nothing but a sliver of darkness. Ederras pushed them open with a creak, revealing the ruins of a cavernous great hall destroyed by fire.

Soot covered every surface. The windows were thick with it, casting the interior into smoky gloom. Benches and tables, charred into shapeless lumps, stood in tumbled heaps near the back of the hall, as if they'd been overturned to serve as barricades for the citadel's last defenders.

The only thing that remained distinct in the burned-out hall was the array of blackened skulls embedded in the walls. They grinned down at irregular intervals, as blasted and damaged as the ones that had been sunk into the bridge. Ederras's skin prickled when he saw them, even though these didn't ignite with eldritch fire. *What other snares do they hold?*

Vhaeros started toward a gaping doorway on the right. Then the dog halted and backed up, his lip curled in a silent snarl.

From the hall beyond, the children came.

They were huddled in a tight cluster. Boys and girls, barefoot in rags, bound at the wrist by rope. Their eyes were big with fear. Thirty feet away, they stopped.

Behind them walked a woman in a hooded cloak that shifted through all the colors of twilight. Blue, violet, gray. Nothing of her face was visible under her cowl except for her eyes, but those eyes shimmered like poisoned stardust. It wasn't a steady glow, like Jheraal's, but a constellation of tiny sparks that spun endlessly.

Two Hellknights flanked her. These, Ederras knew instantly, were the true graveknights of Citadel Gheisteno. The aura of malevolence that surrounded them was unmistakable. Had he encountered them first, he would never have been fooled by the feeble imitations outside.

Yet even now, the lictor hadn't come to them. He'd sent a host of lesser undead instead, with the two last members of the Crux at their head.

One was an impersonal, faceless figure in black plate mail and a skull-crowned helm. A flaming greatsword, its hilt shaped like a roaring dragon, crossed his back. Yellow eyes, fierce and terrible, burned in the darkness behind his visor. *The Master of Blades. Behrion Khollarix.*

The other was a woman, tall and severe. She carried a glassy-bladed scimitar strapped to her hip and wore a lighter version of the Crux's platemail bound together with blue silk. Her helm had been cut back to a stylized crest that left her face bare. It drew a sharp steel point between her brows, then arched up on either side to frame the skull at its center in a double row of spikes. Snow-white hair flowed down to the small of her back.

Paravicar Corellia Leroung. His great-grandfather's former squire had grown into a woman of rare beauty, but that beauty was colder than ice. Death, Ederras suspected, had not changed that in the slightest. It had only preserved what was already there.

Each of the undead knights stood a full head taller than the hooded woman between them, and the smaller figure had nothing like their malign auras. Yet it was she, not they, who spoke. "You came."

"Surrender the children," Ederras said.

The hooded woman—*Sechel?*—laughed. "Surrender? No, I won't be surrendering them, or trading them, or anything else. I just wanted you to see them before you died." She raised a gloved hand in mocking farewell and vanished from sight. On either side of the empty space, the graveknights drew their weapons. The horde of wights and skeletons came forward, their eyes glowing red or else blank and vacant in Citadel Gheisteno's eternal gloom.

Ederras started toward the children, but Velenne held him back. She drew a black wand from its sheath at her hip. "It's a bluff. They aren't going to kill the hellspawn. They want the hearts. I'll take the skeletons. You stop the graveknights."

He nodded and changed his course, advancing on the Master of Blades. Before he was halfway there, Paravicar Leroung intercepted him.

Her lifeless lips were blue as death, and blue fire burned in her eyes. Its reflection shone in the scimitar's crystal blade. "You look so much like Kelvax," she said, and struck.

A hissing trail of ice crystals followed the arc of her blade. Ederras caught the scimitar on his shield. Frost crackled across its golden wings. "He killed you once. I'll do it again."

Her laughter was the sound of shattering ice. The paravicar twisted away, bringing her empty hand up behind the scimitar. Black magic blossomed in her palm, coalescing into a tight knot. "Did he? Kelvax rots in his grave, and I stand here."

The energy leaped from her hand in a ray, striking Ederras in the chest. Weakness shuddered through him, sapping the vitality he'd gained from Velenne's spell. Fatigue snared his feet and turned his sword arm to lead.

He swung at her anyway, calling upon Iomedae to grant him strength. The paravicar brought up her scimitar to parry. Unholy ice screamed against divine fire. Flakes of frost and golden sparks showered through the air, shining through the hazy mist between the two blades.

Ederras won through. His blessed sword smashed through Paravicar Leroung's defenses and into her lightly armored side, crushing the steel plates into her ribcage. Bone and metal crunched inward, leaving a gap the size of two fists pressed together.

She hardly seemed to notice. Again she struck at him, and again he turned the blade aside on his shield, crystal shrilling against feathered gold. Around and around they spun in their dance of black and silvered steel, the paravicar's slashes fast and frequent, Ederras's slower but more telling. Black-tongued bursts of fire erupted at steady intervals behind and beside them, filling the hall with the acrid stench of burning bone as Velenne destroyed the wights and skeletons.

Crushing charred bones under her boots, Jheraal faced off against the Master of Blades. Blood spattered the floor around her, yet despite her wounds, the hellspawn seemed to be getting the better of their duel, in part because Vhaeros had put himself between Velenne and the graveknight and was harassing the undead knight mercilessly.

The Crux Hellknight's platemail was gouged across the thighs and back, ripped by claws that carved steel as easily as melon rinds. Darkness flowed from the ruptured mail like cold smoke. Ederras had just enough time to wonder how Vhaeros had dealt those wounds—*no dog has talons like that*—before the paravicar's scimitar came whirling at him again, and his focus spun back to her.

A cry jerked his attention to the right. Velenne was struggling badly against Sechel, who had blinked back into view. The diabolist had wrapped herself in evasive spells: illusory duplicates surrounded her, and a blurring mist veiled her form. None of those deceptions seemed to deter the assassin, though. Sechel's twin black knives, each crackling with red-violet energy, struck unerringly and with deadly speed. An unseen enchantment turned her blades aside, but only imperfectly. Velenne's chain-paneled dress was dark with blood, and her face was drawn in pain.

I have to go to her. Velenne wasn't made for battle. She was a planner and a plotter, not a soldier. Ederras faltered, distracted.

The paravicar saw it. "You fear for her. Your paramour. Do you know what Lictor Shokneir intends for her?"

"Empty threats." Struggling through the fog of his spell-driven fatigue, Ederras blocked another slash of the icy scimitar and retaliated with a high, sweeping cut of his own. His sword hacked into the plates that protected the graveknight's shoulder, shearing through steel and frost-hard muscle. Iomedae's fury exerted its full force on the paravicar's flesh, charring it away in heatless flame.

Paravicar Leroung laughed in his face. The cold black blood of the dead bubbled at the back of her throat and spilled onto her tongue, limning her teeth between those corpse-blue lips. "He'll kill her. Slowly. Badly. Not with his own hands. With your friend's. He'll use your friend to kill you, too, but I think the woman should go first. So you can watch. And then the lictor will use your deaths to set this empire of devils aflame."

"Is your babbling meant to bore me to death?" Hindered by her spell, Ederras couldn't catch the graveknight's next strike. Her scimitar skittered across his rerebrace, then bit into his arm with icy teeth. A hot flash of pain shot through him, followed a split second later by a numbing blast of cold. His shield dipped, and he strained to bring it up before she could hit him again.

The paravicar's perfect, pallid face twisted in hatred. "If your death hadn't already been claimed . . . but no matter. Much can be done to the flesh short of that. As Ochtel will help you learn."

Ederras's answer was drowned out by a sudden, deafening roar. Even at a remove, the concussive force of the sound was staggering. *Vhaeros?* He looked wildly to where Jheraal and the dog were fighting the other Crux knight.

The Master of Blades was on his knees, brought low by the fiend's unearthly roar. Jheraal clubbed his helm with her heavy mace, crushing its ornamental skull to shards. In an avalanche of sooty plates, the graveknight collapsed.

Somewhere in the heights of Citadel Gheisteno, a sepulchral bell tolled. Again and again it rang its mournful thunder, its echoes reverberating through the deep stones.

Ederras turned to the paravicar in triumph. "You see? You're dead."

Paravicar Leroung laughed again. "I *am* dead. I've been dead for sixty years. You're a fool if you think that frightens me. And I'd be a fool if I didn't know it frightened you."

She pointed a finger at the huddled hellspawn children. "Your kind are easy to deal with. You and your forefather, stupid in all the same ways. Forever controlled by your concern for innocents. Even when those 'innocents' are the spawn of Hell."

One of the children hiccupped a sob. The others were too frightened to hush him. Ederras lowered his sword, just a fraction. He saw Jheraal easing closer from the right. Vhaeros was crouched low, stalking toward the paravicar from behind. The fiend's claws had sharpened and elongated. They looked more like a falcon's talons than anything that should belong on a dog, and they left gouges half an inch deep in the stone.

He had to keep her distracted. "What do you want?"

Paravicar Leroung raised her empty hand, and mist gathered in her grasp. Ice spidered across the blackened steel and drew creaks from the ancient leather beneath. Its shimmering flakes spun faster as she drew upon her magic, intensifying the vortex into a polar freeze that frosted Ederras's eyelashes and stung the breath in his lungs. "First and foremost? For you to watch them die."

She thrust her hand outward, releasing the torrent of lethal cold at the children.

"*No!*"

Jheraal leaped into the blast's path. She thrust her shield out, away from her body, to screen more of the children behind her. Raw elemental cold hammered into her, pounding her breastplate with fist-sized chunks of ice, and the Hellknight collapsed under the onslaught.

Behind her, the children screamed. Some sobbed. Ice shards skipped across the floor, spinning past their feet, trailing threads of bright red blood. But none of the children had been harmed.

"Save them," Jheraal croaked at Ederras. One of the horns on her helm had cracked from the sheer force of the cold. Her shield, which had fallen an arm's-reach away, was rimed to the floor with a rippled glaze of ice. The golden glow of her eyes was fading fast. "Save them."

"Velenne," Ederras called, keeping his gaze fixed on the paravicar as he stepped forward to renew their fight. He couldn't do it. She could. "Please."

"You're asking me to get myself killed." The diabolist's voice was raw, breathless, full of angry fear. "For them. For *children*."

"Help them. If you love me, help them."

She made an inarticulate noise of terror and fury. He heard the metallic tink of the assassin's knife striking Velenne's protective spell, and the wetter sound of one sinking into flesh. But she cried: "Vhaeros! Take the children."

With a snarl of protest, or perhaps frustration, the dog obeyed. Skirting around the renewed battle between Ederras and the paravicar, Vhaeros herded the terrified children toward the door. He wasn't gentle about it. The ones who hesitated got a nip or a growl, or worse, to force them into compliance. But he gathered all of them, and he pushed them out toward the bridge.

As soon as the last of them crossed, a wall of crimson-streaked ice closed off the doorway behind them, preventing pursuit. Just as the wall crystallized into place, Ederras heard the hissing crackle of the assassin's knives carving through the air, an anguished cry from Velenne, and then silence.

Paravicar Leroung smiled at Ederras through the clash of their blades. Black blood coated the insides of her lips as though she'd been supping on shadow. He could smell it on her, cold and dank as the breath of a rain-washed mausoleum. "I *am* impressed. You're an even greater fool than Kelvax was."

"You haven't won yet," Ederras replied grimly, hewing into the graveknight again. Her armor, battered and broken, was barely protecting her anymore, and she was weakening quickly. Another few blows would likely finish her. Then he could heal Velenne, and Jheraal, and—

Pain speared him from behind.

The assassin. Even as the thought occurred to him, the knives jerked out and came back in. Agony exploded in him, carrying oblivion on its back.

"Now I have," Paravicar Leroung said, and then there was nothing more.

22

TWO MORE DEATHS

SECHEL

I t's done."

Defiance and pride colored Sechel's words in equal measure. Defiance of the terror that she always felt around Lictor Shokneir, and of the fear that he might renege on his word. Pride that she had done what the graveknight couldn't, and had captured all three of the assigned targets alive. They were somewhat the worse for wear, perhaps, and in the case of the Thrune woman only barely alive, but she'd fulfilled the letter of her contract. She had earned her reward.

The lictor nodded. He seemed pleased, if it was possible for such a creature to be pleased. "You have served well."

I don't serve you. She bit back the words and hoped he couldn't see her thoughts. "I want my payment. As agreed."

"As agreed." Lictor Shokneir raised his gauntleted hands, cupping them together as if he held an invisible crown for a kneeling king's coronation. The shroud of dark mist roiled around him, rolling off his armored shoulders in a spectral echo of his cloak. "Bow before me."

Instinctively, Sechel bristled. They were alone in the ruins of the citadel's great hall. The castle's mindless servants had carried away the remnants of the fallen Master of Blades, and Paravicar Leroung had returned to her frost-walled chamber of experiments. No one was there to see her abase herself at the lictor's command.

She still hated doing it. But for the promise of humanity . . .

Sechel knelt. Chill mist enveloped her, sapping the warmth from her body, as Lictor Shokneir passed his hands over her. His black-gloved fingers skimmed through the air over Sechel's skin, tracing the contours of her form. Although he never touched her, wracking agony followed his path.

A thousand acid-tipped needles drove into the assassin's flesh, tearing her apart inch by inch. A thousand tiny jolts of lightning followed them, forcing her shattered parts back together. She was destroyed, stripped to pieces, pulverized to dust.

And then she was reborn.

Sechel stood on legs as shaky as jellied eels. She flexed her fingers, stretched her arms, inhaled a deep breath and was astonished at how little she could smell. Every fiber of her being felt familiar and foreign at once.

She stripped off her gloves. Under the fine gray kidskin, her hands had nails. Not the blind, ragged stubs of torn-out claws. Nails.

Sechel pushed back her hood and ran a hand over her head. Instead of the usual bristly stubble, hard enough to abrade stone, she felt hair. Soft. Ordinary.

Her eyes had become ordinary, too. She couldn't see through the shadows so clearly anymore. The far end of the hall was lost in darkness. Before, she could have fired a poisoned bolt through the jaws of any skull embedded in that wall, and it would have been a poor shot if the quarrel's fletchings touched teeth. Now she couldn't even see the skulls.

Her strength was still there, and her reflexes, but the ember of anger that had always burned at her core . . .

. . . was it gone?

Had Lictor Shokneir really taken the taint of evil from her soul? Purified the devils' curse from her heart? Made her *human*, content to find enjoyment in the placid mundanities of life that she'd always mocked to disguise her envy?

I've become weak, she thought, and laughed, inconceivably, for joy.

The lictor's fiery gaze returned her to the moment. "Do you accept this as payment in full?"

"Yes," Sechel said, quickly, before he could take it back. Her hands closed protectively around her transformed fingers. "It's mine."

The skull-crowned helm dipped in a nod. "Then it is done. Our bargain is fulfilled. Now I shall make you another offer."

"What?"

"The deaths of the three in the dungeons."

"You wanted them alive, and now you want them dead?"

Lictor Shokneir's burning eyes flared in irritation. Sechel's levity died on her lips. Her new flesh was too precious to risk.

"They must die in a manner that serves me," he said. The words reverberated not from the graveknight's armored figure, but from the castle around her: floor, walls, ceiling. All at once, booming in unison, driving in at Sechel from all sides. "In Cheliax. In public. At the hands of the hellspawn, so that all can see that the taint of Hell drives those who carry it to the depths of treachery, and that the so-called discipline of the Scourge cannot begin to hold it back."

Sechel nodded. She'd seen what the devilheart chain did when its magic was brought to its final form. With her heart in the lictor's hands, the hellspawn knight would become his slave: a puppet in flesh to do with as he pleased. Apparently what he pleased was making a spectacle of the other two's deaths, which suited Sechel just fine. "What's my role in it?"

"You will find the most effective way to inflame all the empire of devils with their deaths. The temples and the righteous knights must be enraged by the paladin's demise. The cursed legions of House Thrune by the woman's. Find a way to kill them that will set all their kin afire, and the hellspawn will execute your plan."

"How soon?"

"You have until the Master of Blades returns, since the paravicar does not wish to move our captives without him. It may be only one day, or it may be several. In either case, you will be prepared. Death is easy for you, is it not?"

Easier when I hold the knife. She'd have to trust one of the graveknights to control the hellspawn, and Sechel hated relying on others. They were never as competent, never as good. Something always went wrong.

But she was free from the touch of Hell, and cleansed of whatever malign seed in her soul had driven her to murder. Maybe she'd never kill anyone again.

Then why am I annoyed at the thought of someone else botching my targets?

Sechel dismissed the question. It wasn't important. "What's the pay?"

"Silver. Gold. Jewels."

Money. She hadn't worked for mere money in years. Sechel started to curl her lip before she caught herself. She'd need money, if she wasn't going to do the work anymore. Maybe a lot of money. Maybe more than she had now. She had no idea how ordinary people lived. "Fine."

Lictor Shokneir didn't respond. He simply walked away, into the darkness, as if her importance to him was already forgotten.

Sechel tamped down her irritation. She had thought that becoming human would quell her temper, but the lictor's dismissiveness would have sparked fire from wet cotton.

No matter. She had what she wanted.

Mulling over the new problem presented to her, Sechel went to the castle's enchanted garden. How best to make martyrs of the paladin and the Thrune woman?

She knew why Lictor Shokneir wanted that, or thought she did. Sechel had used her time in the citadel to piece together the lictor's motives, wanting to know everything she could about the graveknight who held her hopes in his hands.

It hadn't been that difficult. After years of solitude in Citadel Gheisteno, Lictor Shokneir craved vindication, and his need to justify his deeds made it impossible for him *not* to tell her what he intended. The hardest part had been sorting through his fragmentary speeches and bursts of temper to put the tale together.

Since his days as a living man during the Chelish civil war, the lictor had hated House Thrune. He'd been an outspoken advocate of the view that devils were properly called only to *serve* their summoners, never to master them, and certainly never to couple with them. Those who allowed themselves to be seduced by the infernal were inexcusably weak, and the fruit of such unions were abominations. The spawn were irrevocably tainted, and were quite probably tools of Hell, deliberately created to undermine the bonds and structures of mortal society.

Proof of that proposition, however, had eluded the Order of the Crux for some time. When the world failed to grant him the evidence he wanted, Lictor Shokneir had instructed his subordinates to create their own.

And so the devilheart chain had come into the world.

She stopped before the door that led to Ochtel's garden. It held a large stained-glass window depicting a tree with wide, spreading branches. Flowers and vines covered the hill beneath the tree, and beyond it, a sun or a full moon hung low in the sky. The image was simple and stylized, and every pane of glass that composed it was some shade of gray, but it was the only thing of real beauty in Citadel Gheisteno.

What lay beyond it, Sechel felt, wasn't really part of the fortress. She wasn't the only one who felt that way. It was the entire reason the garden existed.

Pushing past the door, she went in.

The fragrance of a thousand flowers and the green breath of leaves filled the warm, moist air. Trees rose toward the cathedral-high ceiling, brushing the buttresses with their branches. Vines and creepers climbed the walls in a living tapestry adorned with clematis and vivid pink orchids. Soft mosses and silvery-leaved shrubs carpeted the loamy earth. A constellation of tiny, glowing golden lights hung among the plants like captured fireflies. It was these, the creations of Ochtel's magic, that allowed the garden to flourish in a place that never saw the sun.

Somewhere in the greening depths, the druid worked his magic and kept the garden alive, despite the haunted unreality of the fortress that held it and the life-obliterating aura of the castle's cursed master. Somewhere amid the trees, he sacrificed his own life to sustain his plants'.

It wasn't by choice. Ochtel was just a slave, if a gifted one. He was, accordingly, worthy of no real consideration. Sechel put him out of her mind as she walked among the plants, letting their color and fragrance beguile her while she turned the lictor's problem over in her head. How could she arrange two deaths to set Imperial Cheliax aflame?

Treachery. That would be the wedge to break the empire's powers apart. The truce between the righteous faiths of Cheliax and devil-binding House Thrune had always been a fragile thing. Iomedae's crusaders hated fiends, despised the empire's abandonment of its old virtues, and had little love for a royal family that had elevated tyranny into a high art. House Thrune, well aware of their distrust but ever cognizant of political balances, had chosen to make a show of tolerating the Inheritor's faith and accepting its subservience while pushing it toward a slow, quiet death.

The paladin and the Thrune woman, therefore, represented a perfect opportunity to confirm each side's worst suspicions of the other. If that uncertain alliance, instead of solidifying, could be shattered into bloody shards . . .

Sechel vaulted from the ground onto a low-hanging tree branch, slapping a palm against the trunk to steady herself as she landed. Weak as her reborn body was, it had strength enough for that. She perched easily in the tree, balanced on the balls of her feet, and gnawed her lower lip as she mulled over the problem. How to arrange a betrayal?

If the paladin caught the Thrune woman doing something that violated his code—making a sacrifice to Asmodeus, perhaps, or interrogating some innocent using Nidalese tortures—then he might go into a rage at her duplicity. He might accuse her of having betrayed whatever oaths she'd taken that allowed them to work together, and kill her for that offense.

Of course, the "offense" would have to be something entirely permissible, even praised, by Chelish society, but that wouldn't be difficult. Many of the rites and customs of Imperial Cheliax were killing crimes to a paladin.

So the Thrune woman would do something that offended her lover, the paladin would react violently, and the Hellknight would catch him bloody-handed on the scene. Then the Hellknight would kill him in turn, because the Iomedaean fanatic would, predictably, refuse to submit to Chelish justice. He might even shout a few words of defiance before he died. In any case, the Hellknight would give him no chance to surrender—instead of capturing him as the law demanded, she'd kill him on the spot, giving in to the bloodlust that lurked within all hellspawn.

It wouldn't be hard to arrange their bodies to suggest such a scene. Laid out appropriately, the corpses would tell the story clearly enough for a blind man to see. And with the devilheart chain, the lictor could make the Hellknight confess everything, perhaps even fighting the former comrades who came to arrest her.

The Hellknight's missing heart would be a problem, if she were examined. Sechel tapped her lip, thinking hard. Magic might disguise the hole, but self-immolation would be safer. As soon as it looked like she might be captured, the Hellknight could douse herself in alchemical fire. As long as she burned hot enough, there wouldn't be enough of the body left for anyone to identify the hole in the ribcage.

That should spark the conflagration Lictor Shokneir wanted. The flames would need coaxing, of course. They wouldn't consume the empire without considerable encouragement. But as far as one could tear at Cheliax's fragile alliances with a few deaths, it would be as good a beginning as anyone could ask. Betrayal, a murder that undercut the righteous temples' pretensions of virtue, another murder that undercut the Hellknights' pretensions of law.

She was sure she could stage the wounds believably. It wouldn't be difficult. And none of their spirits would contradict the tale told by their bodies. Even if priests or inquisitors tried to call her victims' souls back with magic, they'd have no success.

The diabolist was damned; her soul would be seized by her infernal masters at the moment of her death, leaving nothing for clerics to contact. The paladin would surely refuse to answer Asmodeus's call, and Sechel could make sure that no one other than the Archfiend's priests was permitted to try. That left the Hellknight, whose heart the lictor still held. Would the devilheart chain continue to bind her soul after death? She'd have to ask the lictor. If not, surely he could come up with some other way to block any postmortem testimony.

Sechel smiled, imagining the protests, the imprecations, the curses that Iomedae's so-holy church would level against devil-ruled Cheliax. *And then the empire will burn.*

She dropped off the branch, landing soundlessly on the garden path. Scarcely a leaf fluttered in her passing.

All she needed was to find an obscenity to start it all. Some act of devotion to Asmodeus that would earn praise from his faithful and condemnation from the virtuous churches that still survived in the empire. Something so far beyond the routine rites of the

Archfiend's worship that the Inheritor's faithful would be hard-pressed to blame the paladin for resorting to the sword to stop it. Ideally, something the Thrune woman had actually done in the past, or that would align with her known predilections, so that the revelation wouldn't come as a surprise to court gossips. Instead they'd nod sagely and confirm that, yes, it was just what that woman would do. Some torture from her time in Nidal, perhaps.

Leaving the garden, the assassin started up the stairs to Paravicar Leroung's icy sanctuary in the citadel's north tower. The half-seen flickers of restless spirits flashed and faded in her peripheral vision as she climbed the sooty steps. Citadel Gheisteno was filled with those figments of agony, and although the lictor's favor protected her, Sechel could still feel them prying at her thoughts. Given any chance, the old ghosts of the Crux would wrap their suffering around her, splintering her will under the force of their own and insinuating their memories, their miseries, into her skull.

But she was shielded by Lictor Shokneir's amulet, and none of them could touch her. Sechel ignored them as she ascended through the castle's gloom to the paravicar's tower. A chill in the air, and a melting embroidery of frost over the black stone walls, told her when she was drawing near.

At the top of the stairs, beyond a curtain of snowflakes suspended delicately on strands of silver light, a frozen fairyland unfurled. Ice in white and blue and palest green filled the paravicar's chamber. Her tables, cabinets, chairs, and knives were all fashioned from glittering ice, but so too were the rippled, sinuous patterns that flowed across the walls, the sculptures that erupted from the floor in dazzling prisms, the impossibly fragile trees with leaves of frost and branches of bright snow. The colored lights of a thousand enchantments played through the workshop, splintering sharp and clear across panes of ice or blurring into snow-veiled mist.

Paravicar Leroung's workshop was, in its way, as beautiful as the druid's garden, but its beauty was as wintry as its creator's, and lethal to those who lingered too long. The graveknight kept her sanctuary so cold that it was nearly as perilous for the dead as for the living. Frost-blued zombies and ice-glazed skeletons, casualties of carelessness, littered the laboratory's perimeter. More corpses, and stranger ones, were embedded in her walls.

Sechel didn't enter. She stayed just outside the swaying curtain, a solid shadow against the magical lights, and eventually the paravicar came to her. "Yes?"

The assassin took her time in answering, waiting until her voice was steady. Paravicar Leroung didn't have the lictor's terrifying power, but she was a graveknight all the same, and death hung heavy in the air around her. Sechel could *feel* the life evaporating from her when any of the graveknights came close. Her skin drained of color, her heart slowed its beat, and the taste of cold dirt and phantom worms filled her mouth.

Sechel wasn't even sure they knew when it happened. Perhaps, having been locked away so long in their cursed citadel, the graveknights had forgotten what their presence did to the living.

She *was* sure, however, that Paravicar Leroung would laugh at any show of fear. Therefore Sechel stayed silent and motionless, her arms crossed and hip cocked in a deliberately insolent pose, until she had mastered herself and the paravicar's porcelain face was taut with impatience.

"I need the memory siphon," Sechel said.

The devilheart chain hadn't been the paravicar's first creation. Before perfecting that device, she'd made several others. One of them, the memory siphon, copied its victim's memories and crystallized them into visions that others could watch. Originally intended for clandestine use, it had proved far too slow and obtrusive for that purpose, but it would serve for prisoners in Citadel Gheisteno's cells.

"Why?"

"I need to find religion." Sechel took a petty satisfaction in the uselessness of her answer, but didn't dare leave it at that for more than a moment. "I need to sift the Thrune woman's thoughts. Lictor Shokneir's orders."

"Fine." Paravicar Leroung disappeared behind her veil of snowflakes. She returned a few minutes later, bearing a slender spiral of colorless glass. Wide at one end and narrow at the other, it resembled a cross between an alchemist's condensation coil and an ear trumpet. Rather than offering it right away, however, the paravicar held it back coyly in a black-gloved hand. "But, of course, I'll want a favor in return."

Sechel didn't bother trying to reach for the siphon. "What do you want done to them?"

"Nothing terribly difficult." The pale-haired woman held the glassy spiral out between two fingers, extending it slowly through the drifting fall of her snowflake curtain. "I only want you to listen to all three of them. Find out what they fear. What would hurt them most. Then report that to me before you enact the rest of your plan."

"That isn't in my orders," Sechel said, annoyed. She had no patience for sadism. It was inefficient and self-indulgent, and she'd seen it ruin too many plans. "It's supposed to be done by the time the Master of Blades returns. I don't need the others' memories to do what Lictor Shokneir wants."

"But you need my siphon, and this is my price. Therefore you *do* need their memories." Paravicar Leroung smiled as the assassin reached out to take the glass. "Go. Find their fears for me. Bring them back. I'd like to watch."

23

LOSS

EDERRAS

Ederras awoke in darkness.

He wasn't alone. He could feel the warmth of other bodies near him, and hear someone breathing nearby. More than one someone. The air smelled of blood and sweat and the fermented rotten-meat stink, prickly with alchemical fluids, of arcanely crafted undead.

Blood soaked his clothing, cold and clammy against his skin. The discomfort of it heartened him. It meant the bleeding had stopped.

The weight of his armor was gone, though. His captors had stripped him of sword and mail. Whoever was in the darkness with him was bereft of theirs as well. He didn't hear the clink of chain or plate accompanying those slow, pained breaths.

Cautiously, Ederras sat up. He wasn't surprised to hear chains rattle when he moved, nor to feel them dragging at his wrists. His hands were free enough to allow a minor prayer, though. Calling upon the Inheritor's favor, he prayed for a small blessing of light and touched his right manacle.

The steel flared in the darkness like a tiny sun, light washing over the fleshless faces of the skulls in the fortress's walls and bringing stinging tears to the paladin's eyes. What he saw in its glow stung more.

Velenne lay insensible on the filthy stone floor, her dark hair tangled in the dirt and matted with blood. More blood stained her leather dress and blackened its panels of silvery chain. Her breathing was shallow and too quick, and it caught in her chest as if something were snagging at her lungs. The pale wash of his spell's radiance stole the color from her skin, but even so there was a bruised pallor to her that chilled his heart.

Poison, maybe. What he could see of her wounds looked bad enough already. With poison in her veins on top of what she'd already suffered . . .

Jheraal sat next to her, arms wrapped around her bent knees. Her armor was gone. Ederras had never seen the Hellknight without that carapace of black steel. In cloth and quilted padding, she looked strange as a turtle stripped of its shell. Drying blood gummed her streaked black hair and drew cracked lines across the scales of her cheek. Chains trailed from her wrists and ankles, but she didn't seem to notice them. She wasn't looking at Velenne, and hadn't blinked when Ederras's light blossomed into being. The Hellknight stared into the empty air like a lost soul, or one who expected to lose hers soon.

"Where are we?" Ederras asked, disturbed by her inertia. He had never known the Hellknight to be passive, or anything less than vitally devoted to her cause, but now it seemed like she'd given up entirely. "Why aren't we dead?"

"In the dungeons of Citadel Gheisteno. We've lost." Jheraal's answer was toneless. She never glanced away from the emptiness ahead. "They took our armor, our weapons, Velenne's wands. I don't know why they haven't killed us yet, but I imagine it won't be long. We lost, and it's my fault. I broke discipline. I showed them a weakness, and they used it. I'm sorry. I'm so sorry."

"Don't say that." There was enough slack in his chains for him to reach Velenne. Ederras dragged himself to her side, steeling himself to look at her wounds. "You did nothing wrong. You saved those children, and you didn't cause our defeat. I did that. I let myself lose sight of that assassin."

"Did I save them?" Jheraal turned toward him, finally. Her amber eyes were bleak. There was more blood on the other side of her face, covering her in a grisly half-mask from brow to chin. "Did I save anyone? Or were they cut down by skeletons before they got to that bridge? Torn apart by the fiend we trusted to guard them? What did I *do*, besides doom us?"

"The only thing you could have," Ederras said firmly. "You seized on a chance for hope."

Jheraal didn't say anything to that. She turned away again, staring into the distance, and Ederras brought his light closer to examine Velenne as he reached her side.

It wasn't good.

She was so pale. Even in the dead of winter, there had always been a slight golden cast to Velenne's skin, a touch of rich ochre that he thought beautiful and she found irritating. In her, the blood of Imperial Cheliax was mixed with something else, and it kept her from matching her rivals' fairness. Porcelain pallor had long been the fashionable ideal for Chelish noblewomen, and Velenne had never come close to it.

Until now. It wasn't just the poison, although he was now sure that the assassin's blades had been coated in venom. It was the blood loss that was killing her.

Her blood covered his hands. It was warm, still seeping from her near-drained veins. There wasn't much left. The human body was a fragile, ridiculous vessel: one small cut was all it took for life to pour out. And Velenne had taken many, many more than one.

The assassin had all but torn her apart. Every breath she took was a miracle, and her miracles were fading fast. Hoping he wasn't too late, Ederras steeled himself to ask for one more.

"Iomedae, Inheritor, hear my prayer." The invocation's words came to Ederras easily, familiar as the beat of his own heart, but he didn't hear them. His mind was entirely blank, stripped of every thought except for what he was really praying: *don't leave me.*

Velenne was a diabolist, and she was damned. She'd promised her soul to Hell for her power, and while the Prince of Darkness sometimes granted reprieves to his most useful servants, the Archfiend's mercy was no reliable thing. Ederras had slain enough of Asmodeus's other servants to know that. If she died, she was lost to him.

Fifteen years ago, Ederras had prayed to Iomedae to smite his lover, and he hadn't been sure that his goddess would answer. Now he prayed with every fiber of his being that Iomedae might heal her, and he wasn't sure if the Lady of Valor would answer that call. There was no denying that the diabolist's death would take a great evil from the world.

He prayed anyway. *Let me keep this. If there is any chance for us—any* hope *for something good—let me keep her.*

The magic ignited in his soul, reassuring as the sudden bloom of a campfire on a winter night. It coursed through his hands and flowed into Velenne, drawing her back from the brink of death. Her breathing steadied. The flow of blood slowed, then stopped.

Relief flooded through him, nearly as exhausting as fear. Ederras sank back on his heels, momentarily off-balance, and then straightened and renewed his prayers. The magic came faster, stronger, surer. He no longer feared Iomedae's disapproval of his work. The Inheritor had seen what was in his soul and had expressed her acceptance, if not approval.

She's done no evil while she was with me. Maybe that was close enough to redemption. Close enough to win Iomedae's clemency, at least. For here, for now.

But when the light of his final prayer faded, Velenne didn't wake. Her pulse steadied but remained sluggish. Some of her color returned, but a gray-blue shadow lingered under her eyes, and tormented dreams fluttered their lids.

Jheraal hadn't seemed to notice his prayer, but she lifted her horned head in the silence that followed. "Why isn't she getting up?"

"Poison." Ederras brushed a dirt-flecked lock of hair from Velenne's forehead. She turned blindly toward his touch, murmuring something he couldn't catch, and it dug a barbed hook into his soul. "I don't know what the assassin used, but it's still in her."

"You can't cure it?"

"The goddess's power is infinite, but I'm an imperfect vessel. Poison is tricky—I can heal the damage, but it's still there in her veins. If Velenne's too weak, or the toxin's too strong . . ." *Or if the Inheritor isn't sure the recipient is worthy, or the Prince of Lies has already laid claim to her soul . . .* He pushed those thoughts away. Iomedae wouldn't have healed Velenne if she'd judged the woman unworthy, and the diabolist's soul lingered in her body. It was poison that afflicted her. Only poison. "I have an antidote with the rest of my gear. If we can find out where the graveknights took it—"

Jheraal's laugh was as hopeless as surrender. "How? We can't get out of this cell without Velenne. These chains and bars are way too strong to break, and I don't have any magic to dissolve them. Do you?"

"No. But—" He stopped short, hearing footsteps. An icy, sorcerous blue light appeared, cutting through the dungeon's gloom.

It was Paravicar Leroung, garbed in black steel and blue silk and a halo of bitter frost. All signs of their battle had been wiped from her. The paravicar's armor was immaculate, her pallid skin unscratched.

She seemed surprised, and then pleased, to see that none of them were dying. "I'd thought we might have to send Ochtel to tend you," the graveknight said, looking over her captives before settling her attention on Ederras. "But it seems you don't need the help. You're as holy a fool as Kelvax was." She studied him coolly, stroking the hilt of her ice-bladed scimitar. "Who was he to you? Anything more than a faded name written in a family history?"

"My great-grandfather." Ederras stood to confront her through the cell's bars. "Why do you speak of him with such venom? *You* were the one who betrayed his ideals and turned against his teachings."

"You must be joking."

"Not in the slightest. You were his squire. I found the records in the Dorjanala."

"His squire?" Disbelief widened the paravicar's bright blue eyes, and her lip curled in cold amusement. "Look at me, boy. Do you really think I was just his *squire*?"

For a moment, Ederras didn't catch her meaning. Then he did, and felt his cheeks flush. "That's impossible. He loved—"

"—his wife? Yes, he did. He loved her. In a dull, dutiful, expected way. He had less passion for her than he did for his hunting hounds. The one he *wanted* was me. Even in the beginning, when I was but a squire of seventeen. Even at the end, when he claimed to be sickened by my sins. But you'd know all about that, wouldn't you?"

Her blue-tinged lips curved into a smirk as she looked at Velenne, then back to him. "You Celverian men, so proud and pious, so pristine in your shining armor. But you're just like him. You don't love virtue. It's the taste of transgression you really want. The thrill of touching something wicked. You're worse than he was, though. Even Kelvax never took a Thrune. It didn't go well for him in the end. How much worse do you suppose it'll be for you?"

Ederras shook his head mutely. He wanted to mount a defense of his great-grandfather, but in truth he knew almost nothing about the man. *Had* Kelvax Celverian loved his wife? Had he betrayed her with Corellia Leroung? He had no idea. No word survived to say.

He couldn't really argue about Velenne, either. Everything the paravicar had said was true. Unflattering, and not nearly the entirety of what he felt for her, but true.

Seeing that her barb had struck the mark, Paravicar Leroung laughed. "You can't deny it, can you? All your haughty pretenses are just that. Hollow to their core. Shall I tell you another secret? The devilheart chain, the so-called heresies of the Crux—*they were Kelvax's fault.*"

"That can't be," Ederras protested. "Kelvax was no wizard. He wasn't a Hellknight, either. He was a paladin in Iomedae's grace, and he could have had no part in your infamies."

"Is that what you think? He was a paladin, oh yes. And he *hated* House Thrune. He was the one who seeded the idea: What if there was some way to strip the infernal taint from a soul? What would it take to ensure that someone blighted by devils' blood never acted against the common good? To turn that same devils' blood against the summoners? To undermine the Thrune tyranny?

"Idle thoughts to him, I'm sure. Mere fancies. But they were his thoughts, all the same. It took years of work for me to make them concrete. Eventually I managed, of course. And then he rushed in, all aghast, pretending that the Crux had spun horror out of thin air, when in fact they were his ideas from inception."

"You can't blame him for what you did," Ederras said.

"Can't I? You should be proud of him. He was a better man than you. At least Kelvax fought them. Whereas *you*—well, I can't think of a more profound surrender to House Thrune. Can you?" The paravicar turned on a booted heel and left the dungeon, her wintry laughter trailing after her.

They weren't alone for long. Only minutes after the paravicar's unearthly blue light faded, the orange glow of a torch replaced it.

Their new visitor was the assassin, Sechel, in her twilight cloak. She looked different, somehow. Dimmer, maybe, as if some subtle and deadly magic had evaporated from her. In the glow of her torch, the woman's face seemed entirely ordinary. Waves of sandy hair framed a wide mouth, cool blue-gray eyes, and a slightly snub nose set in an angular, hollow-cheeked face. Neither plain nor pretty, she was so perfectly forgettable that she could have lost herself in a crowd of three.

Beside her stood a seven-foot-tall, grotesquely disfigured man whose lanky black hair couldn't conceal the vicious maiming of his features. Dirty linen draped his body. Behind them, indistinct in the shadows, something nebulous groaned and writhed.

"What do you want?" Ederras asked. He stood, putting himself between the cell door and the other two. "Why are you here?"

Sechel regarded him for a long, unblinking moment. The illusion of ordinariness died as she met and held his gaze. There was such a flat, unfeeling emptiness behind the assassin's eyes that she almost made the graveknights seem warm.

"I'm not here to kill you," she said at last, taking a delicate glass spiral from inside her cloak. Wide and flat on one end, it narrowed through its coils until the far end was a hollow, blunted needle. It didn't look like a weapon, but Ederras tensed anyway. "Not yet."

He tipped his chin at the spiraled glass. "What's that?"

"The Crux knights are curious about you. And your companions." The cloudy glass gleamed in the torch's flame as Sechel tilted it back and forth. "This will tell them what they want to know. It doesn't have to hurt. It doesn't cause any damage. Resisting, though, or refusing . . . that *will* hurt. I can make it hurt a lot. Almost as much as your woman would.

"But I'm human now, and better than I was, so I'll give you a choice. You can accept the siphon, or I can take your lover's face off with a knife. I won't kill her. She'll live. At least until she wakes up. Then I think she'll probably kill herself, because she's too vain to live like that." The assassin watched him through the bars, those blue-gray eyes dead as salt flats. "Or you can accept it, and I'll give you mercy. All of you."

There's a demon's offer. Without looking, Ederras moved his hands apart to measure the distance between his shackled wrists. He might have enough chain to strangle her. "What does mercy mean to you?"

"A quick death. No torture. That's mercy, isn't it? A mercy you've handed out often enough yourself." Sechel shrugged, indifferent to any answer he might make. Handing her torch to the stooped man beside her, she bent over the cell's lock. A swift rake of steel picks, and it sprang open. "I only need you to die. It doesn't have to be badly. But that's up to you."

"I'll do it," Jheraal said, before the door opened and before Ederras could move. He stiffened, turning toward her to protest, but the determination on the Hellknight's face made him hold his tongue. She stood and shouldered past him. "You can use it on me. The paladin won't interfere." The white-scaled woman glanced at him, her eyes flashing from amber to golden fire as she moved from light into shadow. "Give your word that you won't intervene."

With difficulty, Ederras swallowed his protest. He didn't know what Jheraal was doing, but the Hellknight was no fool. She wouldn't throw herself into this without cause. "I won't intervene unless you're in danger."

"So honorable." Sechel's colorless lips curled in a pale imitation of a smile. Opening the cell door, she stepped inside. She kept a fluid, ready stance, effortlessly readjusting her position with every breath she took. The instant Sechel came into their cell, perfectly at ease despite the close quarters, Ederras knew that he'd never have bested that woman while unarmed and in chains. Jheraal had, in accepting the assassin's bargain, saved him from himself.

It wasn't clear what that would cost her. Sechel placed the wide, trumpetlike mouth of the siphon on Jheraal's forehead midway between her horns. The glass adhered to the Hellknight's scaled skin, pulling it up in a brief and awful moment of suction. Jheraal's eyes clouded over with swirling blue fog, and the same fog rose up through the glass, condensing from vapor into liquid as it climbed the siphon's coils.

Tiny shapes floated through the fog. Figures, faces. They were too small and fleeting for Ederras to recognize, and they stretched and shrank as the siphon sucked them up, but he was sure that he was watching Jheraal's memories drawn through the glass.

Sechel watched too, just for a minute, and then she slipped out of their cell and locked it behind her. "Ochtel will stay until it's done. He'll see that you don't get into trouble." A moment later she was gone, melting into shadow so seamlessly that Ederras never saw her leave.

The torch guttered in her wake. Streaks of orange firelight cut across the maimed man's face, illumining him like some monstrous idol carved in flesh. Citadel Gheisteno's fire-blasted skulls grinned around him, darkness locked between their teeth, but their stillness was no greater than the man's own. He hadn't said a word while Sechel had been there, and he said nothing now, simply squatted in silence, unmoving, barely breathing.

Ederras reached for Iomedae's favor. When the goddess's silvery light filled his soul, he reached through the dungeon bars, touching the linen-wrapped wreck of a man on the other side. To his surprise, the silver radiance didn't tarnish in the man's presence. Alone of all the creatures Ederras had encountered in Citadel Gheisteno, this poor wretch wasn't evil.

The paladin cleared his throat. "Ochtel. Did I hear your name correctly?"

For a long, long time, there was no answer. Low groans and clatters echoed through the dungeon's unseen depths. Velenne's breathing was an unsteady rasp. The siphon's cloudy glass swirled with Jheraal's memories, the ghosts of her past rising up in blue spirit-smoke. Ochtel sat inert on the soot-crusted stone of the floor, staring at nothing, never blinking when his torch spat sparks onto his skin.

Ederras began to fear that the man was deaf, or even witless. Perhaps the graveknights had mutilated his hearing and his mind as terribly as the rest of him.

Then, finally, Ochtel stirred. He raised his head, very slightly, and his remaining eye focused on the paladin through the bars. "Yes."

Thank the Inheritor. Ederras reined in his excitement, trying for a gentler tone. Obviously the man had been badly treated by the graveknights, and his manner suggested that he'd responded, in part, by detaching whatever was left of his identity from the wreckage of his body. Coaxing him back to helpfulness would be a delicate task. "Who are you? How did you come to be here?"

"I am . . . I came by misfortune." Ochtel's gaze skittered away like a frightened animal. He darted a hand toward the dungeon's shadows, as if he might find safety there. His voice was a tortured thing, breaking from his lips in blood-flecked bubbles. "An . . . old story. Not wise . . . to speak of it."

"Does it hurt to talk?" Ederras paused. The man didn't answer, but the truth was written in the shuddering hunch of his shoulders and the crust of dried blood at the corners of his mouth. "Will you allow me to try taking your pain?"

Ochtel flinched as if the paladin had struck him. "It is . . . I cannot be healed." His eye was furtive and fearful behind the greasy black ropes of his hair. "This is . . . the lictor's curse for me. A small part of his own. Torment, unending. The knights cannot die. The citadel . . . cannot fall. And I . . . live . . . who should not. In misery."

"What harm can it do to let me try?" Ederras extended a hand through the bars, reaching as far as his shackles allowed. "You're already suffering."

The man's scar-seamed lips quivered. Maybe that was fear, or maybe it was a prayer. Ederras couldn't tell. But Ochtel reached out with a shaking, three-fingered hand to clasp the paladin's. As their fingers met, Ederras drew upon Iomedae's blessing, sending a rush of restorative magic into the crippled man.

It was like no healing Ederras had ever done before. The warmth of the holy power was familiar to him, as was the glow that suffused his body and soul whenever the Lady of Valor granted her gifts to him. But when the magic flowed out of him and into Ochtel, it *changed*. Like a song shifted into another key, or a sapphire that glinted blue in the sun and violet in shade, the magic both stayed itself and became something new as it passed into the man's disfigured form.

Little else seemed to happen. None of Ochtel's scars vanished when Ederras finished his prayer. His wounds were old and long healed; untangling the painful knots they'd left in him was beyond the power of that prayer. The man's spine stayed twisted to one side, his missing eye didn't come back, and his torturously elongated fingers continued to tremble with uncontrollable shakes.

Yet some of the pain seemed to leave him. The agony of his breathing eased. The lines of suffering in his face softened. When the maimed man turned his head back toward Ederras, there was a clarity to his gaze that hadn't been there before.

"It won't last," Ochtel said. The whispery slur of his words had smoothed into a clear tenor. He'd had a beautiful voice, once. "It can't. You've poured life into a leaky vessel, and it's flowing out of this poor shell already. But thank you, all the same. Thank you. I'd forgotten what it was to breathe. Just to *breathe*, and not feel like my lungs were full of smashed glass."

Ederras sat back on the cell floor, letting his chains trail across his knees. "What did they do to you?"

"The lictor wanted to ensure my obedience. I came to the citadel a person, and he saw ore. Something to be smelted down into metal, then forged into a tool. He crushed out the weaknesses, the impurities, the flaws . . . the things that made me human, and less useful as a tool." Something that might have been a smile, or a wince, twitched at Ochtel's ruined lips. "That's what he did to me, with needles and magic and pain. He killed my companions, my lover. Tortured them to death in front of me, so I'd be obedient, or would work harder, or would give him more of myself. I did. I gave him everything, until there wasn't anything left but what you see today."

"Why did you come to Citadel Gheisteno?"

Ochtel's uneven shoulders rose in a shrug. "We thought there was something worth the risk, just as you did. One of my companions—an ambitious, accomplished wizard, not so different from your lady—wanted a spell of the paravicar's devising. The rest of us wanted treasure, or glory, or to cleanse this place's taint from the world. The wizard, she was lucky. She died fighting. The rest of us . . . met with misfortune."

Would Velenne have been luckier if I'd let her go? Ederras didn't want to dwell on that possibility. "You were the only one they kept alive?"

"Yes. Because they had use for me." Ochtel spread his mutilated hand over the dungeon floor. A tiny green seedling sprouted from the dirt between two stones, snaking up toward the torch's light and unfurling tender green leaves. He regarded it with parental affection for a moment, then snapped the seedling off at the base with a quick, efficient pinch.

"You're a druid," Ederras said, surprised. "Why would Lictor Shokneir keep and torment you for being a druid?"

Ochtel cradled the broken plant in his palm. In his hand, it withered as quickly as it had grown. The leaves wilted, then went brown and brittle, in the span of seconds. The stem twisted into a wrinkled curl. He tipped his hand and let it fall back to earth, a crippled brown butterfly. "To make a place of respite for him. A garden to remind him of the world beyond these walls. It gives him . . . peace, I think. But in this cursed place, nothing can grow without magic, and the graveknights' presence makes it . . .

harder. Their aura blights what little I can do, and sustaining the garden's life drains my own. It takes a terrible toll. The pain . . . that was why I fought him, early on. The pain was unbearable. Or so I thought, until the lictor showed me that he could hurt me in worse ways than that."

The druid held his hand up to the bars, showing the stumps of two missing fingers and the impossibly long, scar-seamed three that remained. "He took some of my fingers, and some of my lover's, and cut them apart and stitched them back together. So I'd always be able to hold onto Artuno, he said. So that I'd never be without his touch. Lictor Shokneir made me beg for that kindness."

"That's monstrous."

"Yes. The lictor is a monster." Ochtel slid his hand down the cell's bars. Remembered pain, and deep resignation, touched his voice. "He is a monster, and he has you in his grasp. The greatest kindness you can give your friends is to kill them. Quickly, mercifully. Especially the hellspawn. Lictor Shokneir intends to murder you and your lady, but I don't think he means to torture you. The same won't be true for your friend. He *hates* the Scourge, and he hates hellspawn. If you care for her, you'll spare her that."

"There must be a better way. If you can unlock our shackles, and open this door—"

"Then what?" Ochtel looked upon him with great pity. His breath had begun to claw in his throat again, and his words were breaking on his tongue. Saliva bubbled on his lips, and even by torchlight, Ederras could see that it was bloody. The druid's brief respite from suffering was running out, and his body was returning to ruin. "Will you run, having nowhere to go? Will you fight, having no weapons? They'll catch you again, and punish you for having the temerity to hope. No, there is no escape. Not alive."

"If we could get our weapons—"

Ochtel was already shaking his head. "You cannot kill the lictor. Or his lieutenants. They are *graveknights*. The knights of the

Crux are bound to their citadel, and they will return, no matter what you do. Nothing but misery lasts in this place."

"There must be *something*."

"No." Ochtel said it gently, but with finality.

The siphon finished its work. As the last of its vapor gathered in the coil's needled end, the druid pushed himself to his feet. It was a slow and painful process, requiring him to lean heavily on the wall for support as his legs popped and cracked under his weight. He drew a key from somewhere in his shapeless wrap, then opened the door and hobbled toward Jheraal with lopsided, laborious steps. With great care, he reached down and lifted the memory siphon from the Hellknight. The mist cleared from Jheraal's eyes, and she stirred weakly as her senses began to return.

"Now would be . . . the kindest time," the druid said, retreating from the cell. He locked the door and shuffled away, leaving the torch behind. The beauty of his voice had cracked and gone to dust. "Now . . . before she recovers. Before she can feel anything. Before she understands . . . what has been done. The siphon is not subtle. When she awakens . . . she will know. Best you act before then."

"I won't," Ederras said, but no one was left to hear him. Ochtel was gone, Jheraal dazed, Velenne lost to the venom in her veins. He sat alone in the dungeon's flickering shadows, watching the feeble torch burn.

Eventually it died, leaving him in darkness. The wall's uneven stones bit against Ederras's back as he leaned against them, circling around the cage of his thoughts and finding no way out.

Hope's the key. It always was. But how could he give hope to a man who refused to take it?

And if he couldn't—if there really was no way out, and no greater kindness than Ochtel had suggested—would he have the grace to see that before it was too late?

24

WITHOUT ARMOR

JHERAAL

They know about Indrath.

Jheraal kept trying to push that thought away, and it kept coming back, inexorably, through the fog of her weariness and wounds and despair. She couldn't escape it. In the prison of her memory, there was nowhere to run, nowhere to hide. No cloak of denial that she could pull over her own ugly failure.

They'd stripped away her armor, within and without, and they'd seen all the weakness that shivered underneath. *They know about my daughter.*

She had never imagined that the graveknights would care. Her daughter wasn't the reason she had marched on Citadel Gheisteno. Indrath had nothing to do with Jheraal's investigation, or her companions' tactics and capabilities, or even the internal workings of the Order of the Scourge. The girl wasn't relevant to anything that should have interested Lictor Shokneir or his lieutenants, and for that reason Jheraal had never dreamed they'd seek her out. *Families shouldn't matter for this.*

But to the lictor and his underlings, they did.

Their pursuit of that information wasn't professional. It wasn't even about hunting down and extirpating every last trace of her hellspawn bloodline. Hideous as that would have been, Jheraal could have understood it as a logical extension of a Hellknight's duty. Her own order had taken measures as extreme, and worse. All of them had.

But this wasn't about duty. It was personal, and it was rooted in a hatred so intense, so unreasoning, that even its echoes in the siphon's glass had sickened her.

She opened her eyes.

They were still in Citadel Gheisteno's dungeon. The injuries she'd suffered during their disastrous fight with the graveknights were gone, leaving only the familiar, bone-deep ache that followed magical restoration. Ederras's work, she presumed. She didn't think their captors would have bothered with such mercies.

That healing was the only comfort she found. The torch in the sconce opposite their cell had burned out, leaving nothing but a warm wisp of smoke. Darkness surrounded them, but it was no barrier to Jheraal's infernally gifted sight. She could see every detail of the dungeon, and every one convinced her that they were imprisoned in some nightmarish imagining, not a place that was or had ever been real.

There were no rats in the cells. There never had been. In any ordinary castle's dungeon, rats left scent-marked trails of grease and hair rubbed against the walls. Their tiny pellet droppings littered the corners and crevices, and their squeaks and scratches whispered through the halls. But in Citadel Gheisteno, Jheraal heard nothing and saw nothing, and knew that no living rat had ever twitched a whisker in this place.

Other strangenesses abounded. Despite the damp that should have softened it, and the chafing of their chains and bodies, the soot on the walls didn't rub off. The iron bars grating the cell door didn't show a smudge of rust. The air hung lifeless and clammy around them, undisturbed by natural currents.

Whatever the dungeon's peculiarities, its chains were solid enough, and its bars as well. They weren't going to imagine themselves free. Jheraal turned away from her fruitless examination of the cell and looked, instead, to more ordinary aspects of despair: the weak rise and fall of Velenne's chest, the hopelessness that slumped Ederras against the floor. He'd let the tiny light of his prayer die.

The Hellknight needed to rouse him out of that despair. She dragged her chains across the stones, deliberately, so he'd know she was awake. "They're going to come back with that siphon tomorrow."

"I know." The paladin closed his eyes, tipping his head back against the wall. "I'll volunteer when they do. I should have done that today."

"No. You're going to let them use it on Velenne tomorrow." When he opened his mouth to protest, as Jheraal had known he would, she cut him off mercilessly. "Don't argue. Listen. I didn't offer myself up because I wanted to spare you suffering. I took the siphon so you'd be free to talk to our captors. Do you remember what you told me back in Fishbone Alley? About how you make people become better versions of themselves? We need that. I'm not going to intimidate anyone through these bars. But you can still do what you do. I saw you with Ochtel, how you were able to reach the man he must have once been. You can still inspire. And swaying one of them to our side is about the only chance we've got."

"What does it do?" Ederras asked. "The siphon."

"It steals memories." Jheraal thought about trying to downplay what she'd sensed and suffered through the glass, but it only took her a second to discard the idea. Ederras deserved to know the truth, even if that made it harder for him. He needed to understand what they were enduring so that he could have a chance to bend their captors' loyalties.

She drew a breath. It shook, despite her best attempts at control. Tears burned behind her eyes. The Hellknight stared at the lock of their door, forcing herself to study every meaningless curve of its metal without blinking, until the heat of her grief went away. *No pity, no emotion. You will not be weak.* "It seeks out, and seizes, one of your secrets. Something personal, something that'll hurt.

The siphon didn't hunt out information that might have damaged my career or my order, and it didn't go after anything related to the investigation that led us here. It looked for the secret most likely to wound. That's all they wanted."

"Then that would be—"

"Indrath. Yes. That she exists, who she is, what she means to me. That I never told her the truth of her origins." This time Jheraal got the answer out without quavering. She was nearly as proud of that as any other pain she'd hidden. "They know about my daughter. If they want to hurt me—and they do—they'll take her heart as they took the others."

"I see. I'm sorry you had to endure it." He turned away, staring into the dark without seeing. Trying to hold back the words that gnawed at him, Jheraal knew. She wasn't surprised when, a moment later, Ederras had to say: "You want me to give Velenne to that."

"I want you to save us. More than us. It's not just our lives anymore." *They know about Indrath.* She wanted to howl it. Instead, she said only: "If we get the chain, we can stop them. So that's what we have to do. What *you* have to do."

The silence settled in again, heavier than it had been. Hours trickled away, uncounted and unknowable. Jheraal dozed off when she could, grateful for the small mercy of sleep. She didn't know if Ederras slept, or if Velenne could.

Eventually a pair of zombies came carrying gruel, water, and a latrine bucket. One of them replaced the burned-out torch with a fresh brand. After pushing cups and bowls through a slot in the bars near the floor, the mindless, stinking undead shuffled away.

Jheraal took the gruel, the water, and the bucket. When it came to sustenance, there was no sense refusing. She fished a scrap of rotting skin from one of the cups and a squirming maggot from one of the bowls, flicking them both aside. "Which do you want, the corpse water or the maggot porridge?"

"Nothing wrong with a good maggot porridge," Ederras replied with the same black humor. "It's considered quite a delicacy up in Mendev, you know. Grain untainted enough to host maggots is a treasure. Corpse water, on the other hand, tends to make people sick. So I, being blessedly immune to such things, will take that."

"A true champion of the people." She passed him the fouled cup and tried the other. The water was stale and flat, with an unpleasant mineral aftertaste, but Jheraal was too thirsty to care. She drank it in tiny sips, trying to make it last.

The porridge wasn't any better. Hard, uncooked grains dotted its pasty mush, flavorless except for the charred black bits that had been scraped up from the bottom. Jheraal forced herself to swallow it in globs, because chewing it would probably have chipped her teeth. She ate it, though. All of it. She'd take whatever they gave her.

"You've had prison fare before," Ederras observed, watching her.

"A few times. Worse than this."

"Dare I ask?"

"There'll be time for stories later. We need to make plans now." She jerked a clawed thumb at his neglected gruel. "And eat that. You need to keep whatever strength you can."

"Spoken like a survivor." He ate it, though, and drank his water. "What's your plan?"

"None of the graveknights will bend, and there's no use talking to zombies. We only have two options: Sechel and Ochtel."

Ederras set his empty bowl aside, stacking the cup neatly inside. "Sechel's the stronger, but Ochtel's the easier to reach. Despite all they've done to him, he hasn't given himself over to evil. There's still a glimmer of humanity in him—and still a part of him that wants to be human."

Wants to be human . . . Jheraal narrowed her eyes as a sudden thought struck her. "Did the assassin look different when she came to our cell?"

"Her eyes weren't glowing. And she had hair, which I don't remember seeing before."

"That's part of it, but . . . it was more than that." Jheraal cast her mind back, trying to remember what it was that had struck her about Sechel. Then it hit her, all at once, in a tingling rush of recognition. *The weight of the world was gone.*

The assassin hadn't become kinder, or gentler, or less deadly. But she had become *human,* and she had done it in some way that meant more than a temporary disguise. Jheraal had lived that transformation herself—the glorious, giddy buoyancy that came with having one's anchor of difference cut loose—and she recognized it in another. "She's not hellspawn anymore."

"What do you mean?"

"She's transformed herself. Like I did, with the hat, before I met Indrath's father. *That's* what's different. She's made herself human." The Hellknight sat up straighter in her chains. "Or someone else did."

"Lictor Shokneir? Do you suppose that's why she's been working for the graveknights?" Ederras raised his head, alert to the possibility of hope, then frowned. "But even supposing that's true, how does it help us?"

"I don't know. Not yet. But it tells us something about who she is, and what she wants—and if we know that, then we have the beginnings of a lever." Jheraal shifted in her shackles. She felt naked without her armor, and even more vulnerable that she had to trust in someone else to chisel out the secrets that might save them. A friend, but still . . . "That's what you need to get from Ochtel tomorrow. The rest of that story."

He nodded, turning back to Velenne. At some point while Jheraal was dozing, Ederras had folded the diabolist's bloodstained cloak into a pillow to keep her head off the floor's filthy stones. Now he looked on her with such naked sorrow that the Hellknight glanced away, not wanting to intrude.

"She'll probably take it better than we can," Jheraal said, keeping her eyes locked on a skull outside their cell. It was hard not to see her companions in her peripheral vision, though. The dungeons didn't afford that much privacy. "Doesn't she hurt herself for fun?"

"Not exactly." Ederras lifted a hand to the diabolist's face, trailing his fingers against her cheek. "And I'm as much afraid for *us* as I am for her. If you're right, and what the lictor wants, even more than he wants to hurt House Thrune, is simply to make her suffer . . . then I fear he'll do it by breaking us apart. Velenne's secrets aren't likely to hurt *her*. She's lived her whole life avoiding the risk of blackmail, and I don't think she feels much remorse for any of the evil she's done. But I . . . I might have more difficulty with it."

"Why?" Jheraal lifted a scaled eyebrow at him. "You *know* what she is. You know what Thrunes do. Asmodeans. It can't possibly be a surprise."

"Abstract knowledge is one thing. Details are another." He glanced up, but his hand stayed on Velenne's brow, soothing her through her uneasy slumber. "A woman might know her husband's unfaithful, but finding him in bed with his mistress is another thing entirely. A merchant might know a partner's dishonest, but catching him as he's pocketing stolen gold? Those are moments of rage. Murders. Because *seeing* is different from *knowing*." Ederras's hand stilled, cupping the angle of her jaw. "I love her, you know. Despite it all."

"Then don't let them take that."

"That easy?"

"Doesn't have to be that hard." Jheraal grinned, a grab at levity on the gallows steps. "Or so I've been told."

"I suppose that's true." He smiled, a little, and touched Velenne's dark hair again. Winding it around and around his finger, like a ribbon for a memory. "True enough to try, anyway."

Some time later, Sechel returned. Ochtel was with her, tilted steeply to the side so that his shapeless clothes hung from him like flags in a windless sky. The disfigured man kept three steps behind the assassin, his gaze fixed on the ground.

That wasn't just deference, Jheraal thought. He was trying to hide himself. His face, his thoughts, whatever was left of his private and independent self. Surrender had become its own kind of defiance.

Maybe. If she wasn't just seeing what she wanted to see.

Sechel drew the memory siphon out of her cloak as she came to their cell. "That first session was fascinating. Shall we see what the rest of you have to hide?"

"I'll go next," Ederras said, pushing himself to his feet and grabbing the bars on either side of the door, just as he and Jheraal had agreed earlier. It would have been too suspicious if the paladin had given his lover up easily. He had to put himself out first, and he had to do it desperately, so that their captors' cruelty would make them refuse.

The Hellknight watched him from the corner of her eye while keeping her head down and her shoulders sunk in apparent defeat. This was the riskiest part of their gambit.

She wasn't worried about Ederras's performance convincing their captors. The paladin wasn't a particularly good liar, but for this, he didn't have to be. He didn't need to feign anything. He just had to let his real fear and worry show.

What they couldn't control was whether Ederras's insistence that he go first would affect Sechel's choice of where to place the siphon. Despite her taunts, the assassin hadn't struck Jheraal as much of a sadist. There was an affected artifice to her threats, and a lack of interest in their responses, that made the Hellknight think Sechel was merely going through the motions in her mockery.

The real cruelty, Jheraal guessed, was coming from higher up the chain. The assassin, like a hired torturer, was only carrying out the duties for which she'd been paid.

But if she *had* been instructed to torment them, then it might not matter whether she was personally invested in the results. If she thought Ederras would be hurt more by watching Velenne undergo the siphon, then—

"No," Sechel said. "The Thrune woman first."

Ederras protested, but allowed himself to be pushed aside as the assassin laid the siphon upon Velenne's head. The clear glass clouded with memories, the diabolist's eyes fluttered open over shining blue mist, and Jheraal had the surreal experience of watching someone else succumb to the same magic that taken so much, so intimately, from her.

Almost as soon as the glass was anchored, Sechel left the dungeon, confirming Jheraal's guess that the assassin wasn't interested in watching their pain. Ochtel remained, listless and unmoving long after Sechel had vanished.

"Who is that woman?" Ederras asked at last, turning away from the unconscious diabolist and approaching Ochtel as far as his chains allowed. Anger tinged his words, but it was nearly eclipsed by sorrow, and compassion for whatever struggles had bent the assassin into becoming what she was. Listening, Jheraal was struck with wonder. She didn't think the paladin was feigning any of that. "Why is she doing this? No—wait." He let go of the bars, extending his fingers through them instead. "Allow me to heal you first. It isn't fair to force you into talking otherwise."

Cleverly baited. In accepting the healing, Ochtel would—if there was enough decency left in him—also accept the obligation to answer their questions. *And that one still wants to imagine himself decent.*

The druid stayed frozen for a long moment, but eventually he unfolded himself from his stillness and reached a mutilated hand to meet the offered one. Divine light blossomed between their fingertips, and Ochtel sank back with a groan. If any of the man's wounds had in fact been healed, Jheraal couldn't see it, but the grinding weight of pain seemed to have lifted from him.

"She is a killer," Ochtel said, his eye closed in agonized relief. "She came to the citadel a year ago, tracking a man she'd been sent to murder. Her target was already dead—he was a fool, one of the dozens who came here seeking glory and whose bones now walk in Lictor Shokneir's army—but she did not rest until she found his corpse among all the others. She took his head and his family's locket to prove that she'd found the right one.

"The lictor was impressed. Not only that this assassin was able to survive the citadel long enough to find her quarry among the dead, but that she *would*—that she had the professional pride to find the bones of a man whose soul was sent to the courts of the afterworld long ago. Few would go so far to confirm a kill. So rather than capturing or killing the assassin, he chose to offer her a contract."

"To murder my brother, strip the hearts out of hellspawn, and steal the devilheart chain," Ederras said flatly. "What did he offer to pay her for all these enormities?"

"Transformation. Transcendence. That one has always sought to . . . erase herself. She wishes to be without a history, to become unknowable. She would, if she could, rewrite her existence so that it began anew every time she walked through a door, and ended each time she left.

"But she has—has always had—one desire, despite her pretense that she wants nothing. She wished to become human, and no longer hellspawn, so Lictor Shokneir promised her that."

"He can do that?" Jheraal interrupted, startled out of her silence.

"He can make the promise." Ochtel's eye was a gleam of reflected torchlight behind a lank black curtain of hair. "Would it tempt you, too? You are nothing like her. Why do you want so badly to be something different?"

"Sometimes changing yourself is less painful than trying to change the world." Jheraal met the crippled man's scrutiny without blinking. "But you said the lictor can only make the promise. Not the transformation?"

Ochtel's shrug was as lopsided as the man himself. "Within the walls of Citadel Gheisteno, his power is absolute. Beyond . . . I would be less confident in his promise. Lictor Shokneir can only reshape reality so far."

"I assume Sechel doesn't know that," Ederras said. "Isn't the lictor worried about her being upset when she discovers his deception?"

"What will she do? She is an assassin. Her power is to kill. But Lictor Shokneir cannot die, so he has nothing to fear from her. By the time she discovers that she's sold herself for false gold, he will have everything he wants, and she will have no recourse."

"What else *does* he want? He already has us imprisoned. He has the chain, he has his hearts. I'm surprised he hasn't sent Sechel on her way." The paladin glanced at the siphon swirling over Velenne's insensible form. His jaw tightened, but his tone remained mild. "He doesn't need an assassin to steal our memories. He could do it himself, or send one of his other servants."

"He doesn't need her to steal them," Ochtel agreed placidly. "But to enact them, and use your fears and secrets to take his revenge on Imperial Cheliax . . . that is another tale. He *does* need the assassin for that, because he needs hands that are not shackled to his curse."

"When will Sechel discover that her transformation's a ruse?" Jheraal asked. "What does it take to break the illusion?"

Ochtel's shoulders huddled inward. Under the flickering torch-light, his face looked like a half-melted wax mask. "The lictor's power does not extend past the bridge. He can store a little of his magic in amulets, and he has given one such to the assassin—by the time it fades, the work will already be done. Yet the magic will be broken immediately if she removes the talisman while beyond his reach."

"So if she crosses the bridge and takes off the amulet, she'll discover the truth?"

"Yes." Ochtel's tongue flicked out to touch his scar-seamed lips nervously, but he held the Hellknight's gaze. Then he turned his eye to the blasted, blackened skulls that grinned from the walls all around them. "And if she does, and you are able to use that to win your freedom, then I would ask a boon for . . . this. My aid." His voice was weakening, slipping back toward a crumbled slur, as the Inheritor's magic began to drain away.

Ederras leaned forward in his chains. "What would you ask?"

"Take me . . . with you. Across the bridge. Help me exact a . . . vengeance. One that will last."

"We'll do it if we can," the paladin promised. "Just tell us how."

"Come . . . to the garden. Later. If you are able to . . . win free. If not, there is . . . no point . . . to my dreaming of such things."

After that, the druid said no more. He curled his stilted legs under his shapeless clothing, bent his head and bony shoulders into a ball over them, and went as inert as Havarel's brass golem when it didn't have orders. In the hush that followed, Ederras and Jheraal exchanged a look.

"Can you do it?" the Hellknight asked. Quietly, although she didn't fear being overheard by Ochtel. Not after what he'd just said. "Can you get that thought into her head?"

"What exactly do I have to do?"

"The siphon won't let you lie." Jheraal fought down a shudder, remembering how relentlessly its magic had stripped her defenses away, peeling back the veils of her identity as deftly and cruelly as a scalpel cutting through skin. "It will take everything—*every-thing*—bound up with your memories of pain. If you can make Ochtel's revelation part of that memory, then the assassin will see it and know that it's true. Then we just have to hope she acts on the druid's information, and that he's right about what will break the lictor's falsehood." The Hellknight paused. "Can you do that?"

Ederras nodded. His eyes went to the charred and grinning skulls in the walls, the disfigured lump of Ochtel balled like discarded clay in the corner, the real-and-unreal weight of the chains that bound their wrists and ankles. Then to Velenne, dying slowly in a dream from which he couldn't wake her.

"It won't be hard," he said.

25

TRUTH IN GLASS

SECHEL

Her plan was going perfectly.

The revelation of the Hellknight's daughter would undoubtedly please Lictor Shokneir, and the Thrune woman's memories held everything Sechel needed to enact her scheme. She had the ritual, the setting, and all the prurient details that would outrage both sides of the religious divide—the Iomedaeans that such a thing could be permitted, the Asmodeans that it could be interrupted—and set the court gossips gleefully aflutter.

All that remained was to examine the visions that the memory siphon had taken from the paladin. If nothing there contradicted the story that Sechel planned to tell, then she could set to work arranging the slaughter.

And then, with that last wave of deaths, she'd be free. Free of sin, free of shadow. Free to shake off the dust of her history and make a new way, unencumbered by her past or the infernal stain of her blood.

Her step was light as she made her way back to the druid's garden and pushed open its gray-glassed door.

The greenery enfolded and soothed her, restoring an ache in her soul that Citadel Gheisteno seemed to bruise into even the hardest hearts. Sechel had never been drawn to wild spaces, and had little interest in flowers or trees, but after days in the unrelieved grimness of the dead fortress, she understood why Lictor Shokneir needed this place. She did, too. It was a last, precious reminder of a world that the graveknight had long lost. He couldn't have it anymore, but he could look upon its image and remember.

So could she. And soon enough, when all this was done, she'd be able to walk under a real sun with a real breeze in her hair. She could have all the flowers in the world, not just the tiny, jewel-like handful that Ochtel fed his own life to keep growing in the dark.

As if her thought had summoned him, the maimed man was suddenly before her. One moment the path was clear. The next, the druid was standing in her way, a gaunt, misshapen ghost in a dirt-stained shroud.

It took all of Sechel's training not to react. *No one* should have been able to surprise her. Not here, not anywhere. "What do you want?"

He didn't respond to the harshness of her tone. He didn't even seem to notice it. His words rasped out in a crawl, too mired in pain to manage any other emotion—if he even felt any others after all the graveknights had done to him. "A . . . curiosity . . . only. I wondered . . . what you might have seen . . . in their minds."

"What possible difference could it make to you?"

"As I said. Only . . . curiosity." Ochtel's face was placid, his eye an oasis of unlikely tranquility in a landscape of blasted flesh. "I wonder . . . who we have . . . in our cells. Whether they are . . . as they seem."

Sechel shrugged. Her startlement had worn off, and she wasn't about to let Ochtel spoil her good mood. "So far. More or less. The Hellknight's a Hellknight, although her discipline's not as perfect as she'd like to pretend. The Thrune woman is *exactly* as she seems. Everything they say about House Thrune is true."

"And the paladin?"

"Is the last one remaining." Lifting a corner of her cloak, Sechel let the siphon's cloudy glass shimmer in the garden's starry lights. "I'll have his secrets soon enough. But I don't doubt he is what he claims. Even if I hadn't seen his prayers in battle, the Thrune woman's fears would prove that much."

"What could . . . one such as that . . . fear?"

"Losing." Her patience was waning. She'd indulged Ochtel long enough. Sechel strode deeper into the green, leaving the ruined druid behind. "That's what that woman dreads. Making mistakes and losing."

He didn't try to follow. Sechel walked through yellow-streaked lemon balm and flowering marjoram, rustling the leaves to release their whispering sweetness. It wasn't a thing she would ordinarily have done—usually she avoided scents, as she avoided anything that might betray her presence—but being immured among the unfeeling dead had left her yearning for any touch of life.

Soon, she consoled herself. Soon it would be done.

An immense live oak interrupted the path ahead. Sechel leaped easily up its branches, springing from one to the next until she was twenty feet over the mossy ground. There she perched, comfortable as a gargoyle in a church tower, and drew out the memory siphon.

Each of the visions she'd drawn through the glass had been different. The siphon smoothed and organized its stolen memories, arranging them into something coherent enough for an outsider to follow, but each sequence was shaped by the person who had lived it. The Hellknight's recollections had been orderly and methodical, laid out with careful precision, while the Thrune woman's had revolved around her own aspirations and desires, spiked with stormy flashes of contempt for the weak and admiration of the strong.

The paladin's were lit by a gentle, unearthly glow, visible even within the siphon as a steady golden sheen. The presence of his goddess shone through his memories like sunlight, and like sunlight, it made Sechel feel uncomfortably exposed.

She pushed through the discomfort, drawing the stored visions from the glass. *What do you fear?*

Loss. The answer took shape in wavering, foggy images. The face of a laughing boy running under a fig tree appeared and then melted into that of the scholar Sechel had murdered in Vaneo Celverian. Others came and went: a Thuvian sorceress whose skin shone like fire-warmed brass; a black-bearded man in plate mail scarred by demons' claws; friends and comrades, less distinct. Some fell to fiendish fangs or flames or the gibbering madness of the Worldwound. Some didn't. Not all of the people Ederras mourned were dead, but all were lost to him.

And then there was Velenne. In the paladin's memories, she held a grace that the real woman didn't always show, and such a sense of mourning surrounded her that Sechel had to remind herself that the diabolist wasn't actually dead.

They'll take her. Dread—his, not hers, yet the secondhand emotion was strong enough to clench icy fingers in the assassin's gut—knotted around the thought. Other images swam around it, entangled in the net of the man's worries: Citadel Gheisteno's stern walls and unyielding bars, the endless armies of the dead, and Sechel herself, pitiless and cold, with Ochtel lurking behind her like a one-eyed shadow.

It was an oddly flattering perspective. In the paladin's eyes, she was an adversary to be feared and respected, someone dangerous enough to merit mining information from Ochtel. Sechel, watching her reflection in the siphon's memories, allowed herself a small glow of pride.

Then she paused, frowning, as remembered words drifted to her ears in watery, rippling echoes. *Lictor Shokneir can only reshape reality so far.*

. . . her transformation's a ruse . . .

. . . crosses the bridge and takes off the amulet . . .

. . . the siphon won't let you lie.

Slowly, flexing her fingers against a sudden chilled stiffness, Sechel emerged from her trance. She stared at the oak leaves without seeing them, listened without hearing the sighing breezes, breathed the garden's air without tasting its damp earth or green herbs.

She touched the amulet that hung around her neck. As ever, it was heavy and cold against her skin. An odor of metallic smoke clung to it, always a little stronger than it should be. The Crux's skull, chains, and broken stones were worked into the amulet's face, although the emblem was only dimly visible through the soot that masked the rough-edged metal.

Lictor Shokneir had given her the amulet to ward her against Citadel Gheisteno's many dangers. It shielded her from the soul-searing gaze of the skulls on the bridge, protected her from the graveknights' own devastating auras, and caused the castle's lesser undead to turn blind eyes to her passing.

Does it deceive me as much as it does them?

There was one way to find out. Unfolding from her crouch, Sechel tumbled from the oak's branch onto the garden path and made her way to its door.

If her transformation held once she removed the amulet on the far side of the bridge, then she'd know that Ochtel had, for some inscrutable reason of his own, chosen to lie to their prisoners in order to lure her into a fool's errand. But if it failed . . .

Do you accept this as payment in full? Lictor Shokneir had asked.

And she, so quickly, so blindly, had answered: *Yes.*

An old, familiar anger burned in Sechel's chest as she made her way through the gloomy halls and back to the inner courtyard. The skulls in the walls were blind to her, as were the skeletons clattering in rust-grimed mail and the wights with their milky dead eyes. She walked through the castle, hood thrown back and hands on her knives, and none of them ever glanced her way.

Because of the amulet? Or because they thought she was nothing to fear?

You're being too suspicious. Ochtel might have lied.

The words rang hollow even in her own mind, though. There was no reason for Ochtel to lie, and every reason for Lictor Shokneir to deceive her.

Months of work, dozens of deaths . . . had she done all of that for nothing?

Beyond the citadel's gatehouses, the slim thread of its bridge stretched across the chasm that separated the haunted fortress from the world. Black on this end, gray on the other. Unreal into real.

Sechel hesitated for only a heartbeat before she drew up her hood, crossed beneath the portcullises' iron fangs, and walked through the guard towers' looming silence. Her boots made not a whisper over the bridge's worn skulls. She felt them underfoot, but couldn't see them. Not clearly. Not with her weak human eyes.

If I'm not human, why can't I see? But the thought gave her little consolation. It was too easy to steal sight. Sechel herself could do it half a dozen ways, and she wasn't the deathless lord of a cursed castle.

On the far side of the bridge, she stopped and tipped her face up to the cool mountain night. There was a vibrant breath on the wind, evanescent and inexpressible, that did not exist in Citadel Gheisteno. It was as if she'd stepped from the stark lines of a woodcut back into the color and sensation of the living world. A gray flatness had lifted from her vision, a dullness from her tongue.

She was beyond the reach of the lictor's power. And so, with numb and uncertain fingers, she lifted the amulet from her neck.

At first, nothing happened, and Sechel let herself hope that the druid had lied, or had simply been wrong.

And then, bit by bit, her world began to change.

Starlight filled her vision. Sechel's infernal heritage lifted the shadows from the world, sharpening fuzzy details into clarity and piercing the deepest darkness with quicksilver tones. Her hearing became more acute, as if she were unwrapping a thick woolen scarf from her ears, layer by layer. The wind touched her sensitized skin more keenly, and she felt its caress like a blow.

It wasn't just the citadel's curse vanishing from her awareness. *She* was changing. The weight of her hair left her shoulders. The scrape of her nails in the fingertips of her gloves disappeared. Under the fine gray kidskin, she knew, her fingers would be as they'd always been: stubbed, scarred, deformed. Monstrous.

Ochtel had told the truth. She'd been paid in false gold.

Lictor Shokneir had never transformed her. He'd never had the power. Outside the walls of Citadel Gheisteno, reality was beyond his ability to shape. Only within the haunted fortress could he control it enough to give her the illusion of humanity, and only with the amulet could he sustain that illusion long enough that it might have robbed her of the chance to strike back.

Do you accept this as payment in full?

Sechel squeezed her eyes shut to block out the tears of hurt and rage. The lictor had *cheated* her—of hope, of self-respect, of what should have been her moment of greatest triumph. He had treated her like a child. Like a servant. Like some underling whose wishes could be mocked and cast aside without cost.

But if the maimed druid had been right about one thing, he'd been wrong about another. Sechel's revenge wasn't limited to murder. She'd discovered Lictor Shokneir's treachery in time to pay him back with better coin than that. Something that might hurt even a graveknight who couldn't die.

Replacing the amulet, the assassin retraced her steps across the bridge.

Her false humanity didn't return when she put the amulet back on, but the skulls didn't ignite on the bridge either, so Sechel approached the undead of Citadel Gheisteno with measured care, unsure whether they would treat her as an invader or continue to ignore her.

When she spotted a cluster of walking corpses gathered under one of the rotting pentices, she veered toward them, intent on finding an answer.

Four of the skeletal creatures were clustered under another wearing a skull-faced helm in imitation of the Crux graveknights. The leader wore the rat-gnawed ruins of a foot soldier's leather armor and a soot-crusted breastplate punched through by a cavalry lance. The lesser undead wore nothing save the rags of priestly vestments and their own skins, which had dried and hardened into rawhide crusts over withered muscle and rinds of soapy, cured fat.

Sechel strode forward, scuffing her boots against the courtyard's paving stones so the creatures would look up.

She held her relaxed pose, making a show of studying her foes with contempt, as the creatures' vacant eyes locked onto her and their mouths stretched into hissing grins. The creature that had been holding a picked-over human skull—the scrap they'd all been so fascinated by—tossed it aside.

Snarling and clawing, they came at her in a rush.

Sechel waited until she could smell their fetid breath, and then she dropped the bottle she'd been holding in one hand and drew her enchanted lenses from the band of her hood onto her eyes with the other. Dense white mist flowed from the shattered vial, rising up into an opaque cloud that defeated even the corpses' unearthly eyes.

Not hers, though. Not with those violet-tinted lenses shimmering over her sight and cutting through the fog. Sechel dropped into a crouch as the first of them came at her, letting it lurch off balance as it grabbed at the empty air. The lenses distorted her vision in the mist, but she'd worn them for years and was well accustomed to adjusting. Unerringly the assassin swept her left leg forward, kicking the creature's ankles out from under it. The undead cleric toppled, hissing, and the two behind it went down as well, tangled in its flailing limbs.

They'd be back up in seconds, but seconds were all she needed. Staying low, Sechel danced around the helmed wight's blind graspings and popped up behind it, then drove her twin knives deep into the creature's unguarded back.

Violet-red energy crackled between the black blades, meeting in forked arcs inside the wight's ribcage. The undead creature threw its head back and screamed, and the back of its throat was lit as though with dragon's fire.

It sagged on her blades, dead before she pulled out the knives. Sechel slung its weight off her weapons, throwing the corpse into its rag-robed brethren. That sent them stumbling again, and when she saw the nearest of them grab the twice-dead thing to hurl its impatiently aside, she struck. Two hard upward blows into the surprised creature's chest, another flare of amaranth that flooded its eye sockets and poured from its mouth, and the creature collapsed.

The three remaining undead, frightened now, clustered together in the fog. Eyes darting warily for some sign of motion, tongues flickering through their yellow teeth, they fumbled to find a way out of the blinding white mist.

One raked a claw through the space where Sechel had stood while killing its companion, seeming almost fearful at the chance that it might catch her. Another backed away hurriedly, snatching at nothingness while stretching its foot behind it to feel out a retreat.

That was the moment she'd been waiting for. Soundlessly, Sechel slipped through the mist, raised her boot, and stomped on the fleeing corpse's extended calf. Dead brown bone punched through its shin. The creature jerked its head up, squealing, and Sechel cut its throat twice from behind, one knife scissoring across its spine left to right, the other crossing over in the opposite direction. Magic flared from the black blades, and the monstrosity fell, biting its own withered scrap of a tongue into pieces that hit the ground on either side of its head.

One of the survivors flung itself at the flash of crimson energy, but Sechel sidestepped it easily, her twilight cloak swirling around its claws. She laughed, both in delight and to unnerve them, and kicked one of the dead creatures so that it flopped in the mist. When one of the remainder snapped its head toward the movement, Sechel slid around to its blind side and tore it apart.

The last one turned and fled. Sechel let it clear the mist, just to give it a glimpse of whatever hope it could feel, before she took it down.

She wiped her knives clean on the ragged remnants of the leader's armor, satisfied with her own performance. None of the undead had touched her, and none had needed more than a single pass to drop. *Good.*

Of course, the graveknights wouldn't be so easy. Better to avoid their notice altogether, if she could.

If not . . .

The assassin shrugged to herself as she turned away from the undead guardians' remains and toward the citadel's soot-shrouded chapel. Her cloak melted into the haunted night, blurring her form until she seemed no more substantial than any other shadow flowing along the blackened walls.

If she couldn't hide, she could always kill.

26

THE BONE SMITHY

EDERRAS

"Get up."

Ederras opened his eyes. Sechel was staring at him through the cell bars. He couldn't see any hair under the shifting colors of her hood, although with only their failing torch for light, it was hard to be sure. Gloves masked her fingers, giving him no clue there.

Her eyes told the tale, though. Her eyes, glowing eerily in the dungeon's gloom, and her anger. The assassin had given up her hopes of humanity.

What does that mean for us?

He stood, ignoring the scrape of his shackles. Behind him, Jheraal stirred in her bonds, but didn't rise. "You've already taken the memories you wanted. Why have you come now?"

"'*Why*?'" Sechel echoed mockingly. She unslung the makeshift bundle that had been strapped around her shoulder. "As if you don't know. As if this were anything other than exactly what you prayed for. I watched your memories in the glass. I know what you hoped to achieve with them. And now you have it. So stop pretending to be innocent, and take what you wanted."

Stooping, Sechel untied the knots in the stained brown blanket. She pulled back its mangy corners and laid it out on the floor, letting the metal inside catch the torch's weak flame.

The bundle held a sword, a mace, and a long-bladed knife. Ederras recognized the weapons immediately. The mace, its haft scarred to match a Scourge knight's armor and its leather wrappings worn thin by years of chafing against steel-clad fingers, was unmistakably Jheraal's. The knife was the curved obsidian blade that Velenne carried around for decoration.

And the longsword, its pommel gilded with Iomedae's radiant halo and its silver blade traced with intricate designs, was his own holy brand. Ederras could sense the thrum of its sacred magic even through the bars, striking a chord of communion deep in his soul.

Along with their weapons, the assassin had delivered Velenne's scroll tubes and spell component pouches, Jheraal's collection of unguents and oils, and the padded, stiff-sided case in which Ederras kept his potions.

Flipping a skull-crowned key in a gloved palm, Sechel smirked at the paladin's surprise. "You look disappointed. Did you think you'd have to spend days breaking down my barriers to persuade me? Please. I'm not Ochtel. I don't need you to pretend to care about me as a person, and it wouldn't work very well if you did."

"I've never *pretended* to care about anyone," Ederras retorted. He wasn't ready to let himself hope that she'd really come to set them free. Not yet. This might just be some cruel game the assassin was playing. She had, after all, seized their secrets by magic to better hurt them.

"Then we have that in common." Sechel's smirk spread into a grin, but above it her eyes were hard as murder. She glanced from Ederras to Jheraal. "You'll want to get out of the dungeons soon. I couldn't get your weapons quietly. Had to kill the guardians to retrieve them, and then had to tip my hand again coming here, so the lictor and his dogs will probably be on their way shortly."

"My armor," the Hellknight broke in, standing beside Ederras in the cell.

"Too well guarded for me to risk, and too heavy to move anyway." Sechel shrugged, unconcerned, as she bent to unlock the door. "The rest of your belongings are in the bone smithy, if you want to get them yourselves. Your helms, armor, shields. All the metal bits that *don't* get shoved into people's heads."

"The armor does, actually," Jheraal said. "I'd be happy to give you a demonstration."

Ederras tested the door. It opened, and Sechel stood aside, but he didn't step out. "You're really just going to let us go."

"That depends. Do you *want* to go? Or would you rather stand in your cell asking stupid questions until the graveknights come to finish the job?"

"You'll forgive me for doubting your intentions."

The assassin stepped away, shrugging again as she glanced over her shoulder into the darkness beyond the wall's torch. Ederras couldn't hear whatever she heard, but Sechel tensed and drew her gloved hands to the hilts of her knives. "Doubt them all you'd like, but you'd better move fast if you plan to move at all. You'll find the bone smithy south of the chapel. Behrion Khollarix has returned, so he'll likely be there, along with his honor guard. If he hasn't torn it apart to make more guards yet, your armor will be inside.

"Paravicar Leroung has a workshop near the top of the north tower, and Lictor Shokneir has a throne room above that, where you might be able to find him if he isn't wandering the parapets or headed this way to destroy you. Ochtel keeps to his garden, mostly. I don't expect that one will take part in any fighting. Beyond that, all you have to worry about are their armies of undead and the curse of the citadel itself."

"Fight with us," Ederras urged. "You've seen what we can do. We took down two of the three graveknights here, and that was when you opposed us. With you on our side, we could destroy every walking corpse in Citadel Gheisteno."

Sechel laughed. She lifted a hand to her color-shifting hood, drawing down a curious cloth band fitted with a pair of violet lenses that covered her eyes. "No. No, I don't think so. I've done quite enough to help you already. The lictor thought he could cheat in his bargain with me, so I've done the same to him. That will serve as my revenge.

"Besides," she added, tossing them a second key before melting into the shadows, "I rather like this memory siphon. I think I'll keep it. You can distract the graveknights while I do.

"I should say, in parting, that I haven't told them anything about your memories yet. If I escape, you'll stay protected. If not . . . well, you know what the siphon holds. They'll get all of your precious little secrets if they catch me. So I trust you won't let that happen."

Jheraal scowled, picking up the key. She fitted it to her shackles, unlocking her ankle cuffs before kicking away her chains and opening the paladin's. Holding out her wrists for him to free her hands, the Hellknight nodded toward Velenne. "Best get her up, and quickly. We're going to need her, and her devils, for what lies ahead."

"My antidotes are in the potion case." Ederras unlocked the last of her restraints and went to open Velenne's. With the shackles gone, his raw and blistered wrists stung in the open air, but he welcomed the pain as a token of freedom.

The Hellknight handed him the case. Although Ederras knew its contents by heart, and could have picked out any one of its oils or philters without looking, he conjured a divine light and studied the antidote vial carefully under its white radiance before he uncapped it. A sniff detected nothing amiss. Neither did a cautious taste.

If their captors had contaminated the antidote, he couldn't tell. Wishing he could be surer, Ederras poured the colorless liquid down Velenne's throat, tipping her chin until she swallowed. He followed it with a second potion, the most powerful restorative he had.

A long moment passed. Then she coughed and her fingers curled, and her eyes fluttered open in the dimness, eventually focusing on him. "Where—"

"Dungeons of Citadel Gheisteno," Jheraal answered tersely, pushing the diabolist's returned belongings into her hands. "You spent several days being poisoned. Much as I'd love to give you weeks to recover, we need to get out of here before the lictor's forces corner us in this cell."

"Ah." Wincing, Velenne pushed herself up to a sitting position, then began slotting her wands back into their crimson-banded hip sheath. "Not . . . the best awakening I've ever had, but not quite the worst." She tied her pouches back into place and stood, grimacing as she raked her fingers through her dirt-flecked hair.

Ederras took her elbow to steady her. "Can you fight? If you need another prayer—"

"Save it. I'm sure we'll need all your prayers soon enough." She touched his wrist lightly, drawing some of the sting from her tone, as she slipped her arm from his hand. "I'm well enough to go."

"Are you sure?" He could see the stiffness of her movements, the weariness under her eyes. "Your wounds were grave, and the poison couldn't have helped. And the memory siphon was hard for all of us." He'd been prepared, and it had been hideous to feel those unreal fingers digging through his mind. Velenne, unconscious, had been defenseless and taken unawares. "If you need more time—"

"Then that would be unfortunate, since we don't have it." Velenne canted her head to one side, regarding him with a mixture of affection and regret. "The memory siphon. Is that what that was? I thought it was only a nightmare."

"No. It was a device Paravicar Leroung made. It stole memories."

"I know. It tells you what it does while it's working, even if you're dreaming. Isn't that ingenious? Otherwise you might not be aware you were being tortured." She straightened her earrings and adjusted the choker about her throat, centering its black star sapphire. "So all of that was real."

"What did it take from you?"

"Nothing you'd want to know, my love. That was the entire point." Her lips quirked, regret winning over affection. "They wanted to know what would cause you to cast me aside, or worse. There are, I'm afraid, many such things. Better if you don't ask, especially now. We have more urgent matters."

Jheraal took the torch from the wall sconce, holding it out to Velenne. "What about your dog? Did he get out alive? Did he get the children to safety?"

Velenne started to answer, hesitated, and shook her head. Gentling her tone, she said, "Vhaeros is outside the fortress, that's all I can say. I lost contact with him when he crossed the bridge of skulls. The same magic that prevents my teleportation has severed our link."

The Hellknight nodded, unhappy but unsurprised. "All right. We need our armor. The assassin said it was being kept in the 'bone smithy,' whatever that is. Did you come across any references to such a place while you were studying the citadel?"

Velenne shook her head again, closing her eyes to steady herself against a visible wave of dizziness afterward. "What little I was able to find was almost entirely about the original citadel, before the Order of the Crux was extirpated and this haunted version arose. The most detailed account I could locate of Citadel Gheisteno after its fall was by Gholam of the Thousand Boots, who was . . . not known for his accuracy, let us say. He waxed long and poetic about the terrors of graveknights, and his own bravery in daring to confront them, but he never mentioned a bone smithy.

"Truth be told, now that we've seen the place, I'm not convinced he ever really came here. Little of what we've seen seems to correspond to his descriptions. Gholam wrote that the citadel existed only as the lictor imagined it—'we walked within the lictor's dream, and all was as he dreamed it'—but I wonder whether that wasn't an excuse for passing off his own inventions as fact."

"Fine," the Hellknight said. "If we don't have solid information, then we'll have to charge in blindly and hope for the best." Mace in hand, she led the way out of the dungeon.

Their way out of the dungeon was barred by a wall of animated flesh. That was the source of the pickled-meat odors, and of the moans that Ederras had heard earlier. There must have been at least thirty bodies pressed into that amalgamation of bone and muscle. Jellied blood mortared them together, oozing wetly into the gaps between the flailing arms and raw red ribcages that made up the bulk of the wall.

Little was left of the constituent bodies' clothing, and less of their faces, but the chains that ran through the entire construct made their natures clear. The corpses in the wall were shackled to each other, lashed in place by steel chains that knotted around their limbs and punched through the hollows of pelvis and collarbone.

"This must be what became of Citadel Gheisteno's prisoners." Velenne stood well back from the stinking, moaning wall. "Some of them, at least. The ones whose hearts they didn't take."

"How do we get past?" Jheraal asked. An orc's face pushed through the wall, gnashing his teeth at her. His green skin had been discolored to a sickly gray by the pickling brine, and a band of semi-translucent jellied blood covered the top half of his face in a rubbery mask. Ten feet away, the orc's bent and broken arm thrashed from a tangle of other limbs, clawing at the Hellknight.

"Without a key?" Velenne wrinkled her nose. "Only one option. Cut through."

It was raw butchery, not combat. Ederras hacked through the dense flesh with grim determination, trying to ignore the cold, viscous pink rain that spattered across his clothes. The wall clubbed and kicked at him with the disjointed remains of a dozen bodies, but its blows were as clumsy as those of the skeletons around the bridge. Even without his shield, they were easy to evade.

This was Paravicar Leroung's work, or one of her underlings'. None of the Crux signifers would have undertaken a project of such enormity without her approval. Very possibly, no one else in the Order of the Crux had enough skill to craft one, which meant the wall of corpses might well be her personal creation.

What must his great-grandfather have thought when he walked through this place? What must he have felt upon seeing what his squire had done?

What would you *think, walking through the Midnight Temple of Egorian?*

Ederras cut through the last of the wall's quivering sinews. The corpses lay behind him in oozing shambles, their gelatinous mortar glistening on the dungeon floor. He stepped through the dripping hole in the wall, across a carpet of pulverized flesh, and toward the stairs that led up to the castle.

Jheraal came after him, scowling her disapproval at the remnants of the Crux knights' creation. Velenne followed last, dainty and delicate, stepping high over any bits of gore that might slip beneath her shoe.

Partway up the stairs, the diabolist made them pause for another round of preparatory spells. Diamond dust and bull's hair floated in the air as she imbued them with strength and swiftness, shielded them against fire and ice, and warded herself against blades.

By the time she was finished, the wall of corpses was gone.

The space where it had been was empty. Dry. Nothing remained of the corpses that Ederras had chopped into reeking pieces amid puddles of blood and brine. A span of darkness led back to the cells, without so much as a smudge of ichor on the surrounding stones to mark where the wall had fallen.

"Maybe Gholam wasn't lying," Velenne murmured, looking at the emptiness. "Maybe what we see really is only what the lictor imagines. Those who die in this place are simply . . . forgotten, as if they never existed at all."

"Not everything gets forgotten," Jheraal said. "Lictor Shokneir remembers his prison. He remembers his curse. And when this is over, he'll remember us."

As they came to the ironbound door at the top of the steps, Ederras raised a hand to signal a stop. Reaching for Iomedae's blessing, he extended his senses outward, seeking the spiritual emanations that would warn him whether evil waited ahead.

He found them. One of the souls lurking beyond that door burned nearly as intensely in his spirit-sight as Velenne did behind him. He saw each of them as a pillar of black fire against the silvery, translucent landscape of Citadel Gheisteno—but the one that lay before him had a phalanx of weaker spirits around it, while the diabolist stood alone.

The paladin ended his prayer and turned to his companions. "There is a source of great evil ahead. I believe it must be one of the graveknights. Six servitors are with it. They're weaker than the graveknight, but nevertheless significant."

Velenne uncapped one of her scroll tubes. "How intense was the strongest of their auras?"

"Not quite equal to yours," Ederras answered flatly, looking back at the door as he drew his sword. He disliked seeing her that way. The measure of the diabolist's sins, at least in Iomedae's eyes, had scarcely changed since the day they'd been reunited.

"You're such a flatterer, my love." She sounded amused. "I suspect that's Behrion Khollarix waiting for us, then. I doubt the paravicar would come without her comrades, and I'm not vain enough to think I'd outshine Lictor Shokneir. And the late Master of Blades wields fire."

"What of it?"

"I suggest you allow one of my servants to open that door. Fire holds no fear for them, and if we're lucky, the graveknight will waste his blast on a creature he can't hurt. It's the least they deserve after that ruse by the bridge."

"I don't like you summoning fiends."

"It isn't a question of liking. Vhaeros is gone, and we lost *with* him last time. Without him, our chances are very poor. Both of you are unarmored, and I have no interest in watching you die for a point of pride. We need the devils."

"Can you even bring them here? You said you couldn't teleport in the castle—"

Velenne shrugged, examining her nails. One of them had broken, earning a frown. "It isn't an absolute bar. The citadel's misalignment only makes such spells . . . difficult. I may lose some of them in the transition, it's true, but what does that matter? I wouldn't take the chance with *your* life, but I will with theirs. Why not? Either they'll help us or they'll die. Both should be acceptable outcomes for you, yes?"

"Do it," Jheraal said. "Whatever it takes to bring the graveknights down. Do it."

Ederras studied Velenne for a long, silent moment. Finally he nodded, mouth drawn into a thin line of disapproval, and turned away from her. "Control them well."

The diabolist wasted no time in reading the scrolls that held her unholy invocations. With quick, expert strokes of her curved black knife, she cut open rifts to the smoking chasms of Hell at the conclusion of each spell. A single fiend stepped through each of the tears in their reality, which sealed and vanished into the air as each one emerged. One of them was torn apart by a sudden fluctuation in the gate's dark energies. Ederras saw the bloody tendrils of its beard—or maybe its guts—flailing around its yellow-toothed howl, and then it was gone, sucked away into the void between planes.

The others came through. There were two of them, muscular and horned, their scraggly beards alive and wriggling like mats of nightmare worms. They reeked of brimstone and heated iron. Each carried a viciously bladed glaive with a shaft longer than the fiend was tall.

The first devil hopped up the steps, blood-red hooves clattering on stone, and shoved open the door with a thrust of its sawtoothed glaive. Fire roared out before it had even gotten the door open, rushing through the gap in a sulfurous yellow torrent. The devil giggled—actually *giggled*, a sound hideous in its glee—and lowered its head to rush in with all the joy of a child running through a fountain's spray. Its companion charged up the stairs behind it, vanishing into the flames a second later.

Ederras waited a beat, just enough for the fire to fade into smoke and a few last licking tongues, then followed them out.

In the shadow-swept courtyard of Citadel Gheisteno, the Master of Blades was waiting. He stood motionless, save for the sweep of his charred and crumbling cloak, behind a screen of spear-wielding skeletons in partially molten breastplates and blackened greaves. Yellow fire lit the darkness of his helm, and it was mirrored in the eyes of the dragon carved into the hilt of his enormous greatsword.

He unsheathed that greatsword, holding it high in challenge, as Ederras and Jheraal came out of the dungeon to meet him. His skeletons fought the devils in lethal flurries before him, but Behrion Khollarix paid them no more mind than leaves drifting about his ankles. His burning gaze stayed fixed on the living challengers.

"Your bravery is worthy," the graveknight said. His voice sounded like logs cracking in a bonfire, each word accented with a hiss of unseen sparks.

"I should say the same for you," Ederras called back. "We killed you once already, and here you are, back for more."

"Death refuses me. But it will take you." The Master of Blades swept out his greatsword. The steel dragon's eyes flared, its toothy jaws gnashed around the blade, and the sword became a plume of searing gold. It roared over the spear-wielding skeletons, rushing through their empty ribcages like water sluicing through floodgates.

Ederras braced himself for the blast, wishing he had a shield to raise as cover . . . but the fire washed over him without singing a hair. Velenne's spell had protected him completely.

The skeletons hadn't been as fortunate. Behrion's fiery torrent had burned them with full force, and several had been badly damaged. The devils, grinning, leaped forward to take advantage of their opponents' weakness.

They didn't find it as easy as they might have hoped. The skeletons fell into perfect formation, each one raising its black-tipped spear and shield to defend its comrades as well as itself, and to exploit any weaknesses that its companions might uncover. These were no mindless brutes like the ones Ederras had fought at the bridge; these understood the rhythm of melee as deeply as he did.

Snarling infernal imprecations, the devils skittered around the skeletal phalanx, jabbing their glaives at the warriors. Their sawtoothed blades screeched against steel and bone. Behind the devils, Jheraal came forward, careful, her white-scaled face well guarded.

Ederras shared her unease. It had been ages since he'd faced a real fight without his armor, and all his instincts were wrong without that sheltering steel. His own body felt alien—lighter, less substantial, stripped of its battering mass. He couldn't rely on his helm to conceal the direction of his gaze. Instead, like a boxer, he had to consider whether it might betray his next move.

He drove forward into the skeletons, but hesitation made him vulnerable. The spears came in, and although he sidestepped one and twisted away from another, the skeletal warriors fought with such coordination that each thrust pushed him into the path of the next. The third spear came in fast and confident, and Ederras raised his arm reflexively to catch it before remembering that he had neither shield nor mail.

Red pain tore along his arm. He answered with a blow of his longsword that shattered the skeleton's grin into loose rolling teeth, but the damage was done. Blood ran hot across the inside of his elbow, and the other skeletal warriors pressed forward, black-tipped spears flashing. One gouged his side, scraping against a rib and punching his breath away. Another cut a long, shallow laceration across his thigh.

Then, abruptly, a crackling arc of lightning exploded across them. The skeletal warrior on Ederras's left froze as electricity erupted around it in spitting blue. An indigo corona blazed up around the paladin's sword, filling the air with the scent of ozone. Static energy fizzed around him, pulling his hair up on end and scattering sparks across his clothing.

The lightning leaped up from the paralyzed skeleton to the fleshless warrior on the far end of their line, spreading through the air in dazzling forks that jolted across every skeleton in their formation. Blue-violet coruscations danced across their blackened breastplates and branched through the hollow rings of their ribs. The skeletons' hands clenched convulsively on their spear hafts, bone hammering against wood, as electricity wracked them. Their teeth chattered and trembled in their bony jaws.

Then, all at once, they tumbled to the ground as the electricity released its grip, dissipating into the courtyard's smoky fog with a final lash of burning blue.

Velenne dusted the last motes of her scroll from her fingertips. "I do like enemies stupid enough to stand in a straight line. Such a rare and joyous thing."

No one had time, or breath, to respond to her. Stepping over the remains of his servants, the Master of Blades closed the gap. One of the devils leaped forward to meet him, its glaive thrust forward.

The graveknight knocked the fiend's weapon aside contemptuously and brought his greatsword around in a heavy, shearing blow that beheaded the devil in a single stroke. Mouth still agape in a howl, the head tumbled into the mist, the gristly tendrils of its beard grasping uselessly at its cauterized stump.

The Crux knight kicked the devil's body aside. Ederras came forward to meet him, offering a prayer to Iomedae as he did so. Divine power filled him in a rush, transforming his blade into a blessed brand and granting him a grace and clarity that pushed away his fog of pain. He could see every heat-warped crenellation in the graveknight's armor, every tiny notch in the teeth of his dragon sword. And he *knew*, with perfect premonition, where Behrion Khollarix would strike next, and when.

He couldn't hope to match the graveknight's strength, nor could he survive a direct hit from that sword. Shieldless and unarmored, his only hope was to evade a telling blow long enough to land one of his own.

"You're bleeding," the graveknight said. With each word, his fiery eyes flared behind his helm, like coals stirred by a breath of wind. "Weak. Mortal. Dead, you will be stronger. A worthy soldier, in the end."

"Flattered, but I'll have to pass." Ederras saw the tiny movement of the graveknight's articulated plates, heard the creak of aged leather under all that steel, and was already ducking before the sword came at him. It cut through the air, singeing the back of his neck with its unholy fire.

Lunging forward, the paladin stabbed upward from his crouch, using his longsword like a spear. Iomedae's wrath lent strength to the steel, and his sword plunged through the graveknight's armor as if he'd thrust it into cold black water. White fire blazed through the tiny holes of Behrion's chainmail and flickered along the inner curves of the heavy plate, consuming all it touched.

The graveknight staggered away, snarling, and slammed his greatsword down in a vicious but ill-aimed blow. This time Ederras dodged more easily, and Jheraal struck from the right, slamming her spiked mace into the Master of Blades' cuirass with a thunderous impact that reverberated through the courtyard like the clash of some huge, infernal gong.

Too late, Behrion raised his shield toward the Hellknight. It left his side unprotected, and Ederras—quickened by his goddess's blessing, alight with the joy of fighting for a righteous cause— slashed in once again. Divine fury flared, bright and true as the North Star, and for the second time, the Crux's Master of Blades fell before them.

Bells tolled in the darkness, calling from the high reaches of Citadel Gheisteno's ruined towers to announce the graveknight's fall.

Ederras clasped a hand to his wounded arm, drawing upon the Inheritor's power to heal his injuries and restore his flagging stamina. He repeated the prayer for Jheraal, who'd been struck by several spears herself. The other devil had fallen to the skeletons at some point. He hadn't seen the creature's death, but its corpse lay limp on the stones.

Jheraal grimaced at the bells. "They'll know the Master of Blades failed now. Let's get to that bone smithy before they stop us."

"South of the chapel." Ederras wiped sweat from his brow. His hand came away smeared with greasy black. *The graveknight's flames.* If not for Velenne, those undead would have killed him.

Perhaps that was why Iomedae had chosen to save her, despite her devils and the damnation in her soul. *The gods make use of all their tools.*

Finding the chapel wasn't difficult. East of the courtyard's crumbling pentices, the pointed arches and ornate windows stood out amid the fortress's severity. Whatever religious emblems the chapel may have born, they'd been replaced by skulls nested atop coils of broken chain—Ederras wondered if that had been before or after the citadel's razing and resurrection.

South of the chapel stood the charred shell of a partially roofed building. Sullen red light seeped from its interior, softening its darkness without illumining anything. As the three of them neared, Ederras saw that what he'd initially taken for firewood heaped along the smithy's walls were, in fact, stacks of human bones. Spines, arms, legs. All were blanched and picked clean.

Nothing stirred within the smithy, but he approached cautiously all the same, sword held at the ready. Beside him, Jheraal was equally alert. It was strange to see the Hellknight's clawed hands bare on the haft of her mace, or the grime-streaked paleness of her white scales in the courtyard's swirling mist. He was used to seeing faceless iron where she stood.

Still, it was a comfort to have her there, as it was a comfort to sense Velenne behind him. He'd never thought that he'd find reassurance in a Hellknight and a diabolist, but there it was.

Under the smoky shadows of the smithy's bare, burned rafters, three forges glowed with vermilion light. Gritty bone ash dusted each one's firepot, while human bones were piled along their sides, waiting to be fed into the furnaces. Arcane sigils shimmered in a semicircle on the bricks around each forge's mouth, each radiating a different color: cool azure, fiery orange, and an intense chartreuse that permeated the air around it with sizzling acidic vapor.

The skulls and flayed faces of fiends, both real and wrought in iron, covered the walls in regimented lines. Between them, iron racks held spears and swords, and armor stands supported empty suits of chain and plate, their shoulders dusted with coarse ash.

Ederras took those things for decoration, but neither of his companions did. Jheraal went to look for her own armor among the mounted suits, while Velenne conducted a slower, more thoughtful examination of the smithy's contents.

"Remarkable," the diabolist murmured, surveying the skulls and faces that glowered from the ash-flecked walls. "I hadn't thought graveknights capable of such things."

Ederras glanced over. "What's that?"

Velenne extended a finger to the nearest flayed face. It didn't seem to be that of a true fiend, but rather the preserved face of a hellspawn whose gray, leathery skin resembled a blowfish's belly, all covered in tiny spines. As the diabolist's finger came within a few inches of its mouth, the face suddenly lunged up and snapped at her, straining against the nails that pinned its leathery fringe to the wall.

"They're not dead," she observed, untroubled by the grotesqueness of the magic. She passed her finger down the row, and each of the skulls and tanned faces reacted in some way, cringing or snarling or making soundless cries of pain. All reacted with fear or hate or misery. "They're not really *alive* either, of course, but . . . there's still some emotion embedded in these scraps. Some fragment of who they were. Something that the Master of Blades wished to draw upon, for magic or for inspiration, when he worked upon these forges."

"What did he make here?" Nothing good, not on fires stoked with human bones and tended by the unliving. Yet Ederras was curious, all the same.

"Undead, presumably. Skeletons, zombies, wights. Those spear-wielders we fought in the courtyard." Velenne shrugged minutely. "But more interesting things, too. It's impossible to say what all was made here, but the tools suggest so much. Skull helms that cast their victims' dying agonies and terrors onto the wearer's foes? Cloaks of flensed skin that preserved the hellspawn's' resistance to fire? Armor forged around bones to imprison the soul? Maybe even other graveknights, if a champion of sufficient might fell into the smith's hands. A living person fed into one of these forges, the smoldering remains enclosed in a casket of plate mail . . . might such a person might rise as a graveknight to join the lictor's chosen few?"

Pursing her lips, the diabolist studied the faces more closely. "Few of these are devils, have you noticed? They're almost all hellspawn. For all that the Hellknight orders idolize devils, I suppose even they realized how much easier it was to refine their techniques on defenseless prisoners. Certainly it would have been far easier to evoke their emotions and trap them in bone and skin. Fiends are more difficult to frighten, and much more difficult to preserve."

So many lives. Ederras spent a moment trying to calculate the number of dead represented on the walls, but soon gave up. There were too many, and it was a distraction for which he didn't have time. He needed to find his armor.

But there must have been over a hundred faces and skulls mounted around the smithy's walls, and he had no idea of the numbers that might have been consumed in failed attempts before the magic to preserve the others was developed. Nor could he guess how many had died to create the other things Velenne had named.

How much of this did the Scourge knights see when they marched into Citadel Gheisteno? And why hadn't they written any of it down? Surely, *surely,* these crimes would have attracted condemnation across Cheliax if they'd been known.

"I've found it," Jheraal called from across the room. She held up her horned helm, dislodging the skull that had been set inside it. "They put skeletons in our armor, but they're just skeletons, not undead. Whatever they'd meant to do wasn't finished."

"Good." Ederras saw his own silvered plate near her. He strode over to retrieve it, extracting the bones that had been placed inside. Brittle black filaments, delicate as charred corn silk, connected the bones to the inner surfaces of his armor, but Jheraal was right: whatever they'd been meant to become, the magic appeared to be incomplete.

He held out one of his gauntlets so that Velenne could see the crumbling strands inside. "Should this be a concern?"

The diabolist contemplated it for a second, then waved the gauntlet away. "It will do you no harm."

Brushing the black threads from the metal, Ederras began strapping on his mail. "What is it?"

"The beginnings of a formidable servant. Armor, bone, fire. Yours, I think, might have been desecrated to draw additional power by making a sacrilege of your blessed armor. But it was nowhere near done. Khollarix must have just begun the process when we slew him."

"I'm glad to have stopped that, then." His shield was lying nearby, its golden wings dusky in the smithy's shade. After fastening his gorget, Ederras picked up the shield and strapped it back onto his left arm. "Is there anything we can do to prevent the graveknights from adding more undead thralls?"

"Do you want to spend the time on it?" Velenne waited until he nodded, then lifted a slender shoulder in a shrug. "Burn those bones outside."

"They're not just fuel?"

"Not in the way you're likely thinking. They're the raw materials for the forge, not its fuel. The iron, not the coal. A smith can't make swords without steel, and the knights of the Crux clearly can't make their undead without bodies or bones."

"We can't just destroy the forges?" Jheraal asked. She'd settled her horned helm over her head, and her voice was distorted through its visor. Somehow, that felt more familiar than the Hellknight's unfiltered voice did.

Velenne's black pearl earrings swayed as she shook her head. "It would take far too long, and I'm not certain that we could do it anyway. This entire fortress rose overnight from ashes. Its rooms and furnishings seem to change as easily as pieces of a dream. Gholam wrote that, and we've seen it. If the citadel is shaped by the lictor's thoughts, how could we hope to destroy the smithy? We could tear the whole thing down, walk around a corner, and return to find it standing again, untouched."

"But you think we can destroy the bones?"

"Yes. They're real relics of real lives, not of this place. They came from elsewhere, and they can be destroyed, just as all the lesser undead we've encountered could be. Destroyed, and forgotten."

"Then that's what we'll do," Ederras said. "And then we'll go after the lictor."

"Must we?" Velenne ticked a fingernail over the wands sheathed at her hip. "We rescued the children you were so worried about. If you want to retrieve the devilheart chain, I may be able to find it more directly. It may be in the paravicar's keeping, or in the castle treasury. Confronting the lictor is likely to be very dangerous, and very expensive, for no particular gain. He's a graveknight. He cannot die. The gods have cursed Lictor Shokneir, and we cannot rob gods of their vengeance."

"No," Jheraal agreed, her words hollow through her helm, "but even if you can take us directly to the devilheart chain, the graveknights are likely to be defending it, or else they'll attack us to reclaim it. We'll have to fight them anyway, in that case. Better that we choose the field and come to it prepared."

The Hellknight turned toward the door. "But beyond that, Lictor Shokneir broke the law. You're probably right that we can't steal the gods' vengeance. Fine. We won't. But we won't let it stop us, either. I'm a Hellknight, and I have my duty." She hefted her mace. "That the lictor has to pay the gods' price doesn't mean he won't pay mine."

27

HEARTS IN HELL

JHERAAL

Jheraal crushed a path through dozens of Lictor Shokneir's servants to reach the inner sanctum. Red-eyed wights, zombies clad in shags of rotting skin, unthinking skeletons who tottered into her mace's arc and grinned as its spikes smashed them back to oblivion—all roamed the halls of Citadel Gheisteno, and all stood in her way. She destroyed them without emotion, leaving her companions to finish off the stragglers.

It wasn't fighting. Not really. It was just cutting a path through tangling obstructions, like so many jungle vines. She wanted the master, not these mindless thralls. But as Jheraal hewed a road through the groaning dead, her temper began to rise.

That Lictor Shokneir had subjugated so many lesser undead, binding their shells of skin and bone to serve in the place of the living, was just another confirmation that he had become a hollow mockery of a Hellknight. Only one who was unable to command the allegiance of worthy soldiers would resort to using these miserable things.

It wasn't the worst of his sins. But it was another on the list.

The castle was full of them. Jheraal bashed her shield into the snarls of ghouls on the curving stairs that rose from the great hall to the upper chambers. She kicked the shambling corpses of wanderers and failed fortune-seekers off the catwalks that skirted those chambers, letting their bodies smash on the paving stones below like hideous, overripe fruit.

Her arms ached from the weight of mace and shield. Sweat soaked the linen shirt under her cuirass and dripped salt needles into her eyes. But the dead kept coming, wave after wave, and Jheraal broke them without mercy.

Twice she had to let Ederras or Velenne step to the front when their group was attacked by shadows or wailing ghosts, whose insubstantial forms were not so easy to strike down with her mace. Those added to the smoldering burn of her anger. Incorporeality was a coward's refuge. The use of such creatures was another strike against the lictor.

But none of his servants, whether made of flesh or bone or spectral misery, could stop or even slow the Hellknight and her companions, until the hellspawn came.

There were only five of them, and they weren't outfitted for battle. Two gripped rust-spotted daggers, one wielded a short sword that he held like a club, and the other two had nothing but sticks. None wore any armor. Instead, like the hellspawn whose hearts had been taken in Westcrown, they were dressed in a motley assortment of clothes that spoke to very different walks of life: tanner, dyer, rose-robed priestess of Shelyn, and a man who'd been caught in a purple silk nightshirt. Jheraal had no idea who that one had been, other than someone with money and questionable taste.

All of their clothes were at least sixty or seventy years out of date. They'd been dead a while. But there was one more in their little group, and that one hadn't been dead for long.

That one was the little girl from the bathhouse in Rego Cader, with the froglike skin and the tympanums on either side of her head. She wore the same plain smock she'd had on when Jheraal found her, and the ring with the little yellow stones sparkled on her hand, even though both ring and dress had been returned to her family after she'd died. There hadn't been anything else to give them.

The garments she wore now, Jheraal guessed, had to be illusions of some kind. Perhaps they were figments of the little girl's memory, just as Citadel Gheisteno seemed in some ways to be a creation of Lictor Shokneir's.

Her body seemed real enough, though. She looked solid, not like the shadows and spectres they'd fought on their way to the inner sanctum. All the hellspawn seemed to be corporeal. More than that, there was an intelligence and awareness in their eyes that none of the skeletons or zombies had possessed.

They're really in there. Jheraal wasn't looking at mindless husks. Those people were still in their bodies. They still possessed their own thoughts, memories, and souls.

All they lacked was their control.

There wasn't any obvious sign of that. In a few investigations, Jheraal had run across people who were under the influence of magical compulsion. Sometimes it was blatant: glazed eyes, monotonous speech, jerky movements. Other times, there were no visible cues, and in a few instances the victims themselves hadn't realized that their wills had been subverted.

The hellspawn were somewhere in the latter group. They appeared to be ordinary, living people. Nothing about them suggested that they were undead, and nothing suggested that they had been subjugated by some spell of control.

Nothing, except the fact that they stood arrayed against her in Citadel Gheisteno, armed with sticks and scraps of rusted metal against three professional killers.

Jheraal raised her mace, but she couldn't bring herself to take a step toward them. Even after Paralictor Leroung had used those hostage children to make her falter and fail, even when she *knew* the hellspawn before her had been driven there to test her will— even then, with her own life on the line, she couldn't do it. Her muscles refused to move.

If only they'd been more obviously undead, it would have been easy to smash them aside. If it had only been the adults, her discipline could have carried her through. She knew what had to be done.

But Jheraal couldn't bring herself to wield steel against that little girl, not when she'd seen the terror in those eyes. *She's* in *there.*

Fire stole the choice from her. A gust of heated wind blew past, carrying a ball of flame the size of a marble. Jheraal had just enough time to register the flash of warmth through her armor before the budding fireball reached the hellspawn and exploded into black-edged crimson.

"Keep moving," Velenne said, putting away her wand.

"You couldn't have—" Ederras sounded stunned more than angry.

"No." The diabolist walked through the lingering devastation of her spell. Flames licked at the heels of her boots and reflected from the chain panels of her dress. Scorched bits of cloth tumbled across the stones. There wasn't anything else left. "No, I couldn't have done that some gentler, kinder way. That was the whole point. If it upsets you, I suggest you direct your objections to Lictor Shokneir. He's the one who put those hellspawn there. He doomed them. Not me."

Jheraal tore her eyes away from the blackened burst of stone. Her fists clenched as she watched Velenne stride so casually through the carnage. *That child . . .*

But what could she have done? What could any of them have done? Velenne was right: their deaths had been ordained by Lictor Shokneir, not her. All the diabolist had done was destroy their enslaved husks, just as all three of them had destroyed countless undead in the castle already.

It was the same, and it wasn't. What was *in* those husks had been different. The skeletons and moaning corpses they'd fought had been utterly mindless. The ghouls and shadows had been so twisted by their transformations that only madness and hatred remained in their hearts. The hellspawn, by contrast, had retained their own identities. Jheraal was sure of it. And that was a worse crime by far.

What was the *point* of enslaving ordinary hellspawn? She had imagined that the devilheart chain would transmute its captives to ravening fiends, granting them strength and fierceness far beyond anything they'd had in life. Undeath transformed people into all manner of monsters, and Jheraal had thought that the Order of the Crux must surely have done something similar with the hellspawn they took.

But they hadn't. Those people had just been . . . people. The only extraordinary thing about them was the extent to which they were controlled. That, and their apparent immunity to age. Judging by their clothing, all the adult hellspawn had been taken before the Order of the Scourge had stamped out Citadel Gheisteno. Yet Jheraal would have wagered every clipped copper she owned that none of them had aged a day since their hearts were stolen.

Is that all he wants from us? Eternal servitude?

At the end of the hall, a carved arch framed an unlit spiral stair. Skulls and chains and broken stones were sculpted into the soot-clad wall. Letting her infernal sight pierce the darkness, Jheraal led the way up.

A whisper of ghostly sound reached her as she came to the first landing. A conversation, hushed, intent. Two male voices, one low and urgent, trying to persuade. The other angry, disgusted, struggling to restrain it. Jheraal couldn't make out any words, only fragmentary noises, but the emotions were overpowering.

That was the only warning she had before the memories of the dead overtook her.

". . . to finally bring down House Thrune." Two men, both in Hellknight armor, walked side by side up the torchlit stairs. Two remembered voices, one urgent, one angry.

"It's a lost cause, Behrion. They've won. Your own father signed the peace accords two months ago—have you forgotten? The only ones left fighting are out in the colonies, or beggar-bandits in the woods. It's *over*."

"It can't be over while injustice reigns."

A snort. The other man's face was vague, little more than an olive-tinted smudge in his Crux plate, as if whoever was remembering this scene didn't care to recall him too closely. "They've been ratified by every church and temple in Cheliax. Even the Iomedaeans have recognized Queen Abrogail's authority. Every major noble house has laid down its swords or been destroyed, one or the other. The Scourge and the Rack have conceded, too. Abrogail Thrune is the lawful queen of Cheliax. That means *she* decides what's justice in the empire. *She* decides the law. Not us. I don't like it any more than you do, but we enforce the law. We don't invent it."

"We don't abandon it, either. We don't let devils rule over our land."

"Even if I agreed with you—and I don't—there's nothing we can do. We don't have the numbers to take on an empire."

"We don't have to." Excitement in that voice. A remembered thrill of possibility. The imperative need to make the other man *understand*. "What the paravicar's doing—"

"It's a monstrosity. Madness. Lictor Shokneir has to stop her. Turning people—"

"Hellspawn."

"Fine. Turning *hellspawn* into thralls? Tearing their hearts out, destroying their bodies, binding them into—"

"Safety. *Safety*, Korvai. They can't hurt anyone once they're bound. They can't succumb to the evil in their natures. And they won't ever propagate their taint. Their cursed bloodlines end there. It's brilliant. The lictor is a visionary, and Paravicar Leroung's a genius for finding a way to make it happen."

"Then why are they hiding it?" The blurred man stopped on the stairs. Grabbed a remembered wrist. "Why is this all such a secret? I'll tell you: because it's a horror. If the world knew what they were doing—and that's even without the assassinations—"

A flare of anger at the presumption of the gesture, another at the continued argument. The refusal to appreciate a masterful strategy. "The *inspiration*."

"Inspiration to purges and massacres."

"Inspiration to throw off the yoke of House Thrune."

"Are you that blind? All this is going to accomplish will be the wasted deaths of innocents. This isn't what we're *for*, Behrion. This isn't—"

A knife. The memory of blood. So hot, and then so cold.

Sadness. Just a little whisper of that, almost forgotten in the years since. Mostly satisfaction. That he had not failed when tested. That something as ephemeral as friendship had not held him back from destiny.

"Lead in life, or inspire in death," he told the corpse. And picked up the limp weight of his friend—*paralictor,* a little voice suggested, *he was a paralictor, his murder at the hands of Thrune agents will inspire the rank and file*—and resumed his march toward greatness.

"Are you all right?" Ederras grasped her shoulder, returning Jheraal to the present.

"I'm fine." She swallowed thickly, wishing for water to rinse the taste of bile from her throat. "It was a . . . a memory, I think. The Master of Blades murdering a comrade—a Crux paralictor, a friend of his—and blaming the death on House Thrune to inspire his subordinates to continue a war they couldn't win."

"They did hate us unreasonably," Velenne said from the back, sounding bored and faintly annoyed. The boredom was a pretense, the annoyance probably wasn't. "Always a poor position to take. Hatred drives people into all manner of stupidities. Or, in their case, into cursed oblivion, which might be worse. Are you well enough to continue?"

"Yes. I—yes." She shrugged Ederras's grip away, not unkindly, and resumed her march up the stairs. "I can go on."

"A moment, please." Velenne glanced upward. "We're nearly to the top. It won't be much farther. I'll call the rest of my allies now."

This time Ederras didn't protest, and the diabolist worked her spells with the fluid ease of long practice. Devils clad in fur and fire and plates of ghastly, carapace-like bone emerged into their world, bowed their awful heads to Velenne, and swore words of fealty in hellish tongues. Three iron-barded warhounds and a devil of knife-edged bone formed a phalanx on the stairs around her, and Jheraal wondered whether it was mere accident that, in protecting her, the fiends cut their summoner off from the paladin.

Right now, she didn't care. As far as the Hellknight was concerned, the devils were walking weapons, no more and no less. She only hoped they'd be effective ones. Putting them from her mind, Jheraal marched on.

At the second landing, the haunting whispers returned. This time she heard a woman's voice, cruel and imperious, familiar even in its distorted echoes. Paravicar Leroung. Not a voice Jheraal was likely to forget.

The other voices were weaker and more garbled, not as strongly retained by whatever resonances of pain kept the paravicar's memories here. A man's sobs, a baby's cries, and a deep, rumbling baritone that carried such a commanding presence that it might have been the voice of the fortress itself.

"—serves two purposes," she was saying, with a trace of pride at the efficiency of her design. "First, it preserves the flesh indefinitely. No aging, no decay. The bodies don't even exist until called upon, at which time they can be reconstituted within moments. You can hold your agents until they're forgotten and anonymous, or use them immediately if you want them to be recognized."

A rumble of approbation. As much as anyone ever got from Lictor Shokneir.

Encouraged, she continued. "Second, it allows maximum discretion. The hearts appear to be mere jewels. In their mounts, they might simply be a . . . a pleasant decoration, of sorts. Those who need to know the truth can, of course, be made aware. But as far as the rank and file is concerned, the hellspawn go into the dungeons as prisoners, and are duly convicted and executed—there's no connection between them and the ornaments in the upper quarters."

"Good." Not a trace of a smile, and no warmth in that cold iron voice, but she felt his approval nonetheless. "Show me the extent of your control."

"It's absolute." She sent one of the recent acquisitions forward. He was a shoemaker from Kintargo, part of an entire family of hellspawn that had been condemned to debtors' prison for . . . some reason she'd forgotten. It wasn't important. What *was* important was that the sallow-skinned hellspawn was a new father to a squalling blue-furred ball of infernal corruption. And that he loved that thing, somehow.

She'd taken the shoemaker's heart yesterday. His body, too. The hellspawn man who stood before the lictor now, sweating sulfurous yellow rings through his shirt, was a captive to her chain. Paravicar Leroung held his heart in her hands, in the most literal sense.

The shoemaker had a knife. She'd given it to him. His baby lay at the lictor's feet, crying through a mouthful of sharp blue teeth.

"Show me," Lictor Shokneir said.

Jheraal kept walking, pulling herself blindly up the stairs, as the haunts of Citadel Gheisteno rolled out the bloody tapestry of their tale. She didn't stop. If she stopped, Ederras would ask her what was wrong, or try to take the lead from her, and Jheraal couldn't bear either of those things. The visions only seemed to affect the first person to walk into their grasp, and she could have demurred easily enough. But doing that would have been an admission of weakness, and an acknowledgement that the Crux knights could hurt her, and she refused to give them that.

A Hellknight feels no pain. And she was a Hellknight, truer than they were. She held to her pride, and she went on, showing nothing of the toll that each step took.

Maybe this was nothing compared to what the paladin had seen at the Worldwound. Maybe it was nothing compared to what Velenne had done in Pangolais.

But for Jheraal, who had previously thought herself inured to the evils that humans could do, it was horror and heartbreak, again and again. Years of it. Decades.

She had never imagined anyone could hate hellspawn so badly. Just for existing. She was used to the casual abuse and thoughtless slights that were part of everyday life in Cheliax, but this . . . *this* . . . this went beyond hatred and became something else. Something cold and unfeeling and brutal beyond measure. A crime no law had contemplated.

She had to see it, though. She had to know. Everything. Her people had suffered here, at the hands of those who called themselves her comrades. She would bear witness.

And as the final vision faded, she came to the top of the stairs.

In the room beyond, pale pink lights twinkled on the walls and ceiling in a celestial sphere of rosy stars. Iron chains held them in place, woven into interlocking designs, and although Jheraal couldn't see them from here, she knew that each heart was mounted in a claw-pronged holder worked to resemble a Crux Hellknight's gauntlet. She'd seen them in the visions, and knew what they were for.

Two figures stood before the lights, blotting them out with their bulk. One was Paravicar Leroung, tall and serene. The mane of ice-white hair that spilled from her helm glowed pink at its edges with the radiance of the trapped hearts behind her.

The other was darkness in iron.

"Lictor Shokneir!" Jheraal called. Her voice was strong and clear, as strong as it had ever been when she'd declared herself at an offender's door. "I am Hellknight Jheraal of the Order of the Scourge. I've come to bring you to account for your crimes."

The graveknight laughed. The chill thunder of it boomed from the floor and ceiling and walls all around them, sending the heart-gems shuddering in their claw-knotted web. Undead soldiers stood in armored ranks before him, the plates of their ruined mail sunk deep into soft, discolored flesh. Behind the lesser abominations, a phalanx of black-plated skeletons, identical to those that had defended the Master of Blades, clattered their spears against round shields. Yet the lictor's amused rumble rose above their clamor effortlessly, more a force of nature than a voice. "And what crimes are those?"

Ederras and Velenne had come up the stairs behind her, the diabolist's fiends mirroring the lictor's undead. Jheraal took a step in, allowing them space to fan out to either side. "You stand accused of murdering eight citizens of Westcrown, and of conspiring to murder a Hellknight of the Order of the Rack."

"Eight?" Lictor Shokneir's fiery eyes flared in hellish mirth behind his visored helm. He thrust his great flail up to the innumerable hearts that glowed in the shadows around him. Hundreds, at the least. More hundreds than she wanted to imagine. "Eight deaths are a terrible tragedy, indeed."

She ignored his words as she had ignored those of countless other criminals before him. "You are accused of assaulting agents of the throne in the course of their lawful duties. You are accused of kidnapping, theft, and unauthorized uses of necromancy. You are accused of the hiring of assassins. What say you to these charges?"

"I say that you have come to die a fool's death in service of no legitimate cause." Lictor Shokneir strode forward, scarlet flames igniting about his flail, wreathing its three spiked heads in haloes of unholy fire.

Jheraal nodded solemnly, as if the lictor had confessed his guilt. "Then you do not deny your crimes. I have seen the evidence with my own eyes."

"I deny nothing," the graveknight said, and fire roared from the flail, engulfing Jheraal and the devil beside her in its fury.

The devil's scream was as piercing as an icicle driven into her eardrums. Knotting her jaw against that cry of rage and the lictor's flames alike, Jheraal charged forward. Black fire licked along her scarred platemail. Her hair crisped and smoked inside her helm, filling her nostrils with its acridity. But Velenne's spell kept the worst of the heat from her, and what was left she could ignore. She could. *A Hellknight feels no pain.*

Even as the lictor's flames roared toward them, Velenne hurled her own opening blast. Where the graveknight's magic was black-streaked orange, the diabolist's erupted into solar incandescence, filling the chamber with the blinding white-gold of the sun at high noon. Her spell obliterated the lesser undead instantly, vaporizing the wights and ghouls before any of them could raise a hand. Only the graveknights and their spear-wielders remained, and the latter were visibly damaged, their bones eroded like icicles after a warm spring morning.

Better odds. But for how long? The rosy hearts in the iron-chained nets were twinkling more rapidly now, their lights flickering and fluttering like startled fireflies. Jheraal had seen that magic in the visions, had watched it awaken in the paravicar's hands. *Soon their spirits will answer.*

Ederras stepped out to the side, while Velenne's bony devil came forward to crouch beside Jheraal, its ivory carapace reflecting the hearts' glow in broken ripples. The diabolist herself stayed back, taking cover behind her trio of fiery-fanged warhounds. Paravicar Leroung, surrounded by a whirling cloud of ice motes, drew her scimitar as the remainder of her black-plated honor guard seethed around her. The armored skeletons marched forward, spears leveled in a black-tipped thicket.

The paladin stopped and raised his sword to meet them. A ring of holy fire burst outward around him, engulfing both the graveknights and their servants. Paravicar Leroung winced, squeezing her eyes shut until the white light passed, but the lictor never reacted. His mantle of fog and shadow roiled, then settled about his shoulders once more, seemingly undisturbed.

The skeletons weren't harmed either. As one, they raised their round shields overhead, creating an interlocked canopy. The divine radiance hammered against it like hailstones against tile, somehow deflected by the skeletons' shared defense.

Jheraal heard Ederras curse in frustration, but she didn't have time to see what he did next. As the Hellknight charged forward, bulling through her companions' magic, Lictor Shokneir swung his flail high at her head.

Jheraal ducked, letting the chains tick across the tip of her helm's remaining horn. Fire seared the black iron, blistering her brow. She ignored it and closed in for a retaliatory strike. The lictor had better reach than she did, but if she could get inside the arc of that flail, the advantage would be hers.

All around the room, under the shimmer of their prisoned hearts, the shapes of hellspawn began to form. Tens of them, maybe hundreds. Far too many to fight, even if she'd had the will to cut those innocents down.

She didn't. Instead she called to Velenne: "The hearts! Destroy the hearts!"

The diabolist didn't ask questions. The black wand slid into her hand, and a ball of surging hellfire exploded into the web of hearts. Iron melted. Jewels shattered. A rain of sparkling fragments tumbled down amid the surge of attacking skeletons, losing their enchanted glow and becoming inert as glass even as they fell.

And a dozen hellspawn, their spirits freed, melted into the ether before they'd fully formed.

It didn't stop the skeletons in their molten breastplates, though. The undead marched forward in unified ranks, and Velenne's devils came to meet them with fiery breath and daggered teeth. Beyond them, Ederras squared off against Paravicar Leroung, calling out a challenge that was lost to the roar of Velenne's fireball. His sword was a brand of white fire, so brilliant it seared afterimages into Jheraal's eyes.

She looked away just in time. Lictor Shokneir reversed his flail's arc and swung it back around, low this time, aiming for her side. Jheraal caught the blow on her shield, but it still knocked her back two steps and numbed her arm up to the shoulder. She grunted involuntarily, struggling to keep her feet. The graveknight was inconceivably strong.

"You can destroy all those hearts," he said, "and it won't matter. I'll get more. You can destroy those, too, and I'll replace them as well. Long after you're dead and your name is forgotten, my work will go on."

"It *does* matter." She hit back, bashing something solid through his shroud of dark mist and the tattered cloak that flowed over his black plate. Impossible to tell whether it hurt him, though.

Another fireball erupted over her head, sending down another hail of glittering shards. "They're free of you now. All those hellspawn you murdered and tried to enslave. They're free. And every one of them mattered."

"Others will replace them." Lictor Shokneir struck directly at her face, and despite the spell that quickened her, Jheraal wasn't fast enough to evade him. The best she could do was turn aside, raising her shield arm to guard her head. The flail's spiked heads slammed into her shoulder, wracking her with unholy pain. For a while she lost the breath to make any retort, and could only fight furiously to hold her own against the graveknight.

Through the gaps of her visor, she could see Ederras dueling the paravicar in a swirl of ice and holy fire twenty feet away. The Crux knight cornered Ederras against a wall, her scimitar streaked red with frozen blood. A second wave of divine radiance emanated from the wounded paladin, driving the frost-cloaked paravicar back with a howl of pain before she could finish him. Although the blessed light engulfed Lictor Shokneir as well, the fiery eyes in his helm never flickered.

Across the room, a hellhound fell to a coordinated series of spear thrusts, even as its companion tore apart the skeletal warriors with teeth longer than Jheraal's fingers. With the last of the nearby skeletons reduced to a rubble of bones in its armor, the hellhound turned to Lictor Shokneir and breathed a roaring rush of fire—but its infernal flames did nothing to the graveknight. Not a thread of his black cloak curled in the devil's breath. And then the remaining spear-wielders closed on the hellhound, stabbing and thrusting, and it was lost to Jheraal's sight.

Velenne had nearly finished demolishing the hanging web of hellspawn' hearts. After detonating a final fireball into the last of them, she slid the black wand away and removed another of opalescent glass. She leveled it at the lictor, uttering something the Hellknight couldn't make out. Jheraal felt the small hairs on her neck rise as magic gathered in the room, closing a vise of unseen force about the graveknight . . . and then it vanished, breaking apart before it could take its final form. Somehow, Shokneir had disrupted the diabolist's spell without raising a finger.

The skeletal devil leaped at his back, striking at the graveknight with claws and teeth and a barbed scorpion tail. Its talons tore into the lictor's armor, pulling his attention—and his anger—away from Jheraal.

Not for long. Lictor Shokneir drove his flail into the devil's carapace again and again, each of his swings delivered with brutal force. The fiend fought back, tearing at his armor and stabbing at his cloak, but it couldn't hope to match the lictor's deadly, disciplined fury. Within moments it went down, shrilling in agony. Its body broke into pearlescent shards on impact, scattering ivory plates across the flagstones.

A heavier thud made Jheraal steal a glance to the side, already dreading what she might see. Paravicar Leroung stood over Ederras, who had dropped to one knee. The paladin's sword, its radiance dim as a crushed firefly's, had fallen just beyond the grasp of his failing fingers. His surcoat was white with frost and red with blood, and his head hung low with the pain of a dozen wounds.

"An end to a useless line," the paravicar said disdainfully, kicking his blade away as she raised her own. She stooped, curling a gloved fist under his chin to force his dazed gaze up to hers. "I want you to look at me while you die."

"I don't." Cold as Velenne's voice was, it carried an anger Jheraal had never heard before. Black fire, tongued with crimson, surrounded the diabolist in a mantle of infernal wrath, rising over the back of her head in a ruff as she strode forward. Her face was a mask of pale gold, her eyes alight with reflected hellfire. In that instant, the living woman seemed a more profane embodiment of unholy power than the dead one.

That's *what will save him?* Jheraal thought, stupefied, as she reeled away from another of the lictor's fiery swings and countered with a desperate, clumsy blow at his knees. She'd known the diabolist stood high in her house, but she'd never seen Velenne drop her cultured pretense so completely to show what that *meant*. Now she had, and the sheer force of malevolence that surrounded her made it seem impossible that the lady was mortal blood and bone, not a fiend in flesh.

Velenne lifted her hand, and the hellfire that surrounded her leaped into her grasp. It burst from her palm in a black and red ray, shrieking with the voices of a thousand damned souls. The unholy fire slammed into Paravicar Leroung, knocking her back into the wall and melting the spikes of her half-helm. Liquid steel ran down her face, sloughing skin and bubbled flesh off the paravicar's bones.

The diabolist stalked after her spell, ignoring the stench of burning blood and steaming metal that filled its wake. The remaining skeletons left the last hellhound's corpse and marched toward her, drumming their spears against their shields, but Velenne never turned from her single-minded pursuit of Paravicar Leroung. She stepped in front of Ederras, blocking him from the graveknight's gaze.

"I could take your soul." Fury tightened the diabolist's words. "Had I come on my own, I *would* take it. I would offer your wretched essence to the dukes of Hell, and they would vie for the privilege of torturing you into eternity. But instead, I'll show you mercy you don't deserve, because for *his* sake I swore that I would refrain from such measures." She nodded slightly at Ederras, her eyes still locked on the paravicar. "We of House Thrune hold to our bargains. And I, who care nothing for it, have more honor than you ever did."

Jheraal didn't catch the paravicar's reply. A searing sweep of the lictor's flail forced her to stumble away, using every scrap of her remaining strength to keep her shield up against him. But she saw the dark flash of hellfire scream past, and she smelled its sulfur, and she heard the sudden tolling of the bells that announced Paravicar Leroung's death.

And, a moment later, the clangor of bone and steel as the undead soldiers swept over Velenne. Eldritch energy crackled in

Jheraal's ears, echoing in the steely confines of her helm, but she could see nothing of the diabolist's last stand.

Lictor Shokneir laughed, a sound like a distant rockslide, and pressed his attack on Jheraal. She defended herself as best she could, but she was winded and weary and *mortal,* and he was none of those things. The graveknight fought on endlessly, his stamina as eternal as his false life.

Fatigue weighted Jheraal's mace and dragged down her shield, and finally she failed to stop him. She saw the flail's glowing red ball come in, flashing through the citadel's darkness like a three-headed comet against a starless sky, and tried to pivot away—but she was too tired. Too injured. Too *slow.*

The lictor's flail crashed into the armor over her left thigh. Tendrils of dark energy crackled over the steel, sucking life from the flesh beneath.

Jheraal's leg went numb instantly. She fell forward as it buckled under her weight. The Hellknight threw her shield up to block the deathblow that would surely be coming, even as she knew it didn't really matter. Crippled, she couldn't evade him, and she had no allies left.

"Spells and swords and proud declarations of virtue." The lictor's inhuman voice roiled with contempt. He loomed over her. Darkness filled her dizzy vision, punctuated by a pair of fiery eyes: the last sight she might ever see. "Do you imagine you're anything I haven't seen before? Haven't destroyed before?"

"You never destroyed us," Jheraal spat back. The cold in her leg spread up to her side, stealing away pain and life alike. She fumbled her visor open with a gauntleted hand, showing her hellspawn face. Her eyes burned gold in the shadows, nearly as bright as the lictor's own. She bared her teeth, white and sharp. "You never *could.* Don't you understand that? I'm hellspawn, and I'm of the Scourge, and my kind and my order have flourished in the world. While you—the three of you—surround yourselves with old bones and pretend

you still matter. But you're chained here, alone. Because you've
already lost. You lost before we set foot in your citadel. And you
can't change that, any more than you can die. You can't erase us.
All you've done is convince me that I don't want to erase myself."

The lictor's hatred bought her a moment of crystal stillness.
His shock that a hellspawn would defy him so openly bought
another.

And then she didn't need any more, because Velenne—drained,
drawn, and bleeding badly from a laceration across her temple,
but very much alive—hammered him with a volley of razor-sharp
diamond shards that tore into the graveknight's armor and drove
him briefly, fatally off balance.

Jheraal dropped her mace, letting it dangle from the loop that
secured its haft to her wrist. Lunging up on her good knee, she
grabbed the clasp of Lictor Shokneir's cloak in one hand and his
shoulder with another. With a twist and a heave, she pulled the
overbalanced graveknight down and threw him onto his back, flat
on the ground.

He stared at her with absolute defiance, completely unafraid,
even as she put a boot on his armored chest. His flaming flail,
without the leverage to swing properly, lay limp in his hand. "All
you've done today is meaningless. I cannot die."

"Your death isn't the meaning." Jheraal stripped off her helm
and cast it aside, showing her horns and her scales and her inhuman
eyes. She felt his loathing and pressed harder on her boot, crushing
his armor under her weight. It was the crudest kind of authority,
but she didn't care. It *was* authority, and she wanted him to feel it.
Wanted him to understand, at the end, just how low a hellspawn
had brought him. "Your destruction is. I know what you did, and I
know why you did it. I know how much you hated hellspawn, and
how you tried to make the world see us as monsters. But *you* were
the monsters, weren't you? All along, it was you. And I know how

badly you wanted to keep that secret. How you lied to the men and women who died under your command.

"I know those things, and I'm going to destroy everything you planned for. Your heresies will be announced to the world. No more secrecy to protect the honor of House Khollarix or House Leroung, or even House Celverian. No more hushed whispers to hide the enormity of what you plotted against House Thrune. Everything comes into the light. *Everything.*"

The graveknight's eyes dimmed for a moment, as if a cold wind had blown across those embers. Maybe that was a blink. Maybe it was defeat. She didn't know.

"I will return," he said.

"That doesn't matter." Jheraal gripped her mace, its haft solid and certain in her hands. "The law is the same for everyone. Even you. And the sentence for murder is death."

The mace came down.

And the bells of Citadel Gheisteno sang their deafening song. Tolling, tolling, tolling. Crying long into the endless dark, as their master's spirit fled back to join them.

28

BREAKING CHAINS

EDERRAS

The honor of House Celverian?" Ederras wiped blood and melting frost from his brow. He'd already healed the wound itself, along with the worst of the others he'd sustained during his duel with Paravicar Leroung. Her corpse lay under a mangled section of the iron web she'd built, although he imagined it would disappear soon. None of the dead seemed to stay that way long in Citadel Gheisteno. The lesser ones simply vanished, forgotten, and the others were bound to their curses.

"I meant what I said." Jheraal slid her mace back into its carrying loop. Pain and weariness roughened her voice, but there was deep satisfaction, too. "You'll have to sacrifice a little of your house's dignity, same as the others."

"I don't object to that if it's necessary. I just don't follow what you meant. Khollarix and Leroung were responsible for the crimes done here, I understand that. And I understand that the details of the Crux's perfidies were probably hushed to protect them. But House Celverian had no part in that. Why would our honor be at stake?"

Velenne tilted her head at him curiously. Laughter hovered at her mouth, despite her exhaustion. "Dearest, why do you suppose your great-grandfather hid the devilheart chain?"

"To keep it from falling into the wrong hands," Ederras said, regarding her cautiously. He'd seen what Velenne had done—what she had *become*—when she rained hellfire down upon the paravicar, and it had shaken him profoundly. *That* was what he had saved in the citadel's cells.

And what had saved him, several times over. He didn't quite know how he felt about that. Without her, he'd be dead. With her, he was . . . what?

"Mm." She came closer, mending a dent in his left rerebrace by running a slender finger across the steel. The paravicar's scimitar had hit him hard there, leaving a deep divot in the plate. With a long metal groan, the armor straightened, releasing its painful bite on his arm. "Not at *all* because his paramour—and former squire—had made it, and he wanted to hide the monstrosity of what she'd created? Not to protect whatever honor she might have had? Or his own? Not even a little?"

He frowned down at her. "I wouldn't have."

"Yes, well. That stiff-necked inflexibility *is* a considerable part of your charm." Velenne kissed him lightly and stepped away, leaving Ederras to rub the ache out of his bruised arm. "But I suspect Kelvax was more protective of his lover's good name—or his own. So he hid it. Probably, in part, to conceal what she'd done. And probably, as you say, to keep it from falling into the wrong hands. Unfortunately, since he failed on both counts, the chain will have to go somewhere else now. House Celverian can't possibly hold it."

"Neither can House Thrune." The words were out of his mouth too quickly, too forcefully. She'd have to know that he'd been holding on to that suspicion for a while.

Velenne's eyes narrowed. He saw the rapid flicker of emotions across her face: hurt, pleasure at being hurt, and then annoyance. "*That's* what you thought I came for? To deceive you and take the chain?"

Not anymore. Not if she'd been both wounded and delighted by his guess. That was the one reaction Ederras didn't think she could feign, and he had seldom been so glad to see it. He could lay at least one of his doubts to rest. "It was a possibility."

"In that case it is once again my pleasure to tell you that you're an idiot."

"House Thrune doesn't want the chain?"

"Oh, no, we do. Of course we do. But I didn't come to *steal* it from you. I rather hoped you would see reason and agree that we should have it."

"Why should I agree to that?"

"Because I'm both charming and persuasive. When I want to be, which isn't right now. I'll give you a moment to figure it out on your own first." Velenne turned her attention to Jheraal, who'd been picking up her discarded helm. "Do you have any idea where the chain might be? Neither of our late graveknights was carrying it."

The Hellknight lifted her head and looked around. She started toward the back of the room, under the molten tangle of the spell-blasted iron chains, where a secondary staircase led down. "The assassin said the paravicar had a workshop below the lictor's throne room. We didn't see it on the way up, so I'm guessing it must be down these stairs."

Through a curtain of shimmering snowflakes suspended on threads of silver light, she led them to the paravicar's workshop. Skeletons immured in ice and zombies with withered, frost-furred limbs stood at the periphery like sentinels. Ederras tensed as they walked past, ready for an attack, but none of the frozen undead stirred.

Maybe they didn't need to. Paravicar Leroung's sanctuary was so cold that his breath misted and frost settled on his eyelashes instantly. Even without walking guardians, the chill would drive them out soon.

It was a beautiful place, though. Ice sculptures of astonishing complexity sparkled against walls cloaked in frigid mist. Within those walls, the paravicar had frozen the corpses of animals in horrifying yet strangely artful poses. Needles of pink ice erupted from the veins of birds subjected to lethal blasts of cold, fanning through their feathers like ghostly second wings. A sea urchin had been captured at the moment of exploding into spines and ripples of colored fluid. Around it, fish had been caught in contorted leaps and convulsions, their glimmering scales sheened with ice that exaggerated the fins and flowing lines of their bodies.

There was an undeniable fascination to the paravicar's frozen works of art, yet it was more than cold that made Ederras shiver as he turned away. The bone smithy had been bad enough, but this place was worse. The Master of Blades had sacrificed the lives of others to create tools and weapons. Monstrous, to be sure, but that was a purpose the paladin could understand. This place was filled with death only because Paravicar Leroung had wanted to look upon its leavings.

He moved on. Esoteric magical devices hummed and buzzed across crystal countertops, shimmering in every color Ederras knew and many he didn't. Two immense tables, each fashioned from a slab of ice with runic circles at each corner, occupied the left side of the chamber. Glassy-bladed knives and hooks hung from racks on the walls beside them, and the frost on the floor was pink with a suggestion of blood.

Jheraal stared at the rose-tinted ice. "This was where the lictor had his demonstration. He had a shoemaker cut his own infant's heart out to show the extent of the chain's control." She put her helm back on, leaving the visor open. "That must have been seventy years ago. Maybe more. Before the citadel's fall, before the Scourge razed all of this to the ground. But the blood's still here."

"It might be someone else's blood," Ederras suggested.

"It isn't. I remember . . . too much. Too clearly." The Hellknight's frown was half hidden behind steel. She turned away abruptly, crunching frost under her boots. "But it's different, too.

These knives weren't made of glass back then. They were metal. The originals are in boxes under Citadel Rivad. These are new." She took one down, and then another, setting them side by side on a crystalline countertop.

"This isn't." Velenne took the devilheart chain from a lacquered box on another table. She showed it to the others, draping it across her palms.

Evil radiated from the chain. Ederras scarcely had to draw upon Iomedae's favor to sense that. It was manifest in every detail of the chain's design.

The devilheart chain was a sleek, deadly-looking creation of dark iron ornamented with inlays of red gold, capped at either end by a snarling devil's head. One side was a wolf wearing a blindfold and collar of spiked iron. The other was a not-quite-human skull, horned and shackled and fading into fog. Midway between the two skulls, halfway down the chain's length, was a band of intricate gold puzzlework.

Velenne replaced the chain in its lacquered box and lowered its lid. There was a distinct sense of triumph to the curve of her hands as she let go. "It will have to be broken apart, of course, as it was before. One half to the Order of the Scourge for safekeeping, in recognition and reward for Hellknight Jheraal's role in recovering the artifact. And, naturally, as a rebuke to the Order of the Rack for losing it. The other half to us."

Ederras looked at her, tense but not yet sure if he should object. Broken in two, the chain wouldn't function. "I thought—"

"That we wanted to use it?" Her smile was both affectionate and acerbic. "Yes, my love. We do intend to use it. House Thrune hasn't maintained its power over the cleverest and most challenging empire in the world by passing up useful tools. But it's not my intention to use it to rip the hearts out of hellspawn. That would be terribly inefficient. Peasants don't make particularly good soldiers, as we've seen, and there are simpler ways to enthrall them, if that's one's goal. No, that will not be my recommendation to Her Imperial Majestrix, long may she reign."

"Then what *will* you recommend?"

"That we give it to one of our honored allies. Probably House Oberigo, I think. They were useful to us in this endeavor, and they are a clever, dangerous family. They warrant closer watching."

"You've lost me," Ederras confessed. "Why give it away? Why would Lord Oberigo take it?"

"Because it's an honor," Jheraal said. The Hellknight was watching Velenne closely, a wary respect in her stance. "An honor with a trap in it. After I file my report, House Thrune will probably issue some form of reprimand to House Khollarix and House Leroung, whose scions' sins will become widely known. Of course no overt condemnation will attach to the current leadership of those houses, but—"

"But there will be some small suspicion, yes, as is useful to us," Velenne agreed pleasantly. She walked over to Ederras and pressed the chain's lacquered box into his hands, holding his gaze as she spoke. "A few rumors about who knew what, and how directly their families were involved in covering their deeds. A slight weakening of their positions at court. Renniel Khollarix has been getting presumptuous since marrying his grandson to the Charthagnion girl. A touch of humility will do him good."

"And meanwhile you'll honor your loyal allies, House Oberigo, by making them the stewards of House Thrune's half of the chain, and guardians against any such future treacheries," Jheraal said slowly, sliding the pieces together as she spoke. "Putting your half of the chain all the way out in Westcrown, and passing over any house with the proximity and resources to make trouble with it."

"Indeed. So the Oberigos can take on all the expense and inconvenience of looking after it, and all the risk of our annoyance if they should lose it, and meanwhile we'll have an excuse to inspect their treasury and all their safeguards to ensure that our property is being adequately protected. With periodic re-inspections to see that our standards are maintained, naturally. A great privilege for Lord Oberigo, to be so trusted." Velenne laughed, inclining her head to Jheraal. "And, of course, Houses Khollarix and Leroung will be jealous of his elevation at their expense. A whisper, a word, and they can all entertain themselves plotting against each other forever. Yes. You've seen it exactly. You're wasted on things as small as murders."

"I don't think I am," the hellspawn demurred. "Although I appreciate the compliment."

"No doubt the people of Westcrown are grateful that you bother with them." Velenne returned her gaze, dark and intent, to Ederras. "Do you approve, dearest? Or will you still insist that the perfidious House Thrune must not possess the chain?"

"You frighten me," he answered honestly. Velenne saw too much, too far, too fast. She planned politics even while they fought for their lives in the ruins of Lictor Shokneir's curse. That wasn't a game he'd ever be able to play, not against people like her.

Yet it was, to his surprise, one he trusted her to play on his behalf.

"Good." She slid her palms over his wrists and kissed him again, the box clasped between their hands. "That's the most sensible thing you've ever said to me."

When they emerged from the workshop, the bodies of Lictor Shokneir and Paravicar Leroung were gone. The lattice of iron chains, melted and mangled by Velenne's infernal flames, had been restored to its complicated grandeur, without any trace of the destruction she'd wrought upon them. But the hooks that had imprisoned the hellspawn's hearts were bare, and there was no sign that the curse of Citadel Gheisteno held their spirits in its grasp.

A victory, Ederras supposed, as they walked away from the empty chains. *Some* of the captive dead could be freed from this place.

That thought gave him pause. "The garden."

"What?" Jheraal's eyes burned gold in the shadows of the stairwell.

"Ochtel. He told us to find him in the garden if we were able to win free. I told him that we would."

The Hellknight hesitated, but at length her horned helm dipped in a nod. "All right. I suppose it can't hurt."

The garden wasn't hard to find. They'd passed by its door, marked with a window of gray glass, on their march to the lictor's upper sanctum. No undead had defended that door, though, so they hadn't gone through it then.

Now they did, and on the other side found a vision of beauty in a place that had none.

The druid's garden was a wonderland. Tiny golden lights sparkled among ancient trees, silvery shrubs, and banks of rich green moss. Flowering vines draped the cold black stones of the castle's walls, hiding its charred skulls behind a veil of scented leaves. Tranquility seemed to perfume the air along with the fragrant exhalations of rose and bergamot, peppermint and sweet lime.

In the center of it all, Ochtel sat motionless as a cross-legged gargoyle, his head bowed over his lap. Greasy black hair hid his face. Dirt-smudged linen hid his body. Yet despite all his efforts to make himself nothing, the maimed man could not disappear.

He raised his head as the three of them approached along the garden path. The ruined lips twitched toward a smile, not quite succeeding. His remaining eye gleamed under the shaggy black hair. "I heard . . . the bells."

"We destroyed the lictor," Jheraal said.

"For . . . a time. Yes." Laboriously, Ochtel got to his feet. He had to straighten each of his legs with his hands, forcing the unnaturally long bones into place with agonizing, audible pops. "A . . . measure of vengeance. But . . . I would ask you for more. Now . . . that you have won."

"What?" Ederras asked.

"Freedom." The druid swept a sleeved hand across his body. He wiped bloody froth from the corner of his mouth, breathing hard. "That is . . . the boon I ask of you. The . . . favor. Take me with you. Across the bridge."

There was a certainty in the druid's request that gave Ederras pause. "Why?"

Ochtel didn't blink. For once, the disfigured man met his eyes steadily. "To have . . . a vengeance that will last. I want mine . . . as you had yours."

They took him.

Jheraal and Ederras alternated the burden, carrying Ochtel down the stairs and through the halls when his weakened legs gave out. Despite his height, the druid weighed next to nothing. Under his shroud, he was a skeleton in a parchment shell.

He couldn't have walked across the bridge. Ochtel winced and covered his eye against the blaze of the skulls' green gaze, shuddering on Ederras's back as guilt buffeted his body. The druid never uttered a word of complaint, but it would have been impossible for him to force his tortured form through those wracking waves of memory.

Halfway across the bridge, the paladin understood the second reason Ochtel could never have walked free from his prison. As they left the reach of Lictor Shokneir's will, the druid began to fall apart.

The first time Ederras had seen him, he had thought the man's disfigurements were too severe for him to possibly survive. Outside the bent reality of Citadel Gheisteno, that turned out to be true.

It started with his fingers. Their stitches unraveled, dropping chunks of suddenly dead flesh across the bridge's stones and skulls. Then the decay spread to his limbs. His arms shriveled in the enveloping folds of his shroud. The bones of his legs clacked loose in his skin. Ochtel's hair fell from his scalp, drifting into the dark mist that cloaked the bridge's chasm.

A few steps from the bridge's end, a sigh escaped Ochtel's withered lips. "Artuno," he mumbled, the words so delirious and slurred that Ederras could hardly understand them. "I'm sorry. I'm free. I'm coming."

He was dead before they finished the crossing. Gently, Ederras disengaged the wasted arms from around his neck and lowered Ochtel's remains to the mountain road. There was even less left than he'd imagined. A skull, a torso. Bones clad in fragile, yellowed skin. Everything else had fallen away during their passage. "I wish we could have done more for him."

"He got what he wanted," Jheraal said. "The garden will die without him. That's one thing Lictor Shokneir can't restore. A vengeance that will last, indeed."

"I'll take his bones to be interred with honor. Perhaps he had family somewhere. Friends."

The Hellknight shrugged, unmoved by sentiment. She looked to Velenne. "Can you sense your dog yet?"

"Yes. Come." Gathering her paneled skirts, the diabolist led them up the mountain road.

In a small cave burrowed into the stone, beyond a windswept ledge spattered in fresh blood, they found Vhaeros and the hellspawn children.

The blood didn't belong to the children. A dead drake lay in the cavern's depths, its spiky green scales glazed with a pink slush of half-frozen blood. More blood painted the children's cheeks and chests in pentagrams and circled crosses. One of them wore the drake's horns on her head in a creditable imitation of an Asmodean cleric's headdress. The children sat in a circle around a smokeless crimson fire, chanting clumsily but enthusiastically in unison, while Vhaeros looked on with indulgent amusement.

"What is this?" Jheraal paused at the cave's mouth, taking in the strange and grisly scene.

The children stopped chanting. Turning and standing, the hellspawn girl wearing the drake's horns answered her proudly. "An offering to Our Lord Asmodeus, Prince of Darkness, Ruler of Hell."

"I see." Jheraal absorbed that, then motioned to the drake. "Did you kill that?"

The girl shook her head, blushing and stammering slightly. "N-no. Vhaeros brought us here to stay warm. We'd only been here a few days when the dragon came and attacked us. Vhaeros killed it. He *saved* us. Then he said that we should give thanks and praise to Asmodeus for protecting us with fang and fire in our hour of need."

"Praise to the Lord of Hell!" the other children chorused.

Vhaeros wagged his shaggy tail, offering a fair imitation of a doggy grin that didn't quite disguise the gleam of malicious laughter in his eyes.

"Yes. Praise." Jheraal glanced at Ederras, clearing her throat to hide a smile. "Well, he *did* save them. From a drake. Apparently."

Ederras refused to look at Velenne. He didn't know whether he would laugh or shout at her if he did, and neither would have been appropriate, so he kept his gaze fixed on the children. "Let's wash them off and get them back to Westcrown."

"Can I keep the horns?" the girl asked, clutching them worriedly.

"Yes." Now he *really* wasn't going to look at Velenne. But he knew what the answer would have been, if he had. Laughter. And shouting. Both. Nothing ever easy, and everything he wanted. "You can keep the horns."

EPILOGUE

There was a promotion waiting for Jheraal when she got back to Westcrown. It was the third she'd received for success in a high-profile investigation, and she was beginning to hope there wouldn't be another. Praise was rare from her superiors, and promotions rarer. This one, to a lecturer's position in Citadel Demain, was a considerable gift. It would mean much less danger, and much less unpredictability, than her work as an investigator. It would put her closer to Indrath, too.

Nevertheless, Jheraal preferred to remain in the field. At this stage in her career, promotions meant politics, and that was a game she didn't care for. Better to stay on the streets, where she could serve with clear conscience, and where her talents might actually matter.

There was also a commendation signed by Queen Abrogail, although quite likely the document had been written by a lesser functionary copying from a form. Still, it had been personally signed by Her Imperial Majestrix—no one would dare falsify the queen's signature—and that was an honor that few Hellknights received in their careers.

Beyond that, she'd received invitations to a dozen dinners and parties being hosted by minor nobles of Egorian and Westcrown, a handful of discreet inquiries wondering whether she might be amenable to hiring out for private investigations, and a letter from Indrath, sealed with a thumbprint in candle wax.

Jheraal tossed the invitations and inquiries into the waste-basket beside her desk, placed the promotion and commendation aside in a position of respect, and, with great care, opened her daughter's letter.

> *Dear Jheraal! Did you really fight Lictor Shokneir? And* win? *In Citadel Demain they say you're a hero, that you stormed Citadel Gheisteno with a paladin and the Lady Thrune and killed all the graveknights and saved the souls of hellspawn. Is it true? Really? I want to know* everything . . .

She read the letter, read it again, and then pressed the paper to her chest in silent joy.

For once, Jheraal knew what to write back. For once, she had a story that flowed freely from her hand. A gift she could send her bright-eyed daughter, with love. And truth.

Dear Indrath, she wrote, her pen moving with a speed and confidence she'd never felt before, *it is all true, and I will tell you everything . . .*

About this. About this, she could.

"I have a proposal," Ederras said, late at night in his vaneo.

"Do tell." Velenne folded a hand under her cheek, watching him with avarice and appreciation. She was smiling, slightly, in the heavy-lidded way that she had when she was well content with the world. And with him.

He didn't doubt those smiles anymore. After all they'd endured, and all they'd shared, he had few doubts of any kind remaining where she was concerned.

"Stay with me in Westcrown. Become the lady of my house."

"Oh." She laughed, rolling onto her back and letting her hair trail across the pillows. "Are you proposing *marriage* to me, Ederras Celverian?"

"Yes."

"That's a terrible mistake."

"It might be." He curled a dark lock around his finger, drawing it to his lips.

"It really is, dearest. I warn you now out of love and affection. This was predicted a month ago in Egorian—you don't need to know by whom—and I was authorized to accept. From which it logically follows that any such proposal is advantageous to House Thrune and therefore, probably, not so much to you."

"You can always decline if you're afraid of hurting me."

"Yes, that's always been a paramount concern of mine. You're as delicate as a summer peach." She regarded him with great amusement, tracing her nails along his wrist before digging them into his inner arm, hard, without warning. "Did you learn *nothing* from Kelvax's folly?"

He let go of her hair and caught her hand, bending it back until he saw the strain, and the satisfaction, on her face. "I did learn a few things, actually. Assuming, of course, that the paravicar wasn't just lying."

"Let's assume she wasn't. What would you say then?"

Ederras released her wrist. "That Kelvax should have kept her close, if that was what he wanted. You can't just lecture at someone for a few years, let them go off into the world, and expect all your teachings to be retained forever. The cultivation of virtue is ongoing. It has to be. Every day it's an effort, or else it fails. And he should have been honest with himself about what he wanted, and why. Then, I think, much grief might have been avoided."

"Or not." Velenne's smile took on a reflective, wistful cast. She rubbed her wrist where he'd bent it. Less, he thought, to relieve the ache than to accentuate it. "You won't always be able to keep me close. I do have duties elsewhere. Other allegiances, other obligations. I cannot reconcile those with you. With what you are. I won't ask you to try, either."

"You've managed it these past few months. Is it really so impossible?"

"Months aren't years, and Westcrown isn't Nidal." She leaned up on an elbow to kiss him. "It's tempting to imagine, that I'll grant. But I'm not sure it's anything I can promise you. Understand, please, that these are my own reservations. My superiors don't care so much about preserving your fragile virtue. It's control of your house they want."

He touched her cheek, marveling at the grace of her, at the play of shadows across her skin and the fine beauty of her bones. She was such a strange creature, so fragile and so ferocious. So different from what he'd first thought of her, and yet so much the same. "What about what *you* want?"

"I want many things. They don't all fit nicely together." Velenne pressed against his hand, briefly, then pulled away with a sigh. "Allow me time to think on it. If I agree, we'll have to negotiate terms. Including a house in Egorian. Westcrown is too much a backwater for me to stay here year-round."

"A house is fine. I'm not getting you another ring, though."

"No. Of course not." Languidly she lifted her hand over her head, letting the diamond catch the moonlight. "I'm quite fond of this one. I always have been, you know."

"I know," he said. "I do know that."

A young man in an alley, relieving himself of too much wine.

There was a courtesan in the house waiting for him, and two guards posted by the door. But the night was too cold for the lady to venture outside, and the guards stood in a spill of lantern light that left them blind to the dark. None of them would interfere.

Even if they'd seen her, and even if they'd heard, there was nothing any of them could do to stop her. If they tried, it would simply mean four deaths, not one.

The courtesan stayed in her warm feather bed. The guards stayed in the light. And Sechel unfolded herself from the alley's shadows, and death came to the night.

She took the youth's signet ring when it was done. A heavy piece of gold, its face engraved with some house sigil. Napaciza, maybe, or Charthagnion. Sechel didn't bother keeping track. Her employer had wanted it, and so she had taken it, and that was her only concern.

Maybe he'd been an inconvenient heir. Maybe he'd been an unwelcome suitor. Maybe he'd just made the mistake of slighting someone's favorite racehorse or gladiator or scented dancing girl. It didn't take much to die in Cheliax sometimes.

Who the young man was, and why he'd been chosen, made no difference to her. Sechel didn't care who the corpse behind her might have been.

She didn't care who *she* might have been, either, except that it hadn't happened, and so a road had been closed in her life.

But what did that matter? Many roads were closed to her, and none of them were of consequence. Each mortal was given only one path to tread, anyway. One set of choices. One life, one line.

Hers was one she knew how to walk.

There was a peace in that. In knowing. In accepting. It had been foolish to imagine anything else. To pretend.

I am what I am, Sechel thought, wiping the blood from her knife, and what I always will be.

ABOUT THE AUTHOR

Liane Merciel lives in Philadelphia, Pennsylvania, where she practices law, trains dogs to mix drinks and steal each other's birthday presents, and writes stories featuring swords, castles, and the occasional exploding sea urchin. Her other Pathfinder Tales work includes the novels *Nightglass* and *Nightblade*, as well as the short stories "Certainty" (also starring Ederras) and "Misery's Mirror."

ACKNOWLEDGMENTS

Every book I've ever written has resulted in a debt of gratitude to many, many people who helped along the way, and this one is no exception. In no particular order, I'd like to thank:

Marlene Stringer, my agent, for unfailing encouragement and support.

James Sutter, my editor, for incisive and thoughtful comments, and for pointing out ever-so-gently when I might perhaps have dropped the ball on a few (dozen) continuity errors.

Dave Gross, who E-V-I-S-C-E-R-A-T-E-D an early draft of this manuscript and thereby saved the final version from plunging straight off the Cliffs of Despair. To the extent that this story works at all, it's in large part because he was willing to whack its machinery with a great big mallet until it got back on track and resumed chugging along.

All the rest of the Pathfinder Tales gang for being a wonderfully entertaining bunch of miscreants who make it so much fun to play around on Golarion.

Isabelle Lee, for helping me keep the canon and game rules straight, and for giving Sechel a sweet pair of bifocals.

Pongu and the Crookydog, for forcing me out of my own head and out for walks every once in a while.

. . . and Peter, for not taking it too personally when I make inarticulate angry noises and slam the door at him because *this stupid sentence is not coming out right*. (Also, for procuring comic books for me on request, even though I still won't read Miracleman.)

Thanks, guys. You are, collectively, The Best.

GLOSSARY

All Pathfinder Tales novels are set in the rich and vibrant world of the Pathfinder campaign setting. Below are explanations of several key terms used in this book. For more information on the world of Golarion and the strange monsters, people, and deities that make it their home, see *The Inner Sea World Guide*, or dive into the game and begin playing your own adventures with the *Pathfinder Roleplaying Game Core Rulebook* or the *Pathfinder Roleplaying Game Beginner Box*, all available at **paizo.com**. For an entire campaign's worth of adventures set in Westcrown, check out the Council of Thieves Adventure Path.

Abadar: Master of the First Vault and the god of cities, wealth, merchants, and law.

Alchemists: Spellcasters whose magic takes the form of potions, explosives, and strange mutagens that modify their own physiology.

Archfiend: Asmodeus.

Armiger: Hellknight in training; a squire.

Aroden: The god of humanity, who died mysteriously a hundred years ago.

Aroden's Fall: The death of the god Aroden, which sparked massive natural disasters and societal changes on Golarion.

Asmodean Disciplines: Holy text containing Asmodeus's doctrines for his worshipers.

Asmodean: Of or related to the worship of Asmodeus.

Asmodeus: Devil-god of tyranny, slavery, pride, and contracts; lord of Hell and current patron deity of Cheliax.

Avistan: The continent north of the Inner Sea, on which Cheliax and many other nations lie.

Casmaron: Continent far to the east of the Inner Sea.

Cassomir: Port city in Taldor.

Cheliax: Powerful nation located north of the Inner Sea, whose ruling family gained power by allying the nation with the forces of Hell.

Chelish: Of or relating to the nation of Cheliax.

Citadel Demain: Headquarters of the Hellknight Order of the Scourge, located near Egorian.

Citadel Gheisteno: Headquarters of the former Hellknight Order of the Crux, destroyed by other Hellknight orders only to rise again as a magical manifestation.

Citadel Rivad: Headquarters of the Hellknight Order of the Rack, located near Westcrown.

Clerics: Religious spellcasters whose magical powers are granted by their gods.

Condottari: Branch of the Westcrown guard that patrols canals.

Crown of the World: Frozen continent encompassing the northernmost points of Golarion.

Devil-Blooded: Someone whose ancestry includes a devil.

Devils: Fiendish occupants of Hell who seek to corrupt mortals in order to claim their souls.

Diabolist: A spellcaster who specializes in binding devils and making infernal pacts.

Dorjanala: Former palace now dedicated to Iomedae and Aroden.

Dospera: Ruined northern region of Westcrown, now abandoned save for criminals and monsters.

Dottari: Westcrown's city guard.

Druids: Spellcasters who revere nature and draw magical power from the boundless energy of the natural world.

Durotas: A captain of the Westcrown city guard.

Dwarves: Short, stocky humanoids who excel at physical labor, mining, and craftsmanship.

Egorian: Current capital of Cheliax.

Extraplanar: Something from beyond the plane of reality experienced by most mortals.

Fiends: Creatures native to the evil planes of the multiverse, such as demons, devils, and daemons.

Galt: A nation locked in perpetual and bloody democratic revolution. Fond of beheadings.

Ghouls: Undead creatures that eat corpses and reproduce by infecting living creatures.

Gnomes: Small humanoids with strange mindsets, big eyes, and often wildly colored hair.

Golem: Constructed servitor creature given a semblance of life by magic.

Graveknight: Powerful undead creature whose unholy life force is bound to its armor, in such a fashion that even when destroyed, it reforms again within days.

Half-Elves: The offspring of unions between elves and humans. Taller, longer-lived, and generally more graceful and attractive than the average human, yet not so much so as their full elven kin. Often regarded as having the best qualities of both races, yet still see a certain amount of prejudice, particularly from their pure elven relations.

Halflings: Race of humanoids known for their tiny stature, deft hands, and mischievous personalities.

Hell: Plane of evil and tyrannical order ruled by devils, where many evil souls go after they die.

Hellknights: Organization of hardened law enforcers whose tactics are often seen as harsh and intimidating, and who bind devils to their will. Based in Cheliax.

Hellspawn: Someone with fiendish blood, such as from ancestral interbreeding with devils or demons. Often displayed by horns, hooves, or other devilish features. Rarely popular in civilized society.

House of Thrune: Often called the Thrice-Damned House of Thrune. Current ruling house of Cheliax, after taking power following Aroden's death by making compacts with Hell.

Infernal: Of or related to Hell.

Inheritor: Iomedae.

Inner Sea: The vast inland sea whose northern continent, Avistan, and southern continent, Garund, as well as the seas and nearby lands, are the primary focus of the Pathfinder campaign setting.

Iomedae: Goddess of valor, rulership, justice, and honor. Former disciple of Aroden before attaining godhood herself.

Iomedaean: Of or related to Iomedae or her worship.

Jeggare: Chelish noble family known for its vinyards.

Keep Dotar: Headquarters of the dottari dedicated to patrolling the dangerous ruins of northern Westcrown.

Kellids: Human ethnicity from the northern reaches of the Inner Sea region, often viewed as primitive and violent by more southern peoples.

Lictor: A general of a Hellknight order.

Low Templar: Someone who fights in the crusade against the Worldwound's demons for profit rather than the greater good.

Mendev: Cold, northern crusader nation that provides the primary force defending the rest of the Inner Sea region from the demonic infestation of the Worldwound.

Mendevian Crusades: International military efforts to eliminate— or at least stop the expansion of—the demonic Worldwound.

Midnight Guard: Nidalese spellcasters—primarily shadow-callers—loaned to the Chelish military.

Midnight Lord: Zon-Kuthon.

Midnight Temple: Major temple to Asmodeus, located in Egorian.

Molthune: Expansionist military nation northeast of Cheliax.

Nerosyan: Fortress city and capital of Mendev.

Nidal: Evil nation in southern Avistan, devoted to the worship of the dark god Zon-Kuthon after he saved its people from extinction in the distant past. Closely allied with Cheliax.

Nidalese: Of or pertaining to Nidal; someone from Nidal.

Ninshabur: Legendary ruined empire in distant Casmaron.

Obrigan Gate: Massive gate in the wall separating Westcrown's ruined section from its inhabited regions.

Orcs: Race of formerly subterranean humanoids with green or gray skin, protruding tusks, and warlike tendencies. Almost universally hated by civilized races.

Order of the Chain: Hellknight order devoted to preserving and protecting the existing social and governmental structure. Based near Corentyn.

Order of the Crux: Rebellious Hellknight order destroyed by the other orders long ago for failing to properly respect the law. Originally situated on the border between Nidal and Molthune.

Order of the Gate: Hellknight order devoted to expanding law and order primarily through magic. Based near Pezzack.

Order of the Rack: Hellknight order devoted to restricting dangerous information and protecting society from violent rebellion, cults, and other such threats. Based near Westcrown.

Order of the Scar: Tiny Hellknight order dedicated to hunting down assassins. Based in Cassomir, in the nation of Taldor.

Order of the Scourge: Hellknight order devoted to punishing lawbreakers and oathbreakers, based near Egorian.

Paladins: Holy warriors in the service of good and lawful gods. Ruled by a strict code of conduct and granted special magical powers by their deities.

Pangolais: Capital city of Nidal.

Paralictor: A high-level Hellknight officer.

Paravicar: A leader of a Hellknight order's signifers, equal in rank to a Master of Blades.

Parego: One of the three major regions of Westcrown.

Parego Spera: All still-occupied districts of Westcrown, save for those on Westcrown Island (also called Regicona).

Pathfinder Society: Organization of traveling scholars and adventurers who seek to document the world's wonders.

Plane of Shadow: A dimension of muted colors and strange beasts that acts as a shadowy reflection of the "real" world.

Pleatra: Westcrown's primary slave market.

Prince of Lies: Asmodeus.

Pyrahjes: Giant torches lit by the city guard in Westcrown to help defend against nightly shadowbeast attacks.

Qadira: Desert nation on the eastern side of the Inner Sea.

Regicona: Collective term for all of the districts on Westcrown Island, generally inhabited by the wealthy and powerful.

Rego: A neighborhood of Westcrown.

Rego Cader: Ruined northern portion of Westcrown, inhabited only by outlaws, monsters, and the truly desperate. Also called the Dead Sector

Rego Crua: Slum neighborhood close to Westcrown's ruined sections, but still within the current city limits.

Rego Sacero: Neighborhood of Westcown most devoted to temples and shrines.

River Kingdoms: A region of small, feuding fiefdoms and bandit strongholds far north of the Inner Sea, where borders change frequently.

Rundottari: Westcrown city guard division devoted to patrolling the city's ruined section.

Sarenrae: Goddess of the sun, honesty, and redemption. Often seen as a fiery crusader and redeemer.

Scroll: Magical document in which a spell is recorded so that it can be released when read, even if the reader doesn't know how to cast that spell. Destroyed as part of the casting process.

Shackles: Pirate nation southwest of the Inner Sea.

Shadowcallers: Nidalese spellcasters trained in both arcane and divine magic, blending studious wizardry with religious power granted directly by Zon-Kuthon.

Shadowgarm: Ravenous monster from the Plane of Shadow.

Shadowlands: Plane of Shadow.

Signifers: Hellknight spellcasters who specialize in fighting with magic rather than physical weapons.

Taldan: Of or pertaining to Taldor; a citizen of Taldor.

Taldor: A formerly glorious nation that has lost many of its holdings in recent years to neglect and decadence. Ruled by immature aristocrats and overly complicated bureaucracy.

Taranik House: The Hellknight Order of the Rack's headquarters in Westcrown.

Thrune Ascendancy: Formal name for House Thrune's historical rise to power in Cheliax.

Thrune: See House of Thrune.

Undeath: False life granted through unholy necromantic energies.

Urgathoa: Evil goddess of gluttony, disease, and undeath.

Vaneo: Wiscrani term for a noble's manor house.

Vira: Wiscrani term for a noble's estate.

Wardstone: Magically imbued obelisks that line the Worldwound's border and help hold back the tide of demons.

Westcrown Island: Island where Westcrown's elite reside. Also called Regicona.

Westcrown: Former capital of Cheliax, now overrun with shadow beasts and despair.

Wight: An undead humanoid creature brought back to a semblance of life either spontaneously through a terrible death or malicious personality, or deliberately through necromancy.

Wiscrani: Of or related to Westcrown; someone from Westcrown.

Wizards: Magic users who cast spells through careful study and rigorous scientific methods rather than faith or innate talent, recording the necessary incantations in spellbooks.

Worldwound: Constantly expanding region overrun by demons a century ago. Held at bay by the efforts of the Mendevian crusaders.

Zon-Kuthon: The twisted god of envy, pain, darkness, and loss. Was once a good god, along with his sister Shelyn, before unknown forces turned him to evil.

Turn the page for a sneak peek at

LIAR'S BARGAIN

by Tim Pratt

Available June 2016

3

A CONVERSATION
THROUGH BARS

Rodrick's experience of the nations around Lake Encarthan had given him the impression that it was a land of timbered buildings and towering trees and dirt floors, so he'd expected the capital of Lastwall to be basically an immense fort.

It was with great surprise, then, that he turned his head to see a gleaming city of marble domes, immense archways, gleaming white walls, and elaborately carved eaves. While Vellumis didn't match the majesty of Absalom, or even his home city of Almas, it was without a doubt a *real city*, and Rodrick felt himself begin to relax for the first time in weeks. Yes, he was a prisoner, and if he couldn't talk his way out of his predicament, Hrym would have to freeze a great number of noble crusaders to allow Rodrick to escape, but still, this was a *city*, the kind of place where he was most at home, the kind of place where great good things could happen, the kind of place where fools and their money could be most expeditiously parted.

The cart curved around the outskirts of the city until it finally approached a domed fortress of stone surrounded by a high wall. "The Bastion of Justice," the guard said. "Some of the best dungeons in all of Lastwall down there, I'm told."

Rodrick thought about that. "Best . . . as in . . . most pleasant for prisoners, or best . . . as in . . . most effective at destroying a prisoner's will to live?"

The guard just smiled.

The gates opened, and the cart rolled into the courtyard full of military bustle: crusaders training, grooms doing things to horses, people running to and fro with urgency. The clash of steel on steel, the clang of hammers shaping metal, the smell of forge fires— Rodrick found it all terribly depressing. They were so *organized*. How could anyone stand it?

A crusader with a round helmet jammed on her head approached, frowning. "Do you have a prisoner for us?"

The captain nodded. "One for Underclerk Temple, I think."

The crusader whistled. "Really? Let me see." She climbed up onto the cart, and instantly drew her sword, leveling it at Rodrick. "Why does the prisoner still have a weapon?"

The captain sighed. "Because his sword is sentient and magical and promised to murder anyone who tried to disarm his master."

"It's true," Hrym said. "Except he's not my master. We're partners. He's the junior partner, really."

"No one needs to murder *anyone*," Rodrick said. "This is just a misunderstanding, and it can all be worked out. I'm a fighter for the side of good myself, mainly, just fallen on hard times lately."

The official nodded slowly, but didn't sheathe her sword. "Yes. One for Temple, indeed. Sir, you *do* realize you're in the middle of the capital city of Lastwall, a nation of battle-hardened crusaders?"

"I've noticed, yes. Lovely city, too. Much nicer than I expected."

"Will you hand over the sword, so we can talk without quite so much . . . tension?"

"It's not up to me, I'm afraid. Hrym, would you like to go with this nice crusader?"

"No," Hrym said.

Rodrick gave an apologetic shrug. "Sorry. He can be very stubborn."

The woman rubbed her jaw with her free hand. "All right, then." She shouted, "Clear the courtyard!" in a booming voice, and then sat staring at Rodrick for three full minutes, the force of her attention entirely withering his attempts to dazzle her with a charming smile. After the courtyard had emptied of all personnel, including the big priest and the friendly-ish spear-carrier, the crusader leaned forward and cut the ropes tying Rodrick's feet. She stepped out of the cart and beckoned him to follow. Rodrick struggled upright and climbed out of the cart, his hands still bound in front of him, but both resting on Hrym's hilt.

She led him through deserted hallways of dark stone, and down spiraling stairs, deep into the Bastion of Justice. "Not very well staffed, are you?"

"Everyone is avoiding the area until I have you secured, so if your sword does anything . . . inadvisable . . . casualties will be minimal."

"Good for everyone else. Not so good for you."

She shrugged. "Rank has its drawbacks."

"What if I froze you solid and we ran away?" Hrym said.

"Your wielder would be filled with crossbow bolts the moment he poked his head outside," she replied.

"Ah. That's what I thought," Hrym said.

"Here we are," she said eventually, gesturing.

"Ah," Rodrick said. "Yes. Only the *best* dungeons for me."

Rodrick didn't need long to explore his new home: a small room of bare stone with straw thrown on the floor, furnished only by a bench carved from a single piece of wood, so there were no nails to pry loose or legs to break off to use as weapons. Before he had time to become too bored, a guard opened the barred door and let in a gray-haired, sour-faced man carrying a black bag.

"Hello," Rodrick said. "What's in the bag?"

"Tools of the trade."

"You aren't a torturer, are you?"

The man barked a laugh. "Depends on who you ask. I'm a chirugeon. Mostly I cut off infected arms and legs to keep the rot from spreading, but I'm just supposed to see if you're healthy or not."

"If you try to give him a sleeping draught or harm him in any way, I will bring terrible destruction down on this place," Hrym said.

The man frowned. "A talking sword, they said. I thought they were playing a joke. Oh well. Doesn't matter to me. Swords never need tending on the battlefield, at least not from me. Stand up, would you, and stick out your tongue?"

Rodrick had undergone the occasional physical exam in the past, and this was less invasive than some: the doctor listened to his heart and lungs by pressing an ear to his chest, peered into his mouth and ears and nostrils, made Rodrick cough, prodded at his gums, asked him disgustingly personal questions about his recent bowel movements and whether he had any pain when he passed water. For the most part, Rodrick answered honestly.

"All right, I'm done." The doctor picked up his bag, which he'd never even opened.

"What's the verdict?" Rodrick said.

The man shook his head. "*You* don't pay me. Why should I tell you?" A guard let the chirugeon out, and closed the door, and that was all that happened, for a while.

"I could pick the lock, if there was a lock." Rodrick examined the door of the cell. "The door seems to be sealed by magic, which isn't very sporting."

"Rodrick, I can freeze the bars and you can break them with a kick."

"True. A bit loud, though. Might bring the guards running."

"So I'll freeze *them*, and you kick them as well."

"I see a few flaws with that plan."

"You're softhearted, Rodrick. You should be more like me. I don't have any heart at all, soft or otherwise."

"Even if the prospect of indiscriminate murder didn't give me pause, I'm still hoping for a more elegant solution than destroying the Bastion of Justice and bringing the wrath of the entire nation of Lastwall down on us. They can be quite persistent, I understand, and I'd rather not be pursued across the continent. Though I accept that as a tactic of last resort."

The door at the end of the hall opened with a squeal of rusty hinges. Rodrick wondered if the door made that noise naturally or if they'd worked on it with dirt and sand and steel wool to create the right ominous tone.

A short, stout woman of middle age walked down the hallway at a brisk, no-nonsense pace. Her skin was dark brown, her hair curly and cropped short, with a great deal of gray mixed in with the black. She wore vaguely official-looking black robes with baggy sleeves, and carried a burlap sack in one hand. Rodrick thought she looked rather matronly, until she stopped outside the bars and smiled at him; then she looked more like someone who might eat her young, if the need arose. "My name is Underclerk Temple. I am a humble servant of the Bastion of Justice, and I've been chosen to oversee your case."

In Rodrick's experience those who described themselves as humble servants were usually neither—they tended to be zealous priests or power-mad dictators—so he nodded politely. "Very pleased to meet you. I hope we can straighten this out. It's all just a misunderstanding, really."

"Oh? You didn't try to steal a horse from a group of crusaders?"

"I *did*, but there were mitigating factors –"

"You needed the horse to escape the consequences of an earlier crime, yes, I heard. I don't think there's any misunderstanding. It's a simple case, hardly worthy of my attention. I don't usually bother meeting with horse thieves. I concern myself with a better caliber of criminal. But word reached me of your supposed exploits in the Lake of Mists and Veils, and of course about your wondrous sword, and my curiosity was piqued."

"My wondrous sword and I are happy to answer any questions you might have."

"Oh, I may have some later, but I spent much of last night in correspondence with some associates of mine in Andoran and Absalom—we have magic mirrors, much faster than relying on couriers to carry letters—and I think I have a full understanding of your capabilities and history. I haven't found much in the way of confirmation regarding your claim to have defeated a demon lord, but there's a certain amount of circumstantial evidence, and I have assurances that you at least *believe* your story to be true."

"I'm either a hero or a madman, then?" Rodrick said.

"The difference between those two can be *very* slight," Temple said. "I don't think you're either one, personally. You're a thief, a confidence trickster, and an opportunist who occasionally does the right thing, when there's no more profitable alternative available. You also have a loyal friend who happens to be a magical sword as dangerous as an ancient white dragon."

"Pleased to meet you," Hrym said.

"Oh, good. I was afraid you might say 'Ice to meet you,'" Temple said. "I loathe puns. But, yes, it's . . . interesting to meet you, too, Hrym. We don't usually lock prisoners up with their weapons, but I suppose in this case you qualify as a prisoner, too."

Hrym harrumphed. "Are you a wizard, then? Can you stop me from doing the things I do? Because if not, you should be aware I'm a prisoner for only as long as I *consent* to be a prisoner. Otherwise I'm just a guest in very poor accommodations."

"I am a simple bureaucrat," Temple said. "My talents are organizational, not arcane. Here, Rodrick, catch." She tossed something small and glittering through the bars, and Rodrick snatched it from the air without thinking. He opened his palm and looked down at a ruby the size of his thumbnail.

"Usually I'm the one bribing my guards, not the other way around."

"Burrow," Temple said, and Rodrick screamed as the ruby sank into the flesh of his hand with a sensation like a thousand biting insects swarming across his palm. The gem moved under his skin, and he clamped his other hand tightly around his wrist, but it did no good: he felt the gem slide beneath his gripping fingers and watched as it traveled under the skin along his inner forearm, past the crook of his elbow, scurrying over his bicep and vanishing beneath the sleeve of his shirt. He could still *feel* the ruby moving, like a chip of swallowed ice passing down the throat, but this icy sensation traveled to his shoulder and then down into his chest, stopping in the vicinity of his heart—at which point the sensation vanished entirely.

Hrym was shouting from the bench: "Rodrick! What's wrong! Should I kill everyone?"

"I wouldn't," Temple said mildly. "That gem is . . . let's say . . . an encouragement to good behavior."

"She gave me a ruby, Hrym." Rodrick stared at his palm, which no longer hurt, and which was entirely unmarked. "It crawled under my skin like a burrowing insect and scuttled next to my heart."

"I told you having a heart was a weakness," Hrym said.

"I always thought you meant that metaphorically." Rodrick rubbed at his chest, the banter coming weakly and automatically.

"Metaphorically *too*. Let me guess, Underclerk Temple. If Rodrick disobeys, the gem will, what—explode into crystal fragments, shredding his heart?"

"Not technically accurate, but *practically* accurate, yes. Disobedience equals death."

"And if, say, I flung an icicle through your heart right now, and blew a hole in the wall, and Rodrick and I ran off?"

"That would be rude. It also wouldn't help. If I don't speak a particular phrase each morning, the gem will do its work regardless. Killing me now would sentence Rodrick to death tomorrow."

Hrym chuckled. "This is a promising development, Rodrick."

He stared at the sword. "I . . . disagree. Weren't you listening?"

"Yes, but you weren't, or at least, not closely enough. If she's *threatening* you with death, that means they aren't planning to *put* you to death."

"I'm not sure slavery is preferable to death, Hrym." He still had his hand over his heart, trying not to think of crystal shards ripping him apart from the inside.

Temple clucked her tongue. "No, no. You misunderstand. It's not slavery at all. Think of it as community service. In your home country of Andoran, some minor offenses are punished not with beatings or fines or years in a dungeon, but simply by making the guilty party clean up horse dung on the streets or scrape barnacles off naval ships for a few weeks, yes? This is a similar situation. You will assist me with certain projects, and after a certain period, you will be set free, your debt to society paid. The program is quite enlightened and civilized. I have concluded that you'll be more useful to Lastwall alive than you would be dangling at the end of a rope."

"Ah," Rodrick said. "I see. You want me to embark on some mission that's so dangerous you need someone completely expendable, or so politically questionable that no *legitimate* member of Lastwall's government can undertake. If I succeed, I get no credit, and if I fail in some spectacular way—well, I'm just a rogue criminal, and your government can't be blamed for my reprehensible actions."

"What a marvelous grasp of the situation!" Temple said. "I can already tell working with you will be a delight. Would you like to meet the rest of the team?"

"You mean I'm not the only luckless bastard you've roped into this scheme?"

"No, merely the latest. I'll let you out of the cell, but I'll need you to sheathe Hrym in this." She held up a long scabbard made of green crystal.

"I've had less attractive accommodations," Hrym said.

"But not more restful." Temple tapped a ring on her finger against the crystal, which rang like metal. "This scabbard is made of rare skymetal, brought at great expense from Numeria."

"I knew a man with a skymetal chainmail shirt once, and saw it turn an giant's arrow, an oversized monstrosity that would have pierced plate mail." Rodrick frowned. "Of course, the impact still cracked all his ribs, and one of *those* punctured his lungs, but still, I was impressed. The shirt wasn't made of green crystal, though."

"Probably adamantine," she said. "*This* is made of noqual, and though it looks like crystal, it can be forged like iron. Noqual has fascinating properties . . . mainly the suppression of magic. When we sheathe Hrym here, he'll fall asleep, more or less."

"I don't like the sound of that," Hrym said.

"Nor I," Rodrick agreed.

Temple shrugged. "Consider my situation. I am trying to make an enforceable bargain with a pair of desperate criminals. I can compel Rodrick's good behavior with that gem, but you, Hrym, are a trickier beast to reckon with. Threatening Rodrick seems to make you behave . . . but can I count on that to work forever? In this sheath, you can do no harm. You'll be returned to Rodrick when you're needed to help him with a mission. In the meantime, you won't be bored, and I won't have to worry about you burying the Bastion of Justice in a mountain of ice because you're offended that Rodrick stubbed his toe."

Rodrick shook his head. "Why should we believe you? What's to stop you from selling Hrym off, or presenting him as a gift to some high-ranking crusader?"

"Know this, Rodrick of Andoran." Temple leaned forward, her dark eyes fixed on his face. "I will *never* lie to you. Our relationship depends on my absolute power over your life and death, and that relationship renders most lies unnecessary. I may not tell you the whole truth, but anything I do tell you, you can believe. If you consent to put Hrym away in this scabbard for now, you will be reunited with him later—sooner than you think—and in the meantime, I will introduce you to the other recruits, and explain the particulars of your new situation."

Rodrick touched his chest. He couldn't feel the ruby, but he knew it was there. "Hrym, our choices seem to be either going along with the esteemed underclerk's plans, or dying in a courageous but pointless last stand."

"*I* wouldn't die," Hrym said. "But I would be trapped at the center of a mountain of magical ice. Killing everyone would be satisfying, but the consequences would be boring."

"I have one stipulation, Temple. I assume these little errands you want me to run will be dangerous?"

Temple shrugged. "For someone with your skills? Not very. But accidents do happen."

"In the event of my death, Hrym is to be offered retirement on a pile of gold coins, *not* an eternity of dreamless sleep in a magical scabbard."

"And if I refuse?"

"Everyone has to die someday, Temple," Rodrick said. "If my day has come, I would at least have the satisfaction of taking you with me."

Temple nodded. "Very well. I'll make that amendment to your agreement. You'll have a chance to review the contract." She slid the scabbard through the bars of the cell.

Rodrick took it—the sheath was heavier than it looked—and knelt by the bench. "We'll figure something out, Hrym."

"We always do. Worst case, we can just do what she says. Perform a few tasks, and then take our freedom."

"You believe her?"

"I do. She has a trustworthy face."

"I thought all humans looked alike to you."

"Stop stalling," Hrym said. "At least in that sheath I'll get a moment's peace from your prattling."

Rodrick slid Hrym into the scabbard, which was too long for him but otherwise a good fit, and then passed him through the bars.

Temple tucked the scabbard under her arm like it was a rolled-up broadsheet. She spoke a word of magic and the cell door swung open. She beckoned, and Rodrick followed her out. He briefly considered hitting her over the head, grabbing the scabbard, and fleeing, but it was idle speculation. It was possible she was lying about the gem, but it was hardly a risk he was willing to take.

Temple took him down the familiar corridor, then through a nondescript wooden door and down a spiraling stone staircase that descended below the earth, every landing lit with a magical glowing orb. "The Bastion must be quite well funded," he said. "Most places just use lanterns."

"Ah, but with a single word I can extinguish all these lights, or cause them to flare to blinding brightness, or even to explode in cascades of fire. We're very conscious of security here in the Bastion." She didn't sound threatening at all, which was somehow even more threatening.

After taking the rest of the descent in silence, they reached a heavy door of oak banded in iron, also lacking a keyhole. Temple pressed her hand against it, and the door swung inward.

Beyond was something between a spacious apartment and a palatial office. Amazingly, natural light suffused one corner of the room, which at first Rodrick took to be magic, but then he realized there was a lightwell: a narrow shaft running all the way from the surface to these subterranean depths, shining on a small plot of flowering and leafy plants. The floor was stone, but liberally covered with rugs. The walls were hung with a strange assortment of items: a broken sword, the stuffed head of an orc with unusually prominent fangs, a horned iron helmet with a star-shaped hole on one side. A desk was set up against one wall, beside an apothecary's cabinet full of hundreds of small drawers and a shelf filled with volumes and scrolls. In the middle of the room were several chairs and settees arranged around a low wooden table. There was even a kitchen of sorts: a woodstove with a teakettle on top, a cabinet full of cups and dishes, another full of dry goods, a large stone basin, and even the handle of a water pump. There was a hallway not far from the lightwell, with closed doors on either side and one at the end, open to reveal a set of bunk beds. This was a fully contained set of living quarters, then. As far as barracks went, he'd seen worse.

Rodrick took in the surroundings at a glance, but he spent more time looking over the *people*, though he tried not to make his examination obvious. The most striking of the group was a devilkin woman perched on the edge of the desk, looking entirely human apart from her crimson skin and dark blue lips. She was quite shapely, and dressed to show it off in high boots, tight breeches, and a blouse unlaced halfway down her cleavage. She had long black hair bundled into a ponytail, a pretty face, bright eyes, and a smirk that was several degrees beyond "insufferable": she looked immensely pleased with herself, and as if you should be pleased with her, too, if you had any sense.

Standing in a corner behind her was a tall man wearing a heavy brown winter cloak despite the warmth of the room. His skin was the color of curdled cream, and judging by the gauntness of his face, he must have been calamitously thin and cadaverous under that cloak. His eyes were the same muddy brown as his clothing, though the whites were more like yellows: Rodrick thought of piss in a snowbank. The man looked *ill*, but also like he'd been ill for a very long time, and was getting along fine despite it.

The others sat by the low table, one lounging in an armchair, and the last sitting stiffly upright on a bench against the wall. The lounger was a woman of perhaps twenty-five with the features of someone from Jalmeray or the Impossible Kingdoms—dark skin, dark eyes, dark hair—but dressed in Inner Sea garb, a pale blue blouse and skirt over dark leggings and boots, with a sheathed dagger at her waist. The last was an old man in a baggy shirt with ink-stained cuffs and the attentive and acquisitive eyes of a crow, wearing a pair of pince-nez spectacles. Even so he looked less like a scholar and more like one of those hard, sinewy old men you saw in the country, who could heave hay bales and slaughter cows all day long and still have energy left over to beat their grandchildren.

"Welcome," Temple said, "to the first meeting of the Lastwall Volunteers."

Captain Torius Vin has given up the pirate life in order to bring freedom to others. Along with his loyal crew and Celeste, the ship's snake-bodied navigator and Torius's one true love, the captain of the *Stargazer* uses a lifetime of piratical tricks to capture slave galleys and set the prisoners free. But when the crew's old friend and secret agent Vreva Jhafe uncovers rumors of a terrifying new magical weapon in devil-ruled Cheliax—one capable of wiping the abolitionist nation of Andoran off the map—will even their combined forces be enough to stop a navy backed by Hell itself?

From award-winning novelist Chris A. Jackson comes a tale of magic, mayhem, and nautical adventure, set in the vibrant world of the Pathfinder Roleplaying Game.

Pirate's Prophecy print edition: $14.99
ISBN: 978-0-7653-7547-6

Pirate's Prophecy ebook edition:
ISBN: 978-1-4668-4733-0

PATHFINDER
TALES

Pirate's
Prophecy

A NOVEL BY
Chris A. Jackson

Larsa is a dhampir—half vampire, half human. In the gritty streets and haunted peaks of Ustalav, she's an agent for the royal spymaster, keeping peace between the capital's secret vampire population and its huddled human masses. Meanwhile, in the cathedral of Maiden's Choir, Jadain is a young priestess of the death goddess, in trouble with her superiors for being too soft on the living. When a noblewoman's entire house is massacred by vampiric invaders, the unlikely pair is drawn into a deadly mystery that will reveal far more about both of them than they ever wanted to know.

From Pathfinder co-creator and award-winning game designer F. Wesley Schneider comes a new adventure of revenge, faith, and gothic horror, set in the world of the Pathfinder Roleplaying Game.

***Bloodbound* print edition: $14.99**
ISBN: 978-0-7653-7546-9

***Bloodbound* ebook edition:**
ISBN: 978-1-4668-4733-0

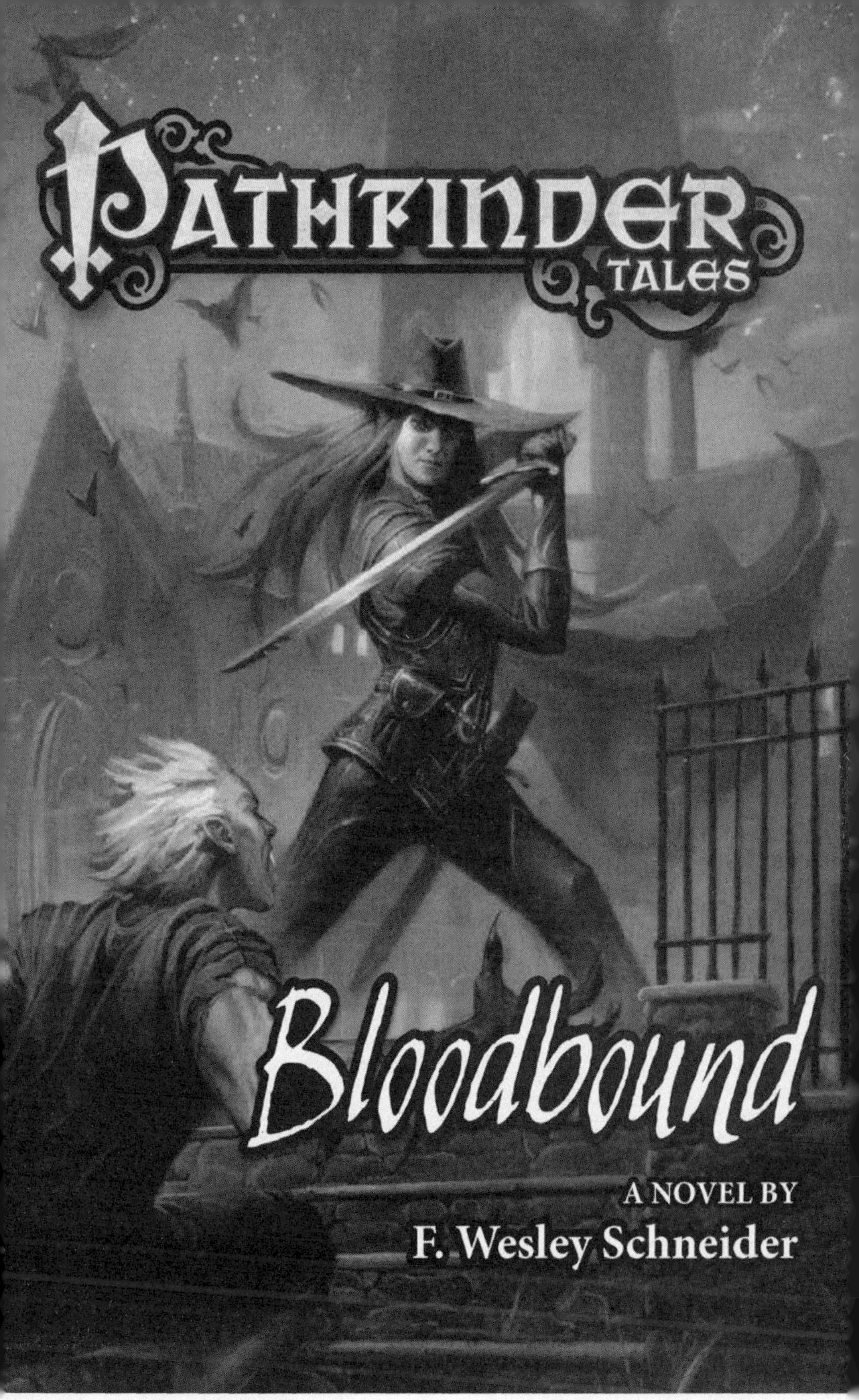
PATHFINDER
TALES
Bloodbound
A NOVEL BY
F. Wesley Schneider

Mirian Raas comes from a long line of salvagers—adventurers who use magic to dive for sunken ships off the coast of tropical Sargava. With her father dead and her family in debt, Mirian has no choice but to take over his last job: a dangerous expedition into deep jungle pools, helping a tribe of lizardfolk reclaim the lost treasures of their people. Yet this isn't any ordinary dive, as the same colonial government that looks down on Mirian for her half-native heritage has an interest in the treasure, and the survival of the entire nation may depend on the outcome.

From critically acclaimed author Howard Andrew Jones comes an adventure of sunken cities and jungle exploration, set in the award-winning world of the Pathfinder Roleplaying Game.

Beyond the Pool of Stars print edition: $14.99
ISBN: 978-0-7653-7453-0

Beyond the Pool of Stars ebook edition:
ISBN: 978-1-4668-4265-6

PATHFINDER
TALES

Beyond the Pool of Stars

A NOVEL BY **Howard Andrew Jones**

Rodrick is con man as charming as he is cunning. Hrym is a talking sword of magical ice, with the soul and spells of an ancient dragon. Together, the two travel the world, parting the gullible from their gold and freezing their enemies in their tracks. But when the two get summoned to the mysterious island of Jalmeray by a king with genies and elementals at his command, they'll need all their wits and charm if they're going to escape with the greatest prize of all—their lives.

From Hugo Award winner Tim Pratt comes a tale of magic, assassination, and cheerful larceny, set in the award-winning world of the Pathfinder Roleplaying Game.

Liar's Island print edition: $14.99
ISBN: 978-0-7653-7452-3

Liar's Island ebook edition:
ISBN: 978-1-4668-4264-9

PATHFINDER
TALES

Liar's Island

A NOVEL BY Tim Pratt

Count Varian Jeggare and his hellspawn bodyguard Radovan are no strangers to the occult. Yet when Varian is bequeathed a dangerous magical book by an old colleague, the infamous investigators find themselves on the trail of a necromancer bent on becoming the new avatar of an ancient and sinister demigod—one of the legendary runelords. Along with a team of mercenaries and adventurers, the crime-solving duo will need to delve into a secret world of dark magic and the legacy of a lost empire. But in saving the world, will Varian and Radovan lose their souls?

From best-selling author Dave Gross comes a fantastical tale of mystery, monsters, and mayhem set in the award-winning world of the Pathfinder Roleplaying Game.

Lord of Runes print edition: $14.99
ISBN: 978-0-7653-7451-6

Lord of Runes ebook edition:
ISBN: 978-1-4668-4263-2

PATHFINDER TALES

Lord of Runes

A NOVEL BY Dave Gross

EXPLORE YOUR WORLD!

paizo.com